"Do as I command!"

Liliath roared this last aloud, the crowd flinching at the power of it. Behind them, in the porter's lodge, a torch flared. The gatekeeper or one of the temple guards had finally roused.

There was the rush of great wings overhead. A sudden warm light and the scent of honeysuckle filled the courtyard. The Night King screamed and fell, and Liliath herself crouched under the weight of power she channeled, but only for a moment, before she stood straighter, shrugging it off. A thick strand of her hair turned white, and lines crawled across her skin, but they were transient changes, soon reversed even as the spark of Palleniel raged and fought against her and she contained it by pure strength of will, at the same time sending Gwethiniel back to finish the job that the angel had only partially completed.

"None may disobey me," snarled Liliath. "You will do as I command."

ALSO BY GARTH NIX

THE OLD KINGDOM SERIES

Sabriel

Lirael

Abhorsen

Clariel

Goldenhand

Newt's Emerald

To Hold the Bridge: An Old Kingdom Novella and
Other Tales

A Confusion of Princes

Across the Wall: A Tale of the Abhorsen and Other
Stories

The Ragwitch

One Beastly Beast: Two Aliens, Three Inventors, Four
Fantastic Tales

Shade's Children

The Left-Handed Booksellers of London

GARTH NIX

ANGEL MAGE

 KATHERINE TEGEN BOOKS

An Imprint of HarperCollins Publishers

Library of Congress Control Number: 2019938847

ISBN 978-0-06-268323-6

Typography by David Curtis

20 21 22 23 24   PC/LSCH   10 9 8 7 6 5 4 3 2 1

First paperback edition, 2020

THIS BOOK IS RESPECTFULLY DEDICATED TO

Alexandre Dumas

AND TO

Richard Lester (director) and
George MacDonald Fraser (screenwriter)
and the entire cast and crew of the films
The Three Musketeers (1973) and *The Four Musketeers* (1974)

AND, AS ALWAYS, TO

Anna, Thomas, and Edward and to all my family and friends.

CONTENTS

HIERARCHY OF ANGELS

SERAPHIM

CHERUBIM

THRONES

DOMINIONS

VIRTUES

POWERS

PRINCIPALITIES

ARCHANGELS

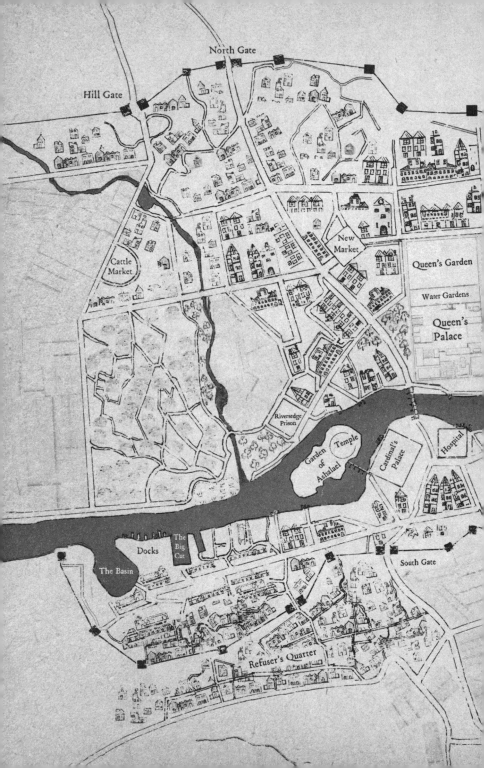

Queen's Gate

King's Wood

Old Market

King's House

River Leire

Unfinished Canal

Tall Island

The Tower

Star Fortress

Mother & Daughter Bridge
Three Firs Island

The Rotunda

Belhalle

Lutace

in the reign of

Queen Sofia XIII

Old Straight Road

P Cross

Gravel Pits

Map by Garth Nix © 2019

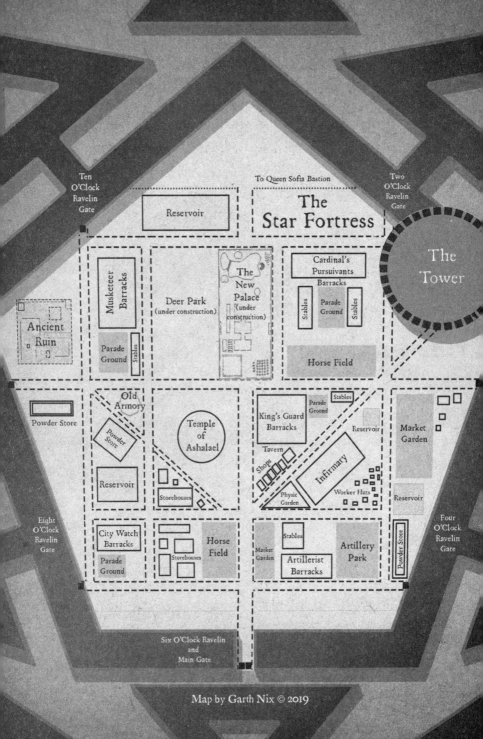

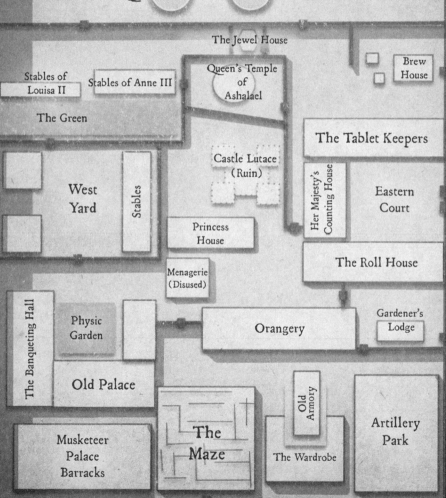

Queen's Palace
in Lutace

Palace Gardens

Queen Louisa X Water Garden

The Jewel House

Queen's Temple of Ashalael

Brew House

Stables of Louisa II

Stables of Anne III

The Green

The Tablet Keepers

Castle Lutace (Ruin)

Her Majesty's Counting House

West Yard

Stables

Eastern Court

Princess House

The Roll House

Menagerie (Disused)

Gardener's Lodge

The Banqueting Hall

Physic Garden

Orangery

Old Palace

Old Armory

Artillery Park

Musketeer Palace Barracks

The Maze

The Wardrobe

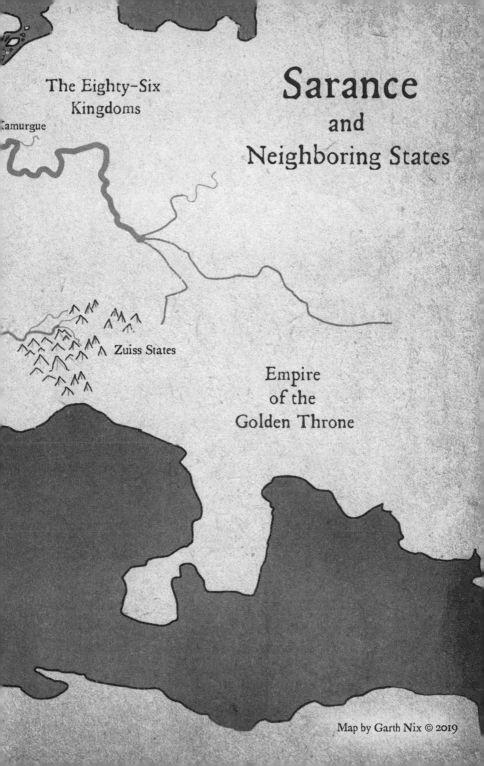

PROLOGUE

"THERE ARE ONLY ELEVEN OF US LEFT, EMINENCE," SAID the young guard. She was obviously very weary, leaning on her sword, which was smeared from hilt to tip in caked gray ash. "I don't think we can hold even this tower for much longer."

"Eleven?" asked old Cardinal Alsysheron, who looked far more ancient than her seventy years. She sat on the ledge of the great arched south window, because there was nowhere else to sit in the belfry atop the tower, most of the space being taken up by the great bell of Saint Desiderus. A massive bronze presence, it was silent now. There was no point ringing out any alarms, and, besides, the bell ringers were dead.

Alsysheron had folded up the long tail of her scarlet robe to make something of a cushion against the cold stone. She wore only one slipper, and her close-shaven head was bare, lacking cap or miter for the first time in many years, the faint white fuzz stark against her deep black skin. The Cardinal had fled very hurriedly from her makeshift bed in the great hall when the creatures had unexpectedly managed to find a way in via the cellars and crypt.

"I did not hear another assault. . . ."

"The Ash Blood took Omarten," answered the guard, giving the plague its newfound name. She wasn't even one of the Cardinal's household. Up until two days before, she had been a very new recruit in the Royal Guard. But when the palace fell to the monsters, she had gone with the survivors along the river, to the cathedral, which had once been a fortress and seemed to offer some slim hope of survival. "We put his body out."

"That was unnecessary," said the Cardinal. "As we have seen, the transformation does not take place after death."

"We didn't want to take a chance," whispered the guard. She leaned forward, deep brown eyes suddenly wide-open, more intense, the weariness banished. She looked very young to the Cardinal, too young to be caparisoned in steel morion and cuirass, with pistols through her once-blue sash, now stained gray with the ash blood of the creatures. "Eminence . . . is it not time?"

"Time for what, my child?"

"To call upon Palleniel!"

Her voice was urgent; she no longer leaned upon her sword but lifted it high. "Surely he can put everything to rights!"

The Cardinal slowly shook her head and looked out over the city of Cadenz, or what she could see of it under the massive, lowering cloud of thick black smoke. There were many fires burning now, kindled when bakers and cooks died from the Ash Blood and no longer banked their fires, fires soon out of control with no one living to fight them. The monsters certainly didn't try. Indeed, at least one of the biggest fires had been started by someone—probably a desperate officer of the City Watch—hoping to keep the monsters on the northern bank of the river, unaware the creatures were not invaders but transformed people—and were thus springing up everywhere.

"Magister Thorran made a report before she died," said the Cardinal. "It is angelic magic that makes the victims become monsters while they still live. Too many mages and priests called upon their angels for healing when the plague first started, or in attempts to defend themselves—I saw it happen myself, as I am sure you did too . . . I am sorry, but I have forgotten your name."

"Ilgran, Eminence. But surely, where the lesser angels fail, *Palleniel*—"

The Archbishop shook her head more stridently.

"I have been slow to penetrate the nature of this, Ilgran," she said. "Perhaps you will be swifter than I when you hear these three things."

She held up her hand, counting on her thin, ancient fingers. Each digit bore a heavy weight of icon rings, some fingers two or three, each icon representing an angel the Cardinal could call upon, though none of these were as powerful as the one depicted on the heavy, gold-chased icon that hung around her neck on a collar of silver-gilt esses.

"First, Esperaviel has flown at my behest to Barrona and Tarille and to the beginning of the land bridge: she confirms the Ash Blood plague does not extend beyond the borders of Ystara, not one yard beyond. Furthermore she could not pass the borders herself—"

"I am not much of a mage, Eminence," said Ilgran, with a faint blush. She had gained her place in the Royal Guard by virtue of her aunt's being a lieutenant, not by the brilliance of her swordplay or expertise with magic. "I do not know Esperaviel. Of what order—"

"A Principality, under Palleniel, her scope the sky of Ystara," continued the Cardinal. "She told me the borders were blocked by the neighboring Archangels, by the power of Ashalael of Sarance in the north and Turikishan of Menorco in the south."

"Gathered to attack us? But why, it doesn't—"

"No, it is not an attack, not from without. They have simply closed the borders to all heavenly beings. All our borders. Listen! The second matter is that Esperaviel reported seeing the Maid of Ellanda, with many followers, crossing the border into Sarance, and third . . ."

The old cleric paused and sighed heavily. She let her hand fall to her lap and then raised it again, reaching to take Ilgran's left hand in her bony grasp, levering herself up to stand somewhat shakily.

"And third, I called upon Palleniel *on the first day*, when the King began to bleed ash. Palleniel answered but would not do my bidding. Another commanded him now, he said."

"What! But . . . that is . . . how? You are the Cardinal-Archbishop of Ystara! You hold the icon!"

"And Palleniel is the Archangel of Ystara. But my icon—the ancient icon of Saint Desiderus—is dull and lifeless now. Did you not notice it? The icon of Xerreniel you bear upon your helmet would jangle and tremble were mine still puissant, to stand so close. I felt its virtue fade as Palleniel retreated. It was then I asked myself, What power could inflict this Ash Blood plague upon our poor people? What power could cause all lesser angels' interventions to go astray, to create monsters rather than the healing or defenses that were sought? Who could do this in *Ystara?*"

"The other Archangels—"

"No," said the Cardinal. "Here in Ystara, Palleniel is paramount. I think the neighboring Archangels have acted to limit the Ash Blood and the creatures it brings, as best they can, in the earthly realms they protect. I sense they are trying to do more, that there is further struggle in the heavens, directed against Palleniel. Because this plague, the monsters . . . it must be *Palleniel's* work. But as always, no angel may come to our world, or act, save at mortal call and direction. And so the pieces come together, for who has the art and power to have made a *new* icon to summon Palleniel himself? And having made it, who would have the arrogance and strength to summon him and set him to such work?"

Ilgran shook her head and frowned, and her mouth quirked in disbelief.

"I suppose it can only be the Maid of Ellanda . . . but why would she want . . . this? It is the death of the kingdom! The death of us all!"

"I do not think she did want this," said the Cardinal. "But as always with angels, one must be very careful. The greater the power, the greater the possibility of unintended harm. We should have seen the logical consequence of her talent to make icons and summon angels. Do I say talent? I mean genius, of course. But she was . . . she is too young. Nineteen is far too young to be made a magister, or bishop, to be given the teaching and allowed the greater orders. Though clearly she has needed neither teaching nor permission. . . ."

"I saw her once. From afar. She had a light in her eyes, a madness," said Ilgran slowly. She was not looking at the Cardinal but out across the burning city. "When she came with her followers to see the King, wanting a charter for her temple. For Palleniel Exalted, whatever that means. . . ."

Ilgran spoke absently, her mind elsewhere, digesting what the Cardinal had just told her. It meant there would be no rescue; she would likely not live to see past another dawn, perhaps not even that long. There were many monsters below, and the cathedral had not been a fortress for a century, at the least. The bell tower had no water, no stored food, and, besides, the gate below was weak. Even without a ram, the bigger monsters would smash it down when they made a determined effort to do so.

"Perhaps we should have allowed her that charter," mused the Cardinal. "But I do not think she is mad. Ferociously single-minded, I grant you. I pity her."

"You pity *Liliath*, Eminence? If it is as you suspect, she has somehow corrupted Palleniel, she is responsible . . . she has brought the Ash Blood plague upon us; she has slain my parents and turned my brother and sister into monsters. If she were here

I would kill her and be glad, if sword or pistol would do what is needed against whatever she has become!"

"Oh, I think cold steel or a bullet would finish her, albeit with difficulty, just as with the monsters," said the Cardinal. "Though you might not get the chance to use sword or pistol, if she does indeed hold Palleniel in her service. She must command other angels, too, more than we ever suspected. But I do pity her, for as I said, this cannot be what she intended. So young, so impossibly gifted, and yet so unwise, all bound up together. I wonder what she actually *did* intend, perhaps—"

Whatever she was about to say was lost, as the first of the monsters who had climbed the ancient, cracked, and open-veined stones of the bell tower launched itself over the battlements and onto her back, cutting the old prelate's throat with its talons as it bore her to the ground.

Ilgran killed one with a sword thrust that left the weapon embedded in the creature's mouth, before she fell. Literally, for as she ducked under the rim of the great bell to throw herself down the open shaft, one of the creatures closed upon her, jaws ravening and horrible, hooked fingers reaching. A pistol remained unused in Ilgran's belt, not fired at the last because the monster looked at her with Janeth's eyes. Her little sister's lively green eyes.

The guard jumped, making no attempt to grab the bell rope. Falling to her death, Ilgran focused every part of her mind on the slightest of hopes those eyes had raised.

There had to be *some* chance that a monster could become human again.

PART I

Liliath

ONE

THE YOUNG WOMAN WOKE IN TOTAL DARKNESS WITH COLD stone under her, and her questing hands felt stone above and to the sides. But the moment of panic that came with this realization ebbed as she remembered why this was so and disappeared completely when she heard the voice.

The voice of power and strength that made her feel complete, made her feel *alive*. With it came a sudden, intense sensation of being enfolded, held close and safe. Not by mere human arms, but within great wings of light and power.

"As you commanded long ago, that which you waited for has occurred, and so I awake you."

"How . . . ?"

Her voice croaked and failed. She swallowed, saliva moving in her mouth and throat for the first time in . . . who knew how long.

She had been stopped for a long time just short of being dead, she knew. She would have seemed dead if anyone could have looked inside the tomb, though the remarkable preservation of her flesh would have given pause to any observers. But the chance of any onlookers had been greatly reduced by her choice of resting place. The great stone coffin, topped with a massive slab of marble, all sealed with lead.

It would have been natural for her to ask how long she had been in the coffin. But that was not her first question. She thought only of what was needful, for her all-consuming plan.

"How many suitable candidates are ready?"

There was a long silence. Long enough for her to think the presence gone. But then the voice came again.

"Four."

"Four! But there should be *hundreds*—"

"Four," repeated the voice.

For a moment, fury coursed through her, extreme anger that her plans—her destiny—should once again go awry. But she fought the anger down. Though she had hoped for many more possible candidates, to allow for error or mischance, four should be enough. Even one might suffice. . . .

"Where are they?"

"In four places in Sarance, but they will come together. Soon."

"And the Order? It continues? You have shown them the signs of my awakening?"

"I have shown the signs. I know not if any survive to see them, or if they have been acted upon. As you know, I am not entire, and mightily resisted . . . only your will anchors me to your world. Almost I wish to *fully* disassociate—"

"You will do as I commanded!"

She spoke urgently, her voice imbued with all her natural power and intense, concentrated will.

"I obey. I am yours entire. I can speak no longer, my—"

The voice stopped. This time the silence was complete. She knew there would be no further speech, no warmth, no sensation of utter security and love. Not now. Tears began to form in the corners of her eyes, but she fiercely blinked them away. She had no time for tears. Ever.

"I love you," whispered the young woman. She felt better saying the words, coming back to herself, to what she had been. Her voice grew stronger, echoing inside the stone coffin. "I will always love you. We will be together. We *will be together!*"

She felt her hands. Her skin still had the soft, velvet smoothness of youth. More important, the rings were all there. She touched them, one by one, letting the power within begin to rise, just a little, before she settled on the least of the nine. The ring on her left thumb. Made from ancient electrum, the band held an oval of ivory, carved to show fine, feathery wings almost obscuring a human face, painted or perhaps enameled, the eyes tiny rubies. The halo above the almost hidden face was a line of gold no wider than a hair.

"Mazrathiel," whispered the woman in the coffin. "Mazrathiel, Mazrathiel, come to my need."

Light shone from the ring, cold like moonlight, though brighter. She shut her eyes against the sudden illumination and felt the lesser presence appear. It came with a sensation of warmth, but this was no more than the welcome heat of a kitchen fire on a cold day, nothing so remarkable as the feeling that had encompassed her whole being before, when she had spoken to *him*. Similarly, she felt the rush of air as if from the folding of wings, and the faint, clear tone of a single harp string, plucked far away.

"Mazrathiel is here," said a faint whisper only she could hear. "What is your will? If it lies within my scope, it shall be done."

The woman whispered, and Mazrathiel did her bidding.

Brother Delfon had always liked the cool quiet of the Saint's Tomb in the lowest crypt beneath the temple. It was very cold in winter, but he had not been sent to a vigil here in winter, not since his sixtieth year. That was more than a decade behind him now, and like all practitioners of angelic magic, he was older than his years. The more fragile followers of Saint Marguerite only stood vigil in high summer, and in truth Delfon would have been spared the task, save that he insisted. He did acquiesce with the suggestion of his superiors that he bring a cushion and a blanket, and sit upon the wooden bench in the corner that served to rest weary pilgrims on the high holy days when they were allowed to visit.

He slumped now, no more than half awake. So it took him some several seconds to notice that he was no longer alone. A sister stood above him, looking at him with a quizzical expression as if uncertain what to make of the elderly monk.

A young sister. She wore a similar habit to his own, the black and white of the followers of the Archangel Ashalael, but there were variations in the width of the white cuffs at the sleeves and in the hem of the robe, and even the blackness of the cloth looked a little different in the light of Delfon's lantern. Slowly he realized it was perhaps a very dark blue, not black at all, and the badge on the breast, picked out in gold, showed a pair of seven-pinioned wings, Archangel's wings. But Ashalael's wings were always shown in silver, and besides, these were surmounted by a strange, nine-tined crown with a halo above, not by the miter of the Cardinal. . . .

But then his eyes weren't what they once were, nor his ears. The same applied to his memory, so he did not long puzzle himself over the badge, or why he didn't recognize this tall, patrician-looking sister. She *was* curiously young, perhaps no more than eighteen or nineteen, surely a novice. But against that, she carried herself like a visiting bishop, or an abbot, and he glanced at her nut-brown hands, nodding as he saw she wore many rings on her fingers, rings set with rectangular or oval pieces of painted and gilded ivory, or intricately engraved gilded bronze. Icons of angelic magic, though he could not immediately see which angels they represented, what powers they could summon.

"I didn't notice you come in, your grace," he said. Her face was a little familiar. Young and beautiful, dark-eyed and almond-skinned, her hair black as a rare slice of jade he had once engraved to make an icon of Karazakiel. Her expression was severe—Delfon could not recall who she was, though she did remind him of someone. . . .

"No, I did not wish you to," said the strange young sister. She held out her right hand, and Brother Delfon took it and brushed his lips in the air several inches above her fingers, his old eyes trying to focus on the face of the angel so beautifully painted on the ivory plaque held in the prongs of the most distinctive and extraordinarily powerful ring. He recognized neither face nor the style of the painter, which was exceedingly odd, for Brother Delfon was a prominent icon-maker himself. He had studied icons all his life, and painted thousands of angels, and in his heyday had been able to channel the power of no fewer than nine very useful, if relatively low-ranking angels into his work.

He could not deal with so many now, but there were still three lesser angels who would answer to him and would lend their power to inhabit the icons he made, which he finished with his own blood.

"I do not . . . I do not recognize your badge, your order," muttered Delfon, releasing the Bishop's hand to shakily point at her habit.

"You do not?" asked the young woman. She laughed, and her eyes sparkled with something of equal parts exuberance and mischief. "It is the blazon of Palleniel Exalted, of course."

Delfon drew back. Surely he had misheard . . .

"Palleniel Exalted," repeated the woman, louder. She seemed to enjoy saying a name that was no longer spoken. Or perhaps even remembered, save by those like Delfon whose lives were bound up in catalogs and listings of angelic beings. Besides, his childhood had been spent near the border of Ystara, the lost country whose Archangel had been Palleniel.

"Palleniel? But he is no more, gone from this world, banished by the other Archangels!"

"But here is his Archbishop, and you have looked upon her.

Not all that you have been told is true."

Delfon frowned and started to speak, but at that moment he finally noticed something behind her, which he should have seen immediately. Words dried up in his mouth as he saw that the Saint's Tomb, the great stone sarcophagus that dominated the center of this circular, vaulted chamber, was no longer as it had been.

The lead-sealed marble lid of the vast coffin had been slid aside. It weighed several tons, and had surely been put there originally only with the greatest effort of engineers, sheerlegs, and rope. Or with the aid of a most powerful angel . . .

The woman saw the direction of his stricken gaze.

"You seem perturbed, brother. But I assure you Saint Marguerite did not object to my sharing her crypt. Indeed, when I crept in I found nothing there, suggesting the predecessors in your order were not entirely truthful about the founding of this place."

"But, but . . . what—"

Liliath sat down on the bench next to the old man and put her arm around his shoulders. He tensed and tried to draw back, but she easily held him close. She was disturbingly strong, and he quickly decided to remain still, though he turned his face away.

"Now, now. Have no fear. I would like to know something of considerable import. To me, at the least, for I suppose it *has* been a long time."

"W-w-what?"

"A long time I have been gone," said Liliath. "I knew it would be, but not in any exact measure. How many years is it since the Doom of Ystara?"

"One hundred and . . . ," whispered Delfon. "One hundred and thirty-six— No, one hundred and thirty-seven years ago."

"It seemed but a night's good rest," said Liliath, almost to herself. "A long time . . ."

She was silent for a while, slim fingers resting on one of the icon rings. Delfon sat next to her, shivering, suddenly as cold as he ever had been in the tomb in winter, in bygone days. He thought he heard the soft flutter of angel's wings, some other summoning, but he couldn't be sure. His head hurt, and his ears felt thick and closed.

"So you are Delfon," said Liliath, pinching his chin and turning his head toward her. He shivered more violently, for he had not told her his name.

She looked even younger close up, and Delfon suddenly remembered where he'd seen her face before, or something like it. There was a handwritten annotation at the end of one of his books about the icon-makers of the ages, with an accompanying sketch. This young woman was the person in that sketch: Liliath, the Maid of Ellanda. The woman who had led the only organized band of refugees to escape from doomed Ystara, dying in mysterious circumstances soon after crossing the border into Sarance.

According to the dozen or so lines added to the end of the book, Liliath had been an incredible young woman, astonishing the world with her ability to make icons and channel angels from childhood, hence her early naming as the Maid of Ellanda. A name possibly rendered ironic later, as rumor had it she was the lover of the King of Ystara, and others, though this was never to anyone's *definite* knowledge.

The notes also questioned a rumor that Liliath was uniquely able to avoid the cost of calling upon angelic powers. To summon angels took something from a mage, some of their living essence. Mages and priests aged swiftly, the more they used their powers, and the greater the angels they summoned.

The great Handuran had quantified this loss in *The Price of Virtue*. A few hours from a span of life to summon a Seraphim was of course of no account, but to call upon a Principality would age the summoner by a year, and an Archangel, several years. One famous example was the Cardinal Saint Erharn the Blessed, who had gone from a vital woman of forty to an ancient, wizened crone and then death in the span of only a day and a night, wielding the powers of the Archangel Ashalael to hold back the sea in the Great Flood of 1309. . . .

Delfon realized his mind had wandered. The young woman was asking him something again. But she could not be the Maid of Ellanda. No, surely not—

"Tell me, you are an icon-maker?"

"Yes," muttered Delfon. He clasped his hands together, as if he might even now hide the stains of paint on his fingers, the dried patches of egg white and raw pigment, bright on his leathery dark brown skin. The pattern of small scars in crosshatched ridges of even darker flesh across the backs of his hands, where his blood had been drawn.

"You still summon as well as paint?"

"Yes. Not often . . ."

"Which angels speak to you? Is Foraziel one?"

"Yes!" exclaimed Delfon, very much surprised. Though he was obviously an icon-maker, he wore no icons on the rope belt of his habit, had no rings, nothing at his neck or wrist to give her a clue as to the particular angels who were his allies in the craft. Given there were ten thousand angels in the host of Ashalael alone, the chance of her knowing which angels he knew was—

"I thought as much," said Liliath, interrupting Delfon's panicked thoughts. "*He* put you here for my awakening."

"He?" asked Delfon, puzzlement mixing with the panic. Though angels did not strictly have a gender, there was a tradition of depicting most of them as either male or female, and traditionally, Foraziel was female.

Liliath ignored his question.

"I need an icon of Foraziel," she said. "I need her power to find what I seek, and I do not want to waste time making an icon of my own."

Delfon nodded dumbly. Foraziel's scope was for finding things and people lost or forgotten. But he could not help gazing at this young woman's strange rings. She had major angelic powers there. One of the lesser ones—and he shivered to think it lesser only because of those neighboring icons—did not show the typical face and halo of an angel but a wheel within a wheel, both rimmed with tiny eyes of diamond. A Throne, one of the strange angels, highest of the First Sphere. Higher than any angels Delfon ever channeled, a being of far greater puissance than little Foraziel. But the other rings held icons that suggested greater angels still. . . .

Liliath flexed her fingers, lantern light making tiny ruby and diamond eyes and gilded halos flash and glitter.

"Sometimes it is a small, specific power that is needed," she said, correctly gauging the tenor of Delfon's thoughts. "Not the awful majesty of Principalities or Archangels."

Delfon bowed his head, his body shaking as if he had suddenly caught the ague. This was all too much for him, this strange sister . . . bishop . . . saint . . . whatever she was, and the power that went with her. The painted icons on her rings were not simply representations of angels, they were direct conduits to great and terrible beings. And she might even have somewhere hidden an icon of the greatest, if she spoke true about being some high priest of Palleniel, who was an equal to the Archangels who guarded the greatest countries of the world.

Though Palleniel had not guarded his country but destroyed its people with the Ash Blood plague, and so now—if mentioned at all—he was called the Fallen Angel, his name used as a curse. . . .

"Is there an icon of Foraziel in this temple?" asked Liliath.

Delfon hesitated, but only for a moment. Whoever this woman really was—presumably some enemy from Alba or the Eighty-Six Kingdoms—she had power far beyond his own, or for that matter far beyond anyone else in the temple, including the abbot. Though how she could be so young, not aged by the powers she called upon . . . it was beyond him, and he knew he had no choice but to honestly answer and obey.

"Yes," he said. "In the workshop. I finished it only a few days past."

"Good," said Liliath. "You can show me the way. I didn't have time to look around on my . . . ah . . . way in here."

"Yes," mumbled Delfon as he slowly got to his feet.

"Good," said the woman again. She held up her hand and touched one of the rings, muttering a name under her breath. Delfon raised one arm to shield his old eyes from the light that came then, but he peeked a little. Whichever angel this woman had summoned, it made quick work of putting the coffin lid back, the strips of broken lead rising to move into place like snakes being charmed to their rest. Within a few minutes, the tomb appeared exactly as it had been when Delfon had begun his vigil at sunset.

The old monk leaned on the wall and looked at the woman, shutting one eye so his best, the right, could better focus. A lock of her hair had turned white, but even as he watched, black flowed back through it, like wine mixing with water. She had not paid the price of using whichever angel had closed the tomb. Or had done so only temporarily.

"You will kill me, I think, when you have the icon?" he said slowly. "So no word can spread of . . . you."

"Yes," agreed Liliath. "I expect that is why *he* called you here, you who are soon to die in any case. Better than any of the younger ones. Palleniel is more compassionate than I."

"Ah," replied Delfon. He did not feel frightened now, which he thought strange. Just curious, and very tired. There had been too much excitement in the past few minutes. And the angel's residual light had frosted the corners of his eyes, making it more difficult for him to see than ever. "Palleniel. Plague bringer. The antagonist."

"Palleniel, yes. Those other names are the invention of others. I did say not all you have been told is true."

"But how can he have called me to be the one here tonight?" asked Delfon, genuinely curious, even faced with the prospect of death. Once an angelic mage, always so, even in great age and final hours. "In this place of Ashalael, in Sarance? Palleniel holds no sway here. And angels do not act of their own volition."

"The orthodox hold it so," said Liliath. She smiled with the satisfaction of secret knowledge. "But in truth, the scope of angels' actions upon this world are not rigid boundaries of *their* making but are defined by long use and custom of *people*, and they can be bent. Or if geographic, pierced in small locales. And some can be given instructions to act upon in time to come. Given sufficient will and power."

Delfon shook his head.

"I cannot believe what you say is so," said Delfon. "Or I would not, save that if you are indeed Liliath . . . I read of you in Decarandal's *Lives of the Magi*. Though it was not Decarandal who scribbled in the final pages . . . whoever that was said Liliath could make icons swiftly, at need, and summon angels previously unknown to any temple. . . ."

"Go on," said Liliath. "I am curious. What else was written?"

"Her skill in icon-making was unparalleled. And the rumors,

the talk that she did not physically pay the toll of summoning . . . but then she died young, only nineteen, in years at least, and so it seemed she had aged after all, if not outwardly. Some thought it a tragedy, a bright promise lost to the world."

"Yet as you see, I did not die," said Liliath. "And I will fulfill my promises. All of them, but one most of all."

Delfon peered at her, not understanding, but recognizing the strength of her feeling. He had seen that intensity in others before, in pilgrims, or those undertaking great tasks, driven by internal forces they often barely recognized themselves. But in this woman it was magnified a thousandfold.

"Come, we must go," ordered Liliath.

"You won't hurt me?" asked Delfon tentatively. "Before, I mean . . ."

"No," agreed Liliath matter-of-factly. "Your heart will simply cease its movement. I think you are already weary, are you not?"

"Yes, yes, I am," muttered Delfon. The angel light around his eyes was spreading, and with it, a welcome warmth. He had not felt so relaxed inside himself, not for many years, his pulse very slow and steady. It made him feel very much as if an extraordinarily comfortable bed lay in his close future, a much more comfortable bed than his own in the cell above them in the temple.

"Not yet, Mazrathiel," whispered the woman. Mazrathiel was a Dominion, of broad scope, encompassing movement of any kind. Including the beating of a heart, though only the most powerful—and selfish—of mages could force an angel to perform a direct act to take a life. "Not until I have the icon, and he is sitting down."

"What's that?" asked Delfon, coming back to himself a little.

"You serve a true and noble cause, one it is a great honor to die for," said Liliath. Her eyes seemed to shine with an inner light as she spoke, and her mouth trembled in a smile. Delfon shivered again, seeing it, feeling so much power and belief in this young woman. Just a girl, really, at least to look at—but one with *such* strength of will and purpose, so many angels at her beck and call . . .

Liliath took his arm and led him to the door, which was already uncharacteristically ajar. "Which way?"

"Left," said Delfon. "And up the winding stair."

He hobbled out, Liliath at his side.

"Tell me," she said. "What has been going on in the world? Who rules Sarance?"

Behind them, the door slowly creaked shut, accompanied by the faint sound of a distant, heavenly choir ending all together on a single, discordant note.

TWO

LILIATH ARRANGED BROTHER DELFON'S BODY ON THE floor by the worktable and closed his eyes with a no-nonsense gentleness. Mazrathiel retreated, eager to be gone after being brought unwillingly to end a life, and he would no doubt be more resistant to further summoning. Not that this concerned Liliath. If she needed Mazrathiel, he would serve, as did all angels whose icons she had made or used. She would brook no disobedience.

The icon of Foraziel the old man had made lay in pride of place on his table. It was good work, more than merely competent. She could feel the potential presence of the angel in the image, which was the most common depiction of Foraziel: an unprepossessing woman of middle age startled by the discovery of some good thing; only the thin halo indicated she was an angel.

"I must know who and where they are," whispered the young woman. "Only four . . ."

But there was no time to call upon Foraziel. Dawn was close now, and Liliath had to leave the temple before discovery. Taking up the new icon, she put it to join a number of others in the secret pockets inside her habit. Decarandal's book on icon-makers with the sketch of her that she had seen in Delfon's mind, via the power of Pereastor, took her a few more minutes to find. She tore out the relevant pages and put them in her pocket too, then left the room, quietly closing the huge oak door behind her.

Despite the passage of time, the temple had changed little from when she had sneaked in to hide herself within the Saint's Tomb, one hundred thirty-seven years earlier. Opening another door, she slipped out into the east cloister. There she paused, gazing out over the large paved courtyard, ill lit by the stars above. There were shapes upon the ground, and snores, indicating the presence of a group of travelers, people of insufficient status to be admitted to guest rooms or dormers, barely respectable enough to be given admittance to the temple and allowed to rest here. Curiously, they were all clad in some light color, hard to discern in the moonlight. Perhaps a greenish blue, or some shade of gray. Like a uniform, though a ragged one, and they did not seem to be soldiers.

Liliath hesitated. There were a dozen or more of these people, and the gatehouse lay beyond the courtyard. Likely some would wake as she passed and complicate matters. One way or another.

In that moment of hesitation, she heard the soft whisk of bare feet on the stone, someone creeping up behind her. Turning, she saw a hooded, gray-clad man, his dagger raised. He struck at her, but she was swifter, moving aside in a flowing, seamless motion that should have given him pause. But it did not.

"I won't kill you," he whispered, telling Liliath that the sleepers in the courtyard were not necessarily his allies, or perhaps he feared the temple guards in the gatehouse would hear and intervene. Many of his teeth were broken, and his left arm hung at his side, withered and useless. But his right arm was very strong, the one that held the knife. "Just slip off those rings like a good lass. And don't think you can call on an angel; I'll gut you in an instant. Wouldn't do you no good anyway, I *am* a Refuser."

"Who do you think I am?" asked Liliath conversationally, neither whispering nor raising her voice. She took note of the word "Refuser" and the tiny spark of Palleniel she could feel coursing through the blood of this would-be thief. Clearly there were many things she should have asked Brother Delfon about and now would have to find out more directly.

"Dunno," said the man, watching her carefully, his dagger ready to strike again. "Old Brill reckoned the stars say to come here, for our great fortune. For once she was right. Get them rings off!"

"You say you're a 'Refuser,'" said Liliath. She could not tell his origin from his skin or facial features. The man's skin was the shade of an ash tree and his eyes green, but no one could discern anything from that. Many ancestral tribes had settled in Ystara and Sarance thousands of years ago, their blood mingling, their descendants coming in all shades from deepest black to the palest of the pale. But that mote of Palleniel inside him could mean only one thing. "So you are a descendant of Ystarans?"

"'Course," muttered the man. He stabbed again, but Liliath leaned back impossibly far, as if she were hinged at the waist. The stroke brushed short of its intended target, her throat. Before he could recover, she flicked back and her hand snapped out and closed on his wrist, twisting his arm so he turned with it and fell on his knees.

She was impossibly strong for so slight and so young a woman. The thief made a gobbling sound in his throat, and his eyes showed white as he looked up at her, unable to comprehend what was happening.

"And being of Ystara means angelic magic does not work upon you?" asked Liliath. "Chances are you would become some fell creature?"

"Yes, yes," said the man. "Don't you try it!"

"Or you would die of the Ash Blood plague," mused Liliath. She could hear sleepers waking behind her, so she dragged the man by his wrist around a little so she could see if anyone else moved in to attack.

"More likely make a monster," gasped the thief. "Kill *you*, for sure."

Liliath did not answer, instead reaching out to that minute fraction of Palleniel inside the man.

"I think it will be the plague," she said, and bent her will upon the mote of him that was also the Archangel.

A second later, specks of gray ash began to form at the corner of the thief's mouth. Ash blossomed around his eyes, and fell from his ears, and oozed from under his fingernails. Liliath let him go and stepped back, as the ash began to flow, slowly but steadily, like almost-congealed blood. The man managed to stay on his knees for a few more seconds, then he fell sideways, and the ash continued to flow from every orifice and pore and scratch, to wearily pool about him.

By the time he was dead, a few minutes later, everyone in the courtyard was awake and watching Liliath, and several lanterns had been lit and held high, creating pools of light and many flickering shadows. She returned the gaze, aware that there was something not quite right about this crowd. There was the expected variation of skin color, and hair, and facial characteristics. All kinds, but . . .

It took her a moment to comprehend that very few of the people stood straight. The majority were bent, or doubled over, or balanced strangely. Uneven, depending on crutches or their fellows. The faces turned to her were missing eyes and noses and teeth, the consequence of disease and injury that, for most, would be no great matter for an angel to heal, or at least improve.

But clearly none of these people had ever felt an angel's healing and cleansing touch.

She met their frightened, questioning, often hostile gazes, taking in their curious all-gray tunics and cloaks, and slowly, one by one they bent down, heads lowering, knees bending, till they offered the obeisance one would give a king or queen. Only one did not incline his head quite so much as the others, and after a moment, looked up and met Liliath's gaze. His skin was the golden brown of heather blossom honey, and he should have been handsome. But his face was marked and scored with deep, crescent-shaped scars of some terrible pox that shuttered one eye and made him look much older than his years, or so Liliath figured from his unobscured eye, which was young and bright, and his voice was youthful.

"So are you really the Maid of Ellanda reborn? Just as all the ancients kept telling us? My great-grandma would have loved, *loved* to see you. Pity she died last week."

"Not reborn," said Liliath quietly. This scarred young man was not properly respectful, though he spoke with some authority, as if he were a leader of this motley crew. "Merely awoken. I take it you are of the Order of Ystara, and you saw the sign?"

She glanced up at the sky as she spoke, at the rectangular patch of stars above the courtyard, hemmed in by the temple buildings on either side. There had been debate since ancient times about whether the night sky was the actual abode of angels or merely a reflection or representation of their existence and power. Whichever it was, the heavens were a fairly reliable indication of the state of various angelic powers.

As would be expected here in Sarance, Ashalael's star shone highest and brightest in the night. But Liliath did not look at that, searching farther to the western horizon and then a little south. Once, Palleniel's star had shone there, not so bright outside Ystara, but still one of the seven most brilliant stars. Now, there was a patch of darkness. Yet, three fingers left of that absence, there shone a very pale, almost violet star. Barely noticeable, even to Liliath, whose eyes were more than human, and who knew exactly where to look. Yet it could be seen, and found by a dedicated night watcher, armed with a telescope and an inkling—or instruction—to look at that part of the sky.

The star was Jacqueiriel's, a small companion of Palleniel's host, whose scope was to bring the sensation of good news, of a happy event to come, within the geographic limitations of Ystara. A little power, for Jacqueiriel could not communicate any detail, and in the days before the plague had been generally used by lovers to send a frisson of a gift soon to be given.

In this case, the angel's star was a portent of Palleniel's reemergence and thus Liliath's own awakening. A visible indication that a message had been sent to the Order of Ystara, or its heirs and descendants.

"The Order?" asked the young man with the scarred face. "There is no Order, no fine folk with blazoned tabards and gold chains and shining swords. There's only Old Brill, who sits at deathbeds and writes down tall tales, and watches the skies. You left us too soon, to see how things would go. Ystarans are not allowed to remember our country, not allowed to remember. We are called Refusers, for it must be our own faults that make the angels deny us, or change us for the worst. We must wear gray, so that no accidents occur, no beasts be made. And we must not be too visible, save as mere creatures of servitude and labor, lest proper folk somehow catch our misfortunes."

"You are still of the Order, no matter your outward appearance," said Liliath. She spoke with utmost certainty. "And you will be healed, and made new, when we return to Ystara and Palleniel comes again."

Her speech was met with silence. Not an awed silence, either, as Liliath expected. More of a beaten-down sullenness.

"You doubt me?" she asked. She looked at the young man, at his pox-ravaged face. He had the spark of Palleniel within, stronger than the others. His ancestor would have been very close to what was desired. It had probably contributed to his leadership among this ragtag group. "What is your name?"

"I am called Bisc. Biscaray, in full. I am the Night Prince," answered the young man. "Night King now, I suppose, since you've offed Franz Wither-Arm, who was our so most noble lord. Unless someone wants to challenge me?"

He spoke this question loudly back at the gathered Refusers. None moved, or answered.

"Night King? You mean you are the lord of beggars and thieves and the like?" asked Liliath. "The underworld of all Sarance?"

The Night King laughed. "Hardly. In Lutace, only, and of Refusers. But lacking other choices, we are by far the most numerous, so we rule the night. As the high and mighty like to say, 'Not all thieves and beggars are Refusers, but all Refusers are beggars and thieves.'"

"Why did you come here, if you doubt I will lead you back to new life in Ystara?"

"Franz ordered it," said the man with a shrug. "Old Brill does read useful things in the sky, from time to time. Our former Night King thought there might be some loot or opportunity in it, and at the worst, a jaunt to the country."

"You saw what I did to him," said Liliath. She smiled, a slight, sly smile. "And yet I still feel your doubt. And though you kneel, I do not sense true obeisance."

"Plague or monster, it could just have been chance," said the new Night King warily. He hesitated, some of the confidence ebbing from his voice. "But I do not entirely doubt . . ."

"You need further proof?" asked Liliath. "Shall I make you whole, your skin smooth, eye no different from its neighbor?"

This next part would be difficult, perhaps too difficult. But if she was successful, it would serve several purposes.

She saw him swallow back some smart retort.

"It would be a suitable test, would it not?" asked Liliath.

Biscaray stood easily and walked to her, stopping a few feet away. He did not kneel again, and his right hand hovered close to the hilt of a blade only partially obscured by his gray cloak. Though the nearest lantern was behind him, Liliath could see the absolute ferocity of the pockmarks, the scarred residue of some disease that had gouged his skin and not just forced his left eye out of place as she had thought, but half concealed it under an outgrowth of scar tissue.

"If you can do as you say, I will acknowledge you are who you say you are, and serve you well," he said quietly. "Fail, and I'll gut you, or my people will."

"Do not fear what I am to do, do not strike against me," said Liliath. She raised her voice, speaking past him to the crowd. "This is but a foretaste of what lies ahead in Ystara, when we return."

She raised her right hand and, still watching the Night King, touched the icon ring that she wore on her left thumb. Gwethiniel, the great healer. There were many angels who could heal, many lesser, but few greater. Gwethiniel was a Power, not to be summoned lightly. The man's hand twitched to his knife, but he didn't draw it. Liliath waited, feeling the distant presence of the angel but not yet summoning her.

"Are you brave enough?" she whispered. She could see a spark of hope beneath the veil of suspicion in his face, though he was trying to show no emotion at all.

"I have staked my life on the roll of dice before," said the Night King with a shrug. "Once the decision is made, what's one more throw?"

Liliath summoned Gwethiniel at the same time she exerted her will against the fragment of Palleniel inside the man, forcing the essence of the Archangel to withdraw. It struggled against her, and Gwethiniel resisted too, not wanting to answer her summons.

"You will obey me," whispered Liliath, speaking to both mindless essence and resisting angel. "You will obey."

"I obey," came the voice inside her mind. Gwethiniel, her normal calm and assured voice overlaid with grating, reluctant obedience. "What is your will?"

"Heal him," commanded Liliath, though she spoke only inside her head. "Do not touch the vestige of Palleniel."

"My scope is restoration of the natural order, oft used in the healing of *mortal* life," said Gwethiniel. "The presence of another prevents my work. I cannot act against one so great, even if he is not fully present."

"You can," ordered Liliath. "I'll hold him back. Do as I command."

"There is great danger," whispered Gwethiniel. "For all."

"Do as I command!"

Liliath roared this last aloud, the crowd flinching at the power of it. Behind them, in the porter's lodge, a torch flared. The gatekeeper or one of the temple guards had finally roused.

There was the rush of great wings overhead. A sudden warm light and the scent of honeysuckle filled the courtyard. The Night King screamed and fell, and Liliath herself crouched under the weight of power she channeled, but only for a moment, before she stood straighter, shrugging it off. A thick strand of her hair turned white, and lines crawled across her skin, but they were transient changes, soon reversed even as the spark of Palleniel raged and fought against her and she contained it by pure strength of will, at the same time sending Gwethiniel back to finish the job that the angel had only partially completed.

"None may disobey me," snarled Liliath. "You will do as I command."

Gwethiniel's wings clapped. Thunder rumbled, but she finished her task and was gone in that same instant, retreating far faster than she had come, even before Liliath's formal relinquishment.

The Night King sat up and felt his face. The pockmarks were gone, his honey-colored skin was smooth and young, his eye in its rightful place. He ran his hands under his jerkin, feeling the skin there, the look on his face one of amazement. He stood up and turned to the others, and every lantern was directed at him as he lifted his head and opened his jerkin to show his smooth chest.

"I . . . I am healed!"

Almost as he spoke, there was a sudden rush toward Liliath, a hobbling, broken, lopsided rush, with arms upraised and voices begging.

"Heal me! Heal me! Help us!"

"I can do no more for now!" called Liliath, raising her hand. She was very weary, despite her inhuman strength, but she did not show it. Could not dare show weakness. There was no visible sign that the summoning had taken any toll upon her, though she could feel the skin of her face repairing itself, faint lines being restored. She smiled a little, to lend the crowd confidence, but also because once again she had forced an angel to do her bidding and had not paid the price, nor ever would. "But *all* will be healed when we return to Ystara."

Still they surged toward her, a mindless, wanting crowd. Liliath dodged back behind one of the columns, readying herself to strike the foremost, for she dared not use angelic magic now. She was too weary and could not control the outcome, and a monstrous change here would probably end with all of them dead. Even herself, though she could not die easily.

But Liliath did not have to do anything. Biscaray roared and cuffed the tide of Refusers aside, throwing the leaders back into the crowd, sending people tumbling across the paving stones. He acted as if they were a pack of dogs after meat, and he the dog handler, fearless despite their numbers.

"Back! Back and down! Down!"

The tide ebbed, Refusers sank to their knees, the moment of their utmost longing passed. But behind them, Liliath heard the gate that penned them in the courtyard for the night being unbarred, and the clank of bolts withdrawn. The temple gatekeeper and doubtless a handful of guards would be with them in a few moments, angry at being awoken before the dawn, particularly by such unwanted guests.

"I need a cloak," said Liliath to Biscaray. "With a hood or hat. And we must leave as soon as possible."

"As you command," answered Biscaray. He spat some orders at a Refuser nearby, who quickly rummaged in her pack, while others dragged the body of the former Night King to the darkest corner of the cloisters. "The leaving won't be difficult. They'll throw us out, I'm sure. And then . . . then do we go to Ystara?"

"No," said Liliath quietly. "I need time to see what has happened since I went to my rest. I had not expected Ystara to *still* be overrun with beastlings. We will need an army to return."

"An army? Every Refuser will gather to your banner, once it is known—"

"No," interrupted Liliath. "We cannot let the news of my return spread, and *never* to those not of Ystara. There are many in Sarance and in the wider world, and even in the heavens, who do not wish Ystara to rise again. Both mortals and angels will resist the return of Palleniel, and they must be tricked into helping us. We will need to be . . . clever."

"That is the way of the Night Crew. We live by our wits and cunning hands," said Biscaray.

"And cunning tongues too, I trust," said Liliath. She startled him with the hint of a salacious wink. She could not really lust after a mere human—the feelings the now almost handsome Biscaray inspired were as nothing compared to her all-consuming love for Palleniel. But the physical act did distract her, offered some relief to the intensity and pressure of the destiny she worked toward.

She would take Biscaray to her bed in due course, Liliath decided. To bind him closer, as she had done before with both men and women, not all of them young and attractive, as he now was.

A cloak was handed to her. Liliath shrugged it on, raised the hood, and wrapped it close. Bending almost double, she slipped in among the crowd as the gate groaned open and the temple gatekeeper strode in, four yawning guards behind, their quarterstaffs already prodding and thwacking.

"How dare you disrupt the peace of the temple!" boomed the gatekeeper, louder than anyone. She paused to look up at the sky, eyes wrinkling at the predawn blue-black expanse entirely devoid of cloud, for she was sure she had heard thunder. But she had been deeply asleep . . . in any case, she had certainly heard sacrilegious chattering and shouting from these vile Refusers.

"Out! Out! Disrespecting our hospitality! Get thee gone!"

THREE

LILIATH HAD NEVER BEEN TO LUTACE, BUT THE PRINCIPAL city of Sarance was not so very different from Cadenz, the chief metropolis of Ystara. Lutace also had a river winding through it—the Leire—though it was not so broad as the Gosse, and the city was mostly flat, lacking the hills of Cadenz.

Lutace did have a much taller and more extensive city wall than the Ystaran city. It was pale yellow brick only a few hundred years old, rather than the gray stone of earlier times. But either the city or royal authorities, or both, had become lax about enforcing the cleared areas necessary for proper defense, with a great sprawl of houses and huts and shacks and shanties built right up to the city wall and over it.

One of the Night Crew's many refuges and hideouts was in the Refuser's Quarter, an extensive slum that began in the dock and warehouse district and flowed over the southwestern city wall to spread out into what had been countryside a generation or two before. Bisc's people had taken over two houses that straddled the wall, the top stories leaning over into each other so it was only a hop and a jump from the attic window of the house outside the wall to the attic window of the one on the inside.

Liliath had commandeered the largest chamber of the city-side house for her own use. Stretching across the entire fifth floor, part of it was temporarily set up as an iconer's studio, with a long workbench situated against the biggest of the dormer windows, for the natural light. Though she did not anticipate staying in the house very long, Liliath had work to do, restoring icons that had suffered a little during her long sleep, particularly those that she had retrieved from the secret caches left by her followers when they first came to Lutace. Angels usually responded better to bright, clean representations.

A great four-poster bed with cloth of gold brocaded curtains occupied the other corner of the large chamber. The bed was fit for a queen and had, in fact, been a wedding gift to some princess of a century or so ago, who had died before the nuptials. It had been stolen from one of the minor, mostly unused royal hunting lodges outside the city, cleaned and finished with a new feather mattress and fine bedclothes. Of course, Liliath knew Bisc had procured such an imposing bed because he hoped to share it with her, but she had not yet chosen to let him do so. The greater the anticipation, the more he would feel under her sway.

Liliath was at the workbench, but she was not restoring an icon. Instead, she took out the one made by Brother Delfon again and leaned close to it, her slim fingers touching the gilded surface. She had started to summon Foraziel twice since she had left the temple of Saint Marguerite, but on both occasions had been interrupted, and the angel had taken advantage of her concentration being broken, proving unexpectedly recalcitrant and elusive.

So now she had to summon the angel in the city, where there were a great many more practitioners of angelic magic, many more angels actively summoned and present in the mortal world, and so a much greater risk of discovery, or curiosity. Liliath was not concerned with this as such, as she was well able to deal with the common run of angels, should some mage send one to investigate. But there was a small risk that Cardinal Duplessis herself might be sufficiently alarmed to summon Ashalael. In the Archangel's own country, Ashalael would find Liliath in an instant, and she would be quickly overcome.

But Liliath considered the chance of this to be very small, because she had learned the current Cardinal who held the great icon of Ashalael was in her late forties but looked sixty or more, already greatly aged by her many summonings. She would not summon Ashalael lightly, probably not at all, save at great need. Liliath felt she could conduct her small workings and deceptions without attracting the Cardinal's attention.

Of course, there were other risks. While the Cardinal might not dare to summon the patron Archangel of Sarance, there was a chance that more earthly agents might stumble upon Liliath, and she had not yet established a suitable identity to hide who she really was. If the Cardinal's Pursuivants—as Her Eminence's soldiers and secret agents were called—found Liliath now, in a safe house of the Night King, she would be hard put to escape without revealing her true identity. The process of becoming someone else, a sleight of hand to misdirect merely human attention, had already begun. But it was not yet done.

Despite the risk, Liliath told herself, she had to summon Foraziel. She could not bear to remain in ignorance of the names and locations of the four candidates.

Once again she frowned at the thought of there being only four but, as quickly, smoothed her forehead, knowing she must not dwell on this setback.

Keeping her fingertips on the icon, Liliath began the summoning. She did not rely on sheer strength of will to force an immediate connection as she usually did, but built the call slowly and more surreptitiously, as she had been taught long ago when she was a precocious child fawned on by her teachers in the temple and first called the Maid of Ellanda.

Foraziel, finder of lost things.

Foraziel, searcher of secrets.

Foraziel, Foraziel, come to my aid.

Slowly, ever so slowly, Liliath felt the angel's presence draw near. The entity was suspicious, not wanting to be summoned, but she could not ignore the thread of power that flowed from Liliath to icon to the heavens where the angels dwelled.

Then he was caught. Trapped by Liliath's fierce, concentrated will.

Foraziel. You will do my bidding. There are four in Lutace who bear the true essence of Palleniel within them. I must know their names and stations and where they are—

I cannot. It is forbidden. I—

You can. You must. If you fail, or retreat from the world before this task is done, the next summoning will be for your unmaking.

Liliath felt the shock and surprise of the angel as she realized Liliath spoke truly. Most angels were not aware their unmaking was even possible, but Foraziel did not doubt it now, unable to escape the shivering, crystal spear that was Liliath's will. She did not know if any other mage had ever discovered that it was possible to end angels, and more.

Given it was always such a surprise to them, she doubted it.

Possibly the greater angels knew. Liliath was not absolutely sure if she could extinguish one of them, and did not wish to risk it. Even unmaking one of the Seraphim or Cherubim was a mighty task, though she had done it numerous times, taking their power into herself. First to become more than human, then to augment certain skills, and then several times more to armor herself against the effects of time, before her long not-quite death.

I obey, as I must. It is within my scope. Within the span of a single hour, I shall return with the knowledge you require.

"Go, then, and do not fail me," said Liliath aloud, her voice harsh and strong.

There was a rush of wings, but as Foraziel was still present in the world, Liliath kept her fingers on the icon, so he should have no chance to slip away without finishing the task. She could dimly feel the angel flitting over the city, now here, now there, as he sought out the four Liliath had specified.

The next hour was spent in pleasant imaginings of the future. Though Liliath was sure to keep her fingers upon the icon, she was almost surprised when she felt Foraziel's unseen presence, her mind absent elsewhere.

I return. I have found what you seek.

Liliath roused herself, bent her will, placed a sheet of thick, linen-rich paper next to the icon.

"Write their names!"

A tiny spark flared on the paper and began to move, leaving a blackened trail, slowly forming the letter "S" in a fine hand. Liliath hissed with impatience and felt Foraziel quail. The angel wrote faster, burning through the paper in his haste, having to quickly blot the tiny flames with unseen hands or the brush of wings or however it was angels interacted with the physical world. Still, the words were clear, whether the letters formed of burnt holes or blackened lines.

- Simeon MacNeel. A student of medicine, at the Hospital of
    Saint Jerahibim the Calm.
- Agnez Descaray. A cadet of the Queen's Musketeers.
- Henri Dupallidin. A clerk in the service of the Cardinal.
- Dorotea Imsel. An icon-maker, student at the Belhalle.

Release me, begged Foraziel.

For a moment, a look of cruel exasperation flashed across Liliath's face. She thought of punishment, extinguishment, absorption. But any of these would certainly alert angels both manifested here and in the heavens, and their human masters. It was tempting, but not sensible.

"Go," she said, waving her hand in dismissal.

After the departure of Foraziel, Liliath put the angel's icon into one of the drawers of the bureau next to her worktable. There were many more icons in the drawer, dozens of them, only a small proportion of the items she had carried in the special interior pockets of her habit, in the Saint's Tomb.

Liliath studied the icons, then slowly shut and locked the drawer. She was tempted, as always, to summon angels merely to test her power over them, to relish their inability to refuse her commands. To test once more that she alone in all the world could remain unaffected by her use of angelic powers, drawing on the angels she had taken into herself rather than her own flesh and blood.

She would remain young and beautiful forever, no matter what she did.

A triple knock, pause, and single knock again at the door alerted her to the return of Biscaray. He was eager to do anything she asked and had put the entire Night Crew at her service: all the thieves, beggars, toshers, scarlatans, goods fishers, night filchers, brawlers, upside folk, and roof crawlers of Lutace. Her healing of him had made him a true believer. He had no doubt Liliath would lead his people back to Ystara. He was clearly also hoping that there he might wield real power, out of the shadows. She suspected he dreamed of becoming king in fact, imagining himself by her side as the new ruler of Ystara.

Only Bisc and the dozen Refusers who had been at the Temple

of Saint Marguerite with him knew who Liliath really was. They had been sworn to secrecy and promised healing and riches from Liliath in return, as well as threats from Bisc that he would kill them if they talked. Even so, they remained a potential threat, so they had been kept close. None had returned to their previous criminal activities; all worked in the wall house now.

"Enter," said Liliath. She stood up from her bench and smoothed down her tunic and breeches. Both were of dark burgundy satin, the tunic cut low, but she wore a wide collar of fine white lace trimmed with tiny diamonds that made it both more modest and more alluring, and the breeches high enough to show her ankles, her gold-heeled shoes accentuating the effect. Only a few icon rings remained on her hands, with another icon pinned to her dress as a brooch. Her long dark hair was gathered under a lace cap, also adorned with tiny diamonds.

The clothes had been bought with funds hidden long ago, like most of the icons in her bureau, for Liliath's return. Though she had not anticipated her sleep would be quite so extensive, or that the refugee Ystarans would become a shunned underclass, the first generation of her followers had carried out her orders to the letter.

Biscaray had personally retrieved the contents of the two most important caches. She had allowed him to see what was inside the small chests he had brought back, astounding him with the wealth her order had brought out, in icons and gems, and coins, the fabulously heavy "double dolphin" gold nobles of Ystara.

One particular treasure from the main cache had absolutely

staggered Biscaray. He'd recognized it at once, both for its almost incalculable worth and because it had been famously stolen from Queen Anne IV of Sarance one hundred and thirty-eight years before: a magnificent jeweled necklace of twelve icons known as the Queen's Collar, or in the folk stories that had sprung up about its theft as the Twelve Diamond Icons, as each of the engraved icon plaques of gilded bronze were bordered with dozens of diamonds.

Liliath had enjoyed seeing his astonishment, and even more the magnification of that astonishment when she told him that she had arranged the theft because she needed to study the icons, which were of the twelve Principalities who served under Ashalael. More important for her purposes, they had been made by the infamous mage Chalconte, the first time engraved metal icons had been proved to work. These icons had been the beginning of the great mage's descent into heresy, though they were not themselves considered heretical.

Liliath didn't tell Bisc what she planned to do with the collar now. She wasn't sure herself, though several plans were evolving, and her mind was constantly weighing up various possibilities.

Biscaray entered and bowed low. He wore a black leather mask, a lumpy, ill-fitting thing that suggested the scars underneath that were no longer there, complete with a smaller hole for his supposedly misshapen left eye. No one could know he had been healed, since this was impossible.

As was required by law, he wore the gray shirt, doublet, breeches, and cloak of a Refuser, but since returning to Lutace, his clothes had become of a finer cut and now featured a narrow band of black lace at the neck and cuffs, as much as, or perhaps a little more than, any former Ystaran refugee was allowed.

"Good evening, milady," said Biscaray. He glanced toward the bed, and then away again, as if it were entirely by chance.

"Milady?" asked Liliath. She smiled and twirled an errant strand of hair that had escaped her cap. "Have I become an Alban noble?"

"If you so choose," said Biscaray. He reached into his doublet and withdrew a sheaf of papers. "You asked me to find someone suitable for you to become, of noble birth, but not yet known at court."

"I did," said Liliath, smiling again.

"I have found three," replied the Night King. "But the Alban is the best. Uh, I suppose you can speak Alban?"

"I can," said Liliath, in Alban. She smiled, a cruel smile, remembering why this was so. One of the angels she had taken within her had been of the Alban host.

Biscaray, his eyes downcast before her, did not see the smile.

"Tell me who I am to be, my trusty knight," said Liliath. She crossed the room and tapped him lightly on the shoulder, as if bestowing an accolade, before going past to look out the high window. She could see his blurred reflection in the thick, flawed glass, broken into nine squares.

"Lady Dehiems, a widow, aged twenty," said Biscaray. "She arrived from Alba two days ago. Her agents bought old Lord Demaselle's house a month ago. She is very wealthy, and under a cloud in Alba, her husband's family believing she killed him in some underhanded way."

"Did she?"

Biscaray shook his head.

"I doubt it. He was old, and she is beautiful."

Liliath turned to look at him. He looked up at her fully for a moment, then down again, mumbling, "Not so beautiful as you. There is a good resemblance, her eyes and skin are dark, her height similar, but her hair is a dark chestnut, not black—"

"Easily matched," said Liliath. "I can call upon Froudriel or Asaravael to do so. Or even simply rhubarb and henna."

"She is the best of those we have found so far. It isn't just her looks. She is rich, estranged from her husband's family and from other Albans, as most nobles have adopted the belief she is a murderer. Politics."

"Is she a mage?"

Biscaray shook his head. "Of no consequence, if anything. She wears an old icon, a cameo of Fermisiel—or so says Erril, I did not recognize the angel myself—"

"Erril? The hunchbacked woman? One of those at the temple?"

"Yes. She is the best of our scholars. If not born a Refuser, I think she would have been a great mage."

"Yes. I remember her," said Liliath. "Fermisiel is nothing. Her scope is color, to make old clothes bright again and the like. So. How many in this Lady Dehiems's household?"

"The doorwarden, three maids, two grooms, a cook."

"She brought an Alban cook to Lutace?"

Biscaray shrugged as if to say that when it came to food Albans were even more inexplicable than in their other strange habits.

"What are her connections here? Relatives? Friends?"

"None that we have found. She was originally from some country part of Alba, in the north. A noble family but fallen. Her beauty alone secured her marriage."

"And you have seen her yourself? We really look enough alike?"

"More than enough, once you change your hair. Besides, she has not stirred from her new house. Few have seen her since she arrived. The crossing of the gulf made her sick, it seems, and she is prone to imagine herself ill."

Liliath thought for a moment. This was a crucial point, where a misstep could have terrible consequences. But she had to assume some new identity, one that would enable her to move and plot and manipulate, to further the great plan. Besides, she did not want to continue living in one room of a criminal gang's refuge, royal bed or not. In Ystara, her chambers in her temple had been as splendid as the King's Palace in Cadenz.

"I may continue that. A sometime invalid, off and on . . . it would suit my purposes. But should she be well enough, she would be received at court?"

"Yes," replied Biscaray. "As I said, a noble family, with royal connections in the past. And the suspicion of murder in Alba will help her here. The Queen is displeased with Alban posturing, and it is rumored that the traitor Deluynes—her former lover— sold the Queen's letters to the Atheling. So . . . an enemy of the Atheling must be the Queen's friend, no?"

"Is she of interest to the Cardinal? Have Her Eminence's people paid her attentions?"

Liliath did not ask about the King. No one cared about King Ferdinand. Queen Sofia XIII notionally ruled Sarance, but her Chief Minister, Cardinal Duplessis, was in most cases the actual governor of the realm, the Queen rarely going against the Cardinal's directives or advice. The King plotted against both, haphazardly, as was also traditional, and of little consequence.

"I do not think so," said Biscaray. He sounded less sure of himself than he had before. "We have seen none of the Cardinal's Pursuivants there, or the Queen's Musketeers, or any of the other agents we know. But the Cardinal tends to perceive more than we would like."

"She must not know about this!" snapped Liliath. "She must not know about me!"

"No," agreed Biscaray. He paced forward and knelt in front of Liliath, his hands folded as if in prayer to an Archangel. "She will not. No one will. I will make sure of it."

"I trust you will, my Biscaray," said Liliath. She dangled one hand and let him kiss it, before moving back to the window again.

"Very well," she continued. "Tonight."

"Tonight?" asked Biscaray.

"Your people are ready?"

Biscaray inclined his head.

"Come here when it is done," said Liliath. "Bring some of her clothes and jewelry."

"It will be late. Before dawn."

"I will be here," said Liliath. She glanced at the bed, then back at Biscaray, and smiled again. "You have done well, Biscaray."

"Thank you, milady," he said.

"There is something else," said Liliath. She gave him the paper with the four names burned on it, black and stark. "These four. I need to know all that can be discovered about them, their families, their lines of descent, where they come from. And they must be watched and guarded. Not too closely—they must not know. But they must be protected, kept safe from harm."

Biscaray studied the list, frowning in puzzlement.

"What is their significance?" he asked. "They seem of little account."

"You will see, in time," said Liliath. "But it is of the highest importance they be watched and guarded well."

"I will order it immediately," said Biscaray. "Watchers and guards."

Liliath gestured for him to rise and offered her hand to be kissed again. When he turned it over to kiss the inside of her wrist, she did not move away but instead caressed him lightly above the ear.

"When will you tell me what you plan?" asked Biscaray. "I do not understand why you want to become an Alban noblewoman, what part it can play in our return to Ystara, these four people . . ."

He tried to draw her closer, but she stepped back and drew herself up.

"I will tell you," she said, but softly, her voice full of promise. "Something of my plans, at least. When it is time."

PART II

The Four

FOUR

SIMEON MACNEEL WAS PONDERING THE ARRANGEMENT of the bones of thumb and wrist as he dissected a hand, so he didn't hear the page's first attempt to tell him he was summoned by Magister Delazan.

Though he was only a first-year student himself, a number of other neophyte doctors watched his dissection. Simeon knew this wasn't because his dissection was so proficient and swift, though it was. It was due to his physical appearance seeming to be at odds with his skill. He was a very large young man, with fingers that even he thought looked rather like black puddings. He had been called "Ox" and "Mammoth" when he first started at the hospital, though those names had faded as he calmly showed his expertise. His parents were well-known doctors in his hometown of Loutain in the province of Bascony, and noting his surprising dexterity, formidable memory, and calm demeanor, they had trained Simeon since he was a child, and he had assisted in almost every imaginable medical treatment and operation. The education offered by the Hospital of Saint Jerahibim the Calm was, for him, more of a formality than a challenge.

That said, though he was effectively already a doctor, Simeon could not practice as one without the formal certification of hospital training, and he had philosophically accepted that he had to put up with repeating much he already knew. And there were always new things to learn, or to discover. Even if this rarely happened in the actual lessons.

"The Magister said you are to attend him at once," repeated the boy. Simeon didn't know the page's name. But he had seen him around before, and he seemed more than usually dejected. Even for a Refuser, who were all typically melancholic.

For a moment Simeon wondered if the boy had finally realized what the future held for him: manual servitude and a life that would be very likely cut short. As a Refuser, angelic magic could not be used upon him, as it would either initiate the Ash Blood plague or transform him into a beastling. The boy was forever cut off from the miraculous cures and protections offered by the very hospital that employed him—and he was very likely to catch one of the quite ordinary diseases they treated here.

But the cause of the boy's hangdog look proved to be closer at hand, explained by his next words. It was merely curiosity defied.

"Magister Delazan wants you to help uncrate a specimen in the old jar room," said the boy. "*We're* not allowed in."

"The old jar room?" asked Simeon, frowning. "Are you sure he wants me?"

"He said 'the big lumpish one,'" replied the boy with a smirk.

Simeon nodded, set his tongs and scalpel carefully down, and stepped back, fingers instinctively closing over the ivory plaque he wore on a leather strap around his neck, whispering the request that would return the angel to rest.

"As you will," whispered a voice in Simeon's mind, and the angelic presence he had been feeling as a slight warmth slowly faded away, with a susurration of air intimating the rush of wings.

The icon was of the Seraphim Requaniel, whose scope was to shield, to wall, to defend. All the students at the hospital were given such an icon and taught how to instruct the angel to defend against the unseen but deadly humors that emanated from the sick and dying, or issued from the dissection of the recently deceased, rather than provide a barrier against physical attacks, which was the angel's other common use.

But as with all such old and oft-used icons issued to the students, Simeon's provided only a narrow channel for the angel's power and was neither very strong nor persisted for long. He had already felt Requaniel's presence fading and would have had to stop soon, even without the page's interruption. Though, of course, even if the icon were stronger, he would probably have had to stop soon anyway. Using angelic magic, even minor magic, took its toll on the practitioner, both in the short and long term.

"Why the old jar room?" asked Simeon, muffling a yawn in his sleeve. "And who exactly isn't allowed in?"

"Me," said the messenger. "And all the messengers and porters."

Simeon looked puzzled. The various specimens and corpses used for private study or the anatomy classes were always handled by the porters. The students and doctors-magisters never did any of the dull, heavy, and often dirty work of carrying such things in and out . . . and why the old jar room?

The puzzlement cleared as he finally figured what the specimen must be.

A beastling.

The fell creatures originally spawned in ruined Ystara, the homeland of the Refusers. Ystara of terrible memory, where the Ash Blood plague some one hundred and thirty-seven years ago had killed at least two-thirds of the population, transformed most of the other third and left a scant remnant to flee to safer lands.

But even these refugees from disaster had suffered terribly, as had their descendants, like the boy before him, for they carried the potential for the Ash Blood plague within them.

The plague turned its victim's blood into a superfine gray dust, which mostly killed them but sometimes caused horrific transformations instead. The Ystarans who'd fled early and survived did not at first seem to have suffered this terrible transformation of blood—until angelic magic was used upon them or they attempted it themselves, when it was found the malady still lurked within them. Their blood would swiftly turn to ash, and they would either die or become hideous monsters.

Consequently Refusers always wore clothes of gray, the color of fine wood ash, to show their nature and thus avoid any accidental brush with magic.

Most people avoided Refusers wherever possible, still fearing the Ash Blood plague themselves, even though there were no recorded incidents of someone not originally from Ystara or not descended from Ystarans becoming afflicted. The incipient plague lay in their blood, and the potential could not be evaded, and it was always passed on to their children, even when they took partners who were not of Ystara. Though this was very rare, for obvious reasons.

Simeon was not afraid of the Ash Blood plague, though he was afraid of beastlings. All sane people were. Refusers found this a small blessing against the fearfulness of the small-minded, who occasionally suggested all Refusers should be killed, thus removing any doubts about them and their plague forever. But this fear was balanced by the even greater one that if they were attacked, Refusers might invoke angelic magic upon themselves and become beastlings.

The original beastlings created in Ystara at the advent of the plague were either very long-lived or had bred, because the country was still infested with them, but they never crossed the borders to the north and south. The only time the rest of the world was troubled by a beastling was when one was made by the meeting of angelic magic and Refuser, usually by accident.

They were always killed as quickly as possible, and usually then burned; so specimens for study were very rare. Simeon had never seen a beastling himself, but he had read several books on beastling dissections, the most recent being the work of Magister Delazan himself, which he required his students to purchase. It was a rehash of earlier works but did feature half a dozen detailed etchings by the famed Katarina Dehallet, and the illustrations at least had made the creatures seem very real to Simeon, and he was fascinated by the variations in their shape, size, and nature.

Beastlings had the same strange, superfine gray dust in their veins as those who died from the Ash Blood plague, and Simeon knew Magister Delazan theorized that it might be possible for Refusers to contract *other* unknown diseases from beastlings, and he would be keen to search for evidence of this in any dissection.

Still, it was probably best to be careful, Simeon thought. He remembered another one of Delazan's theories, which was that beastling blood might be a catalyst that could transform even non-Ystarans . . . which was a truly disturbing thought.

Simeon frowned and touched his icon of Requaniel. He could hardly feel the presence of the angel at all now; the ivory was cold. It could not be used for several days and certainly would not protect him from whatever unseen miasma might emanate from a beastling corpse.

Simeon lifted the chain that bore the icon over his head and stuffed it into the belt purse he carried safely from pickpockets under his student's smock, a shapeless, thigh-length garment of dark blue wool that made many of the more sartorially minded students shudder. Some of the more daring students wore other garments, trusting the standard doctor's coat, worn over the top, would disguise this, but Simeon had never bothered.

"The Magister told me to *rush*," said the messenger suspiciously, watching this preparation. "'Send him straight along,' that's what he told me."

Simeon nodded as he retrieved another icon from his purse, a larger one painted on an almost palm-sized piece of heavy wood, gilded at the edges, with a pin at the back so it could be worn as a brooch. This was an heirloom of his house, a particularly potent icon that had reportedly been created by the famous icon-maker Chalconte several centuries before, and its power had not faded in that time, a testament to his artistry and skill.

Requaniel was depicted in his usual guise, as a golden-eyed, golden-haloed black-skinned man of middle years with a particularly serene countenance. Most icons left it at that, with only a colored background, or perhaps the suggestion of sky or clouds. But in this one, Chalconte had painted the battlements of a great city behind the head of the angel, all done in exquisite detail. Simeon had looked at it through a powerful glass, one the students used to look at animalcules in water or blood, and there were even soldiers on the walls, and banners, and birds in the sky, all of them mere specks to unaided vision.

He had no idea how Chalconte had managed to paint these extraordinarily fine details. Simeon had learned the basics of icon-making when he was first taught to use angelic magic, but he had not pursued that side of the art.

"Please hurry!" urged the messenger boy.

"I am," replied Simeon shortly. He pinned the larger icon on his smock but did not call on Requaniel immediately. This icon was much more powerful than the one provided by the hospital and would require greater concentration and focus. He would need to calm his mind for a while first.

The icon securely pinned on, he waved the boy to proceed and followed at a slightly more sedate pace. Though to tell the truth, he wanted to scurry just as fast as the Refuser, and his heart was beating rapidly at the thought he would soon not only see a beastling but also be able to dissect it and see how it differed from a human corpse.

Magister Delazan was waiting outside the old jar room, accompanied by two Refuser porters, a man and a woman. Not ones Simeon knew, and he glanced at them, puzzled, as they were not typical of the hospital's Refuser staff. The man was huge, even bigger than Simeon, something he very rarely saw. He had the look of the toughs who frequented the river docks, living by theft and banditry. His companion, a woman, was slight and wiry, and her eyes were in constant motion, flicking here and there, taking everything in. This was not how the porters usually behaved. They were stolid, uncomplaining, didn't do anything without direction, and like most Refusers tried to stay in the background whenever possible.

Delazan paid no attention to these unusual porters. He was already dressed in the long black coat the doctors used for bloody operations or when visiting plague-struck houses, and he held his glass-eyed raven mask under one arm, the long beak no doubt stuffed with fresh mint and other herbs. He wore several icons pinned to the breast of his coat, the ever-present Requaniel accompanied by other angels that Simeon did not immediately recognize.

One of the Refuser servants held out a coat and raven mask for Simeon. Clearly the Magister was taking no chances. Even with normal human corpses, sometimes angelic magic failed—the angels withdrew their power, icons suddenly became dull things of paint or even turned to dust. Mundane protections were far inferior, but they provided a small additional layer of safety.

Or the illusion of it, thought Simeon.

Delazan looked impatient, his mouth thin, his pointy chin jutting forward. Not for the first time, Simeon wondered why he didn't grow a beard to disguise just how pointy that chin was. Beards were fashionable; most of the male magisters sported at least a goatee. It would also make up for the lack of hair on Delazan's head, which though not entirely bald, sported only the thinnest gray down. He was far from the oldest magister in the hospital, but he looked old indeed. Simeon thought of him as of his grandfather's generation and would have been shocked to learn Delazan was a little younger than Simeon's father—but would have immediately come to the correct conclusion that this premature aging was a consequence of too frequent use, or too ambitious use, of angelic magic.

"I was beginning to wonder if, given your lack of keenness, I should give the wonderful opportunity that lies beyond this door to Judith Demansur or those Denilin twins," said Magister Delazan as Simeon arrived.

"No, ser, I'm keen," said Simeon, taking the coat and immediately putting it on. "Very keen. Is it a beastling?"

"Yes, or so said the . . . the people . . . who brought it," replied Delazan. "An accident near Malarche, a near-drowned Refuser was not identified, being unclad. A passing bishop tried to infuse his lungs with air by the use of Yazarifiel, but of course the drowned fellow became a beastling and was killed by the

Bishop's guards. The corpse was fortunately claimed by . . . an old acquaintance of mine . . . who ordered it packed in ice and boxed with a layer of straw, and it has been conveyed here in less than three days. I have hopes it will be the freshest specimen I have yet examined. Put on your mask. Is Requaniel with you? That is a very fine icon. Very fine indeed. Not one of the hospital's, I take it?"

"A family heirloom, Magister," said Simeon. "A royal gift originally."

That last part wasn't true; no one knew how the family had come by the icon. Simeon only said it as insurance, since he didn't like the frankly acquisitive look in Delazan's eye. Very old and powerful icons were extraordinarily valuable, and he had been careful not to let it be known he had such a one in his possession. Gossip in the hospital about the Magister said he had enormous gambling debts, and Simeon had been told by a sardonic second-year student that she had seen Delazan bet a thousand livres on a single turn of a card—and lose.

Not that he thought the Magister would blatantly steal it, but it was better not to tempt someone who had great power over the students and was reputedly so badly in debt.

"I will call upon the angel now."

Simeon touched the pinned icon and closed his eyes. The more powerful an icon and the greater connection it offered, the more difficult the summoning. He concentrated for several seconds, repeating the angel's name over and over in his head, while he tried to block out everything else around him. When he felt sufficiently centered, Simeon whispered aloud but so soft even someone standing right next to him would not be able to hear.

"Requaniel, Requaniel, come to my aid."

The angel answered at once, responding to the beauty and power of the icon. Simeon felt the rush of warmth through his whole body that announced the connection was made, and the icon itself shone with a cool light, just a flash that immediately subsided. A moment later, he heard the secret whisper of Requaniel's voice.

Requaniel is here. What is your will? If it lies within my scope, it shall be done.

"Guard me from the things unseen that flock as evil humors in the air," whispered Simeon, hardly even vocalizing the words. It was more he thought them and moved his lips in the pretense of speech. "Keep my body and my self from harm."

Thy bidding is done, said Requaniel inside the young man's mind. *For a time, thou will take no scathe from the tiny enemies unseen by mortal eye.*

The warmth faded back, but Simeon still felt the angel's presence. Only when that comforting sensation left his body, and the icon also grew cold, would Requaniel's shield be lifted. He had used this icon just twice before, but both times the effect had lasted almost a whole day. Far longer than when using the old and weak icon the hospital gave to him as a student.

Not for the first time, he wondered how Requaniel could be here for him so strongly now when the angel was also employed by at least the other dozen students in the dissection class. The orthodox view was that any angel's power was constant, no matter the icon or how many times they were summoned concurrently. But it just didn't feel like that was accurate.

He opened his eyes to meet the glazed glass lenses of the raven mask Delazan had just put on.

"Mask and gloves, Simeon," said Delazan, his voice muffled. "You servants, stay without the door. Admit no one without my word. No one! If it is someone you cannot deny, then knock if you must."

"Yes, Magister," said the Refuser servant, the big one. He had a scar across the corner of his mouth that looked to be from a knife fight. Refusers were often scarred of course. Simeon wondered what it would be like to have to suffer such wounds and scars, without the hope of angelic intervention to take both pain and ugliness away. But only for a moment, the thought wafting in and out of his mind. Chased away by the excitement of dissecting a beastling specimen for the first time.

Delazan opened the door and gestured for Simeon to go in first. A single window high up on one side admitted very little light, and though several lanterns had been lit and set in place, they were situated so as to illuminate only the center of the room. It was quite hard to see out of the raven mask. The glass over the eyeholes was neither very clean nor well placed. Simeon had to keep turning his head from side to side to compensate for the restricted field of vision.

Empty shelves lined the walls, and there was dust everywhere. Once this had been a storeroom for unguents and medicines and herbs and simples, and the shelves would have been packed with bottles and jars of all sizes. But there was a better, larger store-room for such things lower down in the hospital. This one, on the third floor, had been very inconvenient and at some point several years ago everything had been moved.

A single large crate sat in the middle of the room. It was at least nine feet long and four feet wide and high, and had been extravagantly corded with inch-thick rope as well as being nailed closed. Water had pooled underneath it and was flowing slowly to the drain hole in the corner.

Paper notices pasted on each side warned that it was the property of the Order of Ashalael and not to be tampered with, under the seal of the Prince-Bishop of Malarche: great circles of red wax impressed with the coat of arms of the Prince-Bishop, a gold mermaid on a field of blue, supported by silver angel's wings of six pinions, the whole surmounted by an ivory miter.

"Uh, ser, shouldn't we have someone in authority . . . a priest of Ashalael to remove those seals?" asked Simeon. His voice came out very muffled under the mask and sounded strange in his own ears.

"Don't worry about that," said Delazan, waving his hand in easy dismissal. "As I said, this was sent by a friend of mine."

Simeon nodded slowly. Not official, in that case, which was hardly surprising since all beastling corpses were supposed to be burned anyway. But no one would dare use the seal of the Prince-Bishop without authorization. Would they? It all seemed odd . . . but it shouldn't matter for him. He was only a medical student, acting under the orders of a senior magister.

"Let's get the lid off," said Delazan greedily. "I'll cut the ropes. You take that tool there and lever it up. Don't worry about breaking the seals."

"Yes, Magister," replied Simeon, taking up a long chisel as the Magister started to work at the thick ropes with a bone saw.

Simeon was excited too, wondering what kind of beastling lay within. There were at least two dozen different specimens that had been recorded previously. Some were almost human in shape, but others were far closer to animals, or strange hybrids of human and animal. He hoped the ice hadn't melted too much and the corpse was still relatively fresh. It was most unpleasant to dissect waterlogged human bodies, and Simeon supposed beastlings would be no different.

The last rope parted with a satisfying snap. Simeon got the chisel under the lid and pushed down hard, levering up one corner, tearing the warning paper apart. He'd expected to get a whiff of decomposition as he did so, even through the cloaking herbs inside his mask, but he smelled only the mint and lavender stuffed in the snout.

"The other side, boy! Quickly!" called out Delazan. He was in a fever of anticipation, almost hopping from one foot to the other. "Let's see what we've got!"

Simeon levered up the other side. But the lid was still too firmly nailed to open, so he had to run along the sides, forcing the chisel in and lifting the nails every six inches or so. Finally, it seemed to be free enough to move. Delazan, unable to wait any longer, seized one side as Simeon heaved on the other, and the lid came free.

The inside was lined with straw, but only the remnants of ice remained. Judging from the damp stains on the wood, it must have been crammed with heavy blocks. All that was left were small chunks of ice, bobbing about in three inches of water.

There was a beastling within. A nine-foot-tall, vaguely humanoid creature, its entire body speckled with spike-like bristles an inch long, reminiscent of the hunting spiders of the south. Its once-human face was drawn out into a long snout to contain a toothy jaw lined with a double row of small but enormously sharp teeth; its arms were short but very thick and muscular and ended in claws; a spiked tail lay over its strangely jointed legs, which ended in splayed feet of three toes, each with a ripping talon and a recurved spur at the heel.

Its eyes were orange, pupils a jagged black line.

The eyes moved.

Delazan and Simeon both jumped back, struck with the sudden realization that this thing was alive, and not only alive but now unconstrained by lid, rope, nails, and tightly packed ice.

Delazan, in his panic forgetting it would be no use against a creature of Ystara, fumbled for one of the icons pinned to his robe. Simeon ran around the foot of the box, toward the door.

"Help! Help! A beastling!" he shouted, his normal bass voice suddenly shrill, so muffled beneath the mask he felt sure no one outside the room could possibly hear him.

The beastling sat up, ice falling from it, its claws gripping the side of the box, scoring deep lines in the timber. Its jaw opened to emit an incredibly high-pitched screech that shattered jars all round the room.

A hunting call.

It leaped out upon its prey.

Delazan fell under it, screaming, still trying to uselessly summon an angel for his protection. A moment later there was a terrible ripping sound, and the beastling raised its head, jaws now wet with blood, and shrieked again.

The door in front of Simeon slammed open. The two strange porters ran in. The woman had a small crossbow that she fired at the beastling, the bolt thudding into its stubbled hide, to little effect. The other porter grabbed Simeon and flung him into the corridor, before drawing a huge cleaver from under his robe and stepping in front of the arbalist, who was frantically slotting another bolt in place and drawing back the cord.

"Run, boy!" roared the large porter.

Simeon needed no encouraging. He ran, ripping his mask off and throwing it aside.

"Help! A beastling! Help!"

FIVE

THE YELLOW ANTECHAMBER WAS ALMOST AS FAR AWAY AS you could get in the Cardinal's Palace from the center of power. The small, saffron-wallpapered room was usually home to four very unimportant clerks, who merely copied documents rather than drafting anything of importance, and certainly none of them ever expected to speak to the Cardinal herself, or even anyone more important than the Third Secretary, who at least notionally oversaw their work.

So it was with great surprise and no small amount of apprehension that Henri Dupallidin, least and newest of clerks, looked up from his work to find himself the only one present in the Yellow Antechamber as the door was pushed open and Monseigneur Robard burst in with all the preemptory importance of a man who was First Secretary to Cardinal Duplessis, highest priest of the Order of Ashalael, patron Archangel of Sarance—and, more important perhaps, Chief Minister to the Queen and thus generally accepted to be the de facto ruler of the realm.

"Um, good day, ser," said Henri, leaping to attention. He pushed his high stool back so quickly he almost knocked it over, and he did flick several splotches of ink onto the letter he was currently copying.

Robard, splendid in actual scarlet sleeves and hose and a cloth of gold doublet—the Cardinal's colors—looked bleakly at the young, wide-eyed Henri in his low, clerkly version of the raiment, which was dull red and a kind of yellow that only the charitable would associate with any precious metal.

"Where are Dalunzio and Deraner?" he barked. "And . . . er . . . the other one?"

"Ser Dalunzio has the grippe," said Henri after a hasty bow, where his rump threatened to knock the high stool over again. "Ser Deraner . . . I'm not sure. She stepped out earlier. Ah, the other one I know of only by repute; I've never actually met Ser Macallone."

"And you are?"

"Henri Dupallidin, at your service, ser."

"When did you join the Cardinal's service?"

"Last Wednesday, to be exact."

"Is that a mustache or some remnant of your breakfast?"

"The beginnings of a mustache," said Henri defensively, stroking his upper lip. As so often, he wished he'd taken after his brown-skinned mother with her luxuriant hair, but he was apparently the spitting image of his paternal grandfather, with pale skin prone to sunburn and fine red hair, which did not yet grow well on his face, though he hoped it would increase with age. "It will come on, I am assured by Agrippa."

Robard's left eyebrow rose. Agrippa was the most fashionable hairdresser in Lutace this season, his salon frequented by the highest nobles, the most important priests, and the wealthiest merchants. Agrippa was a Refuser, too, which made his rise all the more interesting, his work unaided by angelic magic.

"Well, one of his assistants," conceded Henri. "But Agrippa did nod at me when he walked past."

"I see," said Robard, stroking his own short and tightly curled black beard. Judging from the impressive coils of hair that hung below his cap, he never needed the encouragement and special oils Henri hoped would bring on his own hirsute triumph.

Henri flushed, but Robard did not sound sarcastic or intent on humiliating him, as the other clerks had been wont to do ever since Henri arrived. He supposed it was just the way of things, that the new person would be treated so.

"Well, since you are here and the others are not, perhaps you will do," said Robard. "Henri Dupallidin. Your parents are . . ."

"My father is Sacristan of the Temple of Huaravael in Adianne," said Henri, though his mind was racing. Perhaps he would do for what? As always, he noted the slight lift of the brow as he mentioned Adianne, which was in Bascony, whose inhabitants were popularly held by many other Sarancians to be hot-tempered, rustic simpletons.

"My mother is Ser Perida Dupallidin. She holds a manor directly from the Duchess of Damerçon, who is a cousin."

Henri paused and, judging it best to be completely honest with the Cardinal's chief assistant, added, "A cousin several times removed. The Duchess put me forward to Her Eminence for this position. But I haven't ever actually . . . er . . . met her. The Duchess, I mean."

"You are a second or later child?"

Clearly Henri was not his mother's heir, or his family wouldn't have been asking distant relatives to find him a position, any position. He'd wanted to be a soldier himself—or more particularly an artillerist, as he was mathematically gifted and had a fine hand with a gunner's rule—but there had been no money nor suitable connections to get him into the Loyal Royal Artillery Company. And, of course being of noble, if impoverished, birth, he couldn't join any lesser regiment.

A clerk's position was the best he could hope for, and he had resigned himself to a lifetime in some awful counting house or as a reeve for some backwoods noble, only to have his mother somehow manage to land him a post in Lutace itself, and not only that but in the Cardinal's service. It was far better than anything Henri had expected himself.

"Um, fifth," replied Henri. An economically risky fifth child, given the state of the family finances, which had already been in disarray before he came along. His mother's manor was not rich, and his father's stipend as sacristan of a remote and very small temple was barely enough to keep him, let alone a family. His whole life Henri had been reminded by his older brothers and sisters, if not his parents, that his very existence was the reason there was wine with meals only one day out of seven.

"Good enough," said Robard. "Come with me."

Henri nodded and reached for his scabbarded dagger, which

he had found uncomfortable to leave on his belt when sitting on the high stool. He had brought his sword to the chambers the first few days, until he noticed none of the other clerks did so and made fun of him behind his back.

"Leave that," said Robard. "And brush those crumbs off your doublet."

"Yes, ser," answered Henri, brushing away furiously. He hadn't even realized the crumbs were there, and—curse his luck—there was even a stain of egg yolk, luckily almost the same color as his awful doublet.

"Where are we going?" asked Henri as he stumbled along behind Robard into the corridor, almost running into the First Secretary's gilded spurs.

"To see Her Eminence," replied Robard over his shoulder. "She has a job for you. Rather, she had a job for one of your superiors, but as they are not to be found, it has come to you."

Henri stumbled, flailed with his arms to stop himself colliding with Robard's back, and recovered just enough to pretend that he was merely incredibly eager to attend at once to whatever the Cardinal desired.

Inside, he was both petrified and excited. Even from his few days at the palace, he knew none of the other clerks had even been spoken to by the Cardinal in passing, let alone been summoned to see her. She was a great power, to be viewed from a distance, her commands filtering through a series of lesser beings down to the least of all, which is what Henri was, and there was safety in being so far away from such greatness. He didn't want to attract attention, or at least not from so far on high, or rather he did want attention but not when wearing his stained doublet—

"Do you have any icons on your person?"

"Um, no ser," replied Henri. "I have one, in my lodgings. It is only of Huaravael, one of the family icons, a bit old and worn. Father taught me angelic magic, naturally; I am a practitioner in a small way. And I have dealt with *some* other angels—"

"Remind me," interrupted Robard. "Huaravael's scope?"

"Uh, the properties of air, for the main," said Henri. "Removing smoke, that sort of thing. Not in great quantity, and geographically limited to Adianne. She is a Seraphim, no more."

"If, as may be the case, you are summoned again to see Her Eminence, any icons must be left without. She bears the icon of Ashalael, and even unsummoned, lesser angels quail before such potent majesty, and the icons that connect them with our world will often crumble or burn. Remember."

"Oh, I will, I will, ser!"

Robard did not speak further but hurried his pace still more. Henri galloped along behind, feeling like a particularly stupid horse on a lead. He was taller than Robard, but that seemed undiplomatic, so he slumped down, crouching even more as he saw that they were heading toward the grand staircase that rose from the central reception chamber, a vast thing of gilded rails and scarlet carpet, with the lower steps heavily garrisoned with halberd-bearing members of the Cardinal's Pursuivants in their absurdly highly polished cuirasses over scarlet and gold coats, with beaked morions of gold-etched steel on their heads.

Needless to say, Henri had never been within thirty paces of the grand staircase. It was reserved for the highest officials. Everyone else had to go up and down the usually crowded lesser stairs in the eastern and western wings of the palace.

Now the guards stood aside and saluted with their halberds as Robard strode up the steps, Henri following as close as he dared, jerking somewhat out of his slump as he heard one of the guards behind him whisper to another.

"Who's the hunchback with the Secretary?"

Robard heard too. He paused, glared back at Henri—not at the Pursuivant; they were among the most trusted and valuable members of the Cardinal's retinue—shook his head, and continued.

Henri stretched himself to his full height, almost falling backward down the steps as he overdid it, and strode after Robard, the muscles in his neck tense as he fought to keep his head high against his strong instinct to duck down and present the smallest target possible. That had always been his tactic against his four older siblings, but clearly it was time to develop some other strategies for the wider world.

He tried to calm himself as they left the stairs on the second landing and proceeded through several more large, grand rooms, each full of far better-dressed and obviously more important servants of the Cardinal than Henri, and waiting supplicants too important to be left downstairs. Some of them tried to intercept Robard, but he stalked on, waving them aside. All of them looked at Henri as if he were a stray dog that had somehow got in on the Secretary's heels.

Finally, Robard came to a halt outside two ornately carved doors at the end of a tall vaulted room. A dozen clerks waited along the walls of this room, portable writing desks chained around their necks so they might write wherever they found themselves. Three of the twelve were busily writing, messenger girls and boys waiting to speed away with their missives. The others waited in various attitudes, all of which spoke to long practice of patience, interspersed with frenetic activity.

A pair of Pursuivants guarded the doors, both in uniform but without cuirass, helmet, or halberd, though they had swords at their sides and pistols through their belts.

"First time to see Her Eminence," said Robard, indicating Henri.

The guards moved forward. One took Henri's unresisting wrists and held up his arms while the other searched him, strong fingers probing up from the toes of his shoes, making him flinch as she investigated around his groin and buttocks, continuing up to reach under his doublet and the shirt beneath—not all that clean since he had the doublet to disguise it—and finishing by feeling all around his neck and upward to the crown of his head, fingers ruffling through his hair like a comb.

"No weapons," said the hair ruffler. "No icons."

"What could I have in my hair?" asked Henri, though he immediately regretted speaking at all.

"Garroting wire," answered the hair ruffler. Henri smiled weakly, but she didn't smile back.

Robard knocked on the door.

"Enter!"

Robard opened the door and swept in. Henri swallowed nervously, hesitating on the threshold, till the hair-ruffling Pursuivant pushed him in the back with a whispered, "Go on! She doesn't eat scrawny clerks!"

Henri almost fell into the room, recovering enough to turn this into a clumsy but heartfelt near prostration, going down on one knee and lowering his head almost to the ground. For a moment he studied the design in the thick carpet, so panicked he could hardly take anything else in.

"So, Robard! Who have you brought me? I do not think I have seen this clerk of mine before."

Henri slowly raised his head, still keeping his eyes down. At first he saw only the richly paneled walls, the ornate mahogany legs of several armchairs, a fireplace with a fire laid but not lit—it was summer and the day was warm—and the corner of a desk, the famous ivory-inlaid desk of the Cardinal (though her enemies claimed the inlay was human bone). Fearfully raising his eyes a little farther still, he saw *her*.

Cardinal Duplessis was taller and slighter than Henri, all bones and length. She seemed immensely tall to him, standing by her desk, one elegant, icon-ringed hand resting on the ivory surface. She wore a scarlet robe with a golden belt, and hanging from that belt was an icon that immediately drew all Henri's attention—as it would draw anyone's eyes. It was no more than three inches tall and two inches wide, a small thing of painted timber. There was no gold upon it, no pearls or jewels decorating the rim, none of the adornment found on so many icons. It depicted a . . . Henri blinked, his eyes watering . . . he was looking straight at it, but somehow he couldn't focus. There was a face, he thought, but it wouldn't stick in his mind. A halo above, brighter than the sun, but how could that be painted . . .

It was the icon of Ashalael, of course. Patron Archangel of Sarance, one of the most powerful angelic beings of all, whose scope was not confined to particular actions or objects or things, but was entirely geographic. Someone who could successfully call Ashalael—which would take enormous willpower, focus, and vast experience wielding angelic magic—could perform wonders, as the angel's scope concerned anything at all within the boundaries of the kingdom.

The cost, of course, was also exceedingly high.

Henri blinked again, and looked away, up at the Cardinal's face. She looked amused, which worried him, and he also noticed she wore a great deal of pale crimson face paint, some of it cracking at the corner of her eyes and mouth to show the brown skin beneath. Her silver hair was pulled back and tied with a scarlet ribbon that trailed over her shoulder, and on her head was the blue velvet cap with gold trim of a royal duke, for she held several secular titles too, and was still the Queen's Chief Minister, no matter the King's scheming. The cap had an icon pinned to it, one that Henri could actually look at, a high angel he didn't know, shown as a smiling, motherly woman holding a baby. Only the mother had a horse's head and the baby a foal's head, though the rest of them was human. And the foal had a halo but the mother didn't, so it was the angel . . .

The Cardinal, even with the smoothing of her face paint, looked considerably older than she was, no doubt from the practice of high angelic magic. Henri couldn't remember exactly, but knew she was of an age with his father. Who was forty-four, though the Cardinal looked sixty at the least.

"Henri Dupallidin, the Adianne branch of the family, a remote connection of Damerçon's," said Robard. "Started with us last Wednesday. He was the only one there. I will be asking Dubarry about that."

Dubarry was the Third Secretary. Henri had met *her* when he first arrived. She had handed him his warrant and a portion of his first month's salary—the rest being held back for obscure reasons—and told him to go to the Yellow Antechamber and do what he was told by anyone he met there. Which he had done.

"Dupallidin. You may approach."

Henri didn't so much walk as ooze forward, still crouching low. He kissed the Cardinal's hand, or, more accurately, breathed several inches above those icon rings, and then retreated back to his kneeling position.

"Stand," said the Cardinal mildly. "So you are new to my service. Have you taken vows?"

"Only as a layperson, Your E-em-eminence," stuttered Henri. "To Ashalael, when I started here. Um, I didn't want, I mean I wasn't sure, that is, whether to be a priest . . . it's a big undertaking."

"His father is sacristan to a temple of Huaravael, Eminence," muttered Robard.

"Ah, the Banisher of Smoke in Adianne," said the Cardinal. "But you do not wish to follow in your father's footsteps?"

"Not quite yet," said Henri diplomatically. One thing he knew for sure was that he didn't want to end up as the eternally poverty-stricken sacristan of a small temple in the middle of nowhere.

"Hmmm," murmured the Cardinal. She cocked her head, looking at Henri as if she were considering returning an unfortunate purchase. "There are many who serve me, Dupallidin. The clerks and officials in this palace, my Pursuivants, others in Lutace, across Sarance, and beyond. My people carry out many varied tasks, tasks that are necessary for the good of the people, for the protection of Sarance, and for the glory of Ashalael, our great Archangel and savior."

Henri nodded eagerly, wanting her to see that little as it was, the Cardinal had his utmost support. As did Ashalael, of course, highest of angels and ultimate protector of all Sarancians. Though to be perfectly honest, anyone who offered a chance for him to have some secure position would also have his complete loyalty. . . .

"Sometimes the tasks that must be carried out are difficult and dangerous," continued the Cardinal. "Sometimes they are . . . challenging in other ways."

Henri slowed down with the nodding, uncertain what the Cardinal was getting at.

"I'm not sure you are the person I need for the post at hand," said the Cardinal, and as she spoke, Henri felt the warm touch of angelic magic, the brush of an unseen wing. He looked up and saw Duplessis held an icon he hadn't even noticed, one of several set in a silver bracelet just visible under the cuff of her robe. Henri didn't know which angel she had called, or what it had done, but he suspected it was one of the Thrones who could detect truth, or assist in the reading of surface thoughts.

"I am willing to . . . I *want* to serve you however I can, Your Eminence!"

The words came out without Henri even thinking about them, overruling his deeper common sense that had detected whatever job she had on offer was somehow dubious, or had something wrong with it.

"I know you do, Dupallidin," said the Cardinal. "I know."

She looked down at Henri's face and once again he felt the warmth of angelic magic, like a soft breath against his face, not unwelcome. He heard a silvery harp note, as if coming from some far distant place, his ears just catching the sound. Then there was a sharp stab of icy pain behind his right eye, and he flinched.

"You know the Star Fortress," said the Cardinal.

"Uh, yes, Your Eminence," muttered Henri, blinking the pain away. Who could not?

The Star Fortress dominated the northeastern corner of Lutace. Under construction for the last thirty years, it was built—or was being built—above and around a great lump of rock not quite tall enough to be called a hill. For centuries a lone tower had stood there, built originally to be a lookout but in later centuries serving as an infamous prison, known to all simply as the Tower.

Three decades ago Queen Henrietta IV had decreed a modern fortress be built around the rock, and so the famous engineer Varianna had been hired away from the Prince of Barogno. She had traced out modern ramparts, bastions, and ravelins of brick-fronted earth, ditches to be carved from the stone, sluices made so the ditch could be flooded from the river and a system of magazines, armories, and storerooms to be tunneled into the hump of rock, or converted from the existing excavations.

Varianna's plan also called for the demolition of the Tower, as it interfered with the field of fire for the cannons of the north-eastern bastions. But various political forces had ensured the Tower remained, along with other changes that meant the Star Fortress of Sarance fell short of the perfect specimen of artillery fort envisaged by Varianna.

These shortcomings, and its unfinished state, owed much to the fact that (due to political considerations again) command of the Star Fortress and its construction had been portioned out to the Queen's Musketeers, the King's Guard, the Cardinal's Pursuivants, and the Lutace City Watch.

Each regiment controlled one of the bastions and a ravelin of the Star Fortress as their own, and shared responsibility (not very happily) for Dial Square, the town in miniature built in the central area within the ramparts. To further complicate matters, the great iron or bronze cannons and demicannons and their lesser consorts, the culverins, demiculverins, sakers, and falcons that dotted the bastions and ravelins, came under the aegis of the Loyal Royal Artillery Company.

Despite its purpose to finally provide a properly defensible position within the capital, most people did not think of the Star Fortress in terms of its military use. The old Tower within the newer fortifications still dominated both the skyline and the thoughts of the populace, and the terms "Star Fortress" and "Tower" had mingled, so whenever one or the other was mentioned, the first thought that ever came to mind was: prison.

"The post I had in mind for one of your colleagues of the yellow room," mused Duplessis. "Is in the Tower."

Henri tried to disguise the fact that he felt unable to breathe. He had been so happy to gain his post with the Cardinal. It seemed the first step on the way to financial security and a viable future, both things he had never known. Even more happily it presented the prospect of being able to move to some other position in due course, perhaps even as an officer of artillery. But the prison tower of the Star Fortress . . . even to work there would be terrible . . .

"A new clerk is needed to help with recording what my questioners gather from the prisoners," said the Cardinal. "It is an important post. Second Assistant to the Clerk of Question."

Henri gulped. He knew that most of such questioning was done with angelic magic. But sometimes that didn't work, and there would also be Refuser prisoners on whom angelic magic could not be used. Which meant this Second Assistant to the Clerk of Question would have to sit in on the torturing. Writing down whatever people screamed and mumbled out, in between begging for mercy and, failing that, begging for death.

But it was also a named post, an office. It would mean a much bigger stipend, and would be a stepping-stone to greater things. . . .

"The post comes with an apartment," added Robard, who was watching Henri closely.

He did not add "in the Star Fortress," though Henri knew it must be so.

They were both looking at him. The Cardinal with great detachment, her face so immobile he could read nothing in it. Robard looked faintly scornful, as if all of this was taking too long, that the Cardinal should not be explaining but simply ordering Henri to his new post.

"I only wish to serve Your Eminence," said Henri. His voice trembled, but he managed to get the words out. "However I may do so."

The Cardinal looked down at him. Henri tried to gauge her expression without actually meeting her eyes, but could not. He shivered a little and bent his head down.

"No," said the Cardinal at last. Henri felt the cold piercing his head again, the angel touching his mind, relaying whatever it found there to Duplessis. "No. You are not suitable. I think we need someone . . ."

"Older, Eminence?" asked Robard, when she did not continue.

"More used up," replied Duplessis. Her voice was cold and distant. "No, I cannot use you, Dupallidin."

She waved her hand in dismissal, the gesture suggesting to Henri a terrible finality.

"I am dismissed from your *service*, Eminence?" bleated Henri.

He reared back and stared up at her, face pleading. He felt sick and had to clench his teeth and swallow down the bile that had risen in his throat. To be dismissed meant ruin. He would become a beggar, or die by the roadside trying to get back to his family—

"No, no," said the Cardinal. She smiled, and even though the curve of her lips was not accompanied by any warmth in her eyes, Henri felt a sudden surge of relief. "I do not cast aside a blade because it is ill-tempered. I have it reforged."

She frowned slightly and looked to Robard.

"Pereastor tells me Dupallidin is very talented with numbers," she said. "Place him with Dutremblay as a second assistant, perhaps a surveyor. He will be more useful there than the Yellow Antechamber."

"As you command, Eminence," replied Robard. He made a shooing motion with his hand toward Henri, who began to back out of the room.

"Find those other clerks," said the Cardinal as she walked behind the ivory desk, already picking up papers, half her attention elsewhere. "I will see them together and choose the best suited."

Robard bent his head and followed Henri to the door, pausing to grip the young man by the elbow to spin him around so he walked out forward, rather than continuing his slow, backward crawl.

Outside the Cardinal's chamber, Robard summoned one of the lesser clerks in the waiting room. She rushed over at once, opening the writing desk that was chained around her neck, lifting her quill, and flipping the lid of the inkpot.

"Her Eminence desires this one to be sent to Dutremblay as a second assistant," said Robard. "Issue him a warrant."

Henri only half heard this; he was still staring back at the chamber he'd exited. One of the Pursuivant guards winked at him, but he didn't notice. He was still overcome by the unexpected audience and . . . and his sudden promotion.

Though he didn't know what he was being promoted to . . . or where. He turned back to Robard and waited for an opportunity to speak.

"He is not to go back to the Yellow Antechamber," continued Robard briskly. "Oh, tell Dedene to find all the clerks assigned there, save this one, and bring them to me. At once."

The other clerk bowed low, and Henri bowed again. When he straightened up, Robard was halfway down the hall, golden spurs bright in the shafts of sunlight that speared down from the high windows.

"Second Assistant to Dutremblay," said the clerk as she wrote busily. "To begin today, at a salary of sixteen livres per calendar month, plus—"

"Sixteen livres!" cried Henri. This was four times his current stipend.

"Plus the living allowance of eighteen livres a quarter, paid in advance," replied the clerk. "Not that you'll need so much, given you get quarters."

"Quarters?" asked Henri.

"In the Star Fortress," said the clerk.

"The . . . ?"

"The Star Fortress," repeated the clerk. "You're lucky, it won't be the Pursuivants' Barracks because Dutremblay likes her staff—"

She paused. Henri was staring at her. He knew what she was saying, but his mind couldn't quite get a grip on this unwelcome news, coming so fast on the good fortune of his new wealth. Relatively speaking, given his previous impecunity.

"The Star Fortress," repeated the clerk. "Dutremblay."

Henri croaked something. Had he completely misunderstood his interview? Had he been appointed to the prison tower after all, to assist the Clerk of Question?

Fortunately the clerk was used to people stumbling out of interviews with the Cardinal being rather at a loss for words and correctly interpreted Henri's question.

"Dutremblay is the Queen's Architect! She's overseeing the building of the new palace, in Dial Square. You'll get your own chamber in the part that's already built!"

Henri croaked something else.

"Dial Square! The center of the Star Fortress! Really, where are you from?"

"Damerçon," muttered Henri. He felt light-headed, the room was tilting a bit, and he had to take a deep breath to make it settle.

"Where?"

"In Adianne."

"Where?"

"Bascony," Henri admitted.

The clerk sniffed, finished what she was writing, cast some sand over it to settle the ink, and handed two documents to Henri.

"There you are," she said. "Your warrant, and a draft for the first month's salary and allowance, which you may draw from the treasurer at your leisure. But I would suggest immediately, given it is almost four of the clock, and as it is Saint Tarhern's Day tomorrow, nothing will be done."

It was a weary but pleased Henri Dupallidin who made his way home that evening to his soon-to-be-vacated tiny apartment high in the house of Mistress Trevier, a spice merchant who owed some favor to the Duchess of Damerçon, which had been translated into cheap accommodation for her distant relative.

All in all, Henri decided, it had been a wonderful day, even if filled with some heart-stopping moments and the awful possibility of being immured in a prison to record the laments of torture victims. And though he was destined for the Star Fortress, it would not be to the prison, and he presumed he would be able to come and go as he willed.

Though this might be a big presumption, Henri suddenly thought. What if he had to stay within the fortress all the time, or was allowed out only at certain intervals?

He was thinking about that and not paying attention when he felt a hand pluck at the newly filled purse on his belt. Before he could react, the cord that held it there was cut and a hand snatched it away. Henri spun about, grabbed at thin air, and filled his lungs to shout uselessly "Thief!" as he saw a child in gray Refuser rags duck under the belly of a horse and take the few steps toward one of the narrow alleys that would guarantee escape.

But Henri's shout never came out of his mouth. Instead his teeth made a clicking sound as his jaw snapped shut in surprise. Quick as the thieving urchin was, a woman passerby was quicker. She had grabbed the child, twisted her arm, and extracted the purse in one swift motion, and then when the girl had gone for a knife had twisted that wrist as well.

"I have it, ser!" cried the woman, holding up the purse and kicking the scrawny girl away with a muttered word. Whatever she said, the thief blenched and ran immediately, not even pausing to pick up the small purse-cutting knife, which was lying on the cobbles.

Henri looked around in bewilderment. The people around him averted their eyes and hurried along the street, confirming his suspicion that something odd was going on. He hadn't been in the city very long, but he wasn't stupid. Thieves were simply part of life, and strangers did not intervene unless there was no risk to them at all, or they were close friends or fond relatives of the person being robbed. This woman—clearly also a Refuser, by her gray cloak and head scarf—was either part of some more elaborate scam or was herself a dangerous lunatic.

"Catch, ser!" called the woman, and threw the purse. Henri caught it reflexively and stared as the woman disappeared into the same alley the thief had run along.

"Never seen aught like that before," mumbled someone behind Henri, but when he turned he couldn't see who'd spoken. The tide of people that constantly flowed along Frosting Street was in motion again, parting around him as if he were a suspicious rock.

Henri kept the purse tightly in his hand and rejoined the flow, this time concentrating on the people around him, the holes in the cobbled street under his feet and all the things he should have been focusing on before he was robbed.

But a small part of his mind couldn't help wondering why an older Refuser woman had intervened to stop a younger Refuser street child from stealing from him.

At last he hit on it, his mind clearing. Even somewhat stained and disreputable, his yellow doublet marked him as one of the Cardinal's own. Her Eminence's hand was protection indeed. Even from street thieves.

SIX

AGNEZ TRIED TO RELAX HER GRIP ON THE RAPIER, TILTING her wrist, opening her fingers. The gloves they had given her were not the supple kidskin she was used to but gauntlets of thick buff leather, making her hand bulkier and slow. The rapier was also heavier and longer than her own, not to mention intentionally blunted, whereas her own well-tended sword blade was sharp enough to cut a falling hair.

But this test had to be passed with the gloves and weapon provided, and with her right hand, when she generally preferred her left. Magical aid was likewise forbidden, so the sole icon Agnez possessed, a small plaque carrying the likeness of Jashenael, was tucked in the band of her hat and lay with her sword and cloak in the corner of the room. Though in any case all Jashenael could do was provide a light in darkness, and at that only when the moon was dark or in the first or last quarter. He was only a Cherubim, with a very narrow scope of power.

"Come on, then!" exclaimed the Arms-master, letting her sword point slide a few inches across the paving stones of the courtyard with a shriek of metal on stone. It was just an act,

Agnez knew, to invite a foolish attack. Her mother had taken her to see one of Arms-master Franzonne's exhibition matches on their last visit to Lutace two years ago, and the champion of the Queen's Musketeers was undoubtedly still as lethally fast as she had been then.

"My glove is too big," sniffed Agnez, making herself sound pathetic while also letting her own blade drop as if she couldn't hold it up. But even as the last word left her mouth she suddenly straightened into a stamping lunge right at Franzonne's heart, which for the merest fragment of a second seemed like it might connect, before her rapier was savagely beaten away, and then Agnez was backing and parrying, twisting desperately sideways, and not many seconds later was nursing her bruised hand as her heavy rapier clanged and bounced on the paving stones.

Disarmed so quickly, Agnez knew in a real duel she would be lying on the ground, gasping out her last breath as her bright red blood spread across those pavers.

"Eighteen seconds," said an extraordinarily large, rather bearlike man—a russet bear, for his skin was a red-brown, and though his hair and beard were black they too had a tinge of red, like the last touch of flame in a dying charcoal fire. He wore the same silver-edged black tabard as Franzonne, the uniform of the Queen's Musketeers, in his case garments large enough to make a tent for Agnez.

"You counted too fast," said Franzonne. "Though I compliment you in general upon the achievement. I didn't even see your lips move, Sesturo."

"I counted in my head," said the man calmly. "I *have* been practicing. Shall we say twenty seconds, then?"

Agnez held her breath. This was the first test she had to pass, to last at least a third of a minute against Arms-master Franzonne, sword to sword.

Franzonne looked at Agnez, who tried to restrain the expression that she was sure made her look all too like a puppy hoping to be thrown an offcut from the Arms-master's dinner.

"The 'my glove's too loose' thing was good," said the Arms-master.

"I liked that," rumbled Sesturo.

"She's very young."

"I am almost eighteen!" blurted out Agnez, and then in agonized immediacy, "I beg your pardon, Arms-master."

"Impulsive. Has rustic manners."

Agnez set her jaw tight to stop herself from protesting. She *was* a Bascon, raised in the country, but her mother was not only a former Queen's Musketeer, but also Baron Descaray, of an ancient and noble family whose holder had the unique right to present the Queen with a black rose once a year and ask for a boon in return. Though there were no black roses, and never had been, this was a high honor.

"Perhaps the King's Guard . . ." mused Sesturo aloud.

Agnez bit her lip to stop the protest that almost burst out. The King's Guard, indeed! Everyone knew the Queen's Musketeers were far superior in all respects, particularly in swordsmanship. If Agnez was rejected by Franzonne, she would never apply to the

King's Guard instead. It was a place for young sprigs of nobility who liked to dress up, not fight.

"Or the Cardinal's people," said Franzonne.

Agnez resisted the frown that was threatening to draw her forehead into an ugly scowl. The Cardinal's Pursuivants would be even worse than the King's Guard! Everyone knew they were not honest fighters but mages who always preferred angelic magic over cold steel. They were the Cardinal's spies and police as well as soldiers, and Agnez wanted nothing to do with them. While she had the native talent and had been taught to use icons, she wanted to make her own way in the world, not be carried to the lofty heights she dreamed of on the shoulders of angels.

Captain-General Agnez Descaray of the Queen's Musketeers.

One day, she would hear those words spoken, and not in jest.

But if right now she was rejected by Franzonne . . . Agnez suppressed a shudder, tried to keep her face as impassive as the Arms-master's own. Agnez didn't know what she would do if she couldn't be a Musketeer. Die, she supposed. Leave this outer courtyard of the Queen's Palace and start challenging the most dangerous fighters she could see to duels. At least it would be a quick end, better than an ignominious, humiliating return home.

"No, she is not somber enough for the Cardinal, nor pretty enough for the Guard," said Franzonne. "She might be mistaken for one of their horses."

"The rear end?" asked Sesturo. He squinted at Agnez and made a face.

Agnez clenched her fists inside the stupid oversized gauntlets. But she didn't move, didn't hurl one of those gloves at the Arms-master's face, or leap at Sesturo with fists flailing.

She knew she was generally considered neither pretty nor handsome. Her face might be considered long by some, and her brown skin and black hair were in fact somewhat similar to the bay horses that were among the most common in Sarance. But this was of no matter to Agnez, for it was irrelevant to her fighting abilities.

Not that she would let anyone insult her on any basis whatsoever, including their opinion of her looks.

At least not ordinarily.

"No," said Franzonne. A flicker of what might have been a smile moved swiftly across her face, like a sudden breeze upon still water, gone in an instant. "Not at all horselike in fact, head or tail. We beg your pardon, Descaray. I said that only to test if you could take an insult."

"I can in this place, at this time," said Agnez stiffly. "I would not in other circumstances."

"I also beg your pardon," said Sesturo formally. "Did your mother warn you we would insult you?"

"Not in so many words," replied Agnez. She hesitated, then added, "She told me to be more like Truffo and less like Humboldt."

Sesturo laughed, and that slight smile passed across Franzonne's face again. Truffo and Humboldt were the principal clowns of the play *The Frog King's Revenge*, a classic of Sarancian theater. Truffo was the stolid, straightforward one, always the butt of Humboldt's jokes, the last to react to whatever was going on. Humboldt, on the other hand, was too clever by half and generally the cause of their perpetual state of disarray and trouble.

"So," said Franzonne. "The Queen has approved you in principle, for your mother's sake. You are . . . more than competent with the sword, far better than most. Only one test remains. . . ."

Agnez couldn't help the slight frown that crept up her forehead this time. Another test? Her mother hadn't told anything about *another* test.

"Sesturo?"

The frown grew deeper as Franzonne stepped to the side of the salle and Sesturo levered himself out of his chair and approached Agnez. He was even larger standing up than she had supposed, easily a foot taller than her and much, much heavier. All of it, as far as she could tell, muscle.

"No gouging, no biting," said Sesturo. "Slap the floor with your open hand if you wish to concede."

"We're going to wrestle?" asked Agnez. It came out rather more as a squeak than she would have liked.

"Aye," said Sesturo. "No one may join the Queen's Musketeers who has not put me to the ground, without the aid of weapons."

"For how long?" asked Agnez. She backed up as she spoke and looked quickly about her, hoping to see something— anything—that might help.

"Oh, just down," said Franzonne. "We don't want to make it *impossible*."

Agnez circled Sesturo slowly. Perhaps he was slow, she thought, intently watching his every move. Men of his size were rarely swift. If she could slide in, scissor her legs about his ankles, and twist—

Sesturo wasn't slow.

Agnez had only just readied herself to slide in when he jumped forward and one massive fist clipped the side of her head. The slide became a fall, the huge Musketeer catching the young woman just before she hit the stone floor and doing far more serious damage than she had already suffered from his fist.

"Sesturo!" exclaimed Franzonne. "You've hit her too hard."

"No," rumbled the big man. He gently lowered Agnez to the ground, removing her gauntlets to make a pillow for her head. "She's coming around."

Agnez blinked and took several coughing small breaths. For a few seconds she couldn't work out what had happened. There was an enormous male Musketeer standing over her, and a slighter woman Musketeer a pace behind him.

Then everything slowly coalesced into place. Agnez grunted and tried to get up, but Franzonne came closer, bent down, and easily pushed her back.

"No. You must rest now, for the remainder of the day," she said. "The servants will take you back to your lodgings."

Agnez stared at her and tried to rise again but could not. Her head hurt, and she couldn't focus her eyes.

"I . . . I have failed?" she asked.

"I am not on the floor," said Sesturo. He spoke with a curious tone in his voice.

Agnez didn't try to get up again. For a moment she felt a wave of defeat and despair wash across her, but there was something behind that, some hint in Sesturo's voice . . .

Both of the Queen's Musketeers were looking at her. Waiting for something. Agnez felt she was on the cusp of some action she must take, a last chance . . . but she could barely move, and certainly had no chance of wrestling or knocking Sesturo to the ground.

Though this might not actually be a physical test. She had just supposed it was, and acted accordingly, with Sesturo responding in kind. Agnez looked directly at Sesturo, meeting his gaze, trying to sharpen her focus, to ignore the throbbing pain in her head.

"Ser Sesturo, you look warmed by your exertions . . . would . . . would you care to cool yourself on these paving stones for a few moments?" asked Agnez weakly.

Sesturo's mouth quirked, and he glanced aside to Franzonne. She nodded once, decisively.

"The ignominy!" exclaimed Sesturo in a bass rumble as he first knelt down on one knee and then subsided like an avalanche onto the floor, to lie full length with his arms extended. "Taken down by the merest rustic recruit!"

"Rather, by your own courtesy," said Agnez quietly. She lay back and let a sudden feeling of relief spread through her entire body. Even the pain in her head was receding. "For which I thank you."

"Welcome to the Queen's Musketeers, Cadet Descaray," said

Sesturo, getting to his feet with a long sigh, as if being forcibly woken from sleep to face an unwanted day. He offered a hand to Agnez and, when she took it, hauled her effortlessly upright.

"You will need to stay in bed for the rest of the day," said Franzonne. "I will send word to the hospital for one of the doctor-magisters to visit. Even Sesturo's lightest blows leave their mark."

She took a bronze token from inside the cuff of her gauntlet and tucked it inside Agnez's belt purse.

"The token will grant you entry at our water gate to the Star Fortress. Report to the barracks after breakfast. Not too early."

Agnez nodded and instantly felt bile rise in her throat. She choked it back and fought to stop the sudden dizziness that affected her balance. Sesturo supported her, his hand under her elbow. Franzonne clapped her hands twice, a sharp sound that made Agnez wince. The heavy oaken door groaned open, and four servants entered carrying a litter. As was usual for such mundane tasks, they were all Refusers, clad in the characteristic gray garb that warned they were barred from all angelic magic, for if any were used upon them the results would likely be fatal, either to mage or subject, or both.

"Convey Ser Descaray to her lodgings," commanded Franzonne. "The inn of goodman Hobarne?"

"Yes," said Agnez faintly. She was still fighting off the urge to vomit. "Yes. Hobarne's inn, on Swift Street. But I don't need a litter."

The Refusers brought the litter close, but Agnez waved it away.

She drew herself fully upright and moved away from Sesturo's supporting hand.

"I am perfectly able to walk to the Griffon's Head," she said, lifting her chin. "And there I will not take to my bed, but drink! And play dice!"

"Very good," said Sesturo. "Musketeers should be poor. It makes us fight harder."

Agnez looked aside at him, though the motion hurt her head.

"I shall win," she pronounced. "I bid you good day, Ser Sesturo, Ser Franzonne. Till we meet again on the morrow."

She bowed low to them both, wavered mightily as she came back up, steadied for a moment, and then tottered over to pick up her gloves, cloak, hat, and sword. Holding them together in an ungainly bundle, she strode away—straight into the wall next to the door, slowly sliding down it to end up almost unconscious on the floor.

"A notable effort," said Sesturo. He looked at his fist. "I really did try not to hit her too hard."

"Convey Ser Descaray to her lodgings," repeated Franzonne.

The Refusers nodded in obedience and went to pick up the newest member of the Queen's Musketeers, bundling her and her gear unceremoniously into the litter.

"How many more are waiting?" asked Sesturo.

"A dozen," answered Franzonne. She watched Agnez being carried out. "None of them very likely prospects. But Descaray . . . she is a swordswoman of great promise."

SEVEN

THE UNIVERSITY OF BELHALLE SPREAD ACROSS MANY DOZens of buildings, courts, and gardens on the left bank of the river Leire. Long ago, it had been almost a separate town, surrounded by farmland, the city to the north and west reached only by boat. Over the centuries, bridges had spanned the river, the city had reached out, and now the Belhalle was entirely surrounded, encompassed within the bounds of the city walls.

Among its many buildings, the Rotunda was the best known. Its great glass and copper dome, built with enormous amounts of angelic assistance, was the most visible landmark for miles. It contained the preeminent iconer's studio in Sarance, perhaps in the entirety of the known world. Under the light of the massive windowpane sections of the dome, there were serried concentric rings of workbenches from the middle to the far rim, more than four hundred all told. Those in the outer ring were for students; the closer to the center the better the light, and the more superior, or at least senior, icon-maker.

In the very center of the Rotunda, there was a workbench known as the Assay. It was here, 116 feet below the apex of the dome, that students displayed their graduate work, which they hoped would gain them admittance to the ranks of the magisters. To be a magister of the Belhalle was to be acknowledged an angelic mage of the first rank.

Sometimes, the great and good of the university gathered at the Assay for other reasons, to be watched with awe and sometimes an admixture of cynicism and resentment by the gathered students at the outer workbenches.

But today, the students were absent. The Rotunda had been closed, and proctors stood guard at every entrance. There were only six people gathered around the Assay. The Rector herself, two of the four Procurators, the Scholar-Provost, and the University Bishop. The sixth person was a cheerful-looking short young woman with deep brown skin and thoughtful dark eyes, who wore a student's blue robe over what looked like a groom's leather tunic and breeches, not typical attire in the Rotunda. She had a stick of charcoal in her hand; there was a sharp iconer's pricking knife and a sheet of stiff parchment on the workbench in front of her, next to an open copy of the first volume of the five-volume illustrated compendium of angels, Marcew's *The Inhabitants of Heaven*, an essential reference for icon-makers.

"You do not know this angel?" asked the Rector. She was a stern, sixtyish woman wearing the long black, saffron-edged robe of her office, which was adorned with a half-dozen icon brooches.

"Know," used in this sense, meant an angel a mage had established a connection with and either had already made an icon to summon them or was in the process of doing so. Establishing this initial knowledge often took days, or weeks, or sometimes even months or years for the more powerful angels. Getting to know an angel was a well-known process that could not be hastened.

Or so most angelic mages had always been taught.

"I do not, Your Grace," answered the young woman, whose name was Dorotea Imsel. She was only eighteen, a first-year student at the Rotunda, though she had previously studied at the lesser university of Tramereine, and had in fact graduated from there at the early but not totally unprecedented age of sixteen. The reason she was here, in the center of the Rotunda, surrounded by such luminaries of the Belhalle, was because a talent—or as some called it, a trick—she had exhibited at Tramereine was now to be examined here.

"I opened the book with my eyes shut, fanned the pages, and let it fall as shown," said the Scholar-Provost. He also wore his official robe of black, trimmed with sable rather than gold, and the only visible icon he had was a small cameo set in the pommel of his dagger, visible through the side slit in his robe. "Student Imsel was not yet here and could not have in any way interfered with this process. I felt no angelic presence of any kind."

The others looked at the open pages. The verso showed a full-page illustration of a Seraphim, a human figure with dappled blue-black skin, the characteristic six small wings and a halo not of golden light but of red flames woven together like a laurel wreath. The recto was printed text, with hand-painted illumina- tions in gold leaf and cochineal, mostly around the angel's name and the initial capital of the descriptive text.

This Seraphim was called Kameziel, and her scope was anger. She was generally called upon to quell riots or to calm some murderous person, or in rare cases lift a melancholic individual out of a fit of despond.

"Very well," said the Rector. "A Seraphim . . . should you be successful, the cost will not be too great. Procee—"

Before she could finish the word "proceed" the Rector was interrupted by a disturbance at the main doors, where the proctors first tried to stop someone from coming in, and then when they realized who it was, fell back and allowed her entry.

Dorotea glanced over, and for the first time was jarred out of her calm center. She had not been particularly bothered when the notables of the university asked about her peculiar talent and then wanted her to demonstrate it. She was surprised they had caught wind of it but not worried it would cause her any problems. It was just something she was able to do, and she had never thought it particularly interesting or different. Though one of her old teachers had cautioned her about keeping this talent—and some other things she could do—to herself, and she had largely done so. Not so much from fear or caution, just because it seemed of no great importance and was easy enough to forget.

All Dorotea wanted to do was paint and create icons. She had little interest in the actual application of angelic magic, or summoning angels in general. She simply loved creating icons. Tramereine and now Belhalle were to her the very perfection of all things good, because she could spend all day either studying how others had made icons or in making them herself. She didn't even need to cook or clean but could totally devote herself to her art.

But now Dorotea was belatedly realizing her blessed existence could be threatened by this new interest in her peculiar talent, and that was only the one they knew about. The university authorities were one thing. The woman advancing down the avenue between the work desks was another entirely. Even the jangle of her spurs and the tap of her rapier scabbard on the back of her left thigh as she strode toward them seemed threatening.

She was very tall and dark-haired under the broad-brimmed hat with the red feather. Her face was set, eyes dark and cold. A long scar ran from her forehead down to her jaw and bisected her left eye—an indication that without angelic intervention, she would have lost that eye and be wearing a patch. Her skin was the color of a deep golden pear, and the scar a thin white line, as if someone had sliced just such a fruit and then decided to push it back together, in an unsuccessful attempt to hide the cut.

Though this dangerous-looking woman did not wear the tabard of a Cardinal's Pursuivant with the blazon of the nine-pinioned Archangel, her allegiance was declared by the scarlet of her jerkin and the badge in her hatband of Ashalael's golden wings surmounted by a crowned miter, sigil of the Cardinal of Sarance. Her rank was indicated by her golden sash; and her puissance as an angelic mage by the many icon rings she wore, supplemented by others on her person in the form of brooches and belt-plaques, the latter partially obscured by her sash.

Dorotea felt her own two weak icons tremble and shiver as the woman marched closer, as they had done for one of the Rector's icons. Her own were only of Dramhiel and Horcinael, both Seraphim of very limited scope. The former's minor cleansing and clarification of blood were useful for dealing with hangovers among other things. The latter's scope was the boundary between liquid and solid, so he was often used by icon-makers to speed the preparation of surfaces with gesso.

They would quail for almost any other angel, but even so Dorotea suspected this new arrival, this Cardinal's woman, bore icons for a Power, or perhaps even a Principality. And given this, was probably not the thirtyish she appeared but younger, untimely aged by the angels whose powers she wielded.

Dorotea had never seen her before, but she had no doubt who it was. There were many students at the Belhalle who either worshipped or demonized this woman, according to their political persuasions and ambitions.

She was Rochefort. Pursuivant Captain in the service of Cardinal Duplessis.

"I am not late, I trust," said Rochefort as she arrived, doffing her hat and bowing to the Rector.

"No," answered the Rector shortly, inclining her head as the others bowed. Dorotea was careful to bow quite deeply. "Depending on why you are here, Captain. Does the Cardinal require my presence?"

Rochefort replaced and straightened her hat.

"No, Madam Rector," she answered. "I am here, as you are, to observe some new iconer's trick, as I believe it has been described. You are Dorotea Imsel, I take it? Previously of the University of Tramereine, and before that Darroze? Daughter of Genia Imsel, father officially unknown, but unofficially and in the district well-known to be Destrange, Count of Darroze?"

"I am, ser," answered Dorotea, bowing again. "In all particulars."

"Your mother is known to be an icon-maker of the first order," said Rochefort. She spoke coldly, and though her words seemed complimentary, the tone was not. As proven by how she continued, "Whereas your father is not."

Dorotea frowned, uncertain if she was meant to be insulted. Her father, despite his title, was not held in high regard, at best seen as a genial, handsome idiot. Even by Dorotea and her half siblings. Her mother merely laughed when Dorotea asked how she had come to have a child with Destrange, and said she could not explain it herself. She had a fondness for handsome, not-too-bright men but had not had children with any others, nor had long liaisons in general.

"Pray continue, Student Imsel," said the Rector, not to be intimidated in her own university, even by the Cardinal's right-hand woman.

"I will try, ser," replied Dorotea with a shrug. Her old teacher's warning was now very much at the forefront of her mind. "It . . . I can't always do it."

"Begin," commanded the Rector.

Dorotea nodded and stared at the illustration, letting her eyes go out of focus, taking in the totality of the picture, the feel of it more than the actual visual representation. At the same time, she began to think the angel's name, but in the peculiar way she had developed, where she felt like it was someone else calling and she was merely repeating what this unseen presence said. It was a little mad, she knew, and possibly a sign of some incipient greater insanity, except that it was a technique, a trick, which she controlled. It never happened without her conscious direction, and it also didn't work without a visual representation.

"Kameziel. Kameziel. Kameziel."

She felt the beginning of an angelic manifestation near her, the susurration of six wings, a warm breeze tickling the skin of her face. The others felt it too, and there was a quick exchange of glances, some impressed, some concerned.

Dorotea gave no indication that she could actually *see* the angel, after a fashion, as well as feel and hear its presence. This was something else she had learned long ago was not usual, and so best kept secret. Her hand twitched, and she began to draw, the stick of charcoal moving swiftly over the paper, its soft scratching the only sound, her audience absolutely quiet. They could feel the immanence of the angel too, though Dorotea had touched no icon.

The presence built but not to a full manifestation. The sketch became recognizably Kameziel, or at least a rapidly sketched copy of the far more fully realized usual depiction, as shown in the book. Though this was not at all what Dorotea saw.

She dropped the charcoal, picked up the pricking knife, and cut a tiny notch in the back of her hand, next to the many lines of small white scars from previous cuts. Blood welled up and as quickly as she had used the charcoal stick, Dorotea redrew the icon, this time with a fine brush, painting blood over the charcoal lines, the black drinking up the red.

Blood was needed to fix an icon.

All the time, she shouted the angel's name inside her head.

Kameziel. Kameziel. Kameziel. Kameziel.

There was a clap of many wings, the sound of a struck harp, and Kameziel indicated her approval before departing. The icon, though far rougher than any icon should ever be, and far more hastily made, was judged successful, and the angel would answer to it.

Dorotea sank to the floor, gasping, pressing on the cut with her forefinger to stem the blood. She looked up to see the others inspecting her work, all of them frowning, but Rochefort frowning most of all, the scar on her face not moving when her forehead wrinkled up.

"Her Eminence instructed me that should Student Imsel prove her . . . talent . . . then she is to be taken for her own protection to the Star Fortress."

She reached into her coat sleeve and pulled out a tightly rolled parchment, handing it to the Rector, who reluctantly unrolled it and read it swiftly.

"I am sorry," she said, passing the paper to Dorotea. "It is a fully endorsed letter of durance."

"A what?" asked Dorotea.

"You are to be a guest of Her Eminence," said Rochefort.

"I don't understand," said Dorotea. She struggled to her feet, holding on to the desk, her head swimming. "It's just a trick, ser. It often doesn't work. This is only the fourth . . . fifth time I've managed to do it. What do oddities of icon-making have to do with the Cardinal?"

"Not a student of history, I see, even in your own field," said Rochefort. She indicated the main door with one scarlet gauntleted hand. "A coach awaits us."

"My work . . . my brushes and tools, my books, my clothes—"

"Anything necessary will be provided," said Rochefort. "Come. I have other tasks."

"What do you mean about being a student of history?" asked Dorotea. She let go of the desk and took a few tentative steps toward the door. Rochefort didn't answer, striding away, scabbard tapping again, spurs jangling. Dorotea looked appealingly at the university staff.

All but the Rector looked away.

"You are not the first person to exhibit this . . . er . . . talent," said the Rector. She hesitated. "Those who have done so in the past have not . . . have not always used it wisely, and sometimes it has been the first sign of other abilities, also best not used. But I am sure all will be well, child, and in time you will come back to us."

She sounded like she was trying to convince herself. Her words certainly didn't convince Dorotea. She nodded and walked on, concentrating on putting one foot in front of the other, in keeping her balance. She was exhausted by the creation of the rough icon, as always, but she was also processing this sudden change in her affairs and what it would mean to her various works in progress. She had several icons partially completed and was also assisting some fellow students with their work. What would happen to them?

"Come, girl! Faster!" called Rochefort from the doorway. It was being held open by the proctors, and Dorotea could see other people waiting outside, in scarlet tabards and scarlet hats with red feathers, light reflecting from rapier hilts and silver chasing on pistol butts. It seemed a whole troop of Pursuivants waited outside, dozens of them.

Still weary, Dorotea stumbled to the door. As soon as she stepped outside, blinking at the sunlight, the proctors swung the huge oak and iron doors shut behind her, as if emphasizing her banishment. Pursuivants gripped her arms. Another stripped the icon brooch from her robe, slid the ring with the cameo of Habriliel from her finger, and took her eating knife out of its sheath. It was done deftly, without violence, but it was daunting.

"A precaution, nothing more," said Rochefort. But she was not looking at Dorotea. Rather her cold gaze swept the crowd of students, scholars, and university servants and others who were loitering about on the southern side of the broad thoroughfare that led from the Rotunda back to the Derrecault Bridge. They were curious, of course, to see what brought not only the Pursuivants but also one of the Cardinal's red coaches with the yellow wheels, drawn by a team of six grays in scarlet harness.

And Rochefort as well . . .

Among the blue robes of scholars and students, and the drabber hues of the ordinary servants' clothing, there was a knot of gray—a group of four Refusers, standing out all the more, as no one wanted to get too close to them. It was unusual to see Refusers standing and watching; they usually just scurried about on their invariably menial business.

Dorotea recognized the quartet, with her artist's eye, picking out their features despite their hoods and caps and one a half mask, no doubt to hide some disfigurement. These four Refusers had been trimming the hedges outside her rooms all week, perhaps making more of the work than necessary. Though there were no hedges along the avenue, nor anywhere near the Rotunda, they still carried their long hedging knives.

Another Pursuivant watched with Rochefort and caught her gaze fixed on the Refusers. At the flick of the Captain's finger, he began to walk toward the gardeners, his hand on the hilt of his sword. But before he had taken three steps, they had turned away, first walking swiftly and then flat-out running, diving between students and outraged magisters, making for the alley between the gatehouse of Saint Antony's College and the university stables.

"Stop in the name of the Cardinal!" roared the Pursuivant, drawing a long-barreled pistol. But he did not fire, for the Refusers were too deep into the crowd. Within seconds, they were out of sight.

"Shall we pursue, ser?" asked the Pursuivant urgently. "Riders to the grounds behind Saint Antony's?"

"No," said Rochefort. "Alert the Scholar-Provost that some of the Night King's people were skulking here. Planning a robbery or some such, no doubt. That tall one . . . despite the hood . . . it was almost certainly Griselda, who oversees the beggars and pickpockets in Demarten Place. Pass the word to Debepreval and the other Watch lieutenants to arrest her if she shows up there and report to me."

"Yes, ser."

Rochefort turned her attention back to Dorotea.

"Come. Our carriage awaits. Do not tremble so."

"I'm not trembling from *fear*," said Dorotea, surprised. "It's just the icon-making. It wears upon me far more than a summoning. Temporarily, though. It doesn't seem to have the same long-term effect. . . ."

Rochefort looked at her, eyes narrowing.

Dorotea did not meet her gaze. She was thinking about the effects of the icon-sketching, as she called the process. It did make her feel more immediately weary, but there was no indication it was aging her in the way a summoning would. Though she had not tried it with a powerful angel. Either way, it was probably best she should not repeat the technique unless it was absolutely necessary.

"You are an unusual person," Rochefort said finally. "Most people I take to the Tower of the Star Fortress do more than tremble."

"Hmmm, what was that?" asked Dorotea, distracted by her

thoughts. She only heard the words "Star Fortress."

She tried to remember what she'd heard about the Star Fortress. It had come up in conversation a few times when she first came to Lutace, but Dorotea hadn't paid attention. Though she did suddenly remember the gist of it: that prisoners who went to the Star Fortress didn't come back out again.

"I said most people I take to the Star Fortress do more than tremble," said Rochefort. "Particularly those going to the actual Tower."

"Oh," remarked Dorotea. "I suppose they would. Deluynes was put in there, wasn't she?"

Averil Deluynes had been the favorite of the Queen, but she had been exposed by the Cardinal as being in the pay of the Alban Atheling, having sold him many of the Queen's private letters.

"For a time," replied Rochefort.

Dorotea remembered now. There was an executioner's block in some cavern deep within the rock on which the Tower was built. An ancient stump of oak hardened by angelic magic to be like iron. Many a neck had rested there, waiting the stroke of the ax.

Or a sword, if you were noble, like Deluynes. Though she was said to have lifted her head and ended up not just headless but also in many separate pieces, the executioner getting rattled and chopping away.

"I really don't understand what I'm being arrested *for*," said Dorotea, frowning. "This all seems very arbitrary."

"The Cardinal is naturally concerned with anyone who exhibits a talent such as you have just shown," replied Rochefort, holding Dorotea's elbow to direct the scholar into the carriage. Her grip was harsh, strong enough to leave a bruise, but she did not ease off. "You are being detained for your own protection. You are not being arrested."

"Much the same thing, surely," said Dorotea as she settled back on the seat, grateful it was somewhat cushioned, unlike the bare boards of the conveyance that had rattled and shaken her all the way from Tramereine to Lutace. "This is a very comfortable coach."

Rochefort looked at her suspiciously, as if suspecting sarcasm.

"I've just realized I've never seen the Star Fortress up close," added Dorotea. "I've seen the Tower, of course, from afar. I took a half day off when I first arrived to see the sights. On a tour for new students. But we didn't go north of the Mother Bridge. We saw the Temple of Ashalael, the Queen's Palace, and the King's House, and the city prison . . . I forget what it's called—"

"Riversedge," supplied Rochefort. She still looked at Dorotea, but now her expression was more of bemusement than suspicion.

"Yes, Riversedge. It looked rather damp, I thought."

"It is," said Rochefort. "But most people would prefer to be there than in the Tower."

She slapped the ceiling of the coach. A moment later, it started to rumble away.

Dorotea yawned. The icon-sketching had taken even more out of her than she'd thought. Curling up in the corner, she went instantly to sleep.

Rochefort shook her head slightly, as if unable to believe what she was seeing. A prisoner, being taken to the Tower of the Star Fortress under a letter of durance—which meant no trial and possible lifetime imprisonment—falling asleep as if she had not a care in the world!

EIGHT

"YOU SAY THE *HOSPITAL PORTER* HAD SOME SORT OF . . . small crossbow?" asked the lieutenant of the City Watch, a hard-bitten, sallow-faced woman with suspicious eyes, her blackened cuirass dented, and her cream-and-blue jerkin and breeches showing equal signs of hard wear. She had leaned her demihalberd against the wall but constantly tapped the staff as if to reassure herself it was close to hand.

"Yes . . . yes, she did," answered Simeon. "The other one had a cleaver. They told me to run. I got out the door, and I heard screaming behind me, I'm not sure if it was one of them . . . or . . . or the beastling."

"The beastling that was in a box of ice sent from Malarche?"

"Yes," answered Simeon. "At least that was what the Magister told me. And the ice had melted and the beastling wasn't dead."

"There was no box in the room," said the lieutenant. "No beastling, no strange hospital porters, with or without crossbows. Nor Magister Delazan. Only a great deal of blood on the floor and this."

She held up the two halves of the paper declaring the box to be the property of the Order of Ashalael and not to be opened save with the permission of the Prince-Bishop of Malarche, whose wax seal was appended to the lower half. The seal was cracked and broken.

"You said you cut this off the box?" asked the lieutenant.

"Yes," said Simeon, then quickly, as he saw the trap. "At the Magister's direct command. I asked him if we should not fetch a cleric of Ashalael—"

"But you did cut it?"

"Yes," answered Simeon. "As I said, only when Magister—"

"As this is the only crime I can definitely prove, by your own confession, Simeon MacNeel, I arrest you for degradation of an official document, and also to be questioned for the possible murder of Magister Delazan—"

"What!" roared Simeon. He stood up to his full, imposing height. "I told you what happened!"

The lieutenant took a step back, snatching up her demihalberd. Her sergeant stood closer, half raising his own, full-sized halberd, which did not feature the gold tassels that adorned the lieutenant's smaller weapon.

Simeon looked at the big halberd's long, rusty blade and settled back on his bench. He had been in this cell—one of several the hospital used for unruly patients—for five hours, and things had only gotten progressively worse in that time.

"Let me finish," said the lieutenant testily. "Since the offense proven by your confession was committed against the Order of Ashalael, it's temple business. We'll hand you over to the

Cardinal's Pursuivants and *they* will sort out the rest of your tale, including the murder or disappearance or whatever it is of Magister Delazan. I do not doubt your story is a lie entire, but fortunately I do not need to explore it any further!"

With that, she clapped her helmet back on and left the cell, her sergeant retreating more cautiously, keeping his eyes on Simeon. Only when he was in the doorway, and Simeon still slumped on the bench, did he turn and dash out, pushing the heavy oaken portal shut behind him and lowering the bar.

A few minutes later, Simeon heard the bar raised again. He pushed his back against the wall and stretched his legs forward, wanting to make it obvious he was not a threat, despite his size. He wanted no trouble with the Cardinal's Pursuivants.

It was not one of the Cardinal's officers who entered but old Magister Foxe, the Dean who was in charge of all the first-year students at the hospital. An Alban, he had come to Sarance so long ago it was easy to forget his origins, save that when he was excited or upset he occasionally lapsed into his native tongue.

As he did now, muttering something Simeon couldn't understand, while throwing his arms up and down in either anger or excitement, and tugging at his beard, which though long was thin and ropy. Eventually, Foxe realized what he was doing and switched back to Sarancian.

"Do you realize what you've done, MacNeel?"

"No, ser," replied Simeon. "All I did was obey Magister Delazan, exactly as you are always telling us we should obey the magisters."

"Don't be impertinent," snapped Foxe. "You've brought the Cardinal's attention on the hospital, which is something we do not want. We do not want it, do you hear?"

"I don't want it either," said Simeon. "But truly, Magister, I haven't done—"

"Quiet!" roared Foxe. "Listen. Do not speak. Something else I am always telling you students. Listen!"

"I'm listening, but—"

"Listen! We do not want the Cardinal's attention."

"You already said that—"

"We do not want it. We are not going to have it, because as of this moment, you are no longer a student of the hospital. No, as of yesterday. I will amend the records accordingly."

"But you can't do that!" protested Simeon. "I *am* a student! I have a copy of my indentures; my parents paid the fees—"

"Not a student!" roared Foxe. "Not ours! We'll repay your parents. The indentures will be torn up!"

"You can't even do that," said Simeon. "That's the whole point of both of us having copies. And why do you even want to? I will be cleared by the Pursuivants. Everything I told the Watch lieutenant is true."

"You're a troublemaker! Too clever by half, and Delazan was a fool. We're best rid of both of you. I have the backing of the Conclave of Magisters, I will not discuss this further. You must leave the hospital forthwith!"

"I'm a prisoner, you numbwit!" exclaimed Simeon. "Waiting to be collected by the Cardinal's people!"

Infuriated beyond bearing, Simeon stood up. That was suffi-cient to make Foxe scuttle back to the doorway, where he almost collided with a very tall, dark-haired woman with a scarred face, who easily pushed him aside with one scarlet-gauntleted hand. Foxe squeaked and opened his mouth to utter a sharp retort, but shut it, instead exhibiting a clumsy bow.

Simeon bowed too, as much to the scarlet tunic and gold sash and the badge in the red hat as to the woman who wore them. He knew she must be some high officer of the Cardinal's. Not to mention the air of menace that came with her, the way her long red-leather-clad fingers—several adorned with cameo icon rings—lightly caressed the hilt of her sword. That long blade would be out in an instant and buried in someone's heart, Simeon felt sure, if this woman felt it was required. Not to mention the pair of silver-chased pistols thrust through her belt, and her icons . . .

"Ah, Captain Rochefort!" said Foxe, bowing again. "I am Doctor-Magister Foxe, and I assure you this young man is not, not, not . . . a student of ours. Whatever he may have done, he has done on his own account."

"So I heard," replied Rochefort. "But your statement is belied by the fact that he *is* a student, Magister. Her Eminence is a seeker of truth, not of fancies. We desire this young man to come and tell us his story, and we will test it. Should he prove truthful, as I suspect will be the case, what then?"

"What!" exclaimed Foxe. "All that nonsense about a beastling, and hospital porters with crossbows, none of which were to be found, and Delazan missing?"

"The rather inadequately mopped-up stains on the floor of the . . . ah . . . old jar room are a mixture of the peculiar ash blood of a beastling, conjoined with a rather large quantity of human blood from the now doubtless dead and perhaps not particularly lamented Delazan," said Rochefort.

She tilted her glove, inspecting one of the icon rings, ignoring Foxe. "I would have thought an entire hospital full of doctor-magisters would have noticed that."

Foxe gobbled, lips quivering. Rochefort turned to Simeon.

"Come, Doctor Simeon MacNeel. We must look further into this, but I fully expect you will be returned here by the morrow. Unharmed."

"I had not thought otherwise," said Simeon untruthfully.

He straightened his long coat, lifted his chin, and followed Rochefort out of the cell, leaving Foxe still gobbling, fearing to loose the spiteful words that were doubtless forming in his throat.

Several Pursuivants were waiting near the main gate of the hospital, but Rochefort did not go out onto the broad street of Queen's Avenue. Instead, she led Simeon along the path by the hospital wall, which ran down to the river. The Pursuivants fell in behind.

"Are we not going to the Cardinal's Palace?" asked Simeon. The palace was not far away, perhaps twenty minutes' brisk walk, if the streets were not too busy.

"No," said Rochefort. "The Star Fortress."

"Oh," mumbled Simeon. He felt a sudden empty sensation in his stomach.

"I meant what I said," added Rochefort. "Your story sounds plausible, given what we know of Delazan and his gambling debts. The use of a beastling to assassinate him is unusual but not unprecedented. The trick is to put a Refuser in a box, force an angel to affect them—which is no small deed—and hope it will produce a beastling and not a pile of ash. Difficult, expensive, and likely to fail numerous times before it succeeds—but salutary. The story has already spread among Delazan's favorite haunts, and I am sure a number of other belated debts have suddenly been paid. I am not entirely sure what the Night Crew masquerading as porters had to do with it, or why they would have saved you. Perhaps two of Delazan's creditors both plotted to kill him, one in a more sophisticated fashion, and the plots coincided."

They walked on in silence for several minutes, leaving the path by the wall to take the steps down to the hospital's landing stage, a rather rickety jetty that thrust out into the Leire. One of the Cardinal's barges was docked there, a long and heavy vessel rowed by a dozen scarlet-clad matlows on each side. Two more Pursuivants waited on the jetty, watching the river traffic, and there were two more on board.

With a prisoner, Simeon realized—a tall, pale woman with nasty-looking sun spots crawling across her face. She wore a shapeless Refuser smock and was already clapped in irons, her ankles and wrists manacled. The woman sat on a thwart quietly and did not lift her head as Simeon climbed on board. He tried to look at her without being obvious, the manacles further unnerving him about his own destination. She was perhaps ten years older than he was, and apart from the Refuser clothes, he could not guess at her occupation or why she was there.

"Sit on the second thwart," instructed Rochefort. "Behind the prisoner."

The woman lifted her head as Rochefort spoke but did not utter a word.

"You are not a prisoner," Rochefort added to Simeon. "Merely a helpful witness. We will ascertain the truth of your story with the help of Larquiniel or Pereastor."

She looked at the woman captive, and her face changed, the scarred skin around her eye tightening, her lips curling.

"Unlike this Refuser, who cannot be questioned so gently. It will be the hot irons for you, Griselda."

Simeon flinched at Rochefort's sudden menace, and the mention of torture, but the Refuser seemed unaffected. She stared sullenly back at Rochefort, who scowled and gestured to the boat crew.

"Give way!"

Oars dipped into the river. The barge ponderously left the jetty and turned to starboard. It was upstream to the Star Fortress, and though the river was low, before the autumn rains came, the current was still strong. Twenty-four scarlet backs rose and fell, the long oars moving in perfect unison.

If the destination was somewhere other than the Star Fortress, and the barge not the Cardinal's, Simeon thought it would actually be a very pleasant afternoon to be on the river. He was a little warm, still in his doctor's coat, but he welcomed the sun on his face. He had spent so much time in the past months inside the hospital he had forgotten the joys of sunshine and clean air.

Ahead of them lay the rocky island of Three Firs (the trees long since cut down), spanned by the Mother and Daughter Bridges, six arches on the northern side of the island and three on the southern. The barge turned somewhat to port, making for the widest of the Mother's arches, the easiest for large craft to pass through.

Simeon watched with interest. He'd been on the river a few times but generally only to cross from the Left to the Right Bank when the Queen's Bridge—the one closest to the hospital—was too crowded and it was quicker to spend a half-livre piece on a boat ride.

The Mother was built of white stone, huge blocks of it, and the arches were at least forty feet wide and twenty feet above the current level of the Leire. It must have been built with the assistance of an angel, or several angels, for the stonework was so precise and the blocks enormous.

There was a statue in the middle of the Mother Bridge, of Ashalael, in the Archangel's familiar guise of a patrician-looking woman in classical robes, her wings folded about her. She held a baby in her arms, representing the people of Sarance.

But with the wear and tear over the centuries, Simeon saw the baby's hands had become more like paws and Ashalael's face was now a smooth oval, lacking the features that once would have been there. It seemed odd that the statue was not better looked after, or replaced.

He was just wondering if it would be safe to ask Rochefort about this, or whether it would be considered an offense to the Archangel, when he saw a hooded figure detach themselves from the great throng of people crossing the bridge and lean over the carved stone rail to level a long pistol at the barge, it seemed to Simeon straight at him!

Rochefort saw it too. One of her small silver-chased pistols was suddenly in her hand. Both she and the assassin on the bridge fired at the same time. Simeon crouched as the bangs resounded, and a gust of acrid gun smoke blew across his face, forcing him to squeeze his eyes shut. There were more shots a few seconds later as other Pursuivants fired, and a great deal more choking white gun smoke, accompanied by screaming, with Rochefort shouting over it all to the coxswain to steer the barge to shore.

Simeon felt no pain. Gingerly he opened his eyes and took a breath. He was unhurt. Looking around through the haze of smoke he saw Rochefort standing by the stern, touching an icon ring, whispering. A second later, he felt the rush of air that signaled the sweep of an angel's wings, and the soft harmonic of a plucked harp string.

"'Ware, Captain," called a Pursuivant. "It was a Refuser fired!"

"Pelastriel watches and follows only," said Rochefort calmly. "I am sure I hit the man; he flees. Take Dubois and Depernon, enlist the Watch from the post on the northern end of the bridge. Pelastriel will guide you to the malefactor. I want him taken alive."

The barge shuddered as it met the riverbank. Rowers leaped over the wooden revetment to hold the barge there as three

Pursuivants disembarked and ran off in pursuit of the assassin.

Simeon wiped his eyes and stared about him. At first, he thought no one had been hit by the shot. Then he saw the Refuser, tumbled down in the bottom of the barge, her gray tunic dark with blood.

Quickly, Simeon rolled her over so he could see where she was wounded. The bullet had struck her high in the right arm, delivering a grievous blow. Ripping her sleeve off, Simeon saw arterial blood jet out and jammed his big thumbs against the flow. But it was already useless. The wound was huge, she had lost so much blood already, and without his kit he could not tie off the artery. He could not stop her bleeding to death.

Unless—

"An icon of Beherael! Does anyone have one?"

Beherael's scope was shutting things. The closer of ways, he was called. A door locked by Beherael could not be forced save by a superior angel of appropriate scope (for he was, after all, only a Seraphim). But he could also plug a leak in a pipe, be it lead, copper, or a broken blood vessel.

None of the Pursuivants paid any attention to Simeon.

"Anyone! An icon of Beherael!"

Rochefort, who had been staring at the bridge, fingers on her icon ring to maintain communion with the angel Pelastriel who followed the malefactor, looked back.

"Don't be stupid, boy!" she shouted. "She's a Refuser! Do your best to keep her alive!"

Simeon shook his head, unable to believe what he had almost

done. If he'd had the icon he would have summoned Beherael and then there would have been a beastling on the boat, or the Refuser would die swiftly and surely of the Ash Blood plague.

He just wasn't used to treating Refusers, he told himself. Or it was the sudden shock of the wounding. Though he had treated many bullet and sword wounds, he saw only the aftermath of fighting. Not people shot in front of him.

He tried to keep the pressure on the wound with one hand while he knotted the torn sleeve above it, to fashion a tourniquet. But it was useless. The bullet, he saw now, had continued into the armpit, and there would be further damage to the lung or even heart.

The Refuser gasped something. Simeon bent closer, just managing to catch her final word.

"Ystara!"

A few moments later, she shuddered and died, with an inexplicable look of triumph on her face.

Simeon leaned back on a thwart and sighed. He had lost patients before, but rarely in such a way. If only he had his surgical kit! Even without angelic magic he might have been able to do something. . . .

Rochefort suddenly swore and stamped her red-heeled boots upon the deck. Simeon heard the rush of wings again, as Pelastriel reported back. He didn't know the angel but presumed his or her scope had something to do with observation or tracking.

"Curse them! I said alive!"

She stomped back toward Simeon and scowled down at the

sodden, bloodied mess that had so recently been a living person.

"Refusers! Why am I so troubled now by Refusers!"

"I did my best, ser," said Simeon. He gestured. "But as you see . . ."

Rochefort glared at him, the scar tissue above and below her eye suddenly much paler and more prominent.

"I dislike it when those I wish to question die before they can answer," she said, her voice full of menace. "Remember that. *Doctor*."

Simeon didn't say anything. This was a far cry from the apparently friendly officer who had assured him he would not be harmed. He tried to make himself as small as possible, edged to the gunwale between two rowers, and leaned over to wash his bloodied hands in the river.

"Tip that over the side," ordered Rochefort to the closest rowers, indicating the body. "Then on to the Star Fortress."

"Do we wait for Dubois and the others, Captain?" asked the coxswain woodenly. She did not seem particularly alarmed by Rochefort's rage, but Simeon noticed that while her voice was level, her eyes were cautiously fixed on the Pursuivant officer, much as someone would watch a well-known but potentially very dangerous dog.

"They can walk," said Rochefort. "It will give them time to consider their excuses for failing me."

Simeon washed his hands more vigorously, and wished he had managed to save the Refuser's life, almost as much for his own sake as for hers.

NINE

AGNEZ DID NOT DRINK AND PLAY DICE AFTER BEING CAR-
ried back to the Griffon's Head. Rather she fell into a troubled
sleep, to be woken by a doctor-magister who examined her head
and said the bruise there was already fading and of no account.
She was a surprisingly fast healer. No angelic intervention was
required. She should simply rest, aided by a sip or two of a bitter
cordial the doctor poured from a black glass bottle.

The next thing Agnez knew, it was full daylight, perhaps
even close to noon. Her headache was gone, entirely replaced
by an excitement that rose in her like a starving fish to a lure.
She leaped out of bed to wash, dress, and eat a swift breakfast of
unappetizing gruel from the common pot; armed herself with
sword, two pistols, and a dagger in each boot; and swaggered out
into the street, the crowd parting to allow this obviously dangerous bravo to march swiftly along the Crescent to the Queen's
Pier, there to take a boat to the Star Fortress.

"You want the Queen Ansgarde Bastion or the Queen Sofia
Bastion?" asked the boatwoman with a scowl as she sculled
vigorously at the stern, gray rags bouncing about her sturdily

muscled arms. She was a Refuser, of course, as were the majority of the casual river workers.

"The Musketeers' bastion," replied Agnez shortly, since she didn't know the answer to the question. She knew that each of the five bastions and the five ravelins—smaller outworks—were all garrisoned by different regiments of the Queen's army, and that the Cardinal's Pursuivants also had charge of the old prison tower, but that was all.

"Queen Ansgarde Bastion," grumbled the boatwoman. "They won't let me land you without the word of the day."

"I am a Musketeer," snapped Agnez coldly.

The boatwoman sniffed and looked meaningfully at Agnez's rather provincial outfit, all buckskin and durable cloth, in various shades of muddy brown. But she did not dare say anything, given the obviously well-cared-for weapons that completed Agnez's ensemble.

For her part, Agnez felt once again for the bronze token Franzonne had given her and was relieved to find it. She took it from her purse and held it up, so that the crossed swords surmounted by a royal coronet—the blazon of the Queen's Musketeers—on the obverse were clearly visible to the boatwoman. The Refuser sniffed again but bent more eagerly to her sculling, having to work very hard against the current that flowed more swiftly as they approached the arches of the Mother Bridge.

There was some sort of commotion on the bridge, a gathering of the City Watch, like a susurration of cream-and-blue birds. Agnez couldn't see what had stirred them up, but a score or more of them were milling about, shouting at each other, pushing at the crowd to keep to the northern side as they crossed.

A barge of red and gold with rowers in the same livery was just ahead of Agnez's boat, maneuvering to push through the middle arch against the current. Near the stern, a Cardinal-Pursuivant with the golden sash of a senior officer slowly turned, glaring at everything and everyone. Agnez prepared to glower back, but the officer's eyes did not linger. Whatever she was looking for, she did not see it in Agnez or her boat.

Sitting forward of the officer, a large young man in a doctor's dark black robe that was almost the same color as his skin, draped his hands overboard, washing them clean of . . . blood. Agnez stared at him, struck by the sensation that she'd seen him before. After a moment, he looked back and his brow furrowed, as if he also recognized Agnez. But then the barge disappeared under the bridge, into the shadow of the arch.

Agnez's boat slowed, almost broaching to the current, as the barge shot ahead.

"Ho! Don't slack now!" called Agnez.

"Don't want to get too close to *her*!" spat the boatwoman.

"Who?" asked Agnez. "The barge . . . oh, the Pursuivant. Who is she?"

This earned her the scornful look of the city-born for one from the provinces.

"Rochefort," said the boatwoman. "Captain of the Pursuivants. Taking that poor young doctor to the Tower, I'll warrant."

"Do you know who he is?" asked Agnez.

"Student from the hospital, I reckon," said the boatwoman. "Or was. Don't reckon he'll be going back there."

"He didn't look like a prisoner," said Agnez thoughtfully. "He wasn't bound."

"She doesn't need to tie up her prisoners," replied the boatwoman. "Like a snake, she is, with sword or pistol. Or magic."

The boatwoman spat again and added, malignantly, "Thought you'd know her. Killed her fair share of Queen's Musketeers, Rochefort has."

Agnez stiffened like a dog catching a scent.

"*Killed* Musketeers?"

"Duels. *She* never gets in trouble for breaking the edicts," said the boatwoman. "The Cardinal lets *her* get away with anything—and she always fights to the death."

There were several edicts forbidding the practice of dueling, dating back many years, including the most recent one proclaimed by Queen Sofia XIII herself. But just like back home in Descaray, Agnez knew that the practice continued in Lutace, and she had, in fact, been advised by her mother that if sufficient provocation arose, a challenge had to be given or accepted, regardless of any legal prohibitions.

"A Musketeer does not start fights without good reason," her mother had said. "But if you have good reason, then fight. And win, of course."

As Agnez's mother's concepts of sufficient provocation and a good reason were very broad, Agnez was mentally prepared to duel anyone. Often.

She fingered the hilt of her sword and thought about slaying Cardinal's Pursuivants. She knew the Queen's Musketeers, the Cardinal's Pursuivants, and the King's Guard were rivals, reflecting the political struggles between these three founts of power, and that they fought duels with each other whenever it could be done without being too blatant.

But to the death . . . that was *not* like the duels back home.

There, duels were only prosecuted to first blood. Certainly, every now and then someone would be killed by accident, but most of the time such affairs ended with some scratches, a few slight wounds, needing a doctor-magister and perhaps the healing touches of an angel. A finger might be lost, or some other slight inconvenience, but that was all.

Clearly, matters were different here.

If the occasion presented itself, Agnez daydreamed, she might be the one to teach this Rochefort, killer of Musketeers, a suitably final lesson. . . .

Henri Dupallidin was lost in the tunnels within the great rock the Star Fortress was built upon, and not for the first time. He'd been in the place only two days, but it seemed to him a great deal of his time had been spent in getting lost underground—or under stone—working out where he was and getting back to somewhere he knew.

The fortress had seemed relatively easy to navigate at first. He had followed the road that wound its way around the Six O'Clock Ravelin, the southernmost of the forward defenses, to the long causeway that ran across the very broad ditch that if necessary could be flooded from the Leire.

After showing his warrant, Henri had been allowed to proceed, though he was stopped again where the causeway met the southern rampart, which ran between the Queen Beatrude and the Queen Louisa Bastions, both garrisoned by the City Watch.

Four of the five bastions were named after former queens or kings. The fifth and northernmost proudly bore the name of the current monarch (though she was also the thirteenth of her name). The smaller ravelins, between the bastions but outside the broad ditch, were named after chapters of a clock face.

This all seemed straightforward enough, but once Henri was through the gate he found the passage through the earth and stone rampart slanted down, and instead of brick-faced earth, the walls, floor, and ceiling were of hard-chiseled granite, here and there impossibly smooth, evidence of angelic assistance.

Henri had not been forewarned that the Star Fortress ramparts and bastions were built on and around an enormous hummock of stone, which had been excavated on and off for centuries and built upon many times, particularly in the days of the old Empire, though very little of those ancient works remained.

Though there were many soldiers and workers about, Henri found they universally enjoyed not giving directions, or nonsense ones, and the puzzlement of a new arrival was a major source of fun for those already in the fortress.

By dint of counting his own steps and constructing a mental map based on these measurements, eventually Henri was able to find his way up and out to the very large open area that was surrounded by the ramparts of the fortress. This was known as Dial Square.

Henri knew there would be some buildings there; after all, he had been told about a Pursuivant barracks, and the New Palace he would be helping build. But over the course of several hours wandering about, he discovered a perfectly laid-out town in miniature: a system of well-paved and drained roads; five large brick barracks built around walled parade grounds; there was an infirmary, characteristically whitewashed and many-windowed; two raised market garden fields, fertile earth contained within wooden revetments; two large ponds or reservoirs; a number of long, low commissary stores; a shrine to Ashalael, with a very splendid copper-shingled spire; a tavern with numerous soldiers spilling out its doors to drink around empty barrels; and several rows of shops.

The most important location in Dial Square was the beginnings of the New Palace and its surrounding park. Bounded by a low wall in various stages of construction, the design of the park followed the current trend for a manicured rural scene. There was a model dairy; a cow pasture; a wildflower meadow; an archery field with straw-bale butts; and an apple orchard with perhaps ten of its eventual hundred or so trees in place, holes already dug for near-mature trees in tubs to be transplanted there. A tumbled but artful hill of stone blocks was being built to make a hermit's cave within, and there were several lakes being lined with gravel so the water remained clear.

In the middle of the partially completed park, the New Palace rose up. At least, there was a great deal of scaffolding, a confusion of ladders, and a number of cranes powered by Refusers walking inside huge wheels, surrounding a maze of brick walls that were for the most part only one story high, though some enthusiast had seen the chimneys advanced to their full height.

The New Palace, where Henri was to work and live. It didn't look like any of it was ready to inhabit, and the presence of a large number of tents did not seem promising. But as it turned out, he was granted a chamber in a part of the New Palace that was complete.

The room was not a chamber in the strict sense, as it was destined to be one of the stalls for the Queen's horses. There were twenty more in a line in this part of the stables, all occupied by the Architect's staff. But it had a narrow bed, a writing desk, a chair, and a chest. Not to mention fresh straw on the floor every day, as the Refuser stablehands had already been recruited, though the horses would not move in for at least another six months.

Most important, it was not the Tower.

Henri was reminded of this constantly, wherever he went. Though the bastions themselves were forty feet high, and the embankments between them were thirty feet high, the tower rose up at least ninety feet, and its sick gray stone was very different from the rusty redbrick and pale-white ashlar-faced points of the bastions and ravelins.

The old prison tower. The Tower of Lutace.

Though he saw it all the time, Henri tried to put it out of his mind, and for the most part succeeded, because he was quickly put to work.

Dutremblay, the Queen's Architect, did not need either surveyor or another counting house clerk. But she did need a messenger, and this immediately became Henri's job. Unfortunately, the reason Dutremblay needed a messenger to convey her wishes through the entirety of the Star Fortress and the subterranean regions beneath was because the garrisons within were such independent and recalcitrant principalities.

Henri had no problem finding his way in Dial Square. But under it, in the extensively mined expanse of stone, there were more passageways, chambers, stairs, drains, and just plain holes and unplanned cracks and caverns than Henri had ever imagined. But he had to find his way through them, because the Architect sent messages everywhere, in the vain hope of getting the resources and labor that would enable the New Palace to be finished only two or three years later than planned.

The Queen's Musketeers boisterously governed the Queen Ansgarde Bastion and neighboring ravelins. The Cardinal's Pursuivants garrisoned the Queen Sofia Bastions, the Two O'Clock Ravelin, and the Tower. The King's Guard were to be found in the King Denis Bastion and the Four O'Clock Ravelin. The generally demeaned City Watch had the Queen Louisa and Queen Beatrude Bastions and the Six O'Clock Ravelin.

The artillerists of the Loyal Royal Artillery Company were spread across all the fortifications, insisting on both ancient prerogatives involving their armaments and thoroughly modern technical reasons for why they had to do whatever they wanted to do.

The commanding officers of all the regiments jointly made decisions concerning Dial Square, where each had their main barracks building, and were supposed to equally contribute to the ongoing construction of the New Palace. But, even though this was being overseen by the Queen's Architect, everyone knew it was really the Cardinal's project. Consequently, Captain-General Dartagnan of the Musketeers, Captain-General Dessarts of the King's Guard, the Watch's Deputy-Mayor Chapelain, and Colonel-Artificer Creon of the Artillery Company generally did not cooperate, while pretending to do so.

Consequently Dutremblay was always chasing the skilled tradespeople, contributions of money, building materials, or gangs of Refuser workers that the other regiments were supposed to provide. Every morning, she'd thrust a sheaf of messages into her messenger's hands and send them out to convey the "requests" to the officers notionally responsible for supplying what was required, who were either not to be found or could provide a plausible excuse for not being able to do whatever it was the Architect needed them to do.

Shortly before his most recent geographical embarrassment, Henri had spent two hours tracking down a team of masons employed by the Queen's Musketeers who were supposed to be spending the week working on the New Palace. Having found them chipping stone steps in a dark, seeping cellar far under the Musketeers' Barracks, he had let himself be momentarily distracted and had got turned around on his way back out.

Now he was in a tunnel only wide enough for one person and no taller than the crown of his hat, so he had to hunch down. The taper he held had burned down to the point where wax was melting on his fingers. And Henri was now sure he was *not* in one of the messenger tunnels that would let him quickly ascend to the surface of Dial Square.

To make matters worse, someone was coming from the other direction, or at least a faint glow was approaching, the flickering, pallid kind that suggested another of the ubiquitous tapers everyone carried around.

"Ho!"

A young woman's voice, overhearty for the circumstances, Henri thought. He stopped and raised his taper as high as he could under the low ceiling to try to get the light to fall ahead.

He was surprised and slightly alarmed to see a young woman with a sword at her side and pistols in her belt, though she was not in any uniform. He hadn't seen anyone fully armed within the Star Fortress who wasn't a soldier of one of the regiments.

As difficult as it was to move along this narrow tunnel, she managed to do so with a confident swagger that suggested she had complete right of way. Henri's heart sank as he contemplated having to retreat before her and probably get even more lost than he was already.

Then she was close enough to see him. Instantly her hand flashed to her sword and it came out of the scabbard with a disturbing swiftness and dexterity, not even scraping the walls, which were so close on either side.

"Trick me, would you! You'll pay for that!"

Henri dropped his taper, which immediately went out, and drew the dagger at his side. He managed to parry the half-seen thrust that snaked out at him, pushing the blade away that otherwise would have pinked his arm, but he knew he could not hold off even a moderately competent swordswoman with a dagger, and she was considerably more than competent. As she pulled her sword back to thrust again, Henri retreated along the passage, speaking as swiftly and clearly as he could.

"Hold! I didn't trick you! I don't even know who you are!"

The sword quivered in the air.

"You're not the clerk from the Ansgarde landing?"

"No! I'm one of the Architect's assistants! The Queen's Architect! Dutremblay!"

The sword was lowered still further, and the woman raised her taper so the light fell on Henri's face.

"Hmmm. My pardon, Clerk. Is that a mustache . . . and you have red hair."

"I am aware I have red hair," said Henri stiffly. "I do not believe it is an excuse to run a stranger through. I have a sword at my lodging, if you will allow me to fetch—"

"No, no, I really do beg your pardon. The clerk who smirked when he gave me directions had brown hair. In the dark, with your clerkly habit, I mistook you for him."

"It is true I am temporarily a clerk, but do not let that affright you," said Henri. He was not only scared but angry at the sudden attack. "As I said, I am happy to fetch my sword and we can continue this discussion in a more suitable place. I have heard there is a part of the ditch under the bridge where—"

"You're not the clerk from the landing, but we have met before, haven't we?" interrupted the woman. She still held her taper high, and she was looking intently at Henri's face.

"I do not believe so," said Henri. "Nor do I wish to know . . ."

He faltered as he looked at her. She *was* familiar, now he saw her up close. But he couldn't put a name to her face. It was more a feeling than a memory. . . .

"I do not usually apologize, but I do beg *your* pardon," said the young woman. "Would you be a good fellow and show me the way to Dial Square, and the Musketeers' Barracks?"

"If I knew how to do that, we'd both be better off," he said. "Who are you, anyway?"

The young woman sheathed her sword with a laugh, and doffed her hat, scraping the ceiling. She bent lower and extended her foot in a bow as elegant as possible in the cramped tunnel.

"Well, then, perhaps we may find a way out together. I am Agnez Descaray, a new cadet of the Queen's Musketeers."

Henri responded with a more cautious bow in return. She was so familiar—it was a great puzzle. . . .

"I am Henri Dupallidin," he replied. Being well aware of the animosity between the Queen's Musketeers and the Cardinal's Pursuivants, which he suspected might extend more generally to those in the service of the Cardinal, he considered the clerkly black favored by Dutremblay—rather than his Cardinalist red and yellow—might now be getting him out of trouble, as it had almost gotten him into it a few minutes before. "I am an assistant to the Queen's Architect. A very new one: I only got here the day before yesterday. Which is why I have no idea where we are. I got turned around coming up from one of the cellars. Where did you come from?"

"The river landing at the Ansgarde Bastion," replied Agnez. "The Musketeers there passed me through, but without giving me directions. There was a clerk who recorded my entry . . . he said it was easy to find my way to Dial Square and report to the barracks there. I just had to alternately turn left and right at every intersection. But I have been lost in this warren for hours."

Henri nodded.

"They all love giving false directions to anyone new," he said. "I don't even ask now. Except for Refusers. I think they're afraid not to tell the truth."

"I've seen some Refusers in the distance, but they're always gone by the time I catch up."

"There are hundreds of them working here; it's surprising how much laboring work there is still to be done," said Henri. "They're everywhere. Did you see any steps going up from where you've been?"

"Several," replied Agnez. "But I've kept on the level, like that clown of a clerk told me. Turning left and right . . ."

"If we go back the way I came," said Henri, "I think I know where I went wrong."

He didn't just think that—he was sure of it. He'd counted

steps and turnings on the way down to the cellar, but he'd let the surliness of the workers there distract him into taking the wrong door out. He'd avoided going back because he didn't want to face them again, but now he had an excuse: he would be showing this lost Musketeer the way. He doubted they would show the same dumb insolence to her as he'd experienced. She looked too ready to use all her various weapons.

"As good a plan as any," replied Agnez. She cocked her head and looked at Henri. "I'm sure we have met before . . . not in Lutace. With your red hair and accent I would say—"

"I am a Bascon; it is true," said Henri, drawing himself up and resting his hand on his dagger pommel. "Do you wish to remark—"

"Hold up, cockerel!" exclaimed Agnez. "Are you sure you're a clerk? You seem as keen to quarrel as any Musketeer!"

"I am going to be a soldier," said Henri. "An artillerist, by choice. I am only a clerk for the time being."

"I am a Bascon too," said Agnez. "Descaray is only a little over ten leagues from Farroze."

"Oh," said Henri. "Well, my father is Sacristan of the Temple of Huaravael. . . . Have you been there?"

"Never!" exclaimed Agnez.

"I thought perhaps you had, because I also feel as if we have met before," admitted Henri. "But I've only been in Lutace a . . . short while, and I never left Huaravael before I came here."

"Perhaps we are kindred souls!" exclaimed Agnez. "I will like you all the more if—when we get out of this place—you can show me somewhere to drink a flask of wine! My throat is as dry as the brick dust my boots have been kicking up these past few hours."

"There is a tavern in the Square," said Henri. "But soldiers are only permitted there on certain days, according to their regiment. I think Musketeers have Wednesday and Friday . . . and today is Tuesday."

"I can't believe any Musketeer would accept that!" exclaimed Agnez. "We will drink where and when we please!"

"First we have to find a way out," said Henri. "Follow me."

He bent to pick up his taper but discovered it had been trodden on, the wax pulped and the wick broken. At that moment, Agnez transferred her taper from her left to her right hand somewhat too enthusiastically, and it also went out.

It was immediately very, very dark. Henri thought of all the steps to fall down, the holes where drain covers had not yet been placed, the pit—admittedly in another bastion—he had crossed on a makeshift bridge of planks . . .

"Do you have a quick match, or a flint and steel?" asked Henri. He was pleased his voice sounded calm. "I do not."

"Is it dark of the moon, or the first quarter?" asked Agnez.

"What?"

"Never mind, I'll try it anyway," said Agnez.

A faint glow appeared on the band of Agnez's hat, illuminating the two fingers held against an icon she wore there as a badge. Henri heard her whispering, a name that made the hairs on the back of his neck rise, a common side effect of angelic summoning.

"Jashenael, Jashenael, grant me your light!"

TEN

THE CELL WAS ONE OF THE BEST IN THE TOWER, ALL THINGS considered. It was high up and actually had a window, though it was only an arrow slit that had at some point been crossed with deeply set iron bars. But it admitted both air and light, something entirely lacking from the cells lower down.

Or so Dorotea had been told by the jailer, who asked to be called "Mother." She was a sharp-faced, ruddy-skinned, scrawny woman of middle years with cruel hands who wore an apron marked with what looked like old bloodstains. She'd harped on the relative comforts of the cell, telling Dorotea how lucky she was to be a guest of the Cardinal, rather than an out-and-out prisoner.

Mother had also remarked on the fact that Rochefort herself had handed over a purse for Dorotea's meals and comforts. Without someone paying, Mother told the young student, the plain but edible fare she was given would be replaced by stale bread and water, and the two scratchy woolen blankets and the straw palliasse would disappear.

And there was the window. It provided a limited view, looking southeast, so much of the Star Fortress itself was obscured, save the tip of the King Denis Bastion and the Four O'Clock Ravelin. Nor could she see much of the city, just some outlying houses, and then a few of the closer villages, with fields and pastures and a long, low forested hill that blocked everything beyond it.

But she could see the sky, with all its majesty and marvels, the birds and clouds and weather. And at night, there would be the stars, and whatever insights they might offer on the angelic heavens.

Dorotea liked to look out the narrow window. There wasn't anything else to do. She was not permitted any writing or drawing materials, or books. Apart from the blankets and the palliasse, a wooden spoon and a wooden bowl completed the outfitting of her cell. A shallow drain on the left side of the cell served as a toilet. At dawn and dusk Mother brought a bucket of water, both to flush this out and to wash with and to drink. The water was always tan-colored and full of tiny insects, but it tasted well enough.

Dorotea had been there two days and had adapted to the routine when it was suddenly changed. Mother unlocked her door around noon, when she had only ever appeared, with bucket, at dawn and dusk.

"You've been granted the right to walk about the Square," announced the jailer with a grimace, suggesting she didn't approve of this at all. She jerked her thumb at the door behind her. "Got to be in by dark, and you're not to bring anything back. You'll be searched."

Dorotea didn't move. Her eye was caught by a particular composition of the sky and a lone cloud, framed by the arrow slit. It would make a superb background for an icon of the angel Lailaraille, whose scope was the air, oft used by sponge divers and the like to extend their endurance underwater.

"You hear me?" bellowed Mother. "You can go out! Go on, then!"

Still Dorotea didn't answer, until the jailer came and clapped her hard on the shoulder.

"What? Oh yes," replied Dorotea. She smiled at Mother. "I'm sorry; I was thinking. I'll go for a walk in a minute."

"You're a strange one, and no mistake," grumbled Mother. "You some sort of kin to Rochefort?"

"Hmm?" asked Dorotea. She tore herself away from the window. The cloud had dissipated, and the sky by itself was less interesting. "No, I have no family in Lutace."

"Special privileges," grumbled Mother. "All these 'guests' and 'temporary visitors.' Not like the old days. If you were sent to the Tower, you were sent to the Tower. Be off with you, then! You might not be allowed out again, Captain Rochefort or no Captain Rochefort!"

"Thank you," said Dorotea. She paused to bestow a distracted kiss on Mother's forehead. The jailer recoiled and almost punched her, suspecting she was being made fun of, but hesitated. Rochefort *had* decreed special privileges for this one, and Mother didn't know why. It was best to treat her very carefully. Besides, the kiss had seemed truly innocent.

"Um, how do I get out?" asked Dorotea. "I didn't really notice the way when I was brought in."

Mother shook her head and pushed past the young scholar.

"Don't know what the world's coming to," she muttered. "Follow me!"

She led Dorotea to the winding stair in the southwest corner, down five floors, and out through the guardroom where her consort, peculiarly known to all as Uncle, gave her a knowing glance. Two Cardinal's Pursuivants paused in playing dice to look her over too, but they did not deign to comment. Mother noticed the eyes fixed sharply on Dorotea. There *was* something special about this guest of the Cardinal.

Beyond the guardroom, they crossed the drawbridge to a temporary wooden stair that had been built fifteen years before and was any day now to be replaced in stone.

Dorotea paused to blink in the sunlight that now enveloped her, so much warmer and brighter than the narrow shaft of light that managed to penetrate her cell through the arrow slit. Like most icon-makers, she liked to work in natural light and had been thrilled by the workshops of the Belhalle, where glass perfected by angels made interior spaces seem like outdoors.

"Down the steps," said Mother. "Anyone annoys you, tell 'em you're a guest of Her Eminence, in the Tower. Be back by dusk."

"I can just walk away?" asked Dorotea. "I am puzzled about being a guest who is not exactly a prisoner."

"Me too," said Mother. She hawked up a gobbet of phlegm and spat it over the railing.

"I could just keep walking," mused Dorotea. "Back to the Belhalle, back to my work."

"You're still in the Star Fortress," said Mother, shaking her head. "You can't get out. Even if you could, you'd be arrested . . . I mean be invited to come back."

"I just make icons," said Dorotea. "I really don't understand."

"No one ever does," said Mother, and spat again.

Dorotea looked out upon the square. The side of the tower blocked most of the view, but she could see several buildings, and a raised market garden being worked by a number of Refusers. To her right the out-thrust arrowhead of the Two O'Clock Ravelin was only slightly higher than the rampart, but past that there was the bulk of the Queen Sofia Bastion, a hulking presence of earth encased in stone. There were soldiers marching on top of it, appearing from some unseen stair or passage and disappearing again after crossing her vision for a minute or so.

"Go," said Mother.

Dorotea nodded obediently and started down the steps. She felt her fingers tingling, the kind of itch she experienced when she hadn't been able to draw or paint or make something for a day or more. Not necessarily an icon, though that was what she liked most. She was equally happy sculpting, or messing about with found objects, creating anything. Angelic magic was always fascinating, but it was only one aspect of her creative yearning.

Her pace quickened with the twitching of her hands. No one had said anything about drawing or painting *outside* the prison tower. Provided she did not make icons, surely it would be allowed? She had a few livres in her purse, enough to purchase some paper and sticks of charcoal. Someone would have such things here, an architect or draftsman, perhaps an artillerist or a would-be poet. She could draw caricatures and sell them, just as she had done in Tramereine, to earn money for more paper and perhaps paints and brushes.

Dorotea hurried. Drawing materials beckoned. Soon she would be at work again.

She didn't notice the young Refuser boy who'd been lurking at the bottom of the steps follow her, skipping sideways, dropping back, apparently intent on some game. But always ending up a dozen yards behind Dorotea, and going in the same direction.

Simeon wasn't taken to the Tower but to a comfortably furnished chamber somewhere deep under the Pursuivants' Barracks in Dial Square. There, sitting on a cushioned armchair with his face brightly lit by a massive candelabra of twenty or thirty tall, red candles that dominated the adjacent table, he was interrogated by a weary magister with prematurely white hair, a sharp contrast to his deep mahogany skin, which showed few lines. The magister, using an icon he wore around his neck on a badly gilded chain, summoned an angel whose presence Simeon felt as a cold grip upon his temples, accompanied by very low bass notes, quite unlike the usual bright harp sounds most angels evoked.

Once again, Simeon described the events of the previous day.

"He speaks the truth as he knows it," reported the magister

to Rochefort, who was lounging nearby, sipping wine from a silver flagon made for beer. "Barring some interference with his memory from a more powerful angel—of which Larquiniel can see no trace—what he says happened did in fact happen."

The clerk hesitated, then tapped a closed, lidded icon he wore as a brooch and added, "Do you wish me to summon Pereastor to inquire more deeply?"

Simeon did not know what Larquiniel was, presumably only a Seraphim or Cherubim, but Pereastor was a Dominion. An angel not to be summoned lightly, as the cost would be at least a month of this clerk's life span.

"That will not be necessary," said Rochefort, setting her flagon aside. "Though it would be more convenient if he *had* lied. Deraner, you have taken all this down?"

A sour-faced clerk sitting at the desk by the corner nodded, just as she finished writing in a ledger that was chained to her belt. She cast sand over the page to dry the ink and shut the book.

"Thank you, Ser Habil," said Rochefort to the Magister. He bowed and gestured to the clerk. The clerk nodded again, and followed the Magister out the door.

Simeon swallowed a question he was about to ask, deciding it was better to take the clerk's example and remain silent. But Rochefort saw the nervous movement.

"There is a mystery I do not like about you, Doctor Mac-Neel," she said. "The beastling being set upon Magister Delazan I can understand, given his debts and enemies. It is unusual but not entirely without precedent. But why would these Refusers save you? One, at least, died with Delazan, given the extent of the bloodstains, though they were hastily cleaned up. But who cleared up? Why were the Refusers there? Why take the bodies? Neither Her Eminence nor myself like this kind of mystery."

"I don't know, ser," said Simeon.

"I think I shall have to set a Watch upon you," mused Rochefort. "To see what happens."

Simeon nodded absently. Being watched seemed the least of his current problems. He had been thinking about his future ever since Magister Foxe's outburst. While the dean was a braggart, and a coward, he was also quite careful. He probably had got the backing of the Conclave of Magisters, and it would take some greater authority to get Simeon his place back at the hospital.

But Simeon didn't want to go back to the hospital.

"It would be easier to watch me . . . or those around me . . . somewhere like this, wouldn't it, ser?" he asked.

Rochefort narrowed her eyes.

"I know there's an infirmary in the Star Fortress," Simeon hurried on. "Some of the magisters from the hospital work here, from time to time. I was wondering if perhaps I could—"

"Ah, I see," said Rochefort. "Magister Foxe's declaration that you are not a student. But that can be overborne. You can resume your life at the hospital."

"I don't want to go back," said Simeon. "I was prepared to bide my time, but they teach little of worth there anyway, and I heard the Infirmary here is supervised by Doctor-Magister Hazurain . . ."

"Ah, the fog lifts entirely," said Rochefort.

Doctor-Magister Hazurain was the Queen's Physician, and probably the most famous doctor in all Sarance, though she was originally from Dahazaran.

"What would you do if you are not allowed to work and study at the Infirmary?" asked Rochefort. "Nor go back to the hospital?"

"I suppose . . . I would have to return to Loutain," said Simeon. He did his best not to show it, but he felt despondent about that. He did not particularly need the training provided by the hospital, but he did need the imprimatur of having studied there. Many patients insisted on being treated by a "proper doctor from Lutace." But if he could say he had been trained by the Queen's Physician, Doctor-Magister Hazurain . . .

"Sometimes the needs of the state conjoin with personal ambition," mused Rochefort.

She went to the desk and wrote quickly on a sheet of heavy paper, signed it, and carelessly sealed it with wax poured from the candle and the embossed pommel of her dagger.

"Take this to the chief clerk at the Infirmary," she said, handing it to Simeon. "It recommends you to Doctor-Magister Hazurain, suggests you continue your studies there under her direction and assist in the hospital, with whatever stipend they pay their neophyte doctors."

"Uh . . . thank you," stammered Simeon, taking the folded paper.

"Her Eminence will review my decision," warned Rochefort.

"It is possible it will be rescinded or changed."

Simeon nodded, but it didn't really sink in. This was beyond anything he expected. He had seen Hazurain successfully operate on a depressed fracture of the skull when he first arrived at the hospital, *without* angelic assistance. Simeon had never dreamed he could be one of her students. She was as far above the ordinary doctor-magisters at the hospital as the Tower was above the ditch of the Star Fortress. And to be paid for working in the Infirmary! He wasn't paid at the hospital. He only got his food and lodging.

"Perhaps you can also help me," said Rochefort, almost as an aside. "If anything else odd happens, as with the two Refusers saving you from the beastling. You could let me know. I want to know immediately, at any time. Take this token."

"Yes, ser," said Simeon. He did not reach for the token, though he understood immediately. This was the price of gaining the post with Hazurain. If he accepted it, he must also accept that he was to be some kind of informer for Rochefort. This felt instinctively abhorrent, but he forced himself to consider the matter without emotion. He owed no specific allegiance to anyone else. Rochefort was an officer of the Cardinal, the Cardinal was the Queen's Chief Minister. If the Queen told him he had to spy for the state, he would accept the order. This was no different.

But it did feel a bit like being bought and sold . . .

"Well?" asked Rochefort.

Simeon took the small silver medallion Rochefort offered him. It bore the device of the Cardinal on one side and a stylized representation of Ashalael on the other.

"Show that to any Pursuivant and they will bring me word. Your icons, medical kit, and other possessions will be brought to you," said Rochefort. "There are chambers for the medical staff in the Infirmary. Tell the clerk I desire you to have one of the better ones."

"Yes, ser."

Simeon got up, found himself looming over Rochefort, and hastily bowed. Once again he had to reshape his views concerning the Cardinal's Pursuivant officer. She had seemed kindly enough at first, then she'd frightened him on the barge, and now was cast somewhat in the light of a benefactor. But not an entirely disinterested one.

Simeon hoped he never would need to report anything to Rochefort.

The Pursuivant Captain waved her scarlet-gloved hand negligently. Simeon bowed again and left the room. Just over the threshold he hesitated, facing a dark passage that extended to the left and right, a stairwell ahead of him, and another heavy iron door to his right.

"This way," said one of the Pursuivants who had been on the barge. She was not much older than he was, but infinitely more self-possessed, a kind of Rochefort in the making. She picked up a bull's-eye lantern and sent its narrow beam along the passage. "I will take you up to the gate on to Dial Square and point out the Infirmary."

"Thank you," muttered Simeon. He followed her into a well-lit chamber humming with clerks engaged in mysterious sorting of papers; up a long flight of stairs carved in the rock; then through a guardroom where a group of Pursuivants were firing a small crossbow like the one the Refuser had used against the beastling in the hospital, each of them taking their turn to shoot a small melon or pumpkin perched on top of a bureau.

Past this guardroom, they went out through a proper gateway, under murder holes and a raised portcullis, past more Pursuivants standing sentry, crossed a bridge and then down a right-angled open stair to the vast court that was Dial Square, a town in miniature.

"You see the copper spire of the temple?" asked the Pursuivant. She did not need to say it was a temple to Ashalael; it could not be anything else, not here.

Simeon nodded.

"Head for that. The Infirmary lies a little way east of it, the whitewashed building immediately across the avenue from the tavern."

"Thank you again," said Simeon.

"Patch me up some time," said the Pursuivant with a wink. Simeon was not sure what that meant, but he smiled. He was surprised by the wink, because the Pursuivants had a reputation for puritanical celibacy. Very much unlike the King's Guard, or to a somewhat lesser extent, the Queen's Musketeers.

"Happy to," he mumbled. "That is, I hope it doesn't prove necessary."

"It always is, sooner or later," said the Pursuivant. She winked again and turned on her heel, scabbard clapping against her shapely leg.

Simeon stared for a moment, blushed, turned to fix his gaze on the spire of the temple, and walked off.

ELEVEN

THE TAVERN WAS ONE OF THE OLDEST BUILDINGS IN DIAL
Square, the end house of a terrace of six houses that predated
the construction of the fortress. Its purpose was evident from
the large barrels that sat outside the front door, two currently
in use as makeshift tables, one by a group of dusty masons, and
one by a trio of King's Guards, overspill from the many more of
their regimental brethren inside. The Guards were identifiable
by their dark green doublets and pale green shirts and breeches,
with tabards of yet another green, displaying their blazon: a crown
of five points defaced by a sword, picked out in gold. While the
masons drank beer in wooden flagons, the Guards were drinking
wine in flasks, both groups served by swift-darting Refuser lads
and lasses in gray aprons and caps.

A great noise of soldiers drinking, dicing, arguing, laughing,
and generally carrying on came through the windows, which
were open but heavily barred. A large sign hung from an iron
pole above the door, so faded that the original six golden cups
looked to be no more than daubs of shapeless color.

Now the sign was finally being repainted. An artist in the

robes of a Belhalle scholar perched high on a ladder that had been roped to one of the larger outside barrels to save the painter from being knocked off, a very necessary precaution that had been added to by a Refuser potboy standing at the base to squeak "Mind how you go!" and "Watch the ladder."

"It's crowded," said Henri, who was feeling very pleased with himself for finding the way out of the tunnels beneath the Musketeers' Barracks, though he did not admit to Agnez that they'd come out somewhere quite different than he had expected, emerging into the physic garden of the Infirmary, which lay across the street from the wineshop and was a good two hundred yards from the Musketeers' Barracks. "All King's Guards, too."

"Most of the guards are inside," said Agnez, pointing. "There's space around that third barrel, by the stonemasons. No one's bothering them. Surely you also need to wash away some of that dust? My throat feels like tar paper."

"Aren't you supposed to report to the barracks?" asked Henri. They'd talked as they made their way up and down stairs and along passageways, their way lit by Agnez's icon. He found Agnez easy to talk to, though she held very strong opinions. He was already worried about her finding out he was really in the Cardinal's service, not the Queen's. He wanted to tell her, to get it out of the way, but had yet to find the right opportunity. Or possibly, the courage.

"Oh, I've time for a flask of wine," said Agnez cheerily. "Franzonne said not to report too early."

"Franzonne? The Queen's Champion?" asked Henri. "You've met her?"

"Fought with her," declared Agnez. "That's how I won my place as a cadet."

"You had to defeat *Franzonne*?" asked Henri as they waited for a gap in the traffic. A dozen gardeners in russet smocks and broad-brimmed hats, each carrying a small tree in a tub, were walking past, closely followed by a large group of Refusers hauling a low cart that held a single great oak beam, almost certainly destined for the New Palace. This made Henri feel slightly guilty, since he should have already reported back to the Architect, but not enough to follow them.

"It was a draw," said Agnez as they dashed across the street and took up position around the only barrel that was not already in use as a table. "Essentially. Ho! Varlet. Two flasks of your best wine."

Her clear, confident voice carried over the din of the crowd, and several people turned to look, including the trio of King's Guards. Already drunk, they stared at Agnez and Henri as if suddenly sighting something highly objectionable. Two of them, a slab-faced man with small eyes, and a taller dark woman with a sneering mouth, approached the new arrivals.

"It's Tuesday," said the slab-faced pale man, glaring at Agnez. He was very drunk, swaying on the spot.

"I had wondered," replied Agnez. "It felt like Monday, but I had a niggling doubt—"

"King's Guards drink here Tuesday," added the man. He

made a shooing gesture. "Not country bravos and . . . and inky-fingered clerks."

Agnez looked at her nondescript leathers and raised an eyebrow, while Henri waggled his fingers, to show an absence of ink. The red-faced man grew redder, and the woman's sneer more developed.

"Guards?" asked Agnez. "I thought in all that green you must be gardeners like those fellows with the trees—"

She ducked under a roundhouse blow and stepped back, laughing, as the man spun about. Before he could recover, she kicked him behind the knee and he fell down with a cry of rage and pain. The woman behind him went for her sword, but one of the masons suddenly rose up and embraced her in a bear hug.

"Nay," said the mason, her burly arms stained with stone dust, delineating muscles like iron bands. "No blades."

"Guards! To me!" shrieked the woman, struggling in her captor's grasp.

The third Guard, a more reticent fellow, sighed and stood up but did not put down his flask of wine. There was a sudden cessation of the cheerful noise inside the tavern, the calm before the storm, followed a moment later by the sound of many stools and chairs being pushed back or kicked aside as the Guards prepared to sally forth.

But before they could do so, the ladder for the sign-painting suddenly fell, wedging itself behind two of the large barrels and across the door. As this portal opened outward, the way was now blocked. The Belhalle scholar who had been atop the ladder swung by her hands from the signpost, letting herself drop a moment later.

The scholar landed as the first Guard got up and swung at Agnez again. Distracted by the fall of the ladder, the blow might have connected, save that Henri stepped forward, caught the man's arm, and threw him across his hip, a country wrestling move much favored by his older siblings for use on him until he got very good at it himself. The Guardsman fell heavily, and this time did not rise.

The Guardswoman held by the mason tried to shout again, a puzzled and then panicked look crossing her face as she found herself held so tight she could not draw breath. The mason holding her waited patiently as her struggles grew desperate and then slowed. As she lapsed into unconsciousness, the mason gently deposited the woman next to her companion.

A roar from inside, a shuddering impact, and the groan of the ladder announced that the Guards had found something to use as a battering ram.

The third Guardsman, rather than attacking, ambled over to where his two somnolent companions lay, taking a long drink from his flask as he did so.

"You shoulsdsh go," he mumbled, waving one hand so vigorously he fell over and ended up sitting with his back to a barrel, his wine flask amazingly still steady in his hand. "Others wouldn't understand."

"Understand what?" asked Agnez. "I am quite prepared to fight any number of—"

"No, no," said the burly mason. She gestured at her mates, who were gathering their tools and aprons. "Save it, youngster. They've been drinking all afternoon. There'll be murder done, not mere brawling. Best to be gone."

With that, the masons sauntered away. There was another boom and crash, and a triumphant shout as the ladder splintered but still did not entirely break.

"She's right," said Henri. He looked around. If they went up or down the street they'd be spotted and the chase would be on. But the Guards were also certain to look in the closer shops, something clearly on the minds of the shopkeepers, who were already barring doors and windows.

There was one open gate, just across the street.

"The Infirmary," he said, pointing. He started off in that direction, then stopped, as neither Agnez nor the sign-painter were moving. They were looking at each other, Agnez shading her eyes with her hand, the scholar meeting her gaze with a friendly but distracted smile.

"Come on!"

Whether it was Henri's shout or the sound of the ladder finally being smashed apart and the tavern door flying open, the other two responded, and all three of them sprinted across the street. Unfortunately, even those few seconds of delay meant that the first Guards out the door saw them running and spotted where they were going. A great hue and cry went up, King's Guards falling over each other as they drunkenly charged out into the street.

Somewhere a bell began to ring, summoning reinforcements perhaps, though Henri had no idea for whom. What happened when the King's Guard rioted? Who would bring them to heel?

They got to the gate a dozen paces ahead of their pursuers, slammed it shut, and dropped the bar just in time. Agnez looked left and right and then up at the wall.

The gate boomed as someone charged it, accompanied by a cry of pain. The Guards were throwing themselves at the heavy oak.

"If they roll the barrels over to step up, or find another ladder, they'll be over that wall in a minute," said Agnez.

"They're too drunk," answered Henri, but he was already looking around the courtyard for another way out. The Infirmary proper was an imposing whitewashed building with large arched windows. There was another gate, half-open, which Henri thought led to the physic or herb garden, where he and Agnez had emerged from the depths. If they could get there, they would be—

"Not all too drunk," said Agnez, pointing. Two young Guards had appeared atop the wall. Spotting their supposed enemies, they jumped down and immediately drew their swords, a somewhat comedic action as, despite Agnez's comment, they clearly were very drunk indeed.

Agnez drew her own sword and stepped in front of Henri and the sign-painter.

"There's only one with a sword," said a tall woman with red hair, which had come unpinned and was falling across her face, as her hat had dropped when she jumped off the wall.

"One," agreed the other Guard, whose carefully cultivated mustache and goatee only accentuated the fact it hardly existed, and his smooth saffron skin suggested he couldn't be more than seventeen. "Er . . . is that important?"

"Two can't fight one," said the woman, drawing herself up to a shaky stop and lowering her sword point to the flagstones. "Not the done thing."

"No," agreed the man.

"Have to fight one at a time," said the woman. She looked at Agnez and added, "Only thing, not sure you're a gentlewoman. I'm Debeuil, a cadet of the King's Guard. I can't just fight anyone."

"My name's Descaray, a cadet of the Queen's Musketeers," said Agnez. "But I haven't got my uniform yet."

"Oh, a Musketeer!" said the woman. "That's all right, then. I will charge you in just a moment. I have to . . ."

Her eyes went unfocused and she stared past Agnez, who tried to stop her mouth curling up in a smile. She hadn't seen anyone quite so drunk still standing. Though in this case the standing was more like a wobbling in a small circle.

"I beg your pardon," said Henri smoothly, stepping up. "But I wonder if I might present a solution to the problem of there being only one of us with a sword?"

"Who are you?" asked the male Guard. He was trying to put his sword back in its scabbard and fumbling it, following his own movement around in circles like a dog chasing its tail. "I'm Demaugiron. Not the Marquis, that's m'sister."

"I'm Dupallidin, an assistant to the Queen's Architect," said

Henri. "Now, if you lend me your sword, then two of us will have swords."

"Oh, yes, good idea," said the man. He stopped trying to sheathe his sword, held it under the cross guard, and presented the hilt to Henri, who took it and stepped back.

"I will charge you in a moment," said the woman, blinking. "Remind me what we're fighting about again?"

"We can't fight," said Henri. "There's only one of you with a weapon, and two of us have swords."

"You're right!" exclaimed the man. He thought for a moment. "Perhaps if I could borrow yours?"

"Of course," said Henri. "But then the arithmetic will still hold, only reciprocally. We can't fight at all under these conditions."

"We can't?" asked the woman.

Henri, Agnez, and the sign-painter all shook their heads slowly.

"Because of the 'rithmetic," said the man, nodding wisely. He stood relatively still as Henri sheathed his sword for him. "Well, that's that, then. Where are we?"

"You are in the courtyard of my hospital," said a stern voice, which belonged to a frowning doctor-magister. A clearly very important Doctor-Magister, a woman of fifty or so. Or rather probably of forty, prematurely aged by use of angelic magic. Her black robe was trimmed with gold and she wore a burgundy-colored velvet cap with a golden tassel over her white-blonde hair, which was pulled back and tied with a jeweled ribbon. She had an icon badge on the cap, several icon brooches on her robe, and four icon rings.

Her tone of authority, and appearance, was enough to make all the intruders turn and bow. The two King's Guards fell over and scrabbled to get up.

A far more junior doctor followed in the wake of the Doctor-Magister. He was her physical opposite in almost all respects: a very dark-skinned young man who was at least a foot and a half taller and two or three times broader. His robe was unadorned and the sleeves were stained with dried blood.

"What is happening?" asked the senior Doctor-Magister impatiently, as the gate boomed again. "This noise is very bad for my patients."

"Drunken soldiers, ser," reported Agnez, standing to attention. The gate was charged again, accompanied by the sound of a bone snapping and a howl of pain.

"Hmmph. Injuring themselves to boot. We can't have that."

The Magister held her hands together, two fingers on her left hand resting on one of the icon rings she wore on her right hand. She drew a deep breath and began to whisper.

"Ah," said the sign-painter. "Dramhiel. Headaches all 'round."

For the first time Henri looked at this diminutive scholar properly, and for the second time that day he was struck with the feeling of having met someone before. Though she looked nothing like Agnez, being slighter and much darker in skin and hair, and her lively eyes were almost black, he felt like he also knew her, and had always known her. But he didn't know who she was, which was ridiculous.

"Uh, do I know you?" he asked. He looked at Agnez, his

forehead creased in a deep frown, but she was staring at the young doctor, who was staring back, and for the *third* time Henri had the sense of unsought familiarity, that he knew this large young man as well, or had known him, and somehow forgotten.

There was the clap of an angel's wings, and a distant trumpet note. Henri felt a sudden pain behind his eyes, gone in a moment, but clearly not so quickly sped for the Guards beyond the wall, or the two crouched nearby. A great groaning and sighing began, and muffled asides of "Oh, my head," "My eyes," and "The bone-ache."

"I did not know Dramhiel could cleanse so many at once," said the sign-painter.

"Not Dramhiel," snapped the Doctor-Magister. "His superior, the Throne Azhakiel. A common error, given their near-identical scope. Come, MacNeel. I want to hear your assessment of our patient with the exposed kneecap."

She turned on her heel—a red-painted heel, indicating a high position at court—and stalked away.

The large young doctor looked after her nervously, then back at the other three.

"I have to go," he said. "My name is Simeon MacNeel. We must meet. There is something . . . I don't understand—"

"Yes," said Agnez. She recognized him as the prisoner she had seen on the Cardinal's boat, and now close up, felt the same strange familiarity she did with Henri. "Where? To meet?"

"Here?" suggested Simeon. "At dusk, or soon after."

"Too close to the tavern. The King's Guards . . . ," said Henri, pointing to the two wall climbers who had passed out and were snoring on the spot. "Still Tuesday, their day . . ."

"Oh, all that lot will be unconscious or suffering the worst of hangovers," said Simeon. He glanced at the sign-painter. "Dramhiel . . . or Azhakiel, as I have also just learned . . . cleanses the body, but you pay a very stiff price for sudden sobriety. I suppose I'd better get some of my attendants to bring those two inside. They'll sleep till sundown now."

He waved toward the hospital steps, and a Refuser, who had been watching, nodded and came at a run.

"Guards or not, meeting somewhere more private would be sensible," said Henri. "I have a room in the New Palace—well, a stall in what will be the stables. I'm Henri Dupallidin, assistant to the Queen's Architect."

"Very well," said Simeon. "At the New Palace, then, Henri. And . . ."

"Agnez Descaray," said Agnez. "Cadet of the Queen's Musketeers."

In turn, she looked at the sign-painter, who smiled cheerily but didn't speak.

"And you?" the other three asked, in unison.

"Oh, I'm Dorotea Imsel. I'm an icon-maker, Belhalle scholar . . . hmmm . . . I suppose not right now, because I'm a 'guest' of the Cardinal. In the Tower."

She paused, seeing their shared look of sympathy and horror.

"Oh, I've not been there long. And I'm let out during the day. But I do get locked up at night. So I can't come to meet you all at dusk."

"This time tomorrow?" asked Simeon urgently. Even as the others nodded he was walking away, pausing to speak to the Refuser, who peeled off to fetch stretcher-bearers to take the Guards inside.

"I have to get back to the New Palace," said Henri. But he didn't move.

"And I to the Musketeers' Barracks," said Agnez. She didn't move, either. "It is so strange . . . how can I *feel* I know you all but I *don't* know you? And are there any *more?*"

"Hmm?" asked Dorotea. They could almost see her mind coming back from some other place. "Oh, that's easy. Well, it's not easy. Straightforward, I suppose."

"What?" asked Henri.

"This occurs when people have been summoning the same angel over a short period of time in close proximity," explained Dorotea. "It is the angel we share who creates this sensation. Though I am curious as to which angel a Musketeer, a clerk, and a doctor would be summoning. While I am an icon-maker, I have undertaken very little angelic magic of late myself, I suppose the most frequent—"

"I haven't summoned an angel in six months," interrupted Agnez. "I trust to my sword, not magic."

"Nor have I," answered Henri. "I'm not much of a mage, and I have only one old, worn-out icon. I dare not summon Huaravael unless in dire need—which I can't imagine—for the icon will probably shatter."

"I do not know Huaravael," mused Dorotea, her face now sharpened, her thoughts fully present. "I take it back."

"Take what back?" asked Agnez.

"This familiarity we share," said Dorotea. "It is neither simple nor straightforward. We need to know more. I will think on this tonight."

"Hold! What are you doing?" Henri asked as Dorotea went to lift the bar of the gate.

"I have to finish painting the sign, otherwise the tavern keeper won't let me keep my new paints there," said Dorotea. "I'm not allowed any such materials in the tower."

"But those Guards, you dropped the ladder . . . ," Agnez began.

"Oh, I think they'll be staggering off to bed, at best, or fallen where they drank, like the two who jumped the wall," said Dorotea calmly. "Besides, I didn't drop the ladder."

"You didn't?"

"It was the Refuser boy, the one who was holding it steady. But I was happy he did."

"Why?" asked Henri.

"He was being helpful all morning," replied Dorotea. "Some people just are, I suppose—"

"No, why were *you* happy?"

"Because it made me look down and I saw the two of you, and I thought . . . I didn't think, I *knew* I needed to speak with you," said Dorotea. "Which is very interesting. I will see you tomorrow."

She lifted the bar, opened the gate a crack to look out, seemed satisfied with what she saw, and slipped through the gap. Agnez poked her head out a moment later, her hand on the hilt of her sword.

"She's right," she said. "They've gone. I'd better get to the barracks."

"And I to the New Palace," said Henri. He held out his hand. Agnez took it, and they shook vigorously. The Musketeer cadet smiled.

"We have found an adventure! Good day, brother clerk!"

"I'm only temporarily a cl . . ." Henri's voice trailed off as Agnez slid through the gate and disappeared. He could hear her whistling on the other side of the wall as she marched away.

Adventure. He didn't want an adventure; he wanted stability and financial security. A steady job. Nor did he want to be part of some mysterious kinship with a Musketeer, a doctor-magister, and an icon-maker who was a "guest" of the Cardinal in the Tower.

His mouth quirked as he considered being called "brother," and for the first time realized that he had instantly thought of Agnez as a sister. She was an attractive woman of roughly his own age, if a somewhat frightening one, but not for a moment had he considered her with anything other than fraternal interest.

Agnez already felt as much a sister to him as his actual sisters. Perhaps more so, since they were considerably older and generally treated him with a mild form of contempt.

Then there was the icon-maker, Dorotea. She also was a very attractive young woman, in a different style to Agnez. But again, she raised no feelings in Henri beyond the fraternal. He felt like he had known her forever as well, without knowing anything about her at all.

As if they really were siblings, and had grown up together, but somehow he had forgotten all the details.

It was very strange.

Troubled, Henri peered out the gate before easing himself through, his eyes darting in all directions. He felt he wasn't just watching for irate King's Guards but other threats.

He just didn't know what they were.

PART III

The Pit

TWELVE

DEMASELLE HOUSE WAS A MASSIVE IMPROVEMENT OVER the Night King's run-down headquarters by the city wall. Not only was it in a far more salubrious part of Lutace, Liliath's bedchamber was three times bigger and had tall windows that overlooked the walled gardens of what was essentially a miniature country estate in the heart of the city, and gave her a view of the city beyond.

The changeover had gone without a hitch. For Liliath, at least. The former Lady Dehiems and all her staff, save the children, were no longer of this world. As was the custom of the underworld, their bodies had been put in sacks, weighted down with stones, and put into the river via the sewers. They would not float but would be tumbled along by the river's swift current, and there were lots of hungry eels in the Leire.

Now Liliath was Lady Dehiems. A young and beautiful widow who thought herself ill, having nothing better to do, and so did not leave her mansion or its grounds. Her extensive staff were nearly all Refusers, which was a trifle eccentric but not unheard of, particularly among harsh or penny-pinching employers. It was easier to treat Refusers badly and pay them less than a Sarancian with equivalent experience.

She was pleased to have a valet now, a proper one, called Hatty. Though a Refuser, Hatty was not one of the Night King's people. Or rather, had not previously been one of the criminal denizens of Lutace, though she doubtless knew who her real employer was, and what was expected of her. Biscaray had hired her, the cook, and the pages from other houses. But the gardeners and porters were all fully fledged thieves and cutthroats, including all those who had been at the Temple of Saint Marguerite and so knew who Liliath really was, and the few who didn't had simply been told she was a very important ally of Biscaray's, engaged in a confidence trick that would have an immense payoff, in which they would share.

This was even true, apart from the sharing, Liliath thought, as she looked out over the gardens. She had ordered lanterns of colored glass hung from the espaliered fruit trees and placed along the lower wall of the kitchen garden. The lanterns were pretty but also served the practical purpose of illuminating the approach to the house most likely to be used by sneaking enemies.

Her formerly royal bed had been brought to the new house that morning. Liliath still hadn't shared it with Biscaray, had done no more with him than a lingering kiss in the cool morning when he'd brought her Lady Dehiems's dresses and jewelry. She'd enjoyed that kiss, without for a moment feeling anything more than the same slight pleasure she got from sudden sunshine on a cold morning, or a particularly good glass of wine. She thought he had felt more, which was as it should be.

Now Biscaray was late. She had been expecting him for several hours, and it was near midnight. He had much to report on, most significantly the whereabouts and activities of the four, though she had not signaled that this was her most overriding interest.

Descaray. Dupallidin. Imsel. MacNeel.

Frowning, Liliath left the window and went to her dressing table to pick up a handbell. She gave it several vigorous peals and was answered almost before she set the bell back down, her new valet quietly opening the door from her connecting chamber. Hatty was short and slight, dark-skinned with pale blue eyes, and as was the current fashion for Refuser valets, her head was shaved. She was dressed in simple but elegant dark gray breeches, a dark gray jerkin over a dove-gray shirt with a white rolled collar, and was shod in cork-soled velvet slippers so that she might move soundlessly about on her errands and not disturb her noble mistress.

"You rang, milady?"

"I have been expecting Biscaray for some hours," said Liliath. "I have business to discuss. Inquire of . . . no, ask Sevrin if there has been any word from him. No, better still, have Sevrin come up to me."

Sevrin was the chief of the Night Crew bravos, currently masquerading as the great house's doorwarden, and boss of all the interior staff not of the kitchen, as they answered to Cook. She was surprisingly good at being a doorwarden, possibly from years of infiltrating noble houses in order to rob them.

Hatty bowed and slipped out of the room.

Sevrin appeared only a few minutes later. She had clearly been about to go out, as she was not wearing a senior servant's attire but Night Crew gear: heavy boots, supple leather breeches and jerkin, her arms bare save for steel wrist bracers. She had a long dagger on her belt, which had a cross guard of entwined bronze serpents, well scratched.

"Yes, milady?" asked Sevrin. She gave an awkward bow, for she was nervous around Liliath. Unlike most of the Refusers she had no visible scars. Her brown skin was smooth and clear, her dark eyes bright, and she showed no obvious signs of affliction in wind or limb.

"Where is Biscaray?" asked Liliath.

"Uh," said Sevrin. "He's . . . well, there is a challenge. . . ."

Liliath frowned.

"What does that mean?"

"Bisc didn't want us to bother you," answered Sevrin nervously.

"Tell me," ordered Liliath. She could feel anger rising, anger that some unmentioned difficulty might delay her plans.

"Some of the Night Crew didn't like Bisc becoming Night King," said Sevrin. "Some of those who were close to Franz Wither-Arm. I mean, we couldn't tell 'em what really happened to Franz. So the story was Bisc and Franz fought, and Bisc won. Only some of the crew—those who weren't there—have been saying it wasn't done right and Bisc isn't the proper King."

"So what's happened?" said Liliath crossly, her forehead furrowed. If Bisc was supplanted or perhaps even killed she would have to start again with whoever was in charge now. She needed the Night Crew. "Who is the new Night King?"

"No, no," said Sevrin. "Bisc is still King. For now. He's just been challenged by the Worm."

"Who . . . or what is the Worm?"

"She's the head of the toshers, the sewer hunters," answered Sevrin. "So there's a Court of the Rogue, to decide whether Bisc really is King or not. Only the Worm would never have challenged unless she thinks she's got the numbers, or can run the court quick enough before we all hear where it is. So it'll be Bisc is *not* the King, and he'll be killed for the presumption. Unless we get enough of our folk there to vote the other way."

"Where is this Court of the Rogue?" asked Liliath.

"I'm waiting to hear," said Sevrin. "The Worm sprang the challenge this evening, Bisc had to go straight there, and they nobbled the first two messengers. But there's others, and the Court never meets before midnight. We should hear where it is soon."

"I am extremely displeased to only be finding out about this now," said Liliath coldly. "Who is going with you to this Court of the Rogue?"

"Uh, everyone but Karabin and Small Jack," stammered Sevrin. "They're staying behind to . . . to guard you, milady."

"They can stay to guard the house," said Liliath. "I will come with you."

She went to one of the wardrobes and flung it open, taking out a drab Refuser smock and cloak, flat-heeled boots, a thick leather vest, and one of the padded hoods the ice carriers wore to keep out the cold from the blocks they carried on their heads.

"But, milady!" protested Sevrin. "There *will* be fighting. And Bisc told us you can't risk magic in the city—"

"You have seen me fight," said Liliath, quickly stripping off her pale blue dressing gown to put on the smock and jerkin and tie on the hood, which closed tightly around her face and disguised it well, with only a small oval around her eyes and mouth exposed. She reached into the wardrobe again and drew out a black studded belt on which rested two sheathed daggers, almost small swords, each as long as her forearm from elbow to outstretched finger. She strapped on the belt, drew and inspected the damascened steel of the daggers, then replaced them in their sheaths.

"You have seen me fight," she repeated. "You saw what I did to Franz Wither-Arm."

"Yes, milady," answered Sevrin, her head bowed. "But I thought that was . . . some angel . . . you had summoned to help you."

"No," said Liliath. She moved suddenly, so swiftly Sevrin gasped, finding Liliath at her side, her hand already closed on the hilt of the Refuser's dagger.

"I do not need to summon an angel to help me *fight*," she said. "I am . . . what I am. As this Worm will discover, to her sorrow."

"Yes, milady," whispered Sevrin. "I . . . someone will have come with the news by now. I should go downstairs. . . ."

"Yes," said Liliath. "The sooner we get to this Court of the Rogue the better."

A messenger had arrived by the time they got downstairs, a

one-legged girl, one of the beggars from Demarten Place. All the household staff were gathered around the servants' side door, ready to go out. The girl, still gasping from racing over on her crutches, called out as soon as she saw Sevrin.

"The Pit! It's the statue pit. Rabb and Alizon T caught one of them sewer rats and we got it out of him."

"Have you told the others?" asked Sevrin.

"Yes, they're spreading the word," answered the girl excitedly. "Alizon T went to the Gardens, Rabb went to the Old Dock, Jast to the New, and Little Jast back to Demarten—"

"Good," interrupted Sevrin. "You've done well. Go tell Pieter in the wall house, tell him to bring everyone he can spare."

"And I'm to go too?" asked the girl hopefully.

Sevrin nodded. The beggar spun on her crutches and went out the open door.

"What is this statue pit?" asked Liliath.

"An old gravel pit just south of the city, beyond Nep Cross," said Sevrin. "Where they put all whatshisname's creepy statues of angels."

"*Whose* statues?"

Sevrin shrugged, but the hunchbacked woman Erril, the scholar, spoke up.

"The mage who tried to make statues as summoning icons. A long time ago. The Sarancians are afraid of the statues, so they stay away. His name was—"

"Chalconte," said Liliath slowly. "I know Chalconte's work. None better."

Chalconte had been burned at the stake, for numerous heresies, a decade after he made the Twelve Diamond Icons. Around a century ago—no, Liliath had to add in the years of her slumber—over two hundred years ago now. Liliath had started on her own path in no small part due to a forbidden copy of Chalconte's workbook, which described everything from his astonishingly swift sketching technique for making icons to his experiments with statues and other three-dimensional shapes to summon angels, and then the even more dangerous techniques where he had tried to make "living icons."

"I had thought his statues destroyed," added Liliath. "I will be interested to see them."

"That's one of the reasons the Sarancians fear them," said Erril. "The marble ones can't be broken; the bronze can't be melted down. So they were taken out to the old pit and buried. But when there is a wet winter, the floodwaters from the hill above scour out the pit. Then there is great argument about who is responsible for burying them again, the city, or the temples, or the Queen. This time, the pit has been open for more than five years."

"We have to go, milady," said Sevrin urgently. "It will take an hour to walk to the Pit, and we *must* get as many of our people there as possible before midnight!"

Liliath inclined her head in assent and led her small troop of Refusers out. The servants' entrance steps led to a courtyard, with the stables to the left and a gate to the street, which was closed save for the small sally port that was held open by Karabin, with Small Jack—who was of course a hulking giant—standing by with his great cudgel.

"Admit no one save myself," said Liliath to the two who were to remain behind. "No one. You understand?"

"Yes, milady," answered Small Jack, while Karabin inclined her head to show she understood. She could not talk, and wore a mask below her nose to conceal some sort of horrific injury to her jaw or mouth.

"We can't walk as a group on the streets, milady," said Sevrin hesitantly. "The Watch will be on us, for sure—"

"Do as you would normally," said Liliath. "I will follow you discreetly."

"Yes, milady," said Sevrin. She gave a sign, and one by one, at intervals, the other eight Refusers slipped out onto Delorde Avenue to join the throngs of workers going home; and those beginning night work; and the street sellers hawking pies or jellied eels, firewood or hats, flowers or ironware; and soldiers and bargees and counting-house clerks and scholars tumbling in and out of wineshops and taverns, and Refusers sweeping horse dung and carting rubbish and pickpocketing; and the Watch marching about; all the great bustling crowd of Lutace.

In her room in the Tower, Dorotea looked out her arrow slit. She could see only a small slice of the eastern side of the slowly darkening city, but she liked to watch the tiny sparks of light and blooms of brightness where there were many torches, or a rich house where some great quantity of candles were consumed each night. There were also several small oases of almost daytime brilliance, the product of angelic magic. Typically the work of one of the numerous Seraphim whose scope involved light in some way, or the very often summoned Cherubim Ximithael, whose scope was fire.

There was a knock at the door, which was surprising, since Mother had already come by to deliver Dorotea's evening meal and water bucket. Mother also didn't knock; she merely jangled her keys before opening the door.

That jangle of keys came, but the door did not open immediately. There was another knock, and Dorotea reflexively said, "Come in."

Mother opened the door, but it was Rochefort who came in. She wore her sword but had no pistols in her belt, and her hands were bare. She removed her hat and bowed. Dorotea nodded back, in an absent fashion, her attention still half on the view through the arrow slit, much of her mind remaining with the puzzle of her encounter with the other three young people that afternoon. An angel linked them in some way, she was sure. She had felt it, or thought she had. But the others were not really mages, and there was no recent summoning they had in common . . .

Rochefort said something, bringing Dorotea's thoughts back to the present.

"I brought wine," said Rochefort, holding up a bottle and two pewter goblets.

"Why?" asked Dorotea.

Rochefort did not immediately answer. She sat down on

the straw-stuffed palliasse with her back against the stone wall, stretched out her long legs, spurs screeching a little on the floor, and placed the bottle and the goblets down within easy reach.

"I want to talk to you, Dorotea," she said finally.

"Why?"

"Because you are not afraid of me."

Dorotea raised her eyebrows. Rochefort had her attention now, and she looked at the Cardinal's officer more carefully—at the scar down her face, the wrinkles at the corners of her mouth, at her hands. Rochefort did not meet her gaze, instead attending to the wine, pouring it carefully into the two goblets.

"Very few people are not afraid of me," said Rochefort, holding a goblet out to Dorotea. "It serves its purpose, but sometimes . . . even I wish to see other emotions in those around me."

Dorotea took the goblet and moved to sit down next to Rochefort. She took a sip of the wine. It was very good wine, from Barolle, far better than the sweet, slightly mold-tainted stuff the tavern keeper had given her, in part payment for revitalizing the sign.

"I thought you much older when I first saw you," said Dorotea. "You have spent too much of yourself summoning angels."

"The Cardinal does not spare herself, and as her Pursuivants we follow suit, doing what must be done for Sarance, Ashalael, and the Queen," answered Rochefort. She drank some of her own wine, and said, "I will be twenty-seven tomorrow, as it happens."

Dorotea nodded companionably, though she was a little surprised that Rochefort had used up so much of herself before she was even thirty. She looked at least a decade older than twenty-seven.

All angelic mages knew the cost of their work. Some hoarded their lives, never summoning an angel greater than a Throne. Some played a complicated game of balance, summoning angels (or having others summon them) to repair the signs of age and revitalize failing bodies, but this was a reductive strategy, as angels were loath to redress the work of other angels, be it the direct effect or the side effect, and so a higher-ranking entity had to be employed in each case.

"I will be nineteen next month," said Dorotea. "I wonder if I will still be a prisoner then?"

"You are a guest," said Rochefort hastily. "I have tried to ensure you are housed as comfortably as is possible here."

"I think I am a prisoner," said Dorotea quietly. "And I do not understand why. Perhaps you can tell me?"

Rochefort glanced at her, eyes hot, then back down at the goblet she clasped with both hands. Her fingers were long and elegant, wrists sinewy with muscle. The hands of a duelist.

"Your talent, the icon-sketching. It has been shown before. Many in the temples see it as the first step to other things, leading to certain heresy."

"Who has done it before?" asked Dorotea. "I thought I had discovered the technique myself, but I suppose I should not be surprised. People have been summoning angels for a very long time."

"Chalconte was one, and the Ystaran. The Maid of Ellanda.

They are well-remembered in certain circles."

"Chalconte made statues, didn't he?" asked Dorotea. "To be icons. But he failed."

Though Chalconte's work was not much discussed, she had seen references to him in various standard works on icon-making. And the Degrandin Library of the Belhalle displayed several icons he had made in their green reading room, particularly fine icons, which Dorotea had admired as best she could through the thick glass of the locked display case.

"The statues were but a part of Chalconte's heresies."

"And I thought the Maid of Ellanda was a hero who saved many of her people when Palleniel went mad. Or whatever he did."

"No one knows what happened in Ystara, save that it was done by Palleniel," said Rochefort. "Or if they do know, they have not shared that knowledge. However, Liliath is suspected to have some involvement with whatever occurred. She was the leader of a strange cult devoted to Palleniel. Palleniel Exalted, they called it."

She glanced at Dorotea, then looked back to her goblet, as if she might see something in her dark wine.

"Liliath did bring many thousands out, but she also disappeared soon after, in mysterious circumstances. She was probably killed by someone who blamed her for the Ash Blood plague, because of the Palleniel Exalted cult, which had just been deemed schismatic and was to be broken up. But then she was also involved in purely secular politics and intrigue, so who knows . . ."

"And she sketched icons," said Dorotea, after Rochefort fell silent.

"Yes, she was famous for that," said Rochefort heavily. The Pursuivant looked at Dorotea again, then swiftly away.

"What do you see?" asked Dorotea. "You look away as if I am too bright, like the sun after fog. Or you are ashamed and cannot face me."

Rochefort drank again.

"You . . . there is something about you that reminds me of someone, though you do not look like her," she whispered. "A woman I loved. She, too, I brought to the Tower. This tower."

"With good reason?" asked Dorotea.

"Yes," said Rochefort heavily. "Yes. She was a traitor to the Queen, to Sarance, even . . . to me."

"She did not leave here?"

"Not alive."

Dorotea thought about this for a little while. Rochefort did not look at her again, but drank, refilling her goblet.

"I suppose you are somewhat like an angel and so must work within your scope, which is to do the Cardinal's bidding," said Dorotea. "But I do not think Her Eminence had a good reason to bring me here."

"People are more complicated than angels," said Rochefort.

Dorotea nodded, as if in agreement, but it was a mere politeness. She was not sure angels were any less complicated than people. The concept of scope was a human invention, after all, and over the course of time, angelic mages had learned to get angels to do many different things that had not initially appeared to be within their historically defined scope, begging the question of whether scope really meant anything at all.

They sat in silence, drinking, for several minutes before Rochefort spoke again.

"I am sorry I have brought you here."

"I am not one to worry myself very much about what has happened, or what might happen," said Dorotea. She looked at her foot and wiggled her toes. "I think I take after my mother in that respect. We both make the best of wherever we find ourselves. We walk in sand, not looking back to see our footprints washed away. We enjoy the play of the waves around our feet, and the shells we pick up. Nor do we look too far ahead."

"I must go," said Rochefort, but she did not go.

"Do you think if I asked Her Eminence to release me, she would?" asked Dorotea.

"No," said Rochefort. "But . . . she might if I asked her."

Dorotea looked at her, and this time Rochefort met her gaze.

"Do you want something in return?" asked Dorotea quietly. "While I do take after both my mother and my father in easily taking people to bed, it is always because I simply want to make love with them. Not to gain favors, and never in answer to threats."

Rochefort did not reply, but she moved suddenly, springing up from the palliasse. She left the wine and the goblets, picked up her hat, and strode to the door. She stopped there, grasped the ring to open it, and spoke very low, almost as if to the ironbound timbers and not to Dorotea, who stared up at her.

"I hope you never do have occasion to become afraid of me, Dorotea."

Then she was gone, and the keys jangled as the door was locked.

THIRTEEN

IT STARTED TO RAIN SEVERAL TIMES AS LILIATH LEFT THE city proper behind, and stopped again as often. Big, stuttering drops fell, splashing and drumming for a minute or two, before the wind blew that particular cloud on, and the moon came out again, at least until the next cloud and the next short bout of rain.

At first, the Refusers were just part of the general traffic, but at Nep Cross this all fell away, the night being too late for honest folk to be abroad. A steady stream of gray-clad thieves, robbers, footpads, crimps, cutpurses, beggars, toshers, confidence tricksters, and all the many-splendored folk of the Night Crew flowed out of Nep Cross and took the narrow lane that wound up the low hills to the east, toward the gravel pit.

As Liliath and the Refusers reached their destination shortly before midnight, the wind blew away one rain-stuffed but not actually raining cloud, and in the moment of clear sky before the next cloud arrived, the full light of the moon shone down to show Liliath that the Pit was not a singular hole but three huge excavations, concentric circles, each containing the next, deeper pit within its bounds. A path wound anticlockwise around the rim of the outer pit, turned clockwise for the next, and reversed again and became much steeper for the last, ending in a series of wooden steps and walkways, and finally, a very long ladder down into what would have been total darkness if it were not for the several hundred Refuser Night Crew gathered there already, most of them holding lit torches, here and there the light brightened by a lantern.

Dotted in between the Refusers, all gray in the murk, there were pallid marble, dark granite, and gleaming bronze figures. Some loomed high over the crowd, tall winged statues eight or nine feet tall. Others were human-sized or smaller, though not all were human in shape. There were Thrones depicted, strange geometric creatures of rings and wings and crowns; and other forms, reminiscent of beastlings, though they had wings and haloes to indicate they were angels of some kind.

Liliath felt the presence of Chalconte's statues even before she joined the descent into the depths, in amid a long line of Refusers. She was startled by the sensation of potential angelic presences, for Chalconte's statue-making was, according to everything she had read, a complete failure.

It *was* a failure, she thought, but only by the whisker of a hair. Chalconte had tried to make icons that had height and breadth and weight, theorizing that this would enable easier summoning by anchoring the angel more securely to the mortal world, and thus reducing the cost in the living essence of the summoner.

He had not succeeded in this. The statues had not worked as icons, but with every step, Liliath felt the lingering, residual presence of many angels. Chalconte had managed to trap a spark of the individual essence of each angel within stone and bronze.

Liliath smiled, her small, very white teeth showing like a cat that is pleased to find a mouse trapped in a corner. Chalconte, the famous mage and heretic, had tried over and over again, with statue after statue, to do something that she had mastered early and gone far beyond.

Even better, Liliath could actually draw upon those tiny motes of angelic power that were trapped with the statues. Though she would do so only if it became absolutely necessary, for mages in the nearby city would sense this action, including the Cardinal . . .

"Looks like enough of our lot got the message," whispered Sevrin, as the long shuffle down the walkway paused to allow someone who'd slipped to get up again. She pointed down into the lower pit. "Ours on the right—Bisc is near that fat statue—the Worm and her people are on the left."

"Which one is the Worm?" asked Liliath.

"The woman next to the big lantern-bearer," said Sevrin. "See that stick she's got? That's a tosher pole, got a sharp hook on the end. They use it to snatch up stuff in the sewers, but also a good weapon."

"She's old," said Liliath. The Worm looked to be well over sixty, and was bent from stooping in the sewers, looking for finds. She had lost an ear, from the look of it bitten off, and her hair was reduced to a few wisps that were arranged across her pale head in tight coils, perhaps suggesting a reason for her name. "I had expected a young challenger."

"Cunning is more important than anything else for the Night Crew," replied Sevrin. "Youth or strength or whatever. And the Worm is very cunning. We almost didn't find out about this challenge. Even now I'm not sure . . ."

Sevrin stopped talking as the line of people moved again, and at the same moment, Bisc looked up and saw first Sevrin and then Liliath. Though he was masked as usual, and it was dark, Liliath could tell by the way he suddenly straightened that her presence was an unwelcome surprise. He didn't want her there.

She smiled again, deliberately, forcing herself not to show the anger that boiled within her. This was all unnecessary, and it had the potential to disrupt her plans. That could not be allowed.

As they reached the bottom of the pit, the people ahead peeled off to one side or the other, Biscaray's or the Worm's. There was a gap between the two crowds and now that they were closer, Liliath saw there was yet another pit, one marking the border between the two factions. A hole, in fact, no more than thirty feet in diameter, but she couldn't see how deep it was, suggesting it was very deep indeed. There was a ladder on each side, lashed-together affairs that unlike the more sturdy steps and walkways looked as if they had just been constructed for the evening.

As they walked around the edge of this last pit, Biscaray came to greet them. Here, in public, he did not bow before Liliath or otherwise give her special attention, greeting Sevrin and the others together. But as they walked into the center of his crowd, he leaned in close, a hoarse whisper for Liliath's ears alone.

"Milady! You should not have come here."

"You may need my help," said Liliath. She looked over the pit. "The sides are evenly matched for numbers. When does the fighting begin, and who should die first? The Worm?"

"There won't be a general fight," said Biscaray. "The numbers are too close. The Worm hoped to keep the meet secret and do away with me. But now that hasn't worked, she won't dare start a general melee."

"So we all go back to the city?"

"No. It'll be single combat, down in the hole."

"You against the old lady?" asked Liliath. Her frown could not be seen under the tight closure of the ice packer's hood, but it was suggested by the wrinkle of her nose.

"Her champion," said Biscaray. "Kate Sunless, the woman by her side. She practically never comes out of the sewers, not unless the Worm wants murder done. By night, of course, or underground somewhere. She can see in the dark, they say. That's why they wanted the Court here, of course."

Liliath cocked her head, taking in the taller, younger, and considerably more muscled Kate by the side of the Worm. She wore the ragged remains of a half-dozen different Refuser outfits, tied on in a haphazard but tight fashion, and where her skin was bare on her hands and face and feet it was smeared in whorls of clay or some dark gray paint. She looked away from the fall of light as lanterns and torches moved, and her mouth opened a little, showing teeth that had been painted black and filed to points.

"What weapons does she use?" asked Liliath, for she could see none.

"No weapons allowed in the challenge pit," said Biscaray quietly. "Not here. That's why the Worm chose it. If it was one of our other places—Archer's Mill, say—I'd have the advantage. But here, in the dark of the pit, no weapons . . . I will do my best, but it may be you will need to find a new servant, milady."

"I don't think—" Liliath started to say, but she was interrupted by a sudden shout, quickly picked up and repeated by the crowds on both sides.

"A challenge! A challenge! Who is the Night King? Who is the Night King?"

The Worm was the first to answer. Hoisted up to stand upon the shoulders of a statue of the angel Jeravael, she raised her tosher pole high. Slowly, the shouting faded, even on Biscaray's side, until the pit was quiet, save for the hissing and crackling of the flaming torches and the occasional stifled cough or shuffle of shifting feet.

"Franz Wither-Arm was the Night King," called out the Worm. Her voice was deep and resonant, pitched to carry. She knew how to address a crowd. "But he was killed, far away and in strange circumstances. Biscaray calls himself Night King, but he is not. He has not been acclaimed, he has not faced the challenge. Until now, for I challenge him. I am the Worm, and I am the true Night King!"

Cheers and whoops and chants of "Worm! Worm! Worm!" answered her, all from her side of the hole. Biscaray's followers stood silent, many holding their weapons close, bodies tensed for action.

Slowly, the cheering faded. Biscaray nodded and climbed up on a tall bronze statue of a Throne, setting his feet upon its pinions. He raised his hand, not closing it in a fist, as if he were waving to friends.

"I *am* the Night King," he said. He did not shout, and his voice was a little muffled by the mask he always wore, now hiding the fact he didn't have scars rather than the scarred flesh Liliath had healed. But this only made everyone listen more intently. "So you challenge me, Worm? By acclamation or single combat?"

The Worm's eyes flashed in lantern light, as she looked left and right, a last-minute assessment of the relative strengths of both sides. But it was clear that the numbers were close to equal, and Biscaray might even have more. And there were still Refusers coming down the steps and walkways, and most of the later arrivals would be more likely to support Biscaray than the Worm. Acclamation would favor Biscaray.

"Single combat," she said.

"You dare to face me?" asked Biscaray. "How very brave."

Even some on the Worm's side chuckled at that.

"My champion," said the Worm, not drawn into an angry retort. She gestured down at Kate Sunless, who grinned up at her like a dog to its master.

"Down the pit, as tradition says," continued the Worm. "Tradition you hoped to avoid, Bisc! Stab Franz in the back and all's well, you think, but now you have to go down the hole."

"I didn't stab Franz in the back," said Bisc quite truthfully. But before he could say anything else, Liliath swarmed up next to him, balancing lightly on the outstretched wing, gripping Biscaray's shoulder as if to balance, though she did not need to do so. Rather she pressed her fingers down, repressing whatever he was going to say.

"I am Biscaray's champion," she called. "The Night King does not need to sully his hands with the likes of you."

The Worm stared across at her, old eyes sharp, glinting red in the torchlight.

"And who are you?" she asked. "An assassin, I'll warrant, cost young Bisc a pretty sum. But you can't use those blades in the pit. Got to follow the old ways, our ways."

Liliath shrugged theatrically, and slowly drew her daggers, handing them down hilt-first to Sevrin. She could feel Biscaray tense under her hand, wanting to say something, or do something, but he remained obedient to the pressure of her fingers, stayed under her thumb.

"I've never needed a blade to step upon a worm," called out Liliath. "Or to crush a worm's cast under my boot."

Kate Sunless hissed, baring her sharp teeth.

"It's worms that rule, down in the dark," said the Worm. "In the end, it's worms that eat everything."

"Can't say I ever heard of them killing anyone *first* though," said Liliath. "Biscaray is the Night King. Let's have that proven, and quickly. Who goes down the hole first?"

"You go together," said the Worm. "As is the custom and

always has been. You should know that. What's your name? For remembering you by, once you're gone?"

"I think you'll remember anyway," said Liliath, all trace of banter gone from her voice. "For a little while, for whatever time you have left. But since I am to deal with a worm, why not call me . . . Biscaray's Serpent."

The old woman shrugged.

"Call yourself whatever you like. It makes no difference. Kill her for me, Kate."

Kate Sunless grinned and went to the ladder on her side of the hole. She moved strangely, slightly bent over but agile, like an ape. She did not bow her head but kept her chin up, eyes watching Liliath.

Biscaray leaned close to Liliath.

"You can withdraw," he whispered urgently. "Don't think you can kill her with the Ash Blood plague like Franz. That'll just cause more problems."

"I will simply kill her," Liliath whispered back. "And finish this distraction. You should have told me of it, long before it came to this."

"I . . . I did not expect any challenge," Biscaray spluttered. "But you must not risk yourself. Kate Sunless is deadly—"

"You mean dead, or soon will be," interrupted Liliath. She climbed down from the statue, the crowd parting to allow her to walk to the ladder on her side of the hole.

Opposite her, Kate Sunless spat into the depths and then suddenly raced for her ladder, sliding down it rather than climbing step by step. But Liliath was just as fast, adopting the same technique. The rough wood bit through her soft leather gloves to the skin beneath, but she paid it no attention, digging the sides of her boots in to slow herself as she looked down, gauging just how far it was.

Liliath could see in the dark. All her senses were enhanced. She was stronger and faster than any mortal as well, and so did not fear any enemy.

This overconfidence was almost her undoing. Even as she neared the bottom, at least sixty feet down with perhaps twenty feet to go, she realized the Worm had already cheated. There were people down there, dim silhouettes to her, who thought themselves in total darkness. From the sound of it, waiting ready with a weighted net around the bottom of her ladder.

A dozen feet from the bottom, and the faint outlines and the whites of the eyes of her ambushers visible to Liliath's superior sight, she jumped. Her ambushers swung the net up, but too slowly. She felt its weighted edge brush her back as she landed on one of the net throwers, smashing him to the ground and cushioning Liliath's fall. She struck at his throat at the moment of impact, crushing his windpipe and springing aside almost at the same moment, and swiftly moving away.

There were two others, and Kate Sunless somewhere on the other side. The bottom of the hole was also not clear, as Liliath had once again overconfidently expected. She could make out tall silhouettes, shapes of more intense darkness. The hole was strewn with large boulders and several statues that had fallen, two large, winged human-sized angels and a Throne easily twice their size.

The remaining net throwers were quietly gathering their net for another throw. From their movements, and the way they were poised, Liliath knew they could not see her. But they were toshers, used to hunting treasure and people and rats in the dark sewers and catacombs under the city, their ears attuned to the slightest movement. They were probably listening for her breathing, the panting that came with fear and sudden explosive combat.

Which was unfortunate for them, as Liliath had already stilled her breath and now crouched in absolute silence, listening herself.

The ambushers drew close together, one tapping a message with a single finger on the back of the other's hand. Then they moved as one, hurling the net where their compatriot had fallen, targeting the sound of the remnant twitches of the person's death.

Liliath attacked as they moved forward to feel what they had caught. She kicked the first in the groin, forcing him down as she closed and twisted his head around 270 degrees, the snap reverberating through the hole. Then she caught the falling body under the arms and threw him on his companion, knocking her down. As this second opponent struggled to get free, Liliath found the knife on the man's belt, drew it, and stabbed twice.

But even as she did, something whistled through the air and Liliath screamed, more in anger than pain, as a crossbow bolt pierced the right side of her chest, under the shoulder blade, above her breast.

Kate Sunless was there, one of the Refusers' little crossbows falling from her right hand, a tiny, candle-stub lantern in her left, shuttered so that only the narrowest beam of light came out, enough to aim by. She was drawing a dagger from her sleeve when Liliath threw her knife, the blade flying true to sink into the tosher's left eye.

Kate Sunless fell without making a sound, save the dull thump of her landing.

Liliath stood completely still, listening. She could hear the dull murmur of the crowd far above, but nothing else in the hole.

She felt the bolt, wincing as it moved slightly. Reaching over her shoulder, her fingers touched the head. It had gone right through, and when she breathed out, blood bubbled on her lips. Strangely luminous blood, that shone with its own silvery light.

The bolt had struck her lung, Liliath knew. Any normal person would already be down, close to death. Even altered as she was, Liliath too would eventually drown in her own blood, unless healed with angelic magic.

She had no icons with her, a risk she had taken in case of being searched or some other challenge made to her identity as one of the Refuser Night Crew. No Gwethiniel to make her whole, or Beherael to stop the bleeding, or Herreculiel to hasten the replacement of blood.

Anger rose up in Liliath, eclipsing the pain. She could not die. She had a destiny that could not be altered by mere mortals and crossbow bolts.

She had no icons. But there were the strange, sliced-off portions of angelic power in the statues near her, and up above, and Liliath of all the people in the mortal world knew how to draw upon them and take their raw power into herself.

Indeed, it was made easier for her by Chalconte, for usually she would have to summon the angel first, and dominate it, and slowly strip its power away. But the heretic mage had already done all that. He just didn't know what he had achieved, or how the power he had drawn into his statues might be used.

Liliath held the fletch of the bolt with her right hand and reached around the back to grasp the other end just behind the head. It was not an easy stretch, but she got a good grip—and snapped the bolt.

She did not try to restrain her scream, of equal parts agony and anger. It echoed up and out of the hole, and she heard the crowd grow quiet and saw the glow of lights come closer to the edge as the Refusers looked down and tried unsuccessfully to see what was happening.

Breaking the shaft had massively worsened the wound. Liliath saw her silvery, shining blood gush over her fingers and she found it hard to stay upon her feet, despite the angelic powers she had long ago taken inside her.

That power needed to be augmented, and quickly. Liliath reached out with her mind, feeling the presences in the fallen statues close to her, here in the bottom of the pit. She knew them, took their names into herself, despite their faint resistance, the angels still connected to their greater selves in the heavens. She ignored the plaintive cries inside her head as the fragmented angels tried to escape the bounds Chalconte had laid about them, their marble or bronze prisons. Desperately they tried to flee and not be used so.

But as always, Liliath's will was stronger. She prevailed, took in their power, and made it her own.

The pain ebbed away, but it was still present. She took a deep, slow breath. Blood no longer bubbled around her mouth. The edges of the ragged wound in her chest drew closer yet did not completely close.

She had not taken enough raw angelic power to fully heal herself.

Liliath looked up, at the faintly lighter, red-tinged sky above and around the hole, where the Refusers held their torches.

It was a greater risk, but she had to do it. She could not remain wounded. Besides, the immediate risk was not to her but to the Refusers above. Anyone touching a statue she drew the angel from would suffer the Ash Blood plague, or become a beastling . . .

Liliath reached out once again, mentally questing for the statues, feeling for the strongest remnants, searching out their names and natures. She could feel them all in her mind, all these pathetic stumps of angelic power locked in stone or bronze.

Two were much stronger than the others, probably Virtues or even Powers. One was on Bisc's side of the hole, the other on the Worm's.

Liliath smiled again and focused her will upon Darshentiel, the one on the Worm's side. She felt the remnant flutter and dart in all directions, desperately seeking an escape. But she took it all, reveling in her power and dominion.

Her wound closed completely, her breath came deep and even.

She felt wakeful, and invigorated, every sense sharp as a blade.

She went to one of the Refusers' bodies and tore off a piece of their clothing, using it to wipe her mouth and clothes, removing the stain of her strange, shining blood. It would not do for anyone to see that. But she could not remove all of it. Specks of light clung to her clothes until she dipped the rag into the Refuser's blood and smeared it in place over her own.

That done she went to the ladder and began to climb, swift as a spider, even as the screaming began above. It was not unexpected, but she climbed even faster, hands and feet barely touching the rungs, even as the cries became identifiable, mixed with the sudden bangs of pistol and musket fire, the *thwap* of crossbow strings, and of course, the shouting.

"Beastling! 'Ware beastling!"

FOURTEEN

CARDINAL DUPLESSIS WOKE SUDDENLY, WITH A START. FOR an instant she was unsure what had woken her, before she heard the sound again. She looked out through the gap in the half-closed curtains of her vast, gilded four-poster bed. Her chamber was quiet, the windows shuttered fast, the door shut. The great clock on the mantelpiece ticked as it always ticked, the hands on two and three. What had woken her was a low sound, very low, a deep thrumming that she knew well, though she had not heard it for many a year.

"Anton!" she called as she swung out of the bed and thrust her feet into fur-lined slippers. "Anton!"

The door swung open and her night clerk, Anton, held a lantern high in his hand, adding to the light from the candle stubs in the candelabra on the desk. A Pursuivant stood behind him, her sword already bared. But there was no enemy, no assassin come down the chimney or through the fourth-story windows. The Cardinal was slipping a scarlet robe over her nightgown as she hurried to the bureau, where her most important icons were laid out, necklaces and brooches and rings, and by itself on the topmost shelf, separated from the others, the smallest yet the most potent, that of Ashalael.

"Yes, Eminence?"

"Summon Captain Rochefort. Double the guard here and have the Star Fortress companies alerted to take their posts. All city gates to be closed. Warn Dartagnan at the Queen's Palace . . . tell them a danger comes, I know not what as yet."

"At once, Eminence!"

He disappeared, calling out to the lesser clerks who, like him, worked through the night to write up all the Cardinal had ordered through the day, and be ready for her wakeful nights. The Pursuivant sheathed her sword and stood in the doorway, which remained open.

The Cardinal bent over her bureau. All the icons were shivering, vibrating on the highly polished tabletop, juddering closer to the icon of Ashalael on the shelf above. They were also emitting that low noise, the sound of a slow-plucked bass note on a harp, somewhere very far away. Something had disturbed them, some great or unusual working of angelic magic, not far away.

Andrea Duplessis stared at the icons, wondering if the time had come when she must summon Ashalael, something she both desired and feared. Three times she had summoned the Archangel, and paid the price. Another summoning would probably be the end of her, and as yet, there was no one to stand in her place. At least no one she considered worthy of the terrible responsibility of being Cardinal of Sarance and summoner of Ashalael. Worse, there were so many bad advisers around the Queen that it was not even the Archangel's magic the realm most needed but the sound hand of the Cardinal upon the tiller of the ship of state.

Or so she told herself.

But short of summoning, she could commune with Ashalael, at a lesser though not negligible cost. He would not act, and indeed, sometimes responded in such a distant and mysterious fashion that the communication was worthless, too esoteric to understand.

But she had to do it.

The Cardinal placed one finger on the icon of Ashalael. Immediately, all the other icons stilled. She took a deep breath and, not speaking aloud, directed her will to join the angel in the heavens.

Ashalael! Ashalael! I do not summon thee but wish only words. What stirs in the kingdom of Sarance to fret the heavens so?

No answer came at first. But she felt a presence, a great weight at the far end of a tenuous line, as if she had gone fishing in deep waters and felt the very first faint bite of something huge and distant.

Ashalael! Ashalael! I do not summon thee but wish only words.

Her hand began to shake as she felt the angel drawing closer. She gripped her wrist with her left hand to hold it steady and took in another breath.

The clock on the mantelpiece began to chime suddenly, and the hands ran backward. Small, sparking whirlwinds sprang up in the fireplace, leaping and spinning. The other icons began a jangle of harp sounds, as if someone demented had tried to play four harps at once, with hands and feet. The Pursuivant in the doorway took a step back and became very still.

The Cardinal felt the shadow of great wings upon her, and the room grew cold. She shivered under her marten fur-lined robe and spoke for the third time.

Ashalael! Ashalael!

Words like icicles pierced her brain. Not spoken, just felt.

I am here.

Duplessis struggled to get her question out.

What disturbs the kingdom? Who? Where?

Ashalael answered, after a fashion.

The weight of his voice made the Cardinal wilt and sink to the floor, but somehow she managed to gather enough strength to withdraw her hand from the icon and send the looming presence of Ashalael back to whence he came, as the Archangel, so initially reluctant, became interested in the mortal realm again and desired to fully manifest.

Which, she was now certain, would kill her. That final summoning had to be saved for something of the utmost necessity, something absolutely without question of supreme importance for the kingdom.

"Eminence, do you need assistance?"

"No, no," croaked the Cardinal. She pushed herself upright, clinging to the bureau. Ashalael's answer loomed large in her mind. She whispered to herself what he had said, trying to work out exactly what the Archangel meant.

The killing mage harvests the detritus of angels in the deep wound of stone.

"'The killing mage,'" repeated the Cardinal. She frowned, and winced, as this exacerbated the headache that was rapidly spreading behind her eyes. She had never heard Ashalael use that expression before, nor had she read of it in the reports of past cardinals. But perhaps it was a description, not a name . . . a mage who was killing people. It was very difficult to get angels to directly kill someone, but it could be done. More usually, it could be arranged indirectly, so the angel was not really aware that its work would lead to a death.

Yes, a murderous mage. A killing mage. That was moderately clear.

"The detritus of angels . . ." meant little more to her, though she did vaguely recall seeing that term somewhere. But her head was splitting now; it was hard to think. She turned from the bureau and staggered to a chair, slumping into it.

"Anton!" she called, her shaking, wrinkled hand held over her eyes. "The ginger wine, and a compress for my eyes."

"Yes, Eminence, at once. And Doctor Degarnier? Or shall I send to the Fortress for Magister Hazurain?"

"Yes, Degarnier," mumbled the Cardinal. Her head and eyes ached terribly, and she was suddenly afraid it might mean bleeding in her brain. A stroke, leading to death or impairment, unless averted by angelic healing. "Hurry!"

But even through the debilitating pain, she tried to find her way through the puzzle of Ashalael's answer. "The deep wound of stone" . . . that was also an expression she had read some- where, or heard. She concentrated, bending her formidable will to ignore the pain, the nausea that was rising in her, separating her intellect from her body.

Slowly, memories and thoughts connected, joined new thoughts, coalesced.

Wound in stone . . . a cut . . . a rift . . . ravine . . . a quarry . . . the massive gravel pit south of the city, filled in six times, reopened by floods, used to dump Chalconte's strange statues that felt wrong, not icons, but there was something . . . leftover . . . detritus . . .

"Rochefort! Is Rochefort here yet?"

"Not yet, Eminence. She is not in the palace. Messengers have gone to her house, and to the Star Fortress."

"Send more messengers," muttered the Cardinal. She could not look at the clerk. Though her eyes were closed, lights were flashing under her lids, bright as fireworks. "Tell her, take two . . . no, three . . . troops of Pursuivants to the old gravel pit near Nep Cross. Look for a mage . . . arrest . . . danger."

The lights intensified, and the Cardinal finally surrendered to them, and the pain, and passed beyond into the darkness of unconsciousness.

Agnez was woken by loud and urgent drumming. Immediately she sprang out of her bunk and rushed to don breeches and jerkin, as she had slept in shirt and underclothes. She did not have the full Musketeer uniform yet, but the black-and-silver tabard went on as if she had worn it a thousand times, and she clapped on the distinctive black hat with the silver plumes at the same time as she sat back down to pull on her boots.

The other three cadets in her chamber were not so swift, nor so sure in their movements, with the only light coming from the hooded night lantern that hung above the door. Grumbling and wiping eyes, they were still in various stages of undress by the time Agnez was completely ready, sword and pistols in her belt, musket in her hand, and bandolier over her shoulder.

As she checked the buckle of the bandolier and made sure the cartridges were hanging straight, the door was flung open, and a huge figure stooped to step within, the brim of his hat brushing the lantern even though it was at least eight feet above the floor.

"Ho!" cried Sesturo. "One of the cubs is not so sleepy! Come with me, Descaray. You others, report to Gruppe when you've finished making yourselves beautiful."

Gruppe was the drill master, a saturnine older woman, all grit and corded muscle and a voice that could penetrate a proofed cuirass. Like many of the Musketeers, her name was an invention, as with Franzonne and Sesturo. It was a long tradition among the Musketeers for those of the highest birth to renounce their names and any inheritance, giving all to the service of the Queen. In the case of Gruppe, a considerable pointy-nosed likeness to Queen Sofia suggested she had stepped down from on high indeed.

Agnez followed Sesturo out, pausing only to smile and wave at her fellows, one of whom threw a boot half-heartedly at her. She had met them only the afternoon before, but they had already fought in practice against each other, and Agnez had won, and then lost half her ready money playing Thirteen with them, thus establishing friendly relations on all counts.

The drumming ceased as they left the barracks and marched out onto the parade ground, the three drummer girls and one boy racing to their position at the rear. A few stragglers were also hurrying out to join the company on parade, all veterans. While most of the Musketeers lived in the city in their own quarters, one of the regiment's four companies was always required to stay in the Star Fortress barracks or in the barracks at the Queen's Palace. As were the cadets, though there were only eight at present, those in Agnez's chamber and the one next to it, who clearly had not woken quickly enough for Sesturo either, as none of them were there.

The sun was just coming up, still not high enough to provide much light, particularly with the lingering rain clouds present in massed force, their dark undersides tinted with thin streaks of red from the dawn.

"Stay by me," rumbled Sesturo, sliding into place at the end of the front rank. Agnez stood next to him, mimicking the pose of the others, a kind of relaxed attention, the courteous posture of gentlefolk awaiting important news rather than over-disciplined dogs afraid of a thrashing.

"What's happening?" asked Agnez.

"Who knows," said Sesturo, smiling. He clapped his over-sized gauntlets together. "With luck, we're in for a fight. Here is Decastries to tell us what's up."

He made it sound like Decastries was some kind of simple messenger, when she was, in fact, the lieutenant commanding the company. Decastries was not much to look at, Agnez thought—a middling-sized, middle-aged black woman with silvered hair worn in a long queue under her hat, in a normal Musketeer uniform. The only sign of her rank was a thin golden sash over her shoulder instead of a cartridge bandolier, and she carried no musket.

Decastries was accompanied by several other Musketeers, and a messenger in the scarlet-and-gold uniform of the Cardinal. The messenger seemed unperturbed to be amid Musketeers, following close at Decastries's elbow. Agnez remarked on this to Sesturo.

"No rivalry between us when on duty, or under orders," said Sesturo. He looked down at Agnez. "Every now and then we must fight together. Remember that."

"I will," confirmed Agnez.

"Musketeers!" roared Decastries, and Agnez found herself stiffening to a more rigid posture. The lieutenant might not look imposing, but her voice demanded full attention.

"Her Eminence the Cardinal has spoken with the Archangel Ashalael of a threat to Sarance and Her Majesty the Queen!"

Agnez was surprised that this did not seem to be taken very seriously. Sesturo made a slight snorting noise, and she saw the Musketeer beyond him roll her eyes. Decastries let the ripple of mild suspicion die away before continuing.

"The precise nature of this threat is not known, but we are to stand ready in our bastion and ravelin, and patrols are to go out. The Third Company remains at the palace, and Second and Fourth are also mustering there. Turn out to your posts!"

The company parade exploded like spores from a kicked puffball, Musketeers moving in all directions, hurrying to the gate that opened on Dial Square, to the tunnel leading to the bastion, back to the barracks to fetch forgotten muskets or other gear, and to all other points: stables, armory, and refectory.

Agnez followed Sesturo, feeling very much like a cub hurrying behind a parental bear. The big Musketeer didn't head for gate or tunnel, but toward Decastries, who was using a portable desk held by a servant to write a message, which she handed to the Cardinal's messenger.

"Decastries!" Sesturo called. "Allow me and this cub to go to the palace, to see if the Captain or Franzonne knows what's what."

Decastries looked over, eyes weighing up Agnez.

"You are?" she asked curtly.

"Agnez Descaray, ser," replied Agnez. "Joined yesterday."

"Go with Sesturo," snapped Decastries, already turning away to another Musketeer. "Franico, take a dozen of your choosing to the Old New Bridge. There is supposed to be a troop of the Watch there. They will of course come under your command."

"Come," said Sesturo, tapping Agnez's shoulder, no doubt thinking it a gentle touch. Agnez suppressed a wince and followed, loosening her sword in its sheath.

"We're going to the Queen's Palace?" she asked, trotting to keep up with his lengthy strides. They were heading for the steps down to the tunnel that led to the Queen Ansgarde Bastion. She noticed as they reached the tunnel gate that whereas the day before it had been guarded by a mere two Musketeers, who had been playing draughts, it was now watched over by a score or more, and the portcullis had been lowered halfway down. "To see the Captain?"

She had not yet met the fabled Captain of the Musketeers. Dartagnan was quite old now, perhaps even fifty, but was still a fabled swordswoman. She had been champion for Queen Henrietta IV, and was one of the present Queen's closest confidantes, though she did not seek to manage the government of Sarance, unlike the Cardinal.

"Every now and then the Cardinal jumps at a shadow," explained Sesturo. He paused to put his hand in front of one of the torches in the tunnel's wall sconces and used its shadow to throw a duck shape with his hand. "This may be no more than that. But the Captain will know whatever there is to know. We may also see the Queen herself."

Agnez nodded, unable to speak.

Sesturo glanced at her, his face inscrutable.

"You know the special royal salute? For when you're in uniform, with musket?"

"What?" squeaked Agnez. "What?"

Sesturo laughed, and kept laughing for much longer than Agnez thought necessary, as they marched along the tunnel into the bastion and proceeded via various gates and guarded doors and stairs to the river dock, there to take a boat downstream toward the palace.

Dorotea was also woken by the drums, not just from the Musketeers' Barracks, but also those of the Pursuivants, the King's Guard, the City Watch, and the Artillerists, though the inhabitants of at least one of these places were also being stirred awake by trumpets.

She went to her narrow window, but there was little to see. The first faint illumination of dawn, a red wash under the rain clouds—but there didn't seem to be anything of significance going on, at least nothing in her limited field of view. If the sky had been clear, she would have looked to the heavens and the fading night, though she was not particularly learned in reading the indications of angelic movements in the stars. One day, she hoped to be so.

If she ever got back to the Belhalle to continue her studies . . .

It had rained heavily overnight, Dorotea noted, and there was a pool of rusty water on the lintel of the window, with slow drops still sliding down, assisting in the gradual erosion of the iron bars. Idly, she put her finger in and stirred it around, mixing the pigment. It was surprisingly thick, containing much more rust than she'd expected.

Dorotea took her finger out and looked at the red pigment on her finger. She laughed and quickly sketched a figure on the wall by the window, on one of the smoother stones. The rusty, makeshift paint held surprisingly well, and Dorotea couldn't help but sketch a bit more and fill in some details. First the pursed mouth, then the puff of a breath, and the perfect circle for a halo, done in one swift motion.

She was drawing Zamriniel, an angel she knew very well, one of the first she had made an icon for and had summoned many times. Zamriniel was only a Seraphim, but a very useful one—her scope was to amalgamate like things, provided they were not very big or heavy. The most often called-for use in this context was dust. Zamriniel could gather all the dust in a room into a neat pile. She was one of the best of the angels used for such cleaning, though many mages and priests considered using an angel for a domestic task was close to heresy, unless of course it was for a room in their temple or college—and someone else paid the price of the summoning.

There was a lot of old, old dust in the cell. Gathered in the corners, between the flagstones of the floor, caked in the corners of the ceiling. It would be so much nicer if it was swept clean, neatly piled up by Zamriniel so Dorotea could throw it out the window. And the cost to summon a Seraphim was really so slight . . .

The scab on the back of her hand where she had drawn the few drops of blood for the icon-making demonstration in the Belhalle was easily scratched open. But even as Dorotea found herself dipping her finger in the blood and her mind concentrating on Zamriniel, she managed to stop and draw back.

"Oh, you fool," Dorotea whispered to herself. She wiped the blood on the hem of her robe and then scooped up some of the rusty water to smear across her sketch so now it was just a muddy mark on the stone.

It was hard to do. She felt like her whole body was aching to summon an angel, any angel. It wasn't anyone else's business. The satisfaction of creating a successful icon and a summoning were private things. . . .

Except they weren't. Rochefort had made that clear. Creating a sketched icon and summoning an angel were not to be done lightly, if at all. Perhaps only if she had to escape. Maybe not even then.

Dorotea went back to her straw-filled mattress and pulled the blanket up and then lifted it entirely over her head. Despite what she had told Rochefort, she wasn't entirely able to ignore the future. It was true to an extent, but every now and then even her natural optimism could be overwhelmed, momentarily at least.

But under the blanket, with the world denied, everything seemed a little better. And then just as she had always done since she was a child and escaping problems, Dorotea had no problem falling back asleep, and all was well.

Simeon, in the Infirmary, was not woken by the drums, because he was already at work, setting the broken leg of an artillerist who had slipped on a rain-drenched stair from the ramparts. She was very lucky to be alive, and to have a clean break, so Simeon did not need to call upon any angelic assistance. The woman was a stoic, and his biggest trouble was fending off her three enthusiastic friends who wanted to help, or watch, or comment.

But the friends disappeared as soon as the drums and trumpets started, leaving Simeon to finish binding the broken leg to a splint with the help of one of the Refuser ward attendants. When they were done and their patient helped to a bed, Simeon asked the attendant what the drumming and trumpet blasts coming from the barracks and the bastions was all about, particularly before it was even dawn.

"It happens from time to time," said the Refuser with a yawn. She'd been on duty all night. "Rumors of war, or trouble in the city. I don't know. It's like poking an anthill; the soldiers all boil out. Do you need anything, Doctor? I'm off as soon as Darben gets here, which I hope will be soon."

"No," said Simeon. "I'm for my bed, too. The Magister wants me to assist with the removal of a stone at ten o'clock."

"Really?" asked the attendant. She was more talkative than most of the Refusers Simeon had worked with at the Hospital of Saint Jerahibim, though he had already noted that there was a more relaxed feeling in this infirmary. "Already? You must be a good 'un, Doctor. There's some here she wouldn't let within a dozen paces of a tricky piece of business like that. Good luck."

Simeon found himself smiling foolishly as he wandered back to his chamber, feeling pleased. He had found his place in the world, he felt, and the slant of his progress through life would now surely be ever upward.

Henri slept through the whole thing. He woke up briefly, initially thought the drumming was hail or heavy rain, was puzzled by the occasional trumpet, and in the space of five or six seconds muzzily decided that since no one else was stirring from the neighboring stalls, it had nothing to do with him either, so he rolled over and went back to sleep.

FIFTEEN

LILIATH EMERGED FROM THE PIT ON THE FRINGE OF A WILD melee, with the great crowd of Refusers trying desperately to get to the walkway at the same time, while right near her a combative core of a dozen or more were battling a beastling fresh born from her use of angelic magic. The monster was vaguely human-shaped still, but it was much taller and more slender than the human it had been, perhaps twice the height, with two pairs of clawed arms and long, hinged back legs like a grasshopper's, and its hide gleamed like chitin.

The beastling's red eyes swiveled as Liliath appeared, fixing on her, ignoring the combatants immediately to its front. It charged at once, lowering its wickedly sharp horns, which were already slaked with blood. Several crossbow bolts were stuck in its dun-colored, insectile hide, and it bled gray dust from several other wounds, none of which had slowed it down.

As Liliath leaped aside, the bright flare and terrific boom of an old and very large arquebus came from her right, the heavy ball striking the beastling in the head with a sound like one of the city gates slamming shut.

But still it came on, trampling several Refusers underfoot, ripping them with the burrs on its feet and legs, its head jerking to gore another who had tried to stick it with a dagger. A crossbow snapped, another bolt flowered in the thing's side, and still it staggered forward, those red eyes intent only on Liliath. She jumped over several dead or dying Refusers and scurried up one of the larger statues, the common depiction of the angel Harekiel as a well-muscled woman in a gymnast's tunic, two arms outstretched above her head as if she was about to flip forward, her tall wings folded behind her back. This attempted icon of Chalconte's was not some tiny plaque or cameo, but an eighteen-foot-high statue carved from a massive block of marble.

The beastling rammed the base of the statue, rocking it slightly. But it was too heavy even for the monster to shift. As the beastling reared back and roared in pain, a burly Refuser swung her ax, the blade biting deep into the beastling's head. It stuck there, and she wisely let go as the beastling howled and spasmed in its violent death throes, smacking the statue several times again before it finally died.

Liliath watched from her perch as the axwoman, probably a butcher's menial by her broad gray apron and leather bracers, stood on the beastling's body and worked her weapon free, releasing a slow boilover of its ashen blood.

There were twenty or more Refusers dead or dying around the point where the beastling had emerged from a man or woman, including a young woman lying across her crutches, the messenger who had brought word of the Court of the Rogue to Demaselle House.

The Worm wasn't among the dead, and Liliath couldn't see her elsewhere. There were far fewer lanterns and torches now, and there was an enormous dark mass of Refusers jammed together trying to get on the walkway, and along it. Only the upper reaches were open, where the fleetest people were already sprinting away.

Bisc climbed up next to her. He had blood on his lace-trimmed jerkin, but it was not his own.

"It was a trap," said Liliath. "The Worm had three people down there already, with a net and weapons. And Kate Sunless had a crossbow."

"But you killed them," said Bisc. "Are you hurt?"

"I am not. This blood is not my own. Where is the Worm?"

Bisc pointed to a huddle of Refusers partially concealed by the statue of the Throne. One had a cloak over their head and was bound with rope.

"We have her. When the panic subsides, she will be thrown in the pit."

"No," said Liliath. "I have a use for her."

Bisc did not immediately reply.

"She will still die," said Liliath. "Just in a more useful fashion."

"As you wish," said Bisc.

"You do not seem greatly troubled by all this death and dying," said Liliath, gesturing where lantern and torchlight fell on pools of blood, bodies crumpled and torn, the terribly wounded staring up at the night, unseeing, unable to comprehend what had happened to them.

"Death and dying is a Refuser's lot," said Bisc with a shrug. "We learn this early. I was eight when I caught a pox. My parents weren't Night Crew; they worked as servants for a spice merchant . . . I played with the merchant's children. Florenz and Elen. They caught the pox too, but a doctor-magister came and healed them. But for me . . . I couldn't understand why *they* were suddenly relieved of the heat, the unbearable pain, the sense of wrongness in my flesh, and I was not. When it turned out I would live, I was deemed too ugly, too horrible for my former playfellows. My parents died not much later, of some other plague that angels cured for real Sarancians. There was nowhere for me to go but the Night Crew, and there is never a shortage of death and dying among *us*. I started as a beggar, showing my awful face . . ."

He glanced at the beastling where it lay and added, "As for beastlings . . . I've seen them kill. I've even seen one made before. Franz Wither-Arm organized it, with a mage who was too stupid to realize he'd be offed as soon as he'd done his work. I heard then that we don't really need to wear our grays. The angels know what we are and resist using their powers upon us. That mage said angels have to be forced to use their powers on a Refuser. Is that true?"

"Yes. It is true, the angels do recognize those of Ystara, and they shy away, just as they resist doing obvious harm," said Liliath.

"But they can be compelled, if the summoner has the strength of will. Is there another way out of here?"

She pointed to the throng that still congested the walkways and steps. Even as she did so, someone was pushed over the side, accidentally or with intent. A frail beggar, barely able to walk. Her gray rags fluttered behind her as she fell, screaming.

"There is," admitted Bisc. "But it is not easy. Why should we hurry? The Worm is defeated. Her people are either running or have come over to me. There's no need for haste."

"The creation of a beastling here, using the remnant power in one of Chalconte's statues, has disturbed the heavens," explained Liliath. "The Cardinal will soon be aware *something* has happened, and the general locality. I expect Pursuivants will already be on the way. So we need to get out now."

"There are a series of rope ladders on the southern side," said Bisc. "It's a long climb. No more than six people can be on any stretch of ladder at one time. . . ."

"Provided we are among the six, that appears of little consequence," said Liliath.

Bisc looked at her sharply, then away, nodding slowly.

"We won't be able to go back to the city either, not if there's Pursuivants already on the road . . . it'll have to be the refuge at Nep's Cross, or in the woods above."

"The sooner we go the better," said Liliath. She could feel the distant murmuring of disquiet among angels, like the crash of surf borne far inland by a strong wind.

Bisc climbed down, already calling out orders.

Liliath followed more slowly, reclaiming her daggers from a silent Sevrin.

Five minutes later, they were climbing the rope ladders with the trussed-up Worm being raised on a rope like a bunch of kindling taken up a beacon. On the other side of the pit, the crush continued as the strongest and most able-bodied pushed the weaker ones aside, often over the edge.

The Night King and his officers could have imposed order, if they'd stayed. But Bisc led the way up the rope ladders, and he did not look back.

A tide of red and black, one hundred and twenty Cardinal's Pursuivants in scarlet riding black horses, stormed through Nep's Cross as if late for a battle, effortlessly pushing all other traffic aside, just as it began to get busy, the city and the countryside around waking before the dawn. If they noted the surprising number of Refusers out and about, they did not stop to question them, the fore riders merely shouting at all and sundry to stand aside, the order reinforced with whips or fatally punctuated by the heavy iron shoes of the horses.

Liliath watched the Pursuivants stream past through a tiny window in the attic of the refuge house in Nep's Cross, one of the many Bisc's people had in and around the city. The Night King was close to her, also watching. Behind him were Sevrin and Erril, and a fourth Refuser Liliath didn't know, a small, silent man who limped.

"Three full troops, led by Captain Rochefort," said Bisc quietly. "We were lucky to make it out of the quarry in time . . . and what if the Cardinal summons Ashalael?"

"She has not summoned Ashalael, and she will not," said Liliath confidently. "She is old and fearful and will not call upon the Archangel unless she must. But over long association, summoners develop a form of communion with their familiar angels. It is possible to speak with them without a complete summoning. I am sure Ashalael told the Cardinal something happened in the quarry, but not what, or who. So she has sent her Pursuivants to find out. But she will not discover anything useful."

"I can understand her curiosity," said Bisc with a wry smile.

There was silence for a moment after that, save for the hoofbeats on the paved road outside, where the rearguard of the Pursuivants was passing by with rather less energy than those at the front.

"I suppose we cannot go back until nightfall," said Liliath. "I will miss my bed."

She touched Bisc lightly on the back of his hand as she spoke, but he did not react, other than to nod.

"It would be best to stay here, milady. Whatever else Roche-fort finds at the quarry, she will find our dead people, and then they will want to question any Refuser they think might be one of the Night Crew."

"Well, then," said Liliath. She went to a chest in the corner, with a smashed-in lid, and sat down upon it, her presence making even this ruined object seem like a throne. "We shall have time for you to give me the news I awaited last night and did not get."

"The news?" asked Bisc wearily. He scratched his head. "I . . .

when I heard about the Worm's challenge—"

"The four!" snapped Liliath, unable to conceal her impatience, her need to know. She had already had to wait too long. "What of the four I wanted watched and guarded?"

"Yes," said Bisc. "Though I wish I understood—"

"I will tell you when you need to know," said Liliath dismissively. "Which is not yet."

She took off her cap, and shook her hair free.

"But I have decided on my plan. Your earlier report, you said the four are all in the Star Fortress, but only Dorotea is in some fashion a prisoner?"

Bisc nodded.

"She is the most difficult to watch and guard," he said. "There are no Refusers in the Tower itself. It's easy everywhere else— the Architect's servants in the New Palace, the floor swabbers in the Musketeers' Barracks, the orderlies in the hospital, and everywhere plenty of our children are running about doing odd jobs. I have tried to use people the Pursuivants would be less likely to know, though we . . . I . . . made a mistake with one earlier, when Dorotea was still at the Belhalle. It was corrected."

"Have the four met?" said Liliath. "They would be drawn together."

"They have," confirmed Bisc, his expression one of curiosity restrained. "They plan to meet again, tomorrow . . . no, this afternoon now. At the New Palace."

"Perhaps too soon," said Liliath. "Are you sure we cannot get back into the city?"

"It is not impossible," Bisc allowed. "But risky. I would prefer not to—"

"I need to fetch three of the Diamond Icons, and we will also need the Worm, alive for the moment," said Liliath. "And half a dozen of your most-trusted people. Who will need to secretly enter the Star Fortress. With the Worm."

"That can all be done," said Bisc. "What do you intend?"

"This is the beginning," said Liliath, her voice redolent with promise and authority. "I said we needed an army to help us return to where we must go in Ystara. The Sarancians will provide it, if everything goes as I trust it will."

"What are my people to do with the Worm?" asked Bisc. "And why three of the Diamond Icons?"

"I will elucidate," said Liliath, and gesturing him to draw closer, she put her mouth close to his ear, her tongue darting out to whisper and caress.

PART IV

The Diamond Icons

SIXTEEN

BY THE LATE AFTERNOON, RUMORS ABOUT WHAT HAD happened at the quarry had spread throughout the city, been mixed together and spread again, dissected and reinvented and generally made far more portentous. Agnez, returning to the barracks from the Queen's Palace, found her chambermates were not immune to this sharing of gossip, and after discovering she either had no privileged news or was not going to tell them if she did, they did not hesitate to share their own findings.

"Hundreds of dead Refusers," said the vainglorious popinjay called Gretel Delamapan, whose bed was opposite Agnez's own. "That's what I heard. Most of them in the quarry, but a bunch got themselves killed in a running battle with the Watch and then got done over again by Rochefort's lot when they arrived."

"A renegade mage made a dozen of them into beastlings," added another cadet, Devan Derangue, a slightly older and more somber fellow. He had been in a lesser regiment for a year and thought himself an experienced soldier and wiser head than the others. "For sport, to fight each other, with the audience betting on the result. But the beastlings got out and the crowd panicked."

"Impossible!" sniffed Delamapan, who in addition to vastly superior tailoring, considered herself a more knowledgeable mage than the others. "One beastling, perhaps. A dozen? Impossible!"

Agnez did not add to the rumor-making, simply listening as she changed her shirt, letting the soiled one fall to the floor where the chamber's Refuser servant would pick it up for laundering later. Rebuttoning her jerkin and putting her precious Musketeer's tabard on again, she brushed the plume of her hat straight, set the hat on her head at a rakish angle, and went to the door.

"Hey, where are you off to, Descaray?" called out Delamapan. "Special duties with that great oaf Sesturo again?"

"I'll pass on that greeting to Ser Sesturo in your own words, Delamapan," said Agnez seriously. "Though I may not see him for some time, as I am merely going to drink wine with friends, a pastime I am beginning to suspect you are unfamiliar with."

"Oh, well now, I spoke only in jest . . . ," Delamapan began nervously, her nervous eyes a giveaway that she was visualizing Sesturo's reaction, or perhaps his fists. But as Agnez began to laugh, the other cadet groaned and added, "And though I know you will not say anything to Ser Sesturo, I will guard my tongue more carefully."

"A wise notion," said Agnez gravely. She bowed to the other cadets, not doffing her hat, and they called words of friendly abuse after her as she left, being careful to confine their descriptions only to her and not any more superior Musketeers.

⊛⊛⊛

Henri was waiting by the main south gate of the New Palace at the appointed hour, sitting on a block of stone. The gatehouse had been built, but the walls on either side had not, which made it look rather lonely and odd. Particularly as the gates, though finished, had not yet been shipped on to the massive iron pinions in the gateway, and lay flat on the ground just past the gate, next to a very tall stack of bricks. A crew of Refusers was slowly stacking bricks from one side of this stack to the other, for no apparent reason.

Agnez was first to arrive, striding straight down the road as if it belonged to her. Henri jumped off the block and they bowed to each other, Agnez managing to accent the fact she wore her new Musketeer tabard in her salute.

"Yes, very fine, you are a proper Musketeer," said Henri.

"I am indeed, and you should not forget it," said Agnez, clapping him on the shoulder. She already thought of him as a little brother, even though they were the same age. A smart little brother. Good with numbers, probably not much use in a fight. "I even saluted the Queen today, when she walked past."

"You saw her?" asked Henri, impressed. "Does she look as she does on the coins?"

"Not really," said Agnez. "She is . . . older. The Cardinal was there, whispering in her ear."

"Oh, I've met the Cardinal," said Henri impulsively, ignoring the tone of Agnez's voice. She had spoken as if the Cardinal were some sort of temptress, and the whispering illicit.

"You have! How did you . . . I mean no disrespect, Henri, but . . ."

"Well, I've been meaning to tell you ever since we first ran into each other in that tunnel—"

"What?"

"Only seeing how keen you were to run me through then, and you being a Queen's Musketeer, I hesitated—"

"What?"

"While I am an assistant to the *Queen's* Architect, it was the Cardinal who gave me the post—"

"What?"

"Well, the Cardinal is the Chief Minister, nearly all appointments are made by her, the Queen hardly ever—"

"I know that! Why did the Cardinal give you the post?"

"Well, I was already one of Her Eminence's clerks—"

"You're one of the Cardinal's clerks!"

"Well, only temporarily. I want to be an artillerist, but my family couldn't afford to buy me a commission in the Loyal Royals—"

"You're one of the Cardinal's clerks!"

"Yes," said Henri stiffly. He took a deep breath and said, "Shall I go and fetch my sword?"

Agnez laughed and clapped him on the back again.

"No! If you were a Pursuivant, maybe . . . but since I've had a little longer being a Musketeer, I've learned that the rivalry between our regiments waxes and wanes, and right now wanes, because we must be ready to fight together. When someone in authority works out whoever it is we must fight. I guess we're like brothers and sisters who get to brawling but turn against anyone else who interferes."

"Oh, good," said Henri. "I mean, I've always thought the Cardinal only wants to do what's best, and she is the most competent—"

"Let's not talk politics," said Agnez. "As we will no doubt argue, unless you admit from the beginning the essential principle that the Queen should be her own Chief Minister."

"I'd as soon admit the King should be employed so," said Henri.

"Well, we are agreed there," said Agnez.

"If the Queen employs and trusts the Cardinal as Chief Minister, surely that means you Musketeers should support Her Majesty's decision and thus support the Cardinal?"

"Slippery talk!" exclaimed Agnez. "I said no politics. In any case, all I know is that as a Musketeer, I obey my officers, who obey the Queen. You seem in a more complex situation, being a Cardinal's man yet working for the Queen."

"I would say that in working for the Cardinal I am working for Her Majesty—" Henri began.

"Who's working for the Cardinal?" interrupted Simeon, looming up behind Henri. He was wearing a long doctor's coat as usual, but this one was clean. He had added a hat with a very tall crown, but he was so big the brim looked smaller than it should, everything strangely out of proportion. He had a leather satchel over his shoulder, and at his belt, a surgeon's long and narrow knife rather than a dagger.

"I am," said Henri, with a glance at Agnez. "I am an assistant to the Queen's Architect, but I was appointed by Her Eminence. And before, I was one of her clerks. The Cardinal's, I mean. For a few days. A cousin of mine got me that post, and I was very grateful for it too. We've no money, you see. I mean less than no money, since both my parents have been in debt forever."

"I suppose in a sense I am also working for the Cardinal," said Simeon.

"What!" declared Agnez, and Henri looked surprised.

"What, Agnez? I know Pursuivants and Musketeers cut each other up with regularity, as I've stitched enough of you back together in the hospital. But you must recognize that the Cardinal actually wields all authority in Sarance—"

"The Queen chooses to delegate to the Cardinal her authority!" interrupted Agnez.

"Well, maybe so," said Simeon in a conciliatory voice. "Anyway, as I was saying, I owe my current post to the Cardinal too. Or rather, to her Captain Rochefort—"

"Captain Rochefort? I had an odd conversation with her last night."

The three of them turned out of their huddle at this new interruption, all now surprised. Dorotea smiled and bowed, careful not to drop the block of paper and box of charcoal sticks she held under her arm.

"Why were you—" Henri started to say, but he stopped himself. The gang of Refusers who were stacking bricks were looking over, and there was also a steady stream of other workers, messengers, gardeners, and various types of clerks going through the gatehouse—or around it, since that was just as easy—and any one of the latter two types might be looking for Henri with a task from the Queen's Architect.

Even worse, the Architect herself might appear.

"We can't stay here, or someone will give me a job to do. I was thinking my chamber when we talked yesterday, but it's really only a horse stall, and if any of the other clerks are around they'd be a nuisance . . . but there's a private spot I found. I took some wine to cool there earlier."

"Lead on," said Agnez, brightening.

There was a brief struggle to encourage Dorotea to come with them, as she had started to sketch the gatehouse and the Refusers with their stack of bricks. Once that was sorted with a promise from Henri that he would show her a much more picturesque view, he led them through the gatehouse along the partially paved carriage drive, around the end of the reflecting pool—which had no water in it yet and was still being lined with particularly fine, smoothly glazed bricks—across what would one day be a lawn, past a much smaller but architecturally exact copy of the Temple of Ashalael on Garden Island in the Leire, also under construction, toward a muddy half-empty lake and a tumbled pile of huge stone blocks at the southern end.

"This is the ornamental side of the park," said Henri. "The western end has an orchard, a model dairy, and so on."

"Are we going to perch upon a stone?" asked Agnez, with a

scowl, as they drew nearer. "Why have they all been dumped here?"

"Not dumped. Arranged most carefully, in fact," explained Henri. "They'll be covered in soil and turfed over in due course. Come around the other side, you'll see."

They walked around the jumble of stone and saw that on the side facing the lake the stones had been laid to form a cave, which already had plastered walls inside, a paved floor and an iron stove, whose chimney was cunningly disguised to emerge among the higher stones. It was also furnished, after a fashion, in that chairs had been carved out of smaller blocks of stone, set alongside a rectangular stone table. Henri had earlier borrowed a stack of entirely new horse blankets and had placed them as cushions. He had also cautiously visited the wineshop and bought several flagons of white wine from Jureau, which were benefitting from the lowered temperature in the coolest corner of the cave. Henri had also made a private arrangement with the cooks in the Infirmary, and so the wine was accompanied by several fresh loaves, three cheeses (two hard, one soft, from Bascony and Flarieu) and a dozen small, sweet apples from the North completed the offering.

"The Hermit's Cave," he announced. "A very romantical establishment, except that when it rains and the wind is anywhere in the north, the inside becomes as wet as the lake outside."

"The gatehouse was a better subject for a drawing," said Dorotea. "I dislike these false contrivances. The gatehouse has a purpose, and the unhoused gates lying by it were perfect in their symmetry."

"What about drawing the lake?" suggested Simeon. "Those Refusers fishing or whatever they're doing make a fine subject."

A group of a half-dozen Refusers were wading in a line about fifty yards away, the muddy water up to their thighs. They were all looking down, sometimes bending to rummage with their hands, or poke with short sticks.

Henri looked hard at them and scratched his head under his hat, pushing it to one side so the brim almost touched his shoulder.

"I think that what they are doing is pretending to do something while really avoiding work," he said. "Appearing to be engaged in some important activity is the major pursuit of almost every worker here, be they Refusers or not. I probably should go and find out, but then I am quite keen on avoiding work myself. So I won't."

He sat down at the head of the table, in the grandest chair, no doubt destined one day for the Queen or Cardinal, though it would have many fine cushions in that future and not a few folded-over horse blankets to take the chill out of the stone.

Agnez drew the plug from one of the wineskins and, after pouring a stream down her throat to quench her immediate thirst, filled the simple wooden cups that were all Henri had managed to "borrow" from the temporary kitchen that served all the palace workers. This was a huge, leaky tent set up where a walled herb garden was going to be, though at present this existed solely as a pattern of hammered pegs and constantly replenished chalk lines.

"So, Dorotea, you said you had a conversation with Captain Rochefort last night," said Agnez, once everyone was settled and had a cup and Dorotea had been dissuaded from wandering off to find something interesting to draw.

"Yes, she came to my cell in the Tower," said Dorotea. "I think she was trying to woo me—"

Simeon choked on his wine, Agnez lowered her mug, and Henri tried to act as if this was news he already knew.

"Because I remind her of a woman she loved," continued Dorotea. She frowned. "I think not for myself."

"I thought she was *old*," said Agnez.

"She's younger than she looks," said Dorotea. "The price of angelic magic, of course. She told me she was only twenty-seven—"

"That is fairly old," said Agnez.

This led to a conversation where they established that she was the youngest of the four, by a matter of three months. Simeon was next youngest at eighteen and two months, Henri at eighteen and a half and Dorotea the oldest being weeks short of nineteen.

"Rochefort's birthday is today, as a matter of fact," mused Dorotea. "And she is beautiful, in a way."

"Like a wild falcon," agreed Simeon. "But too beautiful to be safe. I can well understand she looks older, given her magery. I saw her summon an angel, it seemed without any effort of concentration, or consideration of the cost. She sent it to follow a Refuser assassin who shot at her on the river."

Questions flew, and Simeon found himself explaining the whole affair with the beastling and Magister Delazan and his subsequent imprisonment and journey to the Star Fortress, and his good fortune in gaining his new position. He did not tell them he had agreed to inform Rochefort about anything interesting that occurred, though several times he felt a strong urge to let them know.

Simeon's tale naturally led to Henri's, with everyone very interested to hear about what the Cardinal was like in person. They were disappointed when Henri claimed he hadn't really looked at her and all he could recall was the crimson of her face—it was so thickly painted. And like Rochefort, she looked older than she was and also summoned angels very readily. Including the one who had helped her gauge his usefulness.

"The angel looked *inside* your head?" asked Agnez. "Could you feel it?"

"I'm not exactly sure that's what it did," said Henri. "It didn't hurt . . . I just felt a kind of cold presence in my mind . . . and then the Cardinal knew things about me, like I'm good with numbers, which I am, and that I would be terrible as a torturer's assistant; she knew I couldn't work in the Tower . . ."

His voice trailed off as they all looked at Dorotea.

"No one's tortured me," she said. "Yet."

"Why *are* you a prisoner?" asked Simeon. "And if so, why are you allowed out during the day?"

"I'm a 'guest,'" said Dorotea. She explained how her icon-sketching display had led to her being brought to the Tower, and how Rochefort later told her this was because Chalconte and the Maid of Ellanda had both been icon-sketchers and it was suspected this led to full-blown heresy. At least in Chalconte's case. Liliath's was more obscure.

"It seems undue caution," said Simeon. "Just because you can make icons a different way doesn't mean you'll end up making weird statues and claiming people define angel's scopes and they are not immutable."

"Is that what Chalconte did?" asked Agnez. "Yesterday, I heard people in the palace talking about Chalconte's statues—the Queen's Palace, the proper one, not here—"

"This is a proper palace, or will be," protested Henri. Agnez rolled her eyes and continued.

"So Franzonne, that's the Queen's Champion, who I know well, said the alarm this morning was because a whole lot of Refusers got themselves killed and at least one got turned into a beastling. In the quarry where Chalconte's statues were supposed to be buried, only they keep getting washed out by floods. But I didn't know who Chalconte was, and it wasn't appropriate to ask, since the Queen was about to go past. Did I mention I saw the Queen today?"

"It may have come up five or six times already," said Henri. "But who is or was Chalconte? And what's this about statues?"

"Chalconte was a heretical icon-maker who went mad," said Simeon. "One of his many heresies was that if he could make statues work as summoning icons they would anchor the angel they represented more forcefully in the mortal world. They would persist longer and more could be done with them. He failed, of course, but he kept sculpting for years in secret before he was found out and executed."

"How do you know about this?" asked Henri, with a glance at Dorotea, who had not answered his question about Chalconte, though he suspected she knew. But she wasn't paying attention.

"I read up on him, because he made an icon of Requaniel my family owns, which has come to me."

"An icon made by Chalconte?" asked Dorotea, suddenly no longer gazing across the lake at the huddle of Refusers, her focus full on Simeon. "Do you have it with you? May I see it?"

"Yes," said Simeon. He hesitated, before reaching inside his robe to a hidden interior pocket. "But it is a strange thing, that I feel I know you so well that I would do this. The icon is by far the most valuable thing my family owns. . . . I wouldn't usually let it leave my hand. . . ."

Dorotea took the icon reverentially, turning it so the light from the cave mouth fell clear upon it.

"Our . . . bond . . . is mysterious," she said absently, bringing the icon close to her eye and then slowly moving it away again. "I had thought it was an angel we all knew in common, that we summoned. But that has been disproven. So we must ask what else could it be? It is interesting we are all of a similar age, and all Bascons. This is the most extraordinary icon. . . . I cannot fathom how the fine work was done, unless by another angel . . . yet I have always been taught angelic magic cannot be used in the making of icons."

"We *are* all Bascons," said Agnez. She looked around the table: at huge, black-skinned Simeon; small, dark Dorotea; and pale, reddish Henri, and at her own brown hands. "And you feel as . . . as family to me. But surely, we cannot be related. We do not look at all similar."

"I had wondered if we might perhaps share a father at least, as we could not have the same mother given the closeness of age," said Dorotea, handing back the icon to Simeon. "But this seems very unlikely, for a number of reasons. Even despite *my* parents' general absent-mindedness when it comes to bedfellows."

"Impossible," said Henri. He paused. "Well . . . very unlikely. My father has never left Huaravael. He would be arrested for debt, you see, if he leaves the purlieu of his temple. And I do not think he would stray."

"I think my parents would simply have told me if I had any siblings, half or otherwise," said Simeon. "They are both doctor-magisters, both very . . . direct . . . about such things. They gave me Janossa's *Ways of Love* for my fourteenth birthday and *insisted* on talking me through some of its two hundred hand-tinted illustrations . . ."

"Do you still have that?" asked Henri.

"Back home in Adianne," said Simeon.

"We four are unalike in almost all particulars," said Agnez. "And I also doubt my father could have fathered another child. My mother would kill him, as he well knows."

"I'm guessing you take after your mother?" asked Henri.

"She was a Queen's Musketeer," said Agnez proudly. "She

taught me everything I know of the sword."

"I wish I'd been born in your family," said Henri. He looked at Simeon. "Or yours. Mine just has too many other children and a total absence of money. Are your parents rich, Dorotea?"

"My mother probably is, though it's hard to tell. She likes to live in a simple fashion," mused Dorotea. She was looking at the group of Refusers again. "My father isn't officially my father. He's quite eccentric and has lost and found several fortunes."

"How do you find a fortune?" asked Henri. "I would really like to know."

"In his case, when he has money, he gives it away," said Dorotea. She was staring out the cave mouth, intent on the people in the water. "Sometimes, it is used wisely and they give more of it back. One of those Refusers is the boy who dropped the ladder yesterday. He's wearing different clothes and a cap, but it is him."

"We should give him a present," said Agnez. She got up from the table and went to look. "What *are* they doing?"

One of the Refusers had lifted a long pole with a sharp, curved hook out of the water, a cruel shepherd's crook. She didn't say anything, but the other Refusers converged upon her. Several glanced over to the cave and then away again, as if they hadn't really been looking.

"They're searching for something," said Agnez.

"That's a tosher's pole," said Simeon. "The sewer hunters. I've seen them going in and out of the big outfall into the Leire near the hospital."

"I don't think there's a sewer near here," said Henri, who had been made to study the plans of the New Palace. "Though this rock is riddled with tunnels . . . what are they up to?"

As if by accident, four of the Refusers were re-forming their line to block the view from the cave. Behind this line, the other two were almost crawling through the water, sweeping their arms from side to side.

"They don't want us to know what they're looking for," said Agnez. Her hand fell to her sword hilt. "Or what they've found."

"Does it matter?" asked Dorotea. She had taken up her charcoal stick again and was busy sketching the scene, in a few swift strokes capturing the essence of the standing figures, the bent-over waders, the ripples spreading across the water.

"I'd better go and find out," sighed Henri. "If it is something important and Dutremblay learns I was here and didn't do anything . . ."

He bent to take off his boots, but as he did so there was a sudden gunshot from the lake. One of the Refusers reeled back and ran away, throwing himself through the water. Another pursued him, a pistol in her hand. There was a flurry of dagger drawing from the others, an exchange of blows and parries, and a scream of pain.

Agnez plunged into the water, boots and all, her sword in her hand.

"Halt in the name of the Queen!"

SEVENTEEN

HENRI FOLLOWED AGNEZ A MOMENT LATER, HOPPING TO get his foot reseated in the boot he'd almost taken off.

Simeon picked up his satchel and ran around the side of the lake after the Refuser who'd been shot and his pursuer, who were headed for the ornamental bridge that spanned the northern narrows.

The other Refusers spun out of their combat and waded away, one pair toward the western shore, clearly aiming for the serried piles of timber on the future jousting field to the west, where many high stacks of beams for the main palace formed a veritable maze. The second pair headed straight for the eastern shore and, reaching it, clambered out to run for the hole in the eastern perimeter wall where one day there would be another imposing gatehouse.

Dorotea stayed in the mouth of the cave, sketching the action.

It soon became apparent that Agnez and Henri had made an error in entering the lake and were much slower moving through it than the Refusers, who were not encumbered by much clothing, let alone boots or shoes. Swiftly making it to shore, they sprinted to the maze of timbers. Similarly, the "shot" Refuser was either unscathed or greatly assisted by fear, for he reached the bridge and disappeared under it, indicating there was some hidden passage. A minute later, his pursuer followed.

Simeon, seeing his services would not be required, came back, as Agnez and Henri reached the spot where the Refusers had been hunting before they started fighting each other.

None of the Refusers were now in sight, and no one else was paying any attention. The sound of a single gunshot was evidently insufficient to raise the interest of any workers. There were supposed to be guards about, but as per usual the split command meant that whichever regiment was meant to be providing the soldiers never did so unless they were fetched at the Architect's demand, usually by means of a message sent with Henri or one of his contemporaries. This was rarely done, given the New Palace was in the middle of the Star Fortress. What enemies could there be to guard against?

The object the Refusers had been searching for, and had then fought over when they found it, was a body. Strangely, it was not floating facedown, but sitting slumped in the water. Agnez and Henri faltered as they came close, and both raised sleeves to noses.

"Ah, the stench!" exclaimed Henri.

"I have never known a corpse to smell so foul," said Agnez.

"Should we drag it out?" asked Henri. "I wonder why they were fighting over someone dead?"

Agnez shook her head, her nose planted deeply in her sleeve.

"I am a Musketeer," she said. "Not some gravedigger or

corpse robber, and certainly not when the body stinks worse than anything I have ever smelled."

"So, we're just going to leave it here?"

"It is not our business," said Agnez.

"It will probably be mine," said Henri gloomily. "I get all the rotten jobs in this skeleton of a palace."

"I'll bring it in," announced Simeon, splashing up next to them. He wrinkled his nose but did no more. "That stench is not a corpse smell. It is the waft of the sewers; she must indeed be a tosher. But as always with such odors and miasma, there may be a risk of some rot or infection. You haven't touched her, have you?"

Agnez and Henri drew back several steps, both shaking their heads.

"Go and get one of the blankets from the cave and spread it on the bank," instructed Simeon. "I will lay her out there."

"I'll go and see where those two went under the bridge," said Agnez. She drew a pistol from her belt and ostentatiously primed it from the powder flask on her bandolier. "If they're lurking there, I'll roust them from their earth."

"There probably is a tunnel there after all," said Henri with a sigh. "There is everywhere else in this place. I'll get the blanket."

He waded south to the cave, as Agnez waded north. Simeon pinned the icon of Requaniel carefully to his coat, and rested his fingers upon it. Unusually, it immediately vibrated under his fingers, as if the angel it was connected with was eager to manifest. This had never happened before, and Simeon almost drew his hand back. But then the buzzing movement slowed and stopped.

"Requaniel, Requaniel, come to my aid."

The angel manifested in a rush, Simeon feeling it as a sudden burst of warmth everywhere within his body, and he heard the ripple of many harp strings.

Requaniel is here. What is your will? If it lies within my scope, it shall be done.

"Guard me from the things unseen that flock as evil humors in the air," whispered Simeon, the rote incantation. "Keep my body and my self from harm."

It is done and done, answered Requaniel. *Until I am dismissed, or tire of this world.*

Simeon slowly withdrew his fingers from the icon. Requaniel had never seemed so present before, or so distinctive and individual. In fact, Simeon couldn't remember the angel ever varying his responses, as he had just done.

He bent over the Refuser's corpse, holding his breath, examining it without touching at first, before tipping it gently from side to side to see more. This revealed she was a woman, very pale-skinned, quite old, perhaps sixty or seventy. He noticed her thin hair, which was tightly pleated into six or seven strands that were glued or somehow fixed to her scalp, a style he had seen before but not among elderly women. She had quite a few scars on her head as well, pale lines against the darker skin. But they were old, and not the cause of death.

Averting his face and breathing through his mouth, Simeon reached under the water and got his hands under her armpits and gently lifted her up. She was a lot heavier than he expected, which he saw was because she was cradling a well-stuffed satchel of oiled leather, additionally held in place by the strap that was still around her neck.

Grunting with the effort, Simeon half carried, half dragged the corpse and hanging satchel through the water. By the time he got to the closest shore, Henri had come back with a blanket, which he laid out on the edge. Simeon put the old woman down and arranged her legs and her gray robe so she looked a little more as if she had just fallen asleep. Only a little, as she had the pallor and emptiness of death. He had more difficulty moving her arms, as the death stiffness had begun to set in, and her hands were locked around the satchel.

"She died earlier today," he said to Henri, who was still keeping his distance, and his arm up on his face, though his eyes kept straying to the satchel.

"Drowned?" asked Henri.

Simeon shook his head and knelt down on one knee to examine the woman's side. Her robe was rent there, and through the hole discolored flesh could be seen. He pulled the cloth away, revealing a deep puncture.

"Stabbed and tried to run away, but bled to death crossing the lake, I'd say. Early this morning. Which is curious. She must have been facedown till those Refusers sat her up, or we would have noticed her earlier . . . I wonder where she came from, and where she was going? And how she got into the Star Fortress in the first place."

"I wonder what's in her bag," said Henri.

"It's very heavy, that's for certain," said Simeon.

"They have hard lives, and hard deaths," said Dorotea, who had come up quietly, leaving her charcoal and paper back in the cave. "Refusers, I mean."

"They do," said Simeon. "I have always found it difficult that we can do so little when they grew sick or got injured. Even at the hospital, or the Infirmary here, for our own porters and servants, and their families."

He examined the wound again, pointing to the clotted dark red blood.

"Refusers are just like us, save when they are touched by angelic magic," continued Simeon. "Look, her blood is red. No one can explain why angelic magic makes it become gray dust or turns them into beastlings instead. As far as I know they do not even question it themselves."

"They spurned the heavens and were cursed by their own Archangel for their sins," said Henri. "Everyone knows Refusers made their own fate."

"That's not true. No one knows what really happened," said Dorotea, quite sternly for her. "I doubt they had anything to do with it myself. They just suffer the consequences."

"What consequences?" asked Agnez, who had come back, moving as she always did at something between a swift walk and a run. She didn't wait for an answer. "There *is* a tunnel under the bridge, with a padlocked grate. I suppose that second Refuser snapped it shut. It was half-flooded, so maybe it's more of a drain."

"Oh," said Henri. "Yes. There is a water conduit from the river; that must be a branch line. That's on a separate plan. Just to confuse everyone. I suppose if the river isn't too high, you *could* get into the fortress that way. I'd better report it."

"So what were they up to?" asked Agnez. "Who's this? What's in her satchel?"

"Let's find out," said Simeon. He unhitched the strap, lifted the satchel, and took it a few paces upwind of the corpse, before setting it down again to tug at the straps with his large, dexterous fingers, swiftly working them out of the buckles, though the leather was swollen from immersion in the lake.

There was a tightly wrapped oilskin parcel inside the satchel, wound about many times with a waxed cord. Simeon took the package out, its heaviness indicated by a grunt of effort, and placed it down. But as he bent close, the icon pinned on the front of his robe shivered and started to shake again, and he heard Requaniel's distinctive voice call out as if in fear, or perhaps in awe . . .

Simeon drew swiftly back, even as Dorotea leaned forward. They spoke almost together.

"There is a powerful icon in—"

"Angelic magic—"

Henri looked around. The closest people were a group of Refusers being directed by an overseer from the Architect's staff, standing around a sheerlegs atop one of the stacks of timber in the jousting yard, all intent on lowering one of the really big beams to the ground. It would be hard for anyone to see any detail from that distance. But there might be someone particularly sharp-eyed, or just curious enough to wander over . . .

"We should bring it to the cave," said Henri. "Open it there."

"If you have any icons with you, it would be safer to leave them outside," said Dorotea. "Whatever is in here is extremely powerful. I can feel it."

"You can?" asked Simeon. He touched his icon and dismissed Requaniel, before putting the brooch back inside the pouch under his coat. That done, he cautiously picked up the bundle and held it as far away from himself as he could manage. It was extremely heavy for its size, as if it were full of lead.

Or gold, which clearly was what Henri was thinking, judging by the way he couldn't tear his gaze away from it.

Dorotea nodded. "It is a facility some . . . a few icon-makers develop. We become sensitive to the presence of even unsummoned angels. If they are of the most powerful orders."

She said this confidently, but in truth, knew only that *she* was sensitive to powerful icons. No one else had ever mentioned to her that they had the same ability.

"We can't just leave the body here," said Agnez.

"Fold the blanket over her," said Simeon. "There are corpse takers at the Infirmary, I'll send them out."

"What do they do with dead Refusers?" asked Agnez.

Simeon hesitated. He would have lied to most people, but among the four of them he felt he could not do that.

"We . . . er . . . cut up the ones in good condition, to learn more of how everything within the human body is put together," he said. "But this one has been too long in the water already.

She will go to the charnel pits south of the city."

"What about her family, or friends?" asked Dorotea. "Surely someone might want to claim the body?"

"Unless they are present at the death, I don't think anyone does anything to . . . um . . . let them know," said Simeon uncomfortably. "And Refusers end up in the charnel pits anyway. They're not allowed to be buried at the Necropolis or Safavy. And of course not immolated by Ximithael."

"Why?" asked Dorotea. "They cannot become beastlings after death, and the Ash Blood plague cannot harm someone already dead."

"Custom, I suppose," said Simeon. "That's the way it is."

"Hmmm," said Dorotea.

"Come on," said Henri. "Let's see what's inside the package. If there's a powerful icon, it must be valuable, right? And it's so heavy. . . ."

"We should inform some authority," said Agnez, as they walked together back to the cave. "It is very odd to see Refusers bicker so openly. And they are forbidden to have pistols or muskets, let alone use them."

"Let's wait and see what's in this," said Henri.

There was a significant increase in everyone's pace as they neared the cave, which became almost a rush as they got inside and Simeon laid the package on the stone table. Leaving it there, he opened his robe to take out his purse, which he carefully placed on the floor with the wine in the cool corner of the cave.

"Anyone else have any icons?" he asked.

"Rochefort has mine," said Dorotea. "Or some underling has put them in a box somewhere, I suppose."

"I only have Jashenael, in my chest back at the barracks," answered Agnez.

"Similarly, my ancient icon of Huaravael is in my chamber," said Henri.

"Well, then, we may proceed," said Simeon. Everyone clustered around him as he took scalpel to cord once again, cutting each bond with a small, decisive movement. At the last cord, he put the scalpel down, paused for a moment, then opened his satchel and drew out a pair of wooden tongs.

"Oh come on," urged Henri. "Just get on with it."

Simeon stepped back a little and with his arm almost at full extension, used the tongs to hold the oilskin wrapper, while he cut the last of the cords.

"If this is a treasure, it may be trapped," he said. "Have you read Deflambard's *Oddities and Mechanisms*?"

"No," was the universal reply.

"Deflambard collected cunning mechanisms and the like," said Simeon. "One of them was a spring-loaded ampoule of poison contained within just such a tightly bound package as this one. When the last bond was cut, it would burst and shatter, flinging poison-laden fragments of glass into everyone close by. Stand back and avert your eyes."

He did so himself, as far as he could, before opening the tongs. The package did not suddenly burst open, and there were no fragments of poison glass. Simeon shrugged, and using the tongs, unwrapped the oilskin, revealing another layer beneath.

"Well wrapped against water," he said. "Interesting."

Still using the tongs, he folded back the inner layer, revealing the corners and then the entirety of a small bronze chest, eighteen inches long, ten inches wide, twelve inches high. It was suffering a little from verdigris at the edges. It had a catch, but no lock.

Dorotea lowered her head as if suddenly dizzy, and stepped back, holding on to the table with both hands.

"There is at least one *very* powerful icon inside that chest," she whispered.

Everyone was quiet, utterly enthralled by the small bronze box. Very faintly, in the corner of the cave, there was a sound like a hive of bees. The low buzzing of Simeon's icons in his purse.

He reached out with the tongs again, flipped the catch and lifted the lid.

The chest was completely full of neatly stacked piles of large gold coins.

"Gold," said Henri. "Gold!"

"There is a tremendously powerful icon under the gold," said Dorotea, with certainty.

"Ystaran double dolphins!" exclaimed Henri, taking a coin out and balancing it on his palm. "Worth ninety-six livres each! There must be ten in each stack and twenty-four stacks, sweet mercy that's twenty-three thousand and forty livres—"

He took several more out, weighed them in his hand, and laughed with delight. The gap he made in the stack revealed the corner of a paper, which had been hidden under the top layer of coins.

"What's that?" asked Simeon, pointing.

Heads bumped as they all bent in close to look.

"A letter," said Dorotea.

"We shouldn't touch any of it," said Simeon nervously. "Surely it belongs to someone—"

"Us!" exclaimed Henri, giddy with excitement. He took out more coins, revealing the folded letter beneath. A broken seal was on top, only half of it remaining, showing a portion of a seven-pinioned angel's wings and the top part of a heraldic shield, so cracked and broken it was impossible to identify the blazon.

"Seven pinions, so an Archangel, normally a Cardinal's seal," said Dorotea, pointing to the broken wax. "But it's different . . . there'd be the tines of a crown'd miter there . . . so maybe not . . ."

"We need to inform the appropriate authorities," said Simeon uncomfortably.

"Who would that be?" asked Agnez. "Let's look at the letter first."

"The paper looks old," said Simeon. "It might fall apart. We should leave—"

"It's vellum, not paper," said Dorotea. "And very well preserved."

"It might be important," said Agnez.

They all looked at each other and then at Simeon, who reluctantly nodded to affirm the unspoken agreement.

Dorotea gently lifted the letter out and placed it on the table, before unfolding it. The vellum was in good shape, but the writing on the sheet had faded with age. It was still readable, however that didn't help much.

"It makes no sense," said Dorotea. She began to read aloud: "'Wkh djuhhphqw zdv iru doo wkh lfrqv . . .'"

"A cipher," said Agnez.

"An easy one," said Henri, looking over Dorotea's shoulder. "Let's see . . . it's a three-letter shift."

The others looked at Henri, who shrugged.

"I've always been good with numbers. Let's see . . . can I borrow your charcoal and some paper?"

Dorotea tore off a sheet and handed it to him, with a stick of charcoal. Henri quickly wrote down the alphabet and the corresponding cipher letter. Then, tapping with the charcoal on the letters, he went through the message on the vellum page.

"Very well. It says, 'The agreement was for all the icons. You must deliver the remaining three in person to receive the full payment. Perhaps you are unaware that your sister has joined me? We have left Cadenz; do not go there. Bring the icons to my new temple of Palleniel Exalted, at the twin peak three leagues north of Baranais. Do not fail me again, or attempt to hold anything back. Liliath.'"

"Where is Baranais?" asked Henri. He was answered by a cascade of shrugs. No one knew.

"Liliath again," said Dorotea. "And I am sure there is a very powerful icon there, under the gold."

"Well, let's see," said Henri. He took more coins out, stacking them neatly. When the chest was half-empty, it revealed a thick folded cloth in the middle. Henri hesitated and looked at Simeon.

"I know of no traps or devices that could be contained within a folded cloth of that size," said Simeon.

"Are you sure?" asked Henri.

While he hesitated, Agnez leaned in and folded back the cloth, revealing three rectangular icons linked together by S-shaped golden clasps. They were all the same size, roughly that of a human palm. Engraved by a true master, the gilded bronze plaques were bordered by diamonds mounted in gold. Triple rows of diamonds, large ones on the outside rim, medium-sized ones next, and a myriad of tiny diamonds on the inside.

The angels depicted were basically human but had enormous wings of six pinions, the wings four or five times larger than their bodies. One bore a sword, one a shield, and one a trumpet. The first had a face and hands of jet, the second of red bronze, and the third of yellow jade.

"Yamatriel, Samhazael, Triphiniel," whispered Dorotea. "Three of the Twelve Principalities of Ashalael. Though only Samhazael is an active icon. . . ."

"You know what these are?" asked Simeon. It was a rhetorical question; obviously Dorotea knew. Just as he had recognized them immediately, from a dozen books and references.

"How could I not?"

"What are they?" asked Henri and Agnez together.

"Besides a truly stupendous lot of diamonds!" added Henri gloatingly.

"Three of the Diamond Icons of Queen Anne," said Simeon. "Part of the fabled Queen's Collar."

Agnez shrugged. Henri looked blank.

"Very famous icons," said Dorotea.

"Stolen a century or so ago from the treasure house of the palace," added Simeon. *"Personal property of the Queen."*

"Ah," said Henri, his voice suddenly stripped of the elation that had filled it a moment before, as the prospect of being able to claim this extraordinary wealth disappeared. "Well, maybe there'll be a reward. . . ."

"The Queen must be informed at once," said Agnez. "I'll go . . . no, wait . . . I'd better stay on guard. The Refusers might come back."

"I suppose we do have to tell someone," said Henri slowly. "I mean, about the icons, certainly. But what about the gold?"

"We have to tell them about all of it," said Simeon. "The icons, the gold, the letter. I've already been questioned by the Cardinal's people, and I don't want to repeat . . . actually, the Cardinal will need to know too . . . they both need to be informed. But quietly. The fewer people know about this the better. Particularly that we have anything to do with it."

"But there will be a reward!" protested Henri. "Won't there?"

"I'll guard the chest," said Agnez, ignoring this question. "Henri, you've met Sesturo, haven't you? When you've been taking messages around?"

"The giant Musketeer? I know who he is."

"He should be in our barracks. Go to him, tell him what we've found and ask him to come here, and to send word for Franzonne too; she can carry a message to the Queen directly."

"I suppose I can," said Henri slowly. He was thinking through the potential for rewards, and who might give them. "You know, I'm really the Cardinal's man. I should tell the Monseigneur. Though I'll have to take a boat down to the Cardinal's Palace . . ."

"Who is the Monseigneur?" asked Agnez.

"Robard. Her Eminence's Chief Clerk."

"I can probably get word to the Cardinal faster," said Simeon somewhat uncomfortably. "Rochefort gave me a token after I was questioned. Any Pursuivant I show it to will take word to him at once."

"Why did she give you that?" asked Dorotea.

"Suspicion," replied Simeon heavily. "In general, I think. She told me to report anything odd, like when the Refusers saved me from the beastling. This is definitely odd."

Dorotea nodded and her left eye closed a little, a characteristic indication that she was thinking deeply.

"Refusers again," she said. "Chalconte. Liliath. Refusers. I feel like it must all connect in some way . . . not necessarily in a good way."

"You mean there might not be a reward?" asked Henri plaintively.

"I'm sure there will some kind of a reward," said Agnez impatiently. "From Queen *and* Cardinal. That's good, isn't it?"

"Maybe not," said Dorotea doubtfully.

The others looked at her.

"I am not sure it will be beneficial in my case," she said. "But I daresay it will be impossible to leave me out."

"Why would you want to be left out?" asked Henri.

"Those icons," said Dorotea. "They were made by Chalconte the Heretic. And here I am, suspected of some connection with such things, as they suddenly reappear. And two of them are no longer imbued with power, yet are not destroyed. Which should not be possible. And the letter from Liliath, who I am also suspected of being connected to in some way or another, which no one has deigned to explain to me."

"Maybe we could not mention you . . . ," Henri began, but he was interrupted by Simeon.

"No," said the big doctor. "I told you, we will very likely be put to the question."

"But we haven't done anything wrong!" protested Henri.

"That hasn't stopped the Cardinal putting me in the tower," said Dorotea.

No one spoke for a moment.

"And here I was thinking I was finally going to be rich," said Henri.

"Let's put everything back in the chest," said Simeon. "We admit to looking inside, but as soon as we realized about the icons, we sent word to the Queen and the Cardinal. We don't mention the letter unless directly asked. And there's another thing . . ."

"What?" asked Agnez impatiently.

"The connection we feel," said Simeon. "As if we know each other. Which Dorotea thought was because we had all summoned the same angel a lot. We shouldn't ever mention that, unless we have to."

He looked around at the other three, and they all nodded, very solemnly. It was clear that whatever had drawn them together, it would be looked on with suspicion by the Cardinal at least.

"We may not be able to keep that a secret," said Simeon. "But we must try. I'm off to take word to Rochefort. The longer it takes before they hear, the more suspicious it will seem."

"When you put it like that . . . ," said Henri. "I'll go to Sesturo."

"Tell him to hurry," said Agnez. She drew her sword and went to stand menacingly in the cave mouth, casting dire looks in all directions as Henri hurried past her. Simeon retrieved his purse and followed close at his heels. Behind them, Dorotea rested her chin on her folded hands and cast her mind back to those three astonishing icons, resisting the burning desire to fling the chest open and look at them again.

EIGHTEEN

"I AM TOLD THE STOLEN ITEMS ARE ALMOST CERTAINLY lost," said Liliath, handing the Watch officer a meticulously written parchment. "But if there is even a little chance of their return, I must take it. They belonged to my great-great-great . . . oh a far distant . . . grandmother and so are of great personal value, in addition to their worth in gold and gems."

"A ten-thousand-livre reward!" remarked the lieutenant, a craggy, sallow-faced woman whose dented morion indicated a greater affinity with tavern brawls than solving crimes. "Milady, you will have the entirety of the Lutace Watch scouring every pawnshop, thieves' den, smithy, and jeweler's shop in the city!"

"That is my hope," said Liliath. "The second page details the icons, and the coins too were distinctive, gold double dolphins of Ystara."

"Hmmm, 'three old icons, gilded bronze and gold with diamond edges,'" read the lieutenant. "You do not know the angels depicted? That would help."

"I have not looked at them since I was a child," said Liliath.

"They were not common Alban angels, at least. And I am not a mage."

"Well, the diamonds would make them distinctive," said the lieutenant. "Though they're probably prized out and sold separately by now. So there's those three, and the gold—not much hope of recovering any of that; it'll be melted down, and in any case, old Ystaran coins are not that rare—and then let's see, a set of silver draughts, engraved with the likenesses of Alban queens and athelings, in a sandalwood case. That'll be easy to find, if it shows up for sale. Everything was together, you say?"

"I regret it is my carelessness, Captain," said Liliath. "While most of my valuables went into the strong room upstairs, one small bronze chest and the draughts box were left in a traveling case that was stored in the cellars. I had no idea that these . . . these foul criminals . . . could dig their way in from some sewer!"

"Toshers," said the lieutenant, scowling. "The worst kind of Refusers. Thieves and cutthroats, every woman, man, and child."

She hesitated, then added, "There is a possibility, milady, that a direct approach to the Night King . . ."

"The Night King?"

"Self-styled of course," the lieutenant rushed. "Leader of the criminal gangs. Refusers for the most part. If a reward was offered to him . . . or her . . . via intermediaries we know . . ."

"What?" asked Liliath, drawing herself up in full Alban affront. "Are you suggesting paying the very thieves who stole my prized possessions?"

"Er, no," mumbled the lieutenant.

"I will make the reward twenty thousand livres if the culprits are apprehended and executed . . . provided my possessions are also returned," said Liliath coldly. "You may go."

"Yes, milady," croaked the lieutenant. She bowed low and left, rather discomfited.

Bisc came out from behind the screen, frowning.

"Will this not attract the very attention from the Cardinal you wished to avoid?"

"It will *direct* their attention to an Alban exile," said Liliath. "They will be busy investigating my supposed Alban connections. It will also provide my entrée to the Queen. Which in turn will lay the foundation for the army that will take us back to Ystara."

"If everything works out as you plan," said Bisc.

"If *most* things work out," said Liliath. "Not *everything* has to. Have you heard back from the people who dumped the Worm?"

Bisc frowned.

"Heshino reported a few minutes ago, but the others aren't back yet, which is odd. However, it seems from Heshino's report that the play-acting by the lake went as planned, at least. The four took something from the body into the ornamental cave; it had to be the chest. And then a few minutes later, Dupallidin and MacNeel came out, quickly, and headed for the south gate. They'll be followed from there."

"Hmm. They're both Cardinalists, to some degree," said Liliath. "I expected the Musketeer at least to go to the Queen. It should still serve; I cannot imagine Duplessis would keep word of this from Sofia. But if she does, we can ensure she hears of it.

The King too, we must make sure they all know, and are thus tempted."

"What do we do if things do not go as expected?" asked Bisc. "What if you are arrested? Taken to the Tower?"

"Then you must rescue me, dear Biscaray," said Liliath, drawing him in to lightly kiss his forehead.

Agnez spotted them as soon as they started coming out from under the bridge. First one, then another, until four Refusers had emerged, all of them armed with the hooked tosher poles, gleaming wickedly in the afternoon light. Then two more Refusers came out, clearly prisoners, as they had their hands tied behind their backs. Agnez couldn't be sure but she thought they were the two who had fled that way earlier.

"What?" she muttered to herself.

Another four pole-armed Refusers came out. Pushing the two prisoners ahead, they all started south.

Eight to one was slightly beyond the odds she considered she could handle by herself. Three to one, certainly. Four to one, perhaps. She had two pistols, and could account for two enemies at a distance . . . though they might be similarly armed, given that one earlier had broken the law forbidding Refusers the use of firearms. Two more with her sword, at least—but that still left four, armed with those long, hooked poles that had a long reach . . .

"Dorotea!" she called. "Can you fight?"

"What?" came the answer from inside the cave.

"Can you fight?"

"Have you never seen the scholars of the Belhalle riot?" asked Dorotea, coming out to blink in the sunshine and stand next to Agnez.

"No, and it doesn't answer my question either," said Agnez, still watching the Refusers. They had stopped again, pushed the prisoners down on their knees, deep in the water, and gathered about them in a circle.

"I can fight," said Dorotea. "Though I prefer not to. And I only have my eating knife. I suppose I could gather some stones. I have a good throwing arm, and I am a fair shot with a pistol, if you—"

"I am a *very good* shot, so I'll be keeping these," said Agnez.

The dozen Refusers suddenly hacked at the prisoners with their poles and kicked them underwater, in a frenzied few seconds of killing.

"What . . ." Dorotea began to ask.

Agnez took a breath, readying herself to fight if they came on. But all of a sudden the Refusers stopped their savage chopping, and the twelve of them trooped back under the bridge to disappear from sight, with the last one pausing to spit back at the bodies.

". . . was that about?" continued Dorotea.

"I don't know . . . but it seems they are not intent on recapturing the treasure," said Agnez. "Which is as well, since there were too many of them."

"We can always run away if they come back," said Dorotea. "Even with the chest."

"Musketeers don't run away," said Agnez.

"Should we go and have a look?" asked Dorotea. "See who was killed?"

"No," said Agnez. "Those toshers could be just inside the tunnel, lying in ambush. Best to wait for reinforcements."

"I thought Musketeers don't run away," said Dorotea.

"We don't," answered Agnez. "But we don't have to be stupid about where we attack . . . I can hear a horse."

Dorotea cocked her head, hearing the thud and rumble of hooves on the bare earth where one day turf would be laid, accompanied by the jangle of harness. A few moments later, a single horse and rider came trotting around the side of the artificial hill, a rider splendid in scarlet with a gold sash, a red feather in her hat.

"Rochefort," said Dorotea. She smiled faintly, without realizing she was doing it.

"I'd hoped Sesturo and some Musketeers would get here first," muttered Agnez, lifting her sword and resting the blade on her shoulder. She remembered her daydream when she'd first heard of Rochefort, described as a killer of Musketeers, and that one day she, Agnez Descaray, would bring the Pursuivant to account for her murders. Then there was the way Rochefort had treated Dorotea and Simeon, imprisoning one and taking the other to be questioned.

She settled her face into a harsh mask and stared ahead.

Rochefort reined in just short of the cave mouth, her mount stamping up considerable dust. Dorotea coughed, but Agnez ignored it, standing insouciantly and looking up at Rochefort as if this sudden mounted arriviste might be about to ask directions to a flower seller or the like.

"Doctor MacNeel sent word of a discovery," said Rochefort. Her fierce, cold eyes flicked from Agnez to Dorotea. "Where is he?"

"Not back from sending word," drawled Agnez. "Or so I imagine."

"And the discovery?"

"Within," said Agnez. "As you can see, under the guard of the Queen's Musketeers. Hence, no matter for you."

"Agnez!" hissed Dorotea.

"You are insolent," said Rochefort. "Even for a Musketeer. Though I do not like to play the teacher overmuch, it seems that once again a Musketeer requires a lesson in manners. Am I correct in this assumption?"

Agnez shrugged, very slowly, her eyes insolent.

Rochefort sighed, lifted a leg, and slid off her gelding. She tapped it gently on the neck with two fingers, and it obediently walked on several paces, looked back, and lowered its head to crop one of the sad tufts of grass that emerged here and there by the lakeshore. Rochefort slapped some dust off her breeches, flexed her fingers, and drew her sword.

"I suppose I should ask your name," she said. "For the headstone."

"There's no need for this," said Dorotea indignantly. "We sent messages to both Pursuivants and Musketeers to avoid this sort of thing! Agnez, be civil! Rochefort, surely you cannot want to kill a new cadet—"

"My name is Descaray," said Agnez furiously, ignoring Dorotea. "I cannot imagine a Cardinal's Pursuivant has anything to teach a Queen's Musketeer, certainly not in the matter of manners."

"A Bascon, I take it," drawled Rochefort. "Judging by the boasts and the barnyard stench—"

"I'm a Bascon too!" protested Dorotea, but neither combatant heard her, both moving at the same time. Rochefort's sword flashed out, straight at Agnez's heart. She parried the thrust, immediately riposting to Rochefort's head, but Rochefort dodged aside in a swift, fluid motion and beat the Musketeer's blade down even as she stretched out her long left arm and grabbed the front of Agnez's tabard and pulled her off-balance.

Agnez went with the motion, flying forward. Her tabard came off over her head, taking her hat with it, blinding her for a moment. She had an awful second where she expected to feel the swift, white-hot pain of a deadly thrust in her back. But her movement had carried her far enough to avoid an immediate attack—or Rochefort chose not to make one—and she spun around just in time to parry several ferocious thrusts and slashes, giving ground each time.

But as fast as she backed away, Rochefort closed in. The Pursuivant's blade flicked out, searing a line across Agnez's right arm above the elbow. A cut, not immediately dangerous, as she fought left-handed, but a harbinger of things to come. Agnez's world narrowed with the realization that Rochefort was a better swordswoman and would kill her within the next few passes. But at the same time her mother's advice flashed through her mind for just such a situation, when faced by a superior foe.

"Change the ground, for you can change nothing else."

She parried again and this time did not step back but threw herself to the side, sprinted four steps, and jumped up onto the closest great block of stone, the edge of the artificial hill. From there she leaped up to a higher rock, where she turned and readied herself for Rochefort's next assault, ignoring the trickle of blood that was slowly finding its way down the folds in her sleeve.

The assault didn't come. Rochefort stood glaring up at Agnez, but Dorotea had stepped in front of the Pursuivant, and spread her arms wide.

"That's enough," said Dorotea quietly.

"What is this Musketeer to you?" asked Rochefort, the scar across her eye pale as whitewash, the corner of her mouth twitching in restrained rage.

"A friend," said Dorotea calmly. "I think you kill people too easily, Camille."

Rochefort's sword lowered a fraction.

"How do you know my name? And how dare you call me by it?"

"I asked Mother, in the Tower," said Dorotea. "And you called me Dorotea."

Agnez opened her mouth to call out a taunt, to continue the duel, but shut it decisively as her rather limited store of good sense, assisted by suddenly noticing the pain in her arm, managed to overcome her combative ardor, perhaps for the first time ever. Agnez knew she might defeat Rochefort one day, but she would first have to become even faster and more proficient. She did not doubt this would happen, but she had to stay alive first.

Rochefort did not miss the faint movement of Agnez's mouth, the clack of her closing teeth.

"You wished to say something, Musketeer?"

"No," said Agnez, quite truthfully now. She pointed to her cut. "You have taken first blood, ser. Is that not enough?"

Rochefort shook her head slowly.

"Come see what we have found," said Dorotea. She reached out to take Rochefort's left hand. The Pursuivant began to shake it aside, still looking up at Agnez, but Dorotea just moved her hand back again each time until slowly Rochefort's fingers curled around Dorotea's. A moment later, the Pursuivant looked away from Agnez as if she had forgotten her opponent entirely. She sheathed her sword and allowed Dorotea to lead her toward the cave. They paused outside for a moment, and Dorotea whispered something, and as they entered the cave Rochefort was stripping the icon rings from her fingers.

Agnez sheathed her own sword and sat down on the stone block, resting her head on her arms and panting. She felt like she couldn't get enough air, and her arms and legs were burning, besides the throbbing pain from the sword cut on her arm. The effort to move fast enough simply to avoid Rochefort's attacks, without even managing to return them, had taken more out of her than any practice bout ever.

"Dueling against the edicts!"

Agnez straightened up in a flash and stood at attention. She knew that booming voice.

Sesturo, and even more horribly for Agnez, Franzonne, stood beneath the hill, accompanied by a dozen other Musketeers, with Henri bringing up the rear. Henri waved and looked concerned, but Agnez had eyes only for her two superiors.

"We saw you crossing swords with Rochefort," said Sesturo. "I am very surprised to see you still breathing and merely a little bloody. Who was that youngster who faced Her Eminence's captain down, unarmed?"

"Dorotea Imsel. A Belhalle scholar."

"She is brave," said Franzonne.

"She is," said Agnez. "But I would have managed."

She hopped down from the blocks, and gathered up her hat and tabard.

Franzonne and Sesturo exchanged a glance.

"No, you wouldn't have," said Franzonne. "You have great skill with a blade, Descaray, but it is not yet honed to the necessary perfection to go against such as Rochefort. We will practice more together."

"If you must go kicking hornets' nests," added Sesturo, "you had best be better prepared to deal with hornets."

"She insulted me," said Agnez stiffly. "And the Queen's Musketeers."

"You are of no use to Her Majesty if you're dead. Perhaps be more ready with your wit and less so with your sword," said

Franzonne. "What was it your mother told you?"

"More Truffo, less Humboldt," replied Agnez, her cheeks flushing. It was a reprimand, no matter how gently delivered.

"Good advice," rumbled Sesturo. "Now, this assistant to the Queen's Architect says you . . . and your friends, have found something of great significance. May we see?"

"Of course," said Agnez, doffing her cap and indicating the cave mouth. "Inside, on the table. Property of Her Majesty, long lost."

"So we hear," said Franzonne. "And that being so, I believe more guests are coming to the party to celebrate its retrieval. Let us go in before your cave becomes too crowded."

"You will need to leave any icons you bear by the cave entrance," said Henri. "So they take no scathe from the icon of the Principality within."

Franzonne blinked several times, doffed her hat in thanks to Henri, and gestured with it, indicated a semicircle outside the cave, and then to the body under the horse blanket some distance away.

"Gatesby, take guard here, and let's have Degraben and Hroth stand over that dead Refuser there. No one is to draw close, save the officers. Send them in . . . ah . . . warn them about their icons."

Henri coughed and motioned with his hand, holding it level well above his own head.

"Oh, let the big doctor in too, as one of the discoverers," added Franzonne. She pointed to Agnez's arm. "I daresay he will bind up that scratch of yours."

Agnez looked past the knot of Musketeers. A dozen Cardinal's Pursuivants were approaching, with Simeon's head looming above the hat plume of even the tallest. He saw her and tapped his own arm and held up his bag, indicating that he would indeed attend to her sword cut. He had an eye for even a little blood, she thought, before she looked down and saw that it was not so little. Her sleeve was now dark with it, and there was a bloody handprint on the pale rock where she had pushed herself up.

Behind Simeon, a Pursuivant was chasing Rochefort's horse, which had galloped off as the duel began, and beyond them there was a gaggle of City Watch led by a lieutenant with a dented morion; several King's Guards mingling with a few orange-coated artillerists; a crowd of masons and carpenters in white and blue; and finally a cluster of dismal gray, several dozen Refusers bringing up the rear.

"Word travels quickly," whispered Henri, coming up next to Agnez. "At least when the word is 'treasure.' Whatever made you fight Rochefort? Simeon! Simeon! She's fainting!"

"I am not," said Agnez indignantly, though she had slumped a little against the clerk. "I am just tired."

NINETEEN

"THESE ARE DEFINITELY THE QUEEN'S OWN?" ASKED THE Watch lieutenant, looking down at the icons, which were laid out once again on the table, with serried ranks of coins alongside, and the letter next to them, the chest emptied and checked for secret compartments. "But we have received word of just such diamond-edged icons stolen from an Alban noblewoman, and there is a reward. Tw . . . that is, ten . . . ten thousand livres!"

A surprised rumble went around the cave, cut through by Rochefort's imperious voice.

"An Alban noblewoman? What is her name, and when did you receive this news?"

"Lady Dehiems," said the lieutenant, scratching under her dented helmet. She glanced at Rochefort and then at Simeon, who raised an eyebrow, in remembrance of their last encounter. "She reported the theft this morning. Her great-great-something-grandmother's, she said. These three icons, with the diamonds, and a draughts set—anyone seen that? No? Well, and the gold, that looks all here. She bought Demaselle House from old Lord Demaselle. Her cellar was dug into from the sewers, by toshers, no doubt about that now. That dead one by the lake who had the chest, you know who she was?"

"No," replied Rochefort and Franzonne together.

"Called the Worm," said the lieutenant with a disdainful sniff. "High up in the Night Crew. Maybe she was even the Night King, we've never been sure. And those other two floaters? Night Crew, but not toshers, they were thieves from the Demarten Square gang. You can tell because with real toshers the skin on their legs is always sort of wet, like day-old porridge, kind of crusty and wobbly at the same—"

"Enough!" spat Rochefort.

"I'm simply saying there were two sorts of Refuser criminals present," said the lieutenant. "Who turned on each other. One lot got the loot, the other tried to take it."

"I have not heard of this Alban noblewoman," said Franzonne.

The lieutenant got a faraway look in her eyes.

"She's extraordinarily beautiful, even with a widow's cap pulled down—"

"I am not particularly interested in how she looks," interrupted Franzonne. "Why would I have not heard of her?"

"She's only recently come to Lutace. I asked around. She had a husband back in Alba—much older—who died. Some people there think she murdered him, or hastened him along, and he was a relative of the Atheling. So she had to get out. She's *very* rich as well as beautiful. But I don't understand how she would have these icons, if they belong to the Queen—"

"They were Queen *Anne's*," said Franzonne. "Haven't you

ever heard of the Diamond Icons? The Queen's Collar? Stolen a hundred and thirty-two years ago?"

"No," said the Watch lieutenant stolidly. "Before my time."

"This must all be investigated," said Rochefort impatiently. "I will take the chest and its contents to Her Eminence the Cardinal—"

"It is the Queen's property and must go to the Queen," interrupted Franzonne.

"Two of the icons have somehow become . . . disassociated . . . from their angels, but have not crumbled away or fallen into dust," said Rochefort. "Clearly this is a matter for the temple. And the letter, surely you do not think there are better hands with a cipher than the clerks of Her Eminence's shadow chamber? I will take everything."

"What about the gold at least?" asked the lieutenant. "I should take charge of that and return it to Lady Dehiems."

"For the reward, no doubt," sneered Rochefort. "If the gold even makes it to her without sticking to your fingers. As I said, this must all be investigated. I will take everything."

"You will not," said Franzonne. "The icons are the Queen's property, even if long mislaid."

Rochefort's hand fell to her sword hilt. Franzonne's forefinger delicately rested on the cross guard of her sword, the other three fingers balancing for the swiftest unsheathing. Everyone felt the tension in the cave, which instantly spread to the troops outside, who coalesced into their separate groups, women and men readying weapons.

Sesturo started to laugh, booming laughter that echoing inside the cave sounded a little like cannon fire or thunder.

"Look at us, like dogs over a morsel of mutton," he said. "Let us send word to Her Majesty *and* Her Eminence, seeking orders, and wet our dry throats with that wine I spy in the corner."

Rochefort hesitated before slowly nodding in agreement.

"Very well," she said. She crooked a finger at a Pursuivant, who hurried to her side, bending close as the Captain whispered the message she wanted conveyed to the Cardinal. Franzonne summoned a Musketeer for the same service, to the Queen.

"Are you certain these are the same Diamond Icons that belonged to Queen Anne?" asked the Watch lieutenant plaintively, as Henri poured wine for the officers. Simeon, Agnez, and Dorotea stood as far off to one side as they could, not protesting at the usurpation of their chairs and their cups. They did not need to discuss it to know that keeping as much out of the way as possible was the best course of action.

The Watch lieutenant was clearly having trouble letting go of the reward, which she had already apportioned to herself. "Couldn't they be some other icons that have a lot of diamonds on the edges?"

"They are definitely three of the twelve icons from the Queen's Collar," said Dorotea, stepping forward, even as Simeon clutched at her robe to hold her back and keep quiet. "I am sure of it. Can't you see they are engraved metal, not painted? Besides, Chalconte's work is utterly distinctive, even without the diamonds."

Simeon, watching Rochefort as surreptitiously as he dared,

noticed the Pursuivant's eyes narrow at the mention of Chalconte.

"Ah, the brave scholar," said Franzonne. She walked over to her and bent low over her hand. "We saw you step in front of Rochefort's sword. Few people would do that."

"Really?" asked Dorotea. "It seemed the only thing to do at the time. I didn't want her to kill Agnez. Besides, I wasn't really in danger, as Captain Rochefort is responsible for me, after a fashion."

"What do you mean?"

"I am a guest of the Cardinal," replied Dorotea. "In the Tower."

"Really?" asked Franzonne, with a swift glance at Rochefort. "A Belhalle scholar a prisoner in the Tower? Why?"

"She is not a prisoner," interjected Rochefort. "A guest of Her Eminence. That is why she was free to be wandering about here, with Refuser thieves and . . . the like."

She paused and looked over at the four friends, Dorotea standing a pace in front of the others.

"Though I do wonder what the four of you have in common."

"We are all Bascons, Captain Rochefort," said Simeon quickly. "As you noted previously. We are comforted by familiar voices and talk of our homes."

"Not a conspiracy, then," said Rochefort, her voice silky.

"Four Bascons in a dry cave, with some food and drink," said Franzonne, who was from Bascony herself. She laughed. "That is what we would call a festival back home. Besides, what sort of conspiracy could these four youngsters be involved in, particularly one of them being a Queen's Musketeer?"

"I said 'not a conspiracy,'" remarked Rochefort. But she kept looking at the four of them, her eyes lingering on Dorotea, who seemed oblivious to this gaze, though all the others noticed.

There was an uncomfortable silence for a minute or two. The officers drank slowly, each apparently lost in their own thoughts. Sesturo, though not an officer, always behaved as if he was one. He drank twice as much wine as anyone else. The Musketeers, Pursuivants, and constables of the Watch wandered about outside the cave, speaking only to each other or to order the various spectators who kept arriving to go back to their work.

"I beg your pardons, sers," said Henri, after another few minutes of continuing silence. "The Architect may be wondering . . . that is Ser Dutremblay probably needs my attendance, if I could be allowed—"

"No," said Rochefort.

"You'll be wanted, one way or another," said Sesturo kindly. "Dutremblay knows we're here, and that you are with us. I expect half of Lutace knows by now."

Simeon tried to restrain a frown that sparked at this news.

"Not from my Pursuivants," said Rochefort.

"Nor my Musketeers," said Franzonne. "But word gets around. Take heart, you young people, and be patient. I think both Queen and Cardinal will be well pleased with you, for bringing these treasures home."

Henri looked at Agnez, who now sported a clean white bandage on her arm, and raised his eyebrows, eyes smiling. She gave him a slight nod and glanced over at Simeon, who tilted his head and frowned, not in concern, but as if in deep thought, and then he looked at Dorotea, who was staring at the icons on the table, where they had been laid, leaving the gold in the chest.

"I do wonder how those two icons—"

She stopped suddenly and yelped, as Simeon trod on her foot.

"I beg your pardon, Ser Imsel?" asked Franzonne.

"Nothing," squeaked Dorotea.

"Well," said Sesturo, as silence threatened to descend again. "We have wine. And I'm sure Her Majesty would not begrudge us using these gold coins to play some cards, providing we give them back."

He bent down and pulled a metal box out of the top of his massive boot, opening it to extract a set of well-used playing cards.

"I do not play games," said Rochefort. She got out of her chair and stalked to the cave entrance. "I am going to examine the tunnel under the bridge. Send word when the messengers return."

"Certainly," called out Sesturo. He turned to the Watch lieutenant. "Ser?"

"What game?"

"Whatever you wish, as it will not be with my money," said Sesturo. "Perhaps Triple? Franzonne?"

Franzonne made an acquiescent gesture and poured another cup of wine.

"We will need a fourth . . ."

The big Musketeer looked over at the four friends. No one answered at first, then Henri stepped forward reluctantly, as if being dragged by some unseen force.

"I play," said Henri. "A bit."

"Join us, then," said Sesturo.

Henri sat down, and Sesturo dealt each of the players five cards, while the Watch lieutenant began to count out a dozen coins each from the piles on the table. It seemed to grieve her to part with them. She counted very slowly, and her fingers lingered on every single coin as she set them down.

"Eight," she said, placing a coin in front of Franzonne. "Nine . . . ten . . ."

"May I look at the icons again?" asked Dorotea.

"Please do," replied Franzonne, taking up her cards. Her natural authority made her the person everyone looked to as Dorotea asked the question.

The Musketeer sighed as she ran her eyes over the hand she'd been dealt. "I am sure Her Majesty . . . and Her Eminence will welcome any insights you may have. Perhaps you might also enlighten me as to why you are a 'guest' of the Cardinal?"

"I demonstrated a technique of sketching icons, which is swift, though unreliable," replied Dorotea, peering very closely at the central icon, marveling at the detail of the work, finer than seemed possible even with the sharpest burin and the best enlarging glass. Close to, she saw that the angel Samhazael was depicted as a winged woman made entirely of smoke, built up in tiny whorls and eddies no larger than grains of sand.

"I thought I was the first to do this sketching, but apparently Chalconte preceded me, and the Cardinal seems to think that it must lead to making statues and heresy. Oh, and the Maid of

Ellanda sketched icons too, apparently, and maybe she was also a heretic, though I'm not very clear on that or why the Cardinal is worried about someone so long dead."

"Ah, I know what that's about," said the Watch lieutenant with a sour smile. "The Cardinal's always been on the lookout for *that*, we get asked about it regular, we do, being as we have the most to do with the Night Crew, that is, those Refusers who get up to no good. Professionally, as it were."

"Asked about what?"

"The Maid of Ellanda!" exclaimed the lieutenant. She scowled at her cards and rearranged them and then sorted them back into the original order again. "Lots of Refusers believe she's going to be reborn or return or something and improve their lot, that after she led them all out of Ystara she said 'I'll be back, just wait' or something similar, and then she vanished."

"And?" asked Sesturo.

"And so just in case there's something to it, and the Refusers run wild or revolt, we're supposed to report any signs," said the lieutenant. "Of course, not knowing what those signs would be makes it difficult. But if someone starts doing the same magic that Liliath used to do, then maybe she's the Maid reborn, you see what I'm saying?"

"But that's stupid!" exclaimed Dorotea. "I am myself, not some Ystaran savior born again, even if that were possible! And I'm not going to go mad like Chalconte either!"

"I believe you," said the lieutenant. "But I bet that's why you're in the Tower. Liliath."

She cackled and rearranged her cards again.

"It is ridiculous," repeated Dorotea, quite crossly. "I am Dorotea Imsel, none other."

"We have no doubt of that ourselves," soothed Franzonne. She laid three cards down and said, "The flower, the branch, and the tree, a set of three."

"River, bridge, road," said Sesturo immediately, placing three cards of his own. "A superior set."

"I have nothing," said the Watch lieutenant. "I risk no coin." She put her cards back under the remaining deck.

The two Musketeers each picked up three new cards and looked at Henri, who rearranged his hand, sucked his lower lip, and scratched his head in an ostentatious fashion.

"I have a sinking feeling," said Franzonne. "No one who is such a bad actor can also be bad at cards."

"A bee on your flower, a coach on your road, and the sun and the moon *and* the sky," said Henri, placing all his cards down. "Both your sets surmounted and an overarching set, so the bet doubled. My game, sers."

"Bah!" exclaimed Sesturo, throwing his remaining cards in. Franzonne laid her cards down more gently and slid two coins from her pile over to Henri. Sesturo did likewise with one huge finger.

The deal moved to the Watch lieutenant, and they played several more rounds of Triple, the gold coins moving back and forth, but mostly ending up in front of Henri.

At last, the messengers came back, walking together, as had

perhaps been arranged before they left. Rochefort appeared too, boots dripping from wading in the lake, and arranged her tall self against one wall.

"Well?" asked Franzonne.

"The objects are to be taken to the Queen's Palace," said the Musketeer messenger. "Her Majesty wishes to see them at once."

"The Cardinal will be there," added the Pursuivant, with a glance at Rochefort. "Her Eminence also wishes to speak with the four who retrieved this treasure."

"As does Her Majesty," said the Musketeer. "The treasure and the four are to be brought to the Orangery. Captain Dartagnan said to bring the four in via the maze garden door, the treasure by the sally port on the northern wall."

"The Alban noblewoman—Lady Dehiems—has also been summoned," said the Pursuivant. "And the bodies are to be taken to the Infirmary for a complete examination. Anything material found upon them is to be sent to Captain Dartagnan at the Queen's Palace."

"They had nothing," said the Watch lieutenant. "I told you, those other two weren't even toshers. I reckon they'd already been robbed by the toshers who offed them."

"The commotion last night, in the gravel pits beyond the city, involved Refusers fighting each other, though there had to be a mage there as well, since a beastling was made," said Rochefort. She looked at Dorotea and then away again, her face unmoving. "Some of the Refusers have been behaving strangely of late. I think solving this puzzle may be assisted by arresting known members of the Night Crew to see what they know."

"Always happy to help Her Eminence's Pursuivants," said the Watch lieutenant sourly, seeing a great deal of extra work ahead.

"What puzzle?" asked Dorotea. "I really am not part of any puzzle or conspiracy. And I am definitely not the Maid of Ellanda reborn."

"Ah," said Rochefort. "Who told you that?"

"It doesn't matter," said Dorotea. "Except that I think it is a very stupid reason to put someone in prison."

"Something troubles Ashalael, and in turn Her Eminence is disturbed, and we must look into all possibilities," said Rochefort. She hesitated, then added quietly, "As you know, if it were up to me, you would be released."

Neither Rochefort nor Dorotea noticed that everyone else was very interested in their conversation while pretending not to be. As Rochefort stopped talking, Sesturo packed away his cards, making a big production of it.

"Pack up the coins, Dupallidin," instructed Franzonne. She looked at the Watch lieutenant. "We had forty-eight out, as I recall."

"Yes, ser," replied Henri. He glanced at the pile, and added, "Forty-eight. Though there are only forty-seven on the table."

"You seem very adept with numbers," rumbled Sesturo. "I suspect a coin may have fallen on the floor near our friend from the Watch. There."

Henri bent down and picked up the errant coin, which was right next to the lieutenant's boot and, in fact, a moment before might have been under it. He put it with the others, then transferred them all to the chest. Dorotea put the Diamond Icons back on top, handling them very cautiously, with fingertips.

The letter was left on the table.

Rochefort leaned in and picked it up. All of a sudden the four friends tried to look elsewhere, realized this seemed suspicious, and looked back again. All of which looked even more suspicious.

Rochefort either didn't notice or paid their strangled movements no heed. She put the letter on top of the icons, shut the chest, and closed the catch. Then she straightened up and looked at Franzonne.

"I do not care to look ridiculous and have both of us carry something so small but heavy," she said. "Will you allow one of my Pursuivants to bear it hence?"

"No," said Franzonne. "But I understand our large and powerful doctor here carried it from the lake. Would it be agreeable if he were to carry it out? Neither Pursuivant nor Musketeer?"

"Very well," said Rochefort, with a sharp, forestalling look at the Watch lieutenant whose mouth hung open, doubtless a moment before offering to carry the chest herself. "I have ordered two coaches brought to the south gate here, such as it is. I do not understand the ways of architects, to build one thing here, and another there, and the joining of them happens years later or perhaps never. Gates and chimneys, and no walls yet!"

She shook her head and came back to the matter at hand.

"I suggest you and I, Franzonne, and two of our people each travel in the first, with the chest, and these four in the second?"

"If Sesturo may go with them, certainly."

"And my Depernon."

Franzonne smiled and inclined her head in acquiescence.

"That is settled, then," said Rochefort. She paused and added, "I do not believe any Refusers or others will be bold enough to try and seize the treasure, but we had best be on guard."

"I ordered a troop to mount and be ready to accompany us, also at the southern gate," said Franzonne. "I believe that will suffice to discourage any number of . . . er . . . toshers and the like."

"As it happens, I also have a troop waiting there," said Rochefort, her mouth quirking in the faintest of smiles.

"I could get a troop of ours from the barracks," said the Watch lieutenant. "It would take only an hour or—"

"We leave at once," said Rochefort.

"Yes," agreed Franzonne. "The sooner we have this chest safely in the palace, the better. Let us be away!"

TWENTY

THE QUEEN'S PALACE WAS A CLUSTER OF LARGE BUILDINGS of greatly differing antiquity, six hundred years between the first and the last built, connected by a veritable warren of lesser buildings of even greater variation in style, with every construction within the overall palace being executed in a different architectural mode or fashion according to the whims of whichever sovereign ordered their establishment, sometimes tempered by defensive concerns, usually about the Lutacian mob rather than external enemies.

There were dozens of different entrances to the palace, some direct from the surrounding streets or the river, into outbuildings or cloisters. For the most part, people came and went through the eastern gate, where supplicants of suitable rank were admitted into the large outer courtyard, there to while away their days playing bowls, reading, drinking, eating, and always talking, talking, talking in the hope of gaining deeper entry into the palace, there to petition for some sinecure, post, or decision from one of the Queen's ministers or even the Queen herself.

There was little conversation in the coach as it rumbled through the cobbled streets of Lutace, Musketeer and Pursuivant outriders clearing the crowds so that a steady speed could be maintained, even over the bridges. The four friends wanted to talk, it was clear, from the way they looked at each other and mouths opened and tongues moved, only to close and become still again, as eyes flickered across Sesturo and the Pursuivant Depernon.

As they neared the Queen's Palace, the coach ahead with Rochefort, Franzonne, and the treasure turned to follow Sawyers Avenue to the north of the palace, with the Musketeer and Pursuivant troops going with it.

So close to the palace, it was presumed to be safe. Only two outriders remained with the second coach, which rumbled on along the river promenade. Sesturo opened the door to hang outside, surveying the scene ahead, as best he could. The sun had begun to wend its way below the horizon as they left the New Palace grounds and now had set. The coach's four lanterns, one at each corner, supplied a narrow glow about the vehicle, and the street ahead was dark, save for a single torch high in a cresset on the tall, windowless wall that ran along the right-hand side of the street for several hundred paces, a testament to one of those periods where caution had overcome some past queen's desire for an open terrace by the river.

The wall acted as a barrier to waterborne malcontents or rebels, but also to the fog that typically rose from the river as the year began to cool toward winter. It was rising now, wisps of mist rolling across the road and roiling in eddies up against the mellow brick of the wall. The fog was a harbinger of the change of season. Soon the autumn rains would come, colder and heavier than the brief summer showers.

For now, the fog made the street darker and Sesturo's eyes narrowed as he saw a cluster of shapes around the single door in the wall, more than a score of them. But as the coach drew closer, he relaxed and swung back in to sit down.

"The Captain's using us as a decoy from the treasure. She's spread the word to the favor-seeking witlings who infest the courtyard. They think anyone who's ever let inside out of the ordinary way must be important. Pull your hats down . . . or yes, cap . . . Scholar Imsel . . . don't let them get a good look at you, give you anything or hold you back. Go straight inside."

"I stay with the coach," said the melancholy Depernon.

"And I will take the part of rear guard," said Sesturo, flexing his huge, gauntleted hands. "I always enjoy throwing these would-be courtiers around, and some are bound to try to follow."

They heard the coachman bellowing something, and shouts from the outriders, followed by answering cries, people calling out, asking who was in the coach, screeching demands and calling out requests, insisting they should be admitted too, or their letters taken, along with other more incomprehensible pleas.

The coachman shouted again, and the coach rumbled to a stop; Depernon threw open the door and jumped out, surprising everyone by shouting in a very loud and penetrating voice, "Cardinal's business! Make way!"

Agnez was the first to follow the Pursuivant, fending off an attempt by Simeon to help her. Her wound was only a scratch after all, and she had almost forgotten it.

Though the outriders had turned their horses to create a narrow lane between coach and the door in the high wall, and were laying about them readily with their riding crops, the bolder and less socially elevated supplicants were sliding in, even crawling between the horses' legs, calling out and trying to clutch at Agnez's boots. She kicked one aside and hastened to the door, which Depernon was holding half open.

The others followed, pell-mell, with Sesturo behind them, a dozen eager courtiers at his heels. He turned in the doorway, bellowing. His bearlike silhouette in the doorway proved sufficient to dissuade the unwanted followers. The portal was slammed shut behind him and the bar lowered.

"What is this place?" asked Henri, looking around. They stood close together in a tiny exterior courtyard. Enormously tall box hedges grew up on all sides. In the dark it was impossible to see if there was any gap or way through them.

"The Hedge Maze," said Sesturo. He turned to one of the Musketeers who'd been inside and opened the door, and peered closely at him. "Deranagh, isn't it? She'll lead us through."

"I won't," chuckled the Musketeer. "But Errastiel will, I trust."

She touched an icon in her hatband and muttered something, and there was a faint bell-like sound, clear and impossibly distant. A tiny blue light appeared floating in the air in front of the Musketeer. Deranagh muttered something again, and the spark flitted toward a hedge.

"Well, off you go," said the Musketeer. "Errastiel never lingers very long."

Sesturo led the way, finding a gap in the hedge that wasn't visible until he was very close. Even in daylight it would be hard to see, the way the hedges grew together. He also had to crouch low, as did Simeon, though all the others merely had to duck.

Dorotea was last, and she paused to talk to the Musketeer.

"I do not know Errastiel," said Dorotea. "What is her scope?"

"Finding paths," said the Musketeer. "Or showing them. Don't fall behind, ser!"

"Oh yes . . . ," said Dorotea. She looked around but saw neither the glowing mote of the angel nor any mortal silhouette, until Henri stuck his head back out through the gap in the hedge wall.

"Come on!" he urged. "If we get lost we'll be here until morning at least!"

The pathways through the maze were very close, and there were many sudden turnings. Sesturo—an almost disembodied voice already several turns ahead—encouraged them to hold on to each other and for whoever was behind him to grab his belt.

At last, they emerged from the maze into a larger courtyard in between two of the main palace buildings, the Old Palace and the Orangery, their destination that night. The Orangery was only sixty-three years old, its thick redbrick walls and tall windows of angel-clarified glass very much in contrast to the centuries-old stone of the original palace.

Sesturo led them not to the ornate, gilded main doors but around the corner and then along the side of the building, which had no windows, the wall there extra thick to keep the heat in. Halfway along, some 120 paces, they came to a very ordinary door. Sesturo rapped on it, a complicated and secret knock. A moment later a peephole opened, his face was scrutinized, the well-oiled door silently opened, and they were admitted into the Orangery.

The interior of the vast building was all one open space, somewhat intruded upon by the arches at regular intervals to support the roof, which had alternating panels of plastered timber and glass, again of angel-assisted clarity and construction. Huge oil lamps of bronze and more angel glass were suspended on chains from the ceiling, and the southern wall they had come along was dominated by six enormous fireplaces, one every forty paces. Each of these great hearths was attended by six Refusers, who fed heavy lengths of some dark, hard wood—which was stacked in neat pyramids nearby—into these furnaces. The Refusers wore the usual ash-colored clothing, but with the addition of yellow ribbons on their sleeves, an indication they served the royal family and were more trusted than most.

Thanks to the roaring fires, it was very warm inside, particularly after the damp, foggy air outside. The heat was necessary for the orange, lemon, lime, and citron trees that ran very close together. Twenty rows of trees, for the length of the Orangery, with a small central plaza and gazebo in the very middle of the building, which contained a platform and throne for the Queen.

Only the gilded ceiling of the gazebo could be seen by the visitors, but a low susurrus of conversation could be heard through the lines of trees. Sesturo exchanged a few quiet words with the two Musketeers guarding the side door, who quickly and politely searched the party to ensure they had no gunpowder weapons, save Agnez's pistols, who as a Musketeer could be trusted.

That done, Sesturo gestured to the others to follow and led them along one of the corridors between the rows of trees, toward the gazebo but parallel with it, separated by three lines of lime trees.

They were about fifty paces away when there was a sudden blast of trumpets, sounding a fanfare of five notes. Sesturo grimaced and stopped, holding his hand up to indicate a halt.

"What's happening?" whispered Agnez, who was closest. The others gathered around to hear Sesturo's reply.

"The King," he said. "He must have got word about the treasure. Her Majesty will be furious. She won't want you to be seen by him."

"Can we go closer?" asked Henri. "I've never seen the King. Or the Queen, for that matter."

"Neither have I," added Simeon. "And I wouldn't have minded if it stayed that way."

"You have some wisdom, Doctor," chuckled Sesturo. "Too late though. You've attracted the eyes of all the mighty now. Follow me, but stay quiet!"

He led off again, at a much slower pace, crossing several rows at the next gap, drawing closer to the gazebo. The trees here were all oranges and carried a heavy load of ripening fruit, whereas the ones they'd passed earlier were either just in bud or had only young, green fruit beginning.

At the next open intersection of tree rows, there were two

Musketeers on guard who turned quickly as Sesturo approached, swords coming several inches out of scabbards. They relaxed as they saw him, and once again there was a whispered conversation before they moved on again.

"I'll be on duty here soon," whispered Agnez to Henri. "A few weeks, at most. And in a year, I will no longer be a cadet."

Henri nodded and smiled. Though he was not as pessimistic as Simeon, or perhaps Dorotea—though it was hard to tell what Dorotea actually thought—he wasn't entirely sure their newfound attention from the high and mighty would work out as well as they hoped. A year hence they might all be in the Tower. Or worse . . .

Sesturo led them to the last line of trees before the paved square around the gazebo and stopped again, gesturing for them to come close. They could hear the muffled voices of the courtiers around the throne now, and though the trees were so close together they almost formed a hedge, they caught glimpses of them, and the throne gazebo.

"We sneak from here," he whispered, and pointed. "You see that particularly tall tree, directly behind the gazebo, with the very large oranges on it?"

The others nodded, while showing varying degrees of puzzlement, as the oranges were at least twice the size of any others they had ever seen. . . .

"Magic, I suppose," muttered Agnez.

"No," replied Sesturo. "Artifice. They are a gold and copper. That is the first tree placed here, by Queen Louise the Sixth's own hands. Stay behind that tree and wait to be summoned."

"Where are you going?" asked Henri.

"To report to the Captain," replied Sesturo. He pointed through a small gap in the greenery. "She's standing slightly behind the Queen, on her left, as she usually does. See?"

Everyone crowded to look, almost bumping heads, and there was a good-natured moment of silent jostling before an unspoken agreement to take turns eventuated, Henri looking first.

Through the palm-sized gap in the foliage, he could see most of the gazebo. The throne in the middle was not particularly grandiose, more of a high-backed chair, though it was gilded and the cushion was purple velvet fringed with gold. Queen Sofia XIII was leaning back on it, her head tilted to one side, listening to an older woman with a crimson-painted face under a golden cap, wearing long scarlet robes trimmed with ermine, who Henri immediately recognized as Cardinal Duplessis. It was easier to look at her from a distance than when he'd been presented to her. He didn't feel such an urge to stare at the ground. The Cardinal wasn't wearing the icon of Ashalael; he supposed it would cause too much trouble with the lesser icons of those nearby.

The Queen herself was a bit of a disappointment for Henri at least. She was much shorter than the Cardinal, and wore a long, very thick and curly black wig tied with dozens of small gold ribbons, which obscured most of her face. The wig was topped by a small, low crown of gold and emeralds, which was secured with a very narrow jeweled blade rather than a hatpin.

She wasn't wearing a state dress—for the last century women

of noble birth only wore dresses for balls and the like—instead conforming to the current fashion for idealized hunting clothes, in her case a white linen shirt, a doublet of eggshell blue doeskin, with a low ruffled collar and cuffs of golden lace, and in imitation of hunting leathers, breeches of dark linen, which were decoratively laced at the side with golden laces. Her boots were highly polished burgundy, thigh-high, with the tops rolled back below the knees. Her sword leaned against the throne, a straight court sword so heavily encrusted with gems it would be difficult to wield, but the sharp-eyed might notice the scabbard was lined with four small icons, so its purpose was likely more for angelic magic than any mundane combat, though Queen Sofia was not particularly known as a mage.

From the little Henri could see of her face under the wig, she looked quite ordinary, but with a sharpish nose. Her skin was brown, quite dark, and very smooth, but he thought it was probably paint, like the Cardinal's crimson. Her hands were gloved, the gloves set with many small jewels.

On the Queen's left side, Captain Dartagnan stood in a pose of relaxed attention, though her slightly hooded eyes watched the courtiers around the gazebo. Though in her late forties, she was lean and wiry, her hand resting on the hilt of a well-worn sword, a pale scar across the back stark against her deep olive skin. Unlike the Queen's, the sword was entirely without adornment. Her tabard, jerkin, and breeches were the standard Musketeer outfit of black and silver, but the golden sash of her office was not worn over her shoulder as usual but simply wound around her waist, only the knot at the side visible through the slit in the tabard. She wore no icon rings, brooches, or anything else that might be an icon. Being in the presence of the Queen and not being a royal duke like Duplessis, she wore no hat, her razored-short hair as silver as the embroidery of her tabard, her skin as dark as the cloth.

All in all, she looked like an elder crow caught up in a flock of gaudy parrots.

There were only the three of them on the platform of the gazebo; no one else stood near the Queen. Henri shifted a little, trying to see the audience in front, but the angle was wrong.

"My turn," whispered Simeon. Reluctantly, Henri moved aside, and after Simeon had looked, the others each took their turn to gaze at their Queen, the Cardinal, and the Captain-General of Musketeers.

"I wonder what she really looks like," muttered Dorotea.

"Who?" asked Simeon.

"The Queen. I mean, under that wig?"

"Look at a coin," said Henri. "Livre piece, or a gold royal."

"They both use an old portrait," whispered Dorotea. "At least a decade gone. Besides, Depuisne was known for his flattering engravings."

"Who?" asked Agnez.

"Depuisne," said Dorotea. "The Queen's Iconer and Coiner. Not now, Delisieux has the office now."

"How do you know these things?" questioned Agnez.

"How could I not? I presume you know things to do with . . . soldiering and suchlike."

"Why's she wearing a wig anyway?" asked Simeon.

"I suppose her hair's gone gray," answered Dorotea. "Though there are several angels who could fix that. . . . Maybe she just likes wigs?"

"Quiet!" whispered Henri, as loudly as he dared. He was back looking through the gap. "The King's coming up."

There was another minor tussle, but Henri did not give up his spot. However, Simeon, by dint of pushing a branch down, managed to make the gap large enough for all four of them to see, if he looked over the top of Henri's head, Dorotea rested her chin on Henri's shoulder, and Agnez craned in from the side.

"He is quite handsome," remarked Dorotea. "That two-livre piece coined for their wedding doesn't entirely lie. . . ."

The King was a prince of the Eighty-Six Kingdoms, five years the Queen's junior, and known for his love of luxury and diversions. Despite the dissolute lifestyle he had maintained for a dozen years of marriage, he had kept the figure and looks that had been partly responsible for his selection by the then Princess Sofia, though he had long since lost her affection. He was of a height with the Queen and so not tall, his tightly curled hair was still entirely black, and his clear skin shone like the polished ebony of someone years younger. He didn't need to use any face paint.

He too was dressed for the hunt, but in his cloth-of-gold coat with jangling moonstone buttons, double-layered breeches cut in slits to show black and gold, and with black leather boots topped with wound gold wire, he looked more like a very expensive jongleur than a hunter, an impression enhanced by the entirely ornamental gittern on his back, the strap also gold. He played badly and sung flat, but he greatly enjoyed music. Like the Queen, he was not much of a mage, and he wore only one icon ring.

The courtiers stopped talking as the King approached the gazebo and bowed elegantly before the Queen. She turned away from the Cardinal to look at him, and despite the shadow of her great wig somewhat concealing it, the expression on her face was clear. She was not pleased to see him.

"An unexpected visit, Ferdinand. How have you torn yourself away from the opening night of Lamarina's *Three Shepherds of Yore*?"

The King bowed again, doffing his hat, which unfortunately matched his boots, being black leather wound with gold wire, the feather in it a clever construction of gold foil.

"I heard word of a remarkable discovery, Your Majesty," he said loudly. "And wished to congratulate you at once on the recovery of a treasure of state, worth, I am told, many millions of livres."

The Queen did not immediately answer, just staring at him, her slightly bulbous eyes fierce. Her nose in this mood had something of the manner of a sharp-pointed arrow, about to be loosed. The King shifted like a schoolboy caught asking for honey on his morning bread, when there was little chance even of butter.

"He's after money," whispered Henri. "I heard he's in debt everywhere. One of his people even came to the Architect to try and get something from him, had a story about giving up his planned apartments in the New Palace, in return for a payment now. Only he would take the money and not give up the apartments, of course."

"I don't know how the Queen puts up with him," said Agnez judgmentally. "I mean, what does he even do?"

"Since they had the two heirs, you mean?" asked Simeon.

"No, I didn't mean *that*. . . . Never mind," said Agnez.

The Queen leaned across to Dartagnan and whispered something. The Captain-General nodded, then stepped forward and raised her hand. Though it had been fairly quiet, save for muttering, it now became entirely silent.

"Her Majesty desires to be alone," announced Dartagnan.

Immediately there was a shuffling and the muttering resumed. Out of sight of the four peering through the trees, the courtiers started to move away, footsteps sounding on the paved walkways between the rows of oranges.

Being alone meant something different for queens than normal people, Henri concluded, seeing that the Cardinal, Dartagnan, and the King remained, as did a number of servants and Musketeers he could see arranged around the back and sides of the gazebo. Including Sesturo, who crept up as best a giant could, to whisper to Dartagnan, who looked over to where the four friends were watching. But the Captain of Musketeers gave no sign she could see them, or wanted them to do anything.

The Cardinal also turned her head, and though she probably couldn't see them, the four friends all ducked as one.

"Should we leave too?" whispered Simeon.

"No," said Agnez. "Sesturo ordered us to stay until told otherwise."

"Where's Franzonne and Rochefort with the chest?" asked Henri.

"They're probably here too," replied Agnez. "On the other side of the gazebo, waiting like us."

"I used to like oranges," said Simeon mournfully. "I wish we were all somewhere else."

"It's better than the Tower," said Dorotea.

There could be no reply to that.

"So where is this newfound treasure?" asked the King, stroking his mustache and looking around as if someone was about to put it in front of him.

The Queen grew even more cross.

"I said I wished to be alone!"

"Oh, yes, best to wait until all that lot are out of sight," the King said, with supreme self-confidence, waving his heavily ringed hand at the retreating courtiers. "Vultures!"

The Queen sighed, very audibly, and beckoned to Dartagnan again, who leaned in, nodding at some instruction. She backed away and in turn spoke to Sesturo, who left the gazebo and disappeared among the oranges on the far side, emerging shortly after with Rochefort and Franzonne, a Pursuivant and a Musketeer following them, carrying the bronze chest.

"Looks heavy!" remarked the King, with some satisfaction.

TWENTY-ONE

ROCHEFORT AND FRANZONNE APPROACHED THE GAZEBO and bowed low, before stepping aside to let the Pursuivant and Musketeer who were now carrying the chest bring it all the way up to the foot of the Queen's throne. They put it down at her feet and retreated, stepping backward, their heads bowed. The King sidled forward, rubbing his hands together, but stopped as he caught the Queen's piercing eye.

"Open it, please, Dartagnan," said the Queen quietly.

Dartagnan knelt and opened the chest. The Queen leaned forward and looked down. The Cardinal took a step forward too and inclined her head.

Dartagnan lifted out the icons and held them up to the Queen as if she was presenting a plate at a feast.

"These are indeed three of the twelve Diamond Icons, Cardinal?"

"They are, Your Majesty," replied the Cardinal. "I took the liberty of examining them before they were brought in. The letter in the chest also confirms this. But I had no doubts as soon as I saw the icons."

"But you said the letter was enciphered?"

"A very simple cipher," replied the Cardinal. "I read it easily."

Henri sniffed, fortunately not loudly enough for anyone beyond the orange trees that sheltered him to hear.

"Though I have sent a copy to my Shadow Chamber, in case there is some additional layer of meaning, as is sometimes done," continued the Cardinal. "The simple hiding the complex."

"Didn't think of that, did you?" whispered Agnez, digging her elbow sharply into Henri's rib. As it was her wounded arm, both of them stifled cries of pain.

"My, are those Ystaran double dolphins?" asked the King greedily. He had sidled up close and was leaning on the edge of the gazebo. "What's this about a letter?"

The Cardinal glanced at the Queen, who nodded slightly, indicating that the King's question should be answered.

"The letter appears to be addressed to the thief who stole the icons from Her Majesty's glorious ancestor, Queen Anne," replied the Cardinal. "It seems she or he delivered nine of the twelve Diamond Icons but retained the three you see here. The person who had commissioned the theft required the remaining icons to be handed over as well."

"I see," said the King. As always when money was concerned, he got straight to the heart of the matter. "Does this letter state where the other nine Diamond . . . mmmm . . . Icons are? Or more gold?"

The Queen shook her head, very slightly. The King didn't notice, his eyes firmly fastened on the Diamond Icons and the gold.

"This is a matter that must be looked into," said the Cardinal smoothly. "Of significantly greater importance is the fact that two of the icons, very powerful icons for Principalities of Ashalael's host, have become defunct without being destroyed."

"That is indeed of paramount concern," said the Queen. "A grave matter of state we must discuss. You may leave us, Ferdinand."

"Of course, Your Majesty," said the King. He hesitated and pointed at the chest. "Perhaps I might have one of those double dolphins as a keepsake? It is a long time since I have seen . . . held . . . such a wonderful coin."

The Queen sighed and looked to one of her servants standing by the Musketeers over to one side of the gazebo.

"Deruyter, transfer half the gold from the chest to a . . . a purse or bag . . . for His Highness."

"Ah! You are too good to me, Your Majesty!" cried the King. "You know how I delight in fine gold coins."

"I bet he delights in fine gold anything," muttered Henri to the others. It hurt to see the gold he had briefly thought of his own going to anyone, let alone to the wastrel King.

"Quiet," whispered Agnez.

Deruyter, clearly a high-ranking servant from his extravagantly ruffed doublet and long silk stockings gartered in gold and blue, gestured to a lower servant, who gestured to a lower one still, who took off her cloak, fashioned it into a bag by tying knots in the corner, and approached at a crouch to the chest, where she quickly transferred half the contents. The King took it from her with great delight, smoothed his mustache, bowed a little, and strode off.

The Queen looked at the retreating figure of the King with a slightly melancholy gaze. He was still a fine figure of a man, if not much else.

"So, what is to be done with these icons?"

"I would like to take the two that have become quiescent to be studied with my people and the Belhalle magisters," said the Cardinal. "The icon of Samhazael, which remains puissant, should of course go to Your Majesty's treasure house."

"And the gold? I have just remembered that perhaps by rights it belongs to the Alban woman you mentioned."

"That is to be looked into," said the Cardinal. "I am curious how she came to have the icons. Perhaps she is descended from the thief."

"So she may know who has the other icons, or where they are?" asked the Queen, looking directly at the Cardinal. "With other treasure, as Ferdinand suspects . . . nay hopes!"

"The letter has something to say on that," said the Cardinal. She looked around and lowered her voice, this time to a whisper that could not be heard beyond the gazebo. Whatever it was, it made the Queen sit up, and her reply was not in a whisper.

"In Ystara? Not far from the border?"

The Cardinal whispered again, and the Queen lowered her voice. They conversed quickly for a minute or two, completely unaware of the burning curiosity of all around the gazebo, particularly among the four hidden in the fruit trees.

While they were whispering, a Musketeer came up and passed a message to Sesturo. The big man nodded and in turn went to Dartagnan, who listened for a moment, then passed whatever had been said to the Queen. She nodded, said a few more words to the Cardinal, then raised her hand and sat up straight on the throne again.

"Bring Lady Dehiems in," she ordered.

Liliath dressed demurely for the audience with the Queen. She'd been expecting the summons and so took little time to prepare when the Musketeer and the Pursuivant came with a message ordering her attendance at the Queen's Palace. To reinforce her Alban persona, she followed the fashion for faux hunting clothes but in a restrained way, choosing a linen shirt under a primrose yellow jerkin that was dotted with dull iron studs shaped like flower petals in a playful version of a brigantine; breeches of the peculiar checkered cloth of the Alban north, in yellow, green, and black; and hunting boots of soft doeskin, which wouldn't last two hours in an actual hunt, with a single silver spur on her left heel. A jeweled belt and a broad-brimmed hat of yellow felt with a ruby pin completed the ensemble.

She wore no visible icons anywhere on her person, to cement the notion that she was not a mage at all, though she had three on a bracelet hidden under her sleeve. None very powerful, but all useful, for someone who fully knew their scope.

Bisc arrived via the private door as she finished dressing.

"It *was* toshers who killed Wilbe and Raoul," he said. "Still loyal to the Worm, curse them. They followed them in from the river."

"Fortunately Wilbe and the others completed their task before being so careless as to get killed," said Liliath, picking up a pair of gloves. "I would have been most . . . unhappy . . . if my plans had gone awry from such negligence. Fortunately, I have been summoned to the Queen . . . and Cardinal."

"Yes, with only one Musketeer and one Pursuivant to guard you!" exclaimed Bisc. "The Worm's people are still fighting us! If any of them recognize you as Biscaray's Serpent . . . they have ways of moving through the sewers under the city, an ambuscade, you might be shot from hiding—"

"It is very unlikely they will be able to connect Biscaray's Serpent with Lady Dehiems . . . ," Liliath began, stopping as she saw Bisc's face. "What?"

"Hogman. The stooped fellow who was with us at Nep Cross. He was captured some hours ago. He isn't strong; he will have talked. He knows you—Dehiems—are the Serpent."

Liliath snarled, like a beast cornered, and her hands clenched into claws, before she forced herself into a semblance of calm.

"You must redouble your efforts to destroy these pestilent toshers."

"It is being done," replied Bisc. "But it will take time, you need to stay safe—"

"I must go to the palace. Have your people precede and follow, as close as is possible without detection. I will take Sevrin with me as a maid."

"Refusers aren't allowed in the palace," said Bisc. "Leastways, not ones who aren't in the Queen's service. And that lot think they're too good for the rest of us."

"I will be safe enough in the palace, surely," said Liliath.

"I suppose so," grumbled Bisc. "But even the palace has got sewers too, don't they? I never trusted those underfolk. The darkness gets in their heads."

"The Worm had other followers, did she not? Not just the toshers. What of them?"

Bisc snorted.

"They drift where the wind blows. But the toshers . . . they are a real danger."

There was a knock at the door, and Hatty came in. She was nervous and flustered.

"Milady, the Musketeer and the Pursuivant insist you leave for the palace at once!"

"I am ready," answered Liliath. "I will come down in a moment. Has Small Jack brought down the chest as I ordered?"

"Yes, milady. The Musketeer and the Pursuivant insisted on inspecting it before you could bring it to the palace, in case of infernal devices they said, but they've been very quiet since they looked inside."

"Tell Sevrin she will be coming with me, though not into the palace," said Liliath. "I will be down in a few moments."

Hatty fled, as Liliath turned to Bisc.

"You're sure they will be fooled by the letter and the map?" asked Bisc. "The Cardinal has many angels at her command,

and artisans of all kinds."

"Unless she calls upon Ashalael himself, all any lesser angel will be able to say is Liliath wrote the letter and drew the map."

"But you did it this morning!" protested Bisc. "Won't they know it isn't old?"

"Any angel they are likely to call upon will say they are very old documents," interrupted Liliath. "I summoned Azriel, the Principality, whose scope is time and the inanimate. I suppose if they have a priest who dares to call upon a Power and scorns the cost, they might discern that both papers have been somehow manipulated by a high angel indeed. But that will only confirm that both come from long-dead Liliath, Maid of Ellanda, and serve us even better. You worry too much, my Biscaray."

She drew him close and gently stroked his smooth cheek, reminding them both of what she had done for him, and more. "You will look after me, going and . . . coming?"

Bisc brought her hand down and covered it in feverish kisses, until Liliath laughed and drew it away.

"I understand your answer, sir," she said. "To the palace, and the first step of our journey home to Ystara!"

"That Watch lieutenant was right," said Simeon in a hushed whisper. "She is extraordinarily beautiful."

"There's a second chest!" exclaimed Henri, rather too loudly. "Look, behind her!"

The Pursuivant and Musketeer who had escorted Lady Dehiems to the palace were carrying a small bronze chest, identical to the one found on the Worm, and clearly just as heavy.

Henri was not the only one to exclaim. While Lady Dehiems's beauty was the cause of many involuntary sounds, more were due to the presence of the second chest. Even the Queen sat forward on her chair, though it was hard to judge what she was reacting to, the woman or the potential treasure. Dehiems was not typical of her favorites. The late Deluynes, the Queen's most adored but sadly treacherous lover, had been tall and fair, though equally beautiful, in a different way.

Lady Dehiems bowed very low, doffing her hat, which she kept at her side as she straightened up, her head still bent forward a little, eyes properly focused on the shining toes of the Queen's boots.

"Welcome, child," said the Queen. "You have brought unexpected excitement to my court, in both your person and in your train."

"I regret I did not personally bring the first chest to Your Majesty," said Dehiems, her Alban accent very distinct, her "r's" burred. "As soon as I was made aware these chests of my ancestor's properly belonged to the Queen of Sarance, I thought to bring the second one immediately. May I present it to Your Majesty?"

"You may," said the Queen, clapping her hands with pleasure. She gestured to the Musketeer and Pursuivant, who brought the chest forward and threw it open. The Queen looked down, and once again the Cardinal and Dartagnan slowly leaned over, while pretending not to do so.

"More gold double dolphins," said the Queen. She pointed.

"And icons, but not, I think, more Diamond Icons . . ."

"No," said the Cardinal heavily. "I fear not. Please, Dartagnan . . ."

Dartagnan passed several fairly ordinary-looking icons to the Cardinal, who looked at them and sighed.

"Lesser icons. Ystaran, of no great power."

"Ah well," sighed the Queen. "We have been fortunate already."

"There is a paper . . . a drawing . . ." said Dartagnan. She moved a few coins and drew out a folded parchment, which she carefully unfolded. "It looks like a map."

She looked piercingly at Dehiems, who kept her eyes lowered.

"These chests were your grandmother's, five times back?"

"Perhaps six, ser," replied Dehiems. "My mother was not sure, and our family records were lost in the wars between the Atheling Henry's successors, a hundred years gone."

"What do you know of your ancestor?" asked the Cardinal. "Or were told?"

"Very little, Eminence. I only saw the chests once as a child, and then again briefly before I . . . I was married. There was an inventory of my property for the marriage pact. . . ."

She paused, her perfect lips quivered for a moment, and then she bravely carried on.

"Mother said that our ancestor—her name was Isabella— was very rich but had a mysterious past. Her mother—my grandmother—told the family story that when Isabella was no more than fifteen, she left Ystara shortly before the doom, leaving behind even more riches than she had brought with her. But she must still have brought great wealth, for she married the Earl of Merewich, later made a duke. And he was a cousin of Atheling Eardward the Third—"

"Making sure everyone knows she's got royal blood, even if it is Alban," muttered Dorotea, who had not looked at the chest once, her gaze fixed on Dehiems. But not in an admiring, lascivious, or even fascinated way. It was more calculating, as if she wasn't entirely sure what she was looking at and was trying to work it out.

"Of royal descent, rich, beautiful, young," said Henri. He sighed longingly, "And as far beyond my reach as . . . as those golden oranges."

"You could get a ladder for the oranges," Agnez pointed out.

"I could get my head cut off," said Henri.

"We might be looking at a new Queen's favorite," said Simeon slowly, observing how the Queen smiled at Dehiems, and the young woman artfully looked back up through her eyelashes. "She really is astonishingly beautiful, and even more so, attractive."

"What?" asked Agnez.

"The two do not necessarily go together," replied Simeon.

"Sshh," urged Dorotea. "I want to hear what's she saying."

"That is all I know," said Dehiems. "Her name, the family legend about the enormous wealth she left behind. And these two chests, which my mother told me were only to be used in the most dire emergency. Fortunately, my family has never lacked for money, and so they have remained undisturbed and could return to their true owner. Truly I had no notion the icons were the famous stolen ones of your royal ancestor, Your Majesty. . . ."

"Of course, how could you?" said the Queen soothingly.

"Apart from the gold and the icons, the nonsense letter and this drawing—perhaps it is a map, now that you have pointed it out, Captain—the only other property my mother had from Isabella is now lost."

"What was it?" asked the Queen.

"A curious pair of fingerless gloves, of thick but supple leather, that were set with tiny sharp studs on the palm. But they were very old. I don't know what happened to them."

"Climbing gloves," said Dartagnan slowly. "As used by the most proficient of thieves."

"Oh no!" exclaimed Dehiems. She put her lovely, long-fingered hands to her face, all upset. "Surely my ancestor was not the person who stole your icons, Majesty!"

"I bet it was," whispered Henri.

"Come, child. Calm yourself," said the Queen. She tapped the floor of the gazebo by her throne with her boot. "Sit by me here. You are not responsible for some distant ancestor's misdeeds, no more than I am for the actions of Mad Queen Henrietta. You have done the realm a great service by bringing these chests back to Sarance, and even if the first came to me by chance, the second comes from your hand. Wipe those tears away. Your cheeks are too pretty for tear stains!"

"There is something very odd about Milady Dehiems," said Dorotea, frowning.

"Besides being impossibly beautiful and rich and demi-royal?" asked Henri. "And Alban. That is a fault, I agree."

"Not that," said Dorotea.

"What, then?"

"I'm not sure," said Dorotea slowly. "I can't quite—"

"You're jealous of her," said Agnez, in a tone that at least tried to suggest she was not, herself. Though she spoiled this by her next words, "She doesn't wear a sword. Probably afraid of a naked blade."

"I don't think I'm jealous," said Dorotea. She shook her head. "Maybe I'm just tired. When I look at her . . . I don't know . . . it is hard to sleep well in the Tower. I am weary."

"They're talking about us!" exclaimed Simeon, who had remained intent upon what was happening in the gazebo. "Please let whatever happens be quick and . . . and not awful, so we can return to blissful obscurity!"

Agnez and Henri looked at him askance, but Dorotea nodded in understanding. Then all four leaned in, eager to hear whatever was being said.

"I understand I have four young persons to thank for recovering what I had thought was my property but, far more important, is Your Majesty's," Dehiems was saying to the Queen. She was sitting at her feet now, her lovely face turned up admiringly to the sovereign.

"Yes," replied the Queen. She looked around. "Where are they?"

Dartagnan gestured to Sesturo, who hurried off the gazebo,

through a gap in the trees, and lumbered toward the four friends, who hastily leaned back from the viewing spot, stood up, and brushed themselves down and straightened whatever could be straightened or made more presentable. They were about to meet the Queen, and their lives would change. For better or worse.

TWENTY-TWO

"I'LL COME WITH YOU. WE ADVANCE IN A SINGLE RANK, TO within six paces, bow and doff hats," instructed Sesturo. "Hats stay off. Look down unless Her Majesty tells you otherwise. When dismissed, back up four or five paces before turning. I'll lead you out. Ready?"

"Yes," said Agnez, while the others nodded, save Dorotea, who was looking back through the gap in the trees.

"Scholar Imsel?"

"What? Oh, yes . . ." mumbled Dorotea, falling into line behind the big Musketeer. He led them back the way they had come, and through a gap farther away from the gazebo, so that when they emerged in the courtyard they were directly opposite and some sixty feet away, as if they had just arrived or had been waiting somewhere else, out of earshot.

Simeon glanced at Sesturo as they walked on, wondering why the Musketeer had let them eavesdrop, indeed had facilitated it. He felt very nervous about having to face the Queen, even fearful, not least because he knew that, as always, there were political rivalries at work between the Cardinal and Dartagnan and their respective Pursuivants and Musketeers. Not to mention this Lady Dehiems, who both attracted and unnerved him, though not to the extent she clearly upset Dorotea in some way. Though Dorotea was very unusual. . . .

Dorotea was not thinking about the Queen or even the Cardinal, and certainly not about Dartagnan. All her mind was concentrated on the auburn-haired young woman who sat at the Queen's feet, laughing in a restrained but lovely way at something Sofia had just said. Every time Dorotea's gaze fixed on the woman, she felt her eyes blur a little, and she saw several other shapes within the woman's flesh or existing in the same space. But when she blinked, they disappeared. . . .

Agnez was simply happy. Here she was, a Queen's Musketeer, who had done a signal service that had brought her to the notice of the Queen. This was all she wanted in the world, or at least put her firmly on the middle of the road toward her ultimate ambition. One day she would stand at the Queen's side as Captain-General of Musketeers. Perhaps not this queen, but the heir, Princess Henrietta, who was twelve . . .

Henri was wondering if there would be a reward after all and cursed the King for showing up and taking half the gold in the first chest. Maybe what was left would be shared out among the four of them? That would still be a great windfall.

They approached the gazebo close together, with Sesturo off to the left providing a marker and cadence for their marching. When he halted, they managed to do so at almost the same time, and bowed together with a flourish of hats (and one scholar's cap) and went down on their knees.

"So these are our treasure finders!" exclaimed the Queen. "Present them, Sesturo."

"Your Majesty," rumbled the Musketeer. He pointed.

"On the right is our Agnez Descaray, a cadet who, if she lives, seems likely to bring a useful sword arm to Her Majesty's Musketeers."

Agnez lowered her head still farther, though not before the slightest of glances toward Rochefort. Who did not seem to be paying any attention and was looking at the orange trees, not the people being presented. One day they would cross swords again, Agnez knew, with a different result. . . .

"Look up, Musketeer, and tell me how I may reward you for your service," said the Queen.

Agnez looked up, met the Queen's eyes, and quickly lowered her own again, as Sesturo had instructed.

"I wish no more than to continue serving Your Majesty with my sword, and if necessary, my life."

Sofia clapped her hands in delight.

"Prettily said! Just as one of my Musketeers should."

She pointed to the bandage on Agnez's arm.

"But you were wounded in the recovery of the treasure?"

"It's nothing, Your Majesty," said Agnez, resisting an urge to glance at Rochefort again. "I heal swiftly, and as you see, it has been expertly bandaged."

"Bandaged by the giant next to Descaray, Your Majesty, a man almost as large as myself, which I find affronting but bearable, since I too might need him to mend my wounds. He is the apprentice Doctor-Magister Simeon MacNeel, in service to your own physician Hazurain at the Infirmary."

"And you, Doctor MacNeel? What reward might you seek?"

"I, too, need no more than I have," answered Simeon, who had not failed to notice Sofia's delight at Agnez's reply to the same question. "To learn from one of the great doctors of our age, Your Majesty's own physician, is all I have ever wanted."

The Queen clapped her hands again and smiled. She liked these public acts of devotion, particularly when they didn't cost her anything.

"The fellow next to the doctor, who might make half of him, is one of Her Eminence's clerks, currently seconded to serve Your Majesty's Architect, which he does with vigor, forever pestering us poor Musketeers to do as the Architect requires."

"And how might the Queen of Sarance reward you, my clerk?"

Henri opened his mouth to say "gold" or "wealth" but somehow managed to stop himself. Inwardly, he was both furious and despondent—furious at his "friends" who, given the chance at getting something, had let it slip past, and despondent because even worse than that, they had made it impossible for him to ask for anything either. He couldn't request a monetary reward now, when they had simperingly declared it was enough to serve the Queen.

He cleared his throat and said, with as much fervor as he could pretend, "I, too, only wish to serve Your Majesty in my own poor way, as best I can."

"And you, young ser? I do not need Sesturo to tell me you are a scholar of the Belhalle. What is your name, and do you, too, turn away all reward?"

"I am Dorotea Imsel, Your Majesty. Indeed, I am a scholar of the Belhalle, though I do not currently reside or study there. As for a reward, I need nothing . . . but I would like not to have to go back to the Tower."

"The Tower!"

"I am a 'guest' there, Your Majesty," said Dorotea, looking at the Cardinal and then over to the side where Rochefort stood. "I am not entirely sure why."

"Eminence? What does this mean?" asked the Queen.

"Scholar Imsel has been brought to the Tower for her own protection," said the Cardinal smoothly. "She has exhibited a talent for swift icon-making that has only been known in two persons before, the heretic Chalconte and the Ystaran Liliath, sometimes called the Maid of Ellanda. There is a cult among the Refusers who believe Liliath will be reborn and lead them to greatness, though what it leads them to is treachery and rebellion against your gracious Majesty. Given they might believe Scholar Imsel is the reborn Liliath, she needed to be brought within the Star Fortress to ensure her safety. As we have seen with the theft from Lady Dehiems of items these Refusers would believe to be Liliath's, they are as active today as they have ever been, and there is considerable danger."

"Well, then," said the Queen. "It is for the best, child."

Dorotea bent her head deeper, fighting down the strong

inclination to say this was a lot of nonsense. But she had learned a little from her stay in the Tower. Just enough to keep silent, when before she might have opened her mouth.

"Perhaps if it is purely a matter of Scholar Imsel's safety, she might be made more comfortable elsewhere," said someone, a cool, commanding voice. Dorotea glanced up. It was Dartagnan talking, the Captain of the Queen's Musketeers.

"The Queen's Musketeers would be pleased to offer safe accommodation within the Star Fortress at our barracks," continued Dartagnan. She forestalled whatever the Cardinal was going to say by a direct appeal to the Queen. "Perhaps for all four of these young people? If Your Majesty thinks it suitable?"

"Yes, of course, Dartagnan. An excellent notion. But what of this Refuser cult, Cardinal?" asked the Queen. "These thefts and murders displease me! What is being done?"

The Cardinal looked at Dartagnan without expression, then back to the Queen. Everyone present knew they had just seen a brief skirmish of the powers that circled the throne, and this time Dartagnan had won. Though it seemed she had won a prize of no importance, the moving of an inconsequential prisoner.

To Dorotea, it seemed a great deal.

"The cult is largely centered in the criminal conspiracy commonly known as the Night Crew. All Refusers known to be members of this gang will be arrested at dawn tomorrow, Your Majesty," said the Cardinal, with utmost certainty. "Under the direction of Captain Rochefort, with the assistance of the City Watch."

Rochefort inclined her head, her scar stark, both eyes glittering. She looked ready to go forth on her task at once, eager to gather up Refusers and set them in chains.

"And what will be done with them, Ser Rochefort?" asked the Queen.

"The leaders will be taken to the Star Fortress for questioning, Your Majesty," replied Rochefort. "Those who seem physically capable will go to the galleys at Malarche, the others dispersed to the city prisons of Loutain and Mouen."

"There are great numbers to be arrested?" asked the Queen, turning to look at the Cardinal again. "I trust you will bear in mind, Eminence, that many Refusers perform useful work, and while I want any malcontents and traitors dealt with, we must not lose our willing workers."

"Your Majesty knows I have long advised *all* Refusers be cast out of the kingdom," said the Cardinal, her voice hard. "They . . . or their ancestors . . . defied their Archangel and were punished for it, unto their children's children and beyond. But as always, I bow to Your Majesty's compassion."

"How many, Cardinal?" asked the Queen, her voice now fractious.

"A thousand, perhaps two," replied Duplessis. "Of the more than twenty thousand counted in the last census, a decade hence. As they breed rapidly, lacking the grace to forestall or arrest conception granted by Hereniel or Shapanael, there are certainly more than that now."

The Queen sat silently for a moment, frown invisible under

her wig but lines tightening around her eyes. She looked down, meeting Dehiems's gaze.

"And what do you counsel, Lady Dehiems? You have been wronged by these sewer-dwelling Refusers."

"I say they should answer for their crimes," said Dehiems. "In any case, all the world knows Your Majesty is kindness itself to all your people, even Refusers, who do not deserve such attention. If they behave as criminals, then they should be treated as such."

"Yes," replied the Queen. "Yes, you are right."

She laid her hand on Dehiems's shoulder, and the young woman looked up at her again, both smiling. The Queen started to say something but was interrupted by a slight cough from the senior servant, Deruyter. It was a familiar and known interruption.

"Yes, yes, what is it, Deruyter?"

"The Ambassador from Menorco awaits in the Amber Presence Chamber, Your Majesty, as you instructed."

"Bah!" exclaimed the Queen. "I had forgotten."

She looked back down at Lady Dehiems.

"You must come to my levee tomorrow, my dear, but for now . . . matters of state. Cardinal, you will wish to see the Ambassador?"

"Of course, Your Majesty."

Lady Dehiems somehow slid off the gazebo floor and onto her feet and down into a low bow, all in one graceful motion, before backing away, continuing beyond Agnez and the others.

The Queen glanced over at the four friends still kneeling in front of her.

"We thank you again, sers, for your service to the kingdom."

The words sounded like rote, something she had said a thousand, ten thousand times. So did the words that came next.

"Deruyter! Purses!"

Once again, Deruyter signaled a lesser servant, but this time that woman did not pass the task on to an even lesser one. Instead, she brought a gilded box to the Queen, who reached in and drew out a small velvet purse.

"Descaray."

Agnez looked up but did not move.

"Approach. I don't bite, my brave Musketeer!"

Agnez stepped forward slowly, bowing over the Queen's offered hand and taking the velvet purse, then retreating back to kneel again. This process was repeated three more times, but when Dorotea, who was last, returned, Sesturo made a shooing motion and started to retreat himself.

The audience was over. The four young people backed as instructed, turning as they got far enough away. Lady Dehiems was ahead of them, being led by two Musketeers to the main doors of sculptured bronze. They treated her with extreme courtesy, likely as much to the perception she had already captivated the Queen as for her own undeniable charms.

Sesturo took the others a different way, through a gap in the trees and along another avenue between citrons, and pointed toward a door guarded by more Musketeers.

"Derossignol or Rotrou will show you the way out around the Roll House, into the Eastern Court," he said.

He bowed courteously and returned back toward the gazebo. The others returned the bow and watched him for a few moments, then headed toward the door, one of the Musketeers there raising his hand in greeting. The other was perched on one leg, writing in a small notebook. She didn't look up.

Henri looked in his purse as they walked on, sighed, and shut it again. Simeon, who was next to him, raised an eyebrow.

"Silver," whispered Henri. "We bring gold and the fabled Diamond Icons, we get sixty livres each, if I'm any judge of this weight. Which I am. I can't believe none of you asked—"

"I'm just glad to be leaving with my head unpromised to the ax," said Simeon. "The sooner I get back to the Infirmary the happier I'll be."

"It's all right for you," grumbled Henri. "I suppose you even meant it when you said you didn't want anything more than to cut people up and hobnob with angels over weeping sores or—"

"We didn't really do anything anyway, Henri," said Agnez. "We were just in the right place to find that body."

"Yes," said Dorotea thoughtfully. "The workings of luck must never be discounted, but I wonder—"

She was interrupted by sudden noise on the glass panels in the roof above, which made everyone look up. But it was only rain, heavy drops splashing down. Just a few at first, with a *tap-tap-tap* and then suddenly a rapid drumbeat as the rain intensified.

"We don't have our cloaks," said Henri sourly. "And I bet we won't get to ride back to the fortress in one of the Cardinal's coaches."

"You might be wrong about that," said Simeon, glancing back over his shoulder. "We are pursued."

Rochefort was striding toward them, her red heels clacking on the floor in counterpoint to the beat of the rain on the roof above. She inclined her head to Sesturo as they passed each other. He waved a sort of salute, perhaps ironically.

"One of us is, anyway," whispered Henri to Agnez.

Agnez didn't reply, stiffening up to her full height as Rochefort drew closer, like a cat arching its back as a trespasser approached its territory. Predictably, the Pursuivant ignored this, addressing Dorotea.

"I am pleased you are leaving the Tower, Ser Imsel," she said stiffly. "Her Eminence has asked me to tell you that should the accommodations of the Musketeers be not to your liking, a guest chamber is available in the Pursuivants' Barracks. Her Eminence has also ordered one of her coaches to carry you all on to the Star Fortress."

"That is kind of you, in this weather, ser," said Simeon.

"Kindness has nothing to do with it, Doctor," said Rochefort. "Her Eminence considers you to be under some threat. We do not know why the Refusers are fighting each other, why the Worm had the treasure, or what your retrieval of the treasure may mean. You may be marked for their retribution. Or in Scholar Imsel's case, of abduction, if they truly believe she is Liliath returned."

"I am not Liliath! How many times must I say it?"

"I believe you," said Rochefort. "I do not think even the Cardinal truly thinks otherwise. But . . . ah . . . Her Eminence does wish to . . . discuss . . . this with you tomorrow at noon. I will escort you from the Musketeers' Barracks at eleven of the clock. Please be ready."

"I don't have a watch," said Dorotea mulishly.

"You can hear the temple bells easily enough," said Rochefort, unruffled by this sally. She held out her red-gloved hand. "Come! I am pleased you will be out of the Tower, even if it is to be with Musketeers!"

Dorotea took Rochefort's hand and bowed over it, very correctly.

"I shall be happy when I am back in the Belhalle, behind a parapet of books, with my brushes, paints, and plaques, and this Liliath nonsense is forgotten," she said. "But I do thank you, Captain."

"I must return to Her Eminence," said Rochefort. She looked over the four of them and sniffed. "Only the Musketeer has a sword? Wear your blades in the future; caution is necessary. I make the perhaps unwarranted presumption you know how to use them."

Even as both Henri and Agnez bit back replies, she turned on her heel and strode away.

Derossignol greeted them with the cheerfulness of a bored sentry and kicked Rotrou in the leg she was standing on, which almost made her fall over. She shut her book and made a mock stab at Derossignol's face with her Simonio pencil, a particularly fine one where the graphite core had been encased in wood and that in turn had been fitted into a silver sleeve engraved with scenes from famous plays.

"Descaray, is it not? And the treasure seekers?"

"Treasure finders," said Agnez, exchanging a salute with him, while Rotrou busied herself sliding her book under her cuirass. "Sesturo said one of you would lead us to the East Courtyard, where our carriage awaits."

"'Our carriage awaits'!" cried Derossignol, nudging Rotrou. "What it is to be a Musketeer cadet these days! I would have thought a long march in the wet would be just the thing for you, Descaray. But I suppose your companions, whom I trust you will introduce me to, would not like it so much."

"No, we would not," said Henri, with a perfunctory bow. "I am Dupallidin. That is Scholar Imsel and Doctor MacNeel."

"I am pleased to make your acquaintance," said Derossignol, with continued good humor. "Many say I talk too much and do too little. I will make amends now by leading you to your destination, which will please Rotrou as well, as she may continue writing her play."

"I am writing a poem, not a play," said Rotrou. "And now it is interrupted I may as well take our visitors, who are young, and even in a short space of propinquous proximity with you might well be corrupted."

"Surely 'propinquous proximity' is a redundancy," said Dorotea.

"Ah, a true scholar!" cried Rotrou, who at most was only three or four years older than the four friends. She linked her arm through Dorotea's and gestured to Derossignol. "Unbar the door, let the cold winds in and us out, good Derossignol."

"I am, as usual, diverted at the point of victory," grumbled Derossignol. He slid back a viewing port and looked out carefully, before unbarring the door and pulling it open. A cold wind howled in, the temperature outside having fallen a great deal, a shock after the hothouse air of the Orangery.

"Quickly now!" encouraged Derossignol, who was already beginning to push the door closed again. "Mustn't let out the warm!"

TWENTY-THREE

THE RAIN WAS VERY COLD. THE PARTY HURRIED ALONG the wall of the Orangery, from one pool of dim light to the next, cast by storm lanterns hung on hooks every twenty paces. They tried to stay under the eaves to avoid the splashing overflow from the gutters, but it was impossible, and in turn each of them was soaked by a sudden cascade.

Shivering, they rounded the corner of the Roll House and made it to the locked grille at the western end of the Southern Lane, where two fully cloaked and rugged-up but nonetheless miserable Musketeers returned the watchword with countersign and allowed them entry, Rotrou returning eagerly to the warmth of the Orangery.

The lane was a narrow gap between the Roll House and the Queen's Counting House, and fortunately the roofs some six floors above overlapped, so they were momentarily out of the rain. It was dark though, save for a single torch in a cresset halfway along.

"Maybe the Zuiss have it right in becoming a republic," grumbled Henri, but he didn't say it loud enough for Agnez to hear, as she would doubtless take offense at the merest slight to the Queen.

There was another grille at the other end of the lane, and more sodden, heavily cloaked Musketeers. They let the four now sodden and chilled visitors out into the Eastern Courtyard, where they immediately ran underneath the closest colonnade, the courtyard being lined on three sides with deep cloisters. These were currently thronged with all those courtiers lacking funds or energy to seek proper accommodation elsewhere, or who feared they would not be admitted again if they left. Most were huddled around the half-dozen massive iron braziers that were irregularly refueled by palace servants, more gold-ribboned Refusers who carted baskets of firewood on their backs.

Usually the courtyard would be full, even at this hour, with courtiers talking and dancing and playing music, practicing their swordplay or demonstrating their riding skills. But the cold rain had sent everyone away or into the colonnades. The huge, open paved area was deserted, save for two of the Cardinal's coaches, each drawn by six steaming horses, who had been hurriedly put into their bright scarlet winter blankets a month early.

"There's Lady Dehiems," said Agnez, pointing. The Alban noble had come a different and obviously much drier way, and she wore a hooded cloak, a fur-lined vision of warmth in dark blue wool. A Musketeer and Pursuivant were helping her move through the courtiers who had clustered to her like midges to a swamp picnic, trying to attract her attention with emphatic bows and flourishes, all of which she ignored.

A gold-ribboned Refuser came up to Agnez and offered the four of them oiled leather parasols for the walk across to their carriage. But even as they took them and opened them up, the rain grew louder and then louder still. The cold intensified, and the heavy drops translated into hailstones.

"Quickly!" called Agnez, leading the way. Grooms had come out from where they were sheltering under the coaches to hold the horses' heads, but even the Cardinal's extremely well-trained steeds were made anxious by the hail.

Lady Dehiems was heading for the closer carriage, a parasol held over her head by her accompanying Pursuivant, who had beaten the Musketeer to the honor. They were about halfway there, with the four friends well behind, when the hail suddenly stopped, a few remnant lumps of ice pinging and bouncing about before coming to rest, the entire courtyard now white as snow, with hail piled in lines where it had barreled down from the roofs of the colonnades.

In the sudden silence, there was the groan and shriek of metal on stone and a large, verdigris-covered iron grille covering a drain in the very middle of the courtyard was pushed up onto one edge and then fell over with a resounding clang, followed a second later by an eruption of ragged gray-clad figures wielding hooked tosher poles, cleavers, rusted axes, and clubs made of donkeys' jawbones.

They charged at the closest people: Lady Dehiems and her two escorts.

Agnez was the first to react, throwing her parasol aside to

draw a pistol and fire in one swift motion. But the priming had gotten wet, and the pistol merely sparked and fizzled. She threw it aside and drew her sword, scuffing the ground to clear her boot heels of any embedded hailstones. The others had no swords, but the parasols were heavy, iron-ribbed affairs. They quickly closed them, readying them for use as makeshift clubs.

Lady Dehiems turned and ran back past the four friends as the Pursuivant and Musketeer faced the rush of toshers. There were twenty or more attackers, and there was only a quick exchange of swordplay and polework before they rushed on, leaving Musketeer and Pursuivant dead or dying with several toshers around them, their blood conjoining to mar the pristine whiteness of the layer of hail.

"Alarm! Alarm!" shouted the Musketeers at the various doors and gates, but rather than advancing to combat the toshers, they did as they were supposed to do, which was lock and bar gates and grilles to deny access into the palace proper, and ready their muskets.

Most of the courtiers retreated as far as they could get to the colonnade walls, but a dozen or so rushed out, slipping and sliding in their best red-heeled boots through the six-inch-deep strands of hail, drawing court swords and blunt, ornamental daggers. Just as in the Orangery, none save Musketeers were allowed to bring gunpowder weapons into the palace.

Lady Dehiems was very swift, even running across hail-strewn pavers. She stopped behind Agnez and the others as gunfire blasted out from the windows in the counting house above, the

Musketeers stationed there beginning to shoot. Three toshers went down, and two more fell over them and scrambled about in the hail, but the rest came on, their eerie silence as unnerving as their sudden attack.

"Stay close together!" shouted Agnez. "'Ware the poles!"

As the leading toshers struck, thrusting with poles and trying to get in close with their cleavers and clubs, there was the sudden bright sound of harp strings.

"No!" screamed Dorotea, parrying a pole with her parasol. "They're Refusers! No magic!"

But it was too late. Someone among the courtiers had panicked, and there was a clap of thunder as angelic wings clashed together and a rush of sandalwood-scented air blew across the courtyard.

The Refusers paused as if struck by a much harsher wind, just for a moment. The pause was long enough for Agnez to kill one with a thrust to the heart, draw her sword back, twist, and slash open the throat of another; for Simeon to wrench a tosher pole out of the hands of one Refuser, turn it about, and smack the former wielder on the head; and it saved Henri's life as it gave him a vital half second to dodge a swipe from a cleaver that would have disemboweled him.

The moment passed, and the Refusers came on to attack again, the four friends clustered close together, with some courtiers now with them, desperately trying to stop the toshers outflanking the small group of defenders.

Whatever the angel was supposed to do—and Dorotea thought she recognized the presence of Sarpentiel, whose scope was consciousness, either raising or lowering, typically to sleep—did not, of course, happen. But the Refusers were slower, their blows missing, their thrusts awry, and then . . .

They started to bleed gray ash.

Slowly, at first, from ears and mouth, but then from their eyes and existing wounds, and as they realized what was happening for the first time they made noises, shrieks of pain and fear and rage. A few redoubled their attacks, as if in their last moments they might take their enemies with them, but they were already too weakened. Most crumpled where they stood, and within half a minute all the attackers were down, writhing in the hailstones, rivers of ash slowly pouring from them as they died.

"Back! Step back!" ordered Agnez, doing so herself. She held her sword ready.

"'Ware beastling!" shouted Simeon, who was deathly afraid one or more would emerge, as terrible as the one that had been in the box in the hospital.

For a few seconds, it seemed that all the Refusers would simply die of the Ash Blood plague. Simeon was the first to notice something else happening, and he pointed with his tosher pole.

"There!"

Two toshers lay sprawled together, apparently twitching in their death throes. But as Simeon had seen, these were not the fading movements of a dying mind desperately trying to instruct the body. The ash blood was not flowing *out* of the bodies. It was flowing around and over them, and as it spread it was thickening, congealing, changing color and consistency.

The two bodies merged into one, and tendrils of black ash struck out to gather mounds of hail, drawing them into the new, conjoined body, which continued to change very swiftly even as it melded together, growing larger, extending limbs, extruding claws.

An overbrave courtier, closest to the birthing monster, stabbed at it with her court sword, but a hand already broadened and made leathery gripped the blade and snapped it off, flinging the sharp point back at the woman to pierce her eye. She dropped to the ground and everyone stepped back, the urge to flee upon them. A strong sense of panic was in the air, the moment when a battle is won or lost.

"Hold fast!" shouted Agnez. She tried to look up at the counting house, but the combat had pushed them back almost under the roof of the colonnade, and the Musketeers upstairs no longer had any field of fire, nor did those behind the iron grilles of the north and south passages.

Somewhere within the palace, trumpets were sounding the alarm, quickly followed by the harsh rattle of drums.

Henri threw his umbrella away and grabbed a tosher pole, Dorotea and the few surviving combative courtiers following his example. In front of them, the beastling rose up on its haunches—more like a massive dog's now, not human legs at all—and its body straightened, chest inflating and arms stretching. Its head was expanding slowly, like a hot-air balloon inflating, the skull plates beneath grinding horribly. It moved its long jaw from side to side, as if testing it, and snapped at the air, showing newly grown teeth.

Off to the sides, courtiers were screaming and banging on doors and gates, begging to be let out. There were orders being shouted above and in the passageways, and at the main gate to the east. But all this might as well have been happening on the moon to the few who stood facing the beastling, readying themselves for the inevitable attack.

"On my word, charge it all at once!" shouted Agnez. "Charge!"

She rushed forward and lunged straight at the center of the beastling's torso, where she hoped its heart would be. The others surrounded it, stabbing with tosher poles and court swords. But Agnez's lovingly sharpened sword did no more than prick the skin that had hardened into something like proofed plate, and the duller tosher hooks and the brittle steel of the court swords could not penetrate at all, and several broke.

With a high-pitched screech, like a hawk's but much louder and more terrifying, the beastling sprang forward at Agnez, its clawed hands trying to embrace her. Its arms were so surprisingly long it almost succeeded, and it would have grabbed anyone less athletic than Agnez, who flung herself backward, feet scrabbling in the hail.

Its next grab would have gotten her, but Henri thrust a tosher pole between the beastling's legs, and he and Dorotea pushed and leaned on it with all their weight and strength, greatly augmented by sheer terror. The pole broke, but not before the creature was sent sprawling. It shrieked again and pushed itself up, slipping on the hail-wet stone, ignoring another round of attacks from weapons that still could not pierce its hide.

"Try and hold it down!" shouted Simeon. Throwing his tosher pole aside, he ran to the nearest brazier of hot coals, paused for the merest moment, and then picked it up by its tripod legs, ignoring the burning embers that spilled down the front of his doctor's robe. Grunting from the effort, he half carried, half dragged it to where the others were desperately trying to pin the beastling down, even as it snapped their tosher poles and broke more ornamental swords.

Simeon reached the beastling just as it got up again, leisurely reached out, and gripped one of the courtiers, crushing him and biting down on his head at the same time. Simeon upended the brazier with a cry of extreme effort, flinging a hundredweight of burning wood and embers into the monster's eyes and mouth.

Even as he did so, he flung himself aside into a pile of hail, his robe having caught alight. He rolled away, smoke and steam billowing from his body, as the blinded beastling struck out wildly around itself, screeching and howling in a terrible high pitch that sent the coach horses madly careening around the courtyard, frothing in fear, grooms hanging off the traces, their screams and shouts adding to the general cacophony of terror.

Everyone backed well away from the beastling again, picking up more tosher poles or any other weapon that came to hand. All except Agnez, who stood ten feet away, carefully drying the pan of her second pistol with her handkerchief before priming and loading it, her motions swift and assured.

As she rammed the shot home, someone behind her who sounded like Dorotea said urgently, "Shoot under the jaw when it lifts its head."

Agnez nodded, cocked the lock, and took a single pace forward, right hand on her hip, her shooting arm extended, steady as ever. The beastling must have felt or heard the movement, for it turned toward her and sprang forward, lifting its head to shriek, exposing softer skin under its jaw. As it did so, Agnez fired. This time the spark and flash followed on the instant by a resounding crack.

She ducked aside as the beastling came on, but it was only momentum that carried it forward. It went a few paces past her and collapsed in a horrid morass of melted hail, mud, and blood, amid the bodies of toshers and courtiers. Gray ash gushed from the wound in its throat.

Agnez drew a very long, deep breath, stilled her slightly shaking hand, and immediately went to work reloading her pistol. Henri and Dorotea rushed to Simeon, who was hauling his smoking doctor's coat over his head.

"Are you burned?" asked Dorotea.

"Nothing serious," said Simeon, looking at his hands, which had been peppered with sparks and embers. "There is much to be said for a good doctor's coat. But there must be others . . . we must get the wounded under cover at once—"

Henri was shaking his head.

"There are no wounded," he said. "I think they're all dead."

Simeon looked around. None of the bodies on the ground were moving at all, or making a sound. Over near the gate, the grooms had managed to calm the bolting horses and were walking them again. Everyone was either alive and basically unhurt, or dead.

"I'll make sure," he said, shaking his head as he went and knelt by the closest body. He had been taught that in battles there were always far more wounded than dead, usually at least ten to one. But the sharpness of the beastling's claws and teeth and its incredible strength had meant that even glancing blows were mortal.

He needed no more than a quick glance to confirm Henri's assessment, but even as he checked the last one, someone called out that the Musketeer who had been with Lady Dehiems was actually still alive. Readying his satchel, Simeon ran over, his huge boots sending broad splashes from the puddles of melted hail.

Courtiers started to come out from under the colonnades. Some of them were even strutting, as if they had been involved in the brief combat themselves.

Agnez came over to Dorotea and Henri. She gripped the scholar on the shoulder and said, "Thank you for telling me to shoot it under the jaw, I would have aimed for the—"

"I didn't tell you anything," said Dorotea.

"Well, who was it?" asked Agnez, looking around. Several of the courtiers who had fought with them were close by, looking at the bodies of the toshers, not touching them but stirring the strange pools of ash blood with their swords. More clustered around Lady Dehiems, who stood close by, immobile and apparently stunned by her brush with violent death.

"I don't know," said Dorotea. She looked around but couldn't see anyone obviously holding or touching an icon. "I'd like to know who summoned Sarpentiel as well. We were very lucky only one beastling was made. It could have been all of them."

Agnez opened her mouth, but no words came out. She shut it, gulped, and tried again. Her voice was not as forceful and commanding as she would have liked.

"Very lucky."

A clang of iron announced the opening of the grille doors and a tide of Musketeers washed in. Word of a beastling had obviously gotten to them, for most were bearing halberds, and Franzonne, in the lead, had a grenade in one hand and a burning length of slow match to light it with in the other. Sesturo was behind her, carrying a massive battle-ax that looked like it had been wrenched off a wall where it had been serving decoratively, as there were silver wires trailing from the shaft and spike.

Orders were barked out, and Musketeers ran across the courtyard, a number concentrated around the open drain in the middle. Franzonne and Sesturo approached the blackened and burned body of the beastling, with the broken brazier and bent tripod nearby. They looked at the corpse for a moment. Sesturo prodded it with the spike of his battle-ax and murmured something. Franzonne nodded, bent down, and thrust the glowing end of the slow match in a patch of still-melting hail, putting it out. Her breath frosted out as she did so, and Agnez suddenly felt the full onset of her cold, sodden condition and shivered. Franzonne, perhaps sensing the movement, looked at her and waved, then both she and Sesturo headed over toward the young Musketeer.

"I could do with a hot dinner and a blanket," said Henri. "No. Three blankets."

"I wasn't hungry till you said that," said Dorotea. "Now I am."

"You must come to Demaselle House; it is nearby," said the Alban noblewoman, who had come out of her trance of fear or whatever it was. "Allow me to give you a feast, and mulled wine and—"

"They have orders to return to the Star Fortress, milady," interrupted Franzonne. She bowed, holding the grenade behind her back. "Sesturo here and a troop of Musketeers will escort you to your carriage and thence to your house."

Lady Dehiems's eyes narrowed for an instant as if in anger, but the expression was so swift no one but Dorotea saw it, for no one else watched the Alban so carefully.

"Oh, of course, Ser Franzonne," she said. "I fear Her Eminence is correct, that these . . . what do you call them . . . *towzers?* . . . bear a grudge against my friends here, for taking back my, or I should say, Her Majesty's treasures."

"It seems so, milady," replied Franzonne, easily. "Sesturo?"

"Milady?"

The big Musketeer gestured toward the closest carriage, which was now being cautiously driven over toward them, taking a wide berth around the sprawled bodies of people and the beastling corpse.

"I thank you again," said Lady Dehiems to the four friends, looking at each of them with great attention. All looked back, with varying degrees of admiration and interest: Agnez somewhat scornful, for the Alban had not even tried to fight, but her mind was mostly elsewhere, wondering what she might have done differently to kill the beastling sooner, or what possible tactics she could have employed if there had been more than one; Henri, thinking that a rich and beautiful spouse might be the way to secure his future, but Lady Dehiems was already far beyond his reach, likely to be the Queen's favorite; Simeon, attracted too by her beauty, but also intellectually puzzled—there was something in the way she moved, which was not at all usual, though he thought not an injury, maybe she was double-jointed; and finally, Dorotea, who kept moving her head a little from side to side, because when she looked at Lady Dehiems out of the corner of her eyes she didn't see an astonishingly beautiful young woman at all, but caught glimpses of a number of strangely overlaid and blurred figures of fire and intense light, backed with enormous wings. . . .

TWENTY-FOUR

IT WAS NEAR MIDNIGHT BEFORE THE FOUR FRIENDS GOT back to the Star Fortress and, at Franzonne's insistence, straight to the Musketeers' bathhouse, in the middle of their barracks. This luxurious establishment was built on the remains of a much earlier and larger bath complex, a relic of the old empire. There were a number of broken, empty pools, but there were still four small ones around the original central pool, which was kept the hottest. A dedicated staff of Refuser servants fueled the furnace and mixed the water, all of them, they had been assured, of long and faithful service and definitely not connected with the toshers of the Night Crew.

Despite this assurance and the presence of at least another dozen Musketeers in the other pools, Agnez kept her sword and pistols on a stool by the side of the hot pool, and Henri borrowed a sword and kept it handy too. They were offered long white bath shirts, flimsy items of clothing some people wore in the baths, but they declined, though Agnez was careful to keep her boots with her weapons. Nudity in a bathhouse or at home among friends was quite acceptable to Sarancians, not a taboo as it was to Albans and some others. Agnez was not bothered by the thought of fighting toshers while naked, but boots were a practical necessity.

The four of them warmed themselves quickly with full submersion in the hot pool and some good-natured splashing and dunking, before paddling over to one side to rest on the ledge that allowed them to sit up to their armpits in the pool. Apart from Simeon, where the water only came up just above his waist. But the air in the room was warm anyway, from the hot pools and the tubs of hot stones, which the Refusers splashed cool water on to send gouts of steam up into the air.

Though, as far as they knew, no one had ordered the other Musketeers to give them the main pool for themselves. No one else jumped in, though there was a constant stream of Musketeers in and out, and much use of the other pools.

Almost every arriving Musketeer called out congratulations in general to the four friends for fighting the toshers and the beastling, adding particular comments to Agnez for her finishing shot, and to Simeon for hurling the enormously heavy brazier. Many told him he should become a Musketeer and not bother with being a doctor, but if he insisted on being one, he was the kind they wanted around, as he had saved the life of the Musketeer with Lady Dehiems, a woman called only Jannos, who clearly was very well-liked in the regiment.

But beyond these words, the Musketeers did not stay to talk. Even so, overhearing the conversations in the other pools, the four learned that following the outrageous and unprecedented attack within the palace grounds, the arrests of known members of the Night Crew had been brought forward from the next dawn and were in process now, with greater force, including not only the Cardinal's Pursuivants and the City Watch but also the Musketeers. Even three troops of Colonel Derohan's greencoats, the nearest army regiment, were marching in from their quarters, six leagues away in Charolle.

They also heard that Franzonne herself had led a troop through the drain hole in the Eastern Courtyard and into the sewers, discovering that the maps held by various civic authorities were hopelessly inaccurate, whether for the network of drains and sewers constructed over the last three hundred years or the much earlier natural passages that ran through the rock, which, like at the Star Fortress, underlay much of the city. Several skirmishes had been fought with toshers, and it seemed likely the campaign to arrest and deport the presumed criminal elements of the Refuser population would be much more extensive and bloody than anyone had thought.

"This has been a very strange day," said Simeon, splashing hot water up onto his barrel-like, furry chest. He had a surprising amount of body hair for so young a man, particularly as his face was relatively smooth, and he did not sport a beard.

"Doesn't the water hurt your hands?" asked Agnez.

"No. Didn't you see? I admit I delved into my satchel. The Infirmary has given me a number of icons to use, and I called upon Innenael, whose scope is pain. In any case, these burns are mild, not bad enough to even blister," said Simeon.

"There is something very wrong with Lady Dehiems," said Dorotea suddenly, making the others start.

Henri started splashing loudly, while quickly looking around to make sure the Musketeers in the closest pool weren't listening.

"Sssh!" he said in an urgent whisper. "You saw how the Queen treated her! She's practically the new favorite already."

"She . . . she has an angel or angels *within* her. Always there."

"How do you know this?" asked Simeon. Everyone leaned in close, Agnez slipping off the ledge to tread water, continuing the splashing noise to cover the conversation.

"I saw them," said Dorotea. "When I looked out the corner of my eye. You know, to the side."

Henri and Simeon exchanged a troubled glance.

"What do you mean?" asked Agnez.

"Well, when I sort of squinted and looked not exactly at her, I saw shapes of fire and light in the same place as her body," said Dorotea. "The suggestion of wings . . ."

"I can see all sorts of things if I squint and look off to one side!" exclaimed Agnez. "Everybody does!"

"Hmmm," said Dorotea. She squinted and looked at each of the others, very slowly.

"Now you mention it, I think . . . there is a sort of similar fire in all of you as well. Like a reversed shadow . . . light not dark . . . of angelic wings."

"In us!" exclaimed Simeon, louder than he meant to. They all looked around, but the other Musketeers were still talking among themselves, and those in the closer pool were now passing around a wineskin, which was taking all their attention.

"Did you hit your head?" continued Simeon. "There was a lot going on; I didn't see. . . . Did you slip on the hailstones?"

"Yes," said Dorotea honestly, to a general sigh of relief, which abruptly stopped when she added, "But not enough to fall over. This is very interesting, because I couldn't see this . . . shadow . . . in you three before I saw it in milady. And it's not the same . . . similar, but not the same. I wonder . . ."

"Dorotea, you are already in trouble with the Cardinal's thinking you might be Liliath reborn," said Henri. "If you go around saying you can see angels in people, then they might think you're Chalconte reborn as well! And you particularly mustn't say there's something wrong with Milady Dehiems!"

"Has anyone got a mirror?" asked Dorotea.

"What?"

"Are you sure you didn't hit your head?" asked Henri. "In case you hadn't noticed, we are all naked in this bath. How could we have a mirror?"

"I meant close by," said Dorotea. "I want to squint at myself."

"Squint at yourself?" asked Agnez. "Simeon, you need to feel her head. She must have fallen over. Or even . . . did you get hit by the beastling or a tosher?"

"No!"

"Let me see," said Simeon, slipping off the shelf and wading closer. He started to probe at Dorotea's head, pressing with his fingers at key spots, but she backed away, and he had to let go or hold on to her hair. He chose to let her go.

"I keep telling you, I haven't hit my head, or had my head hit or anything," protested Dorotea. "I don't know what it means that I can see what I see. I need a mirror to see if I can see it in myself as well, because maybe that would explain why we all feel as if we are close family!"

"Can you see anything in the Musketeers over there?" asked Simeon.

Dorotea looked across, bobbing up out of the pool, squinting and looking off to one side, at the Musketeers in the closest pool, four women and three men, who were still idly drinking from the wineskin they passed hand to hand.

"No," she said, shaking her head and sinking back into the warmth.

The other three looked at her. Simeon frowning in deep thought, Henri worried, Agnez squinting and looking to one side to see whether she could see anything herself.

"There's a throat mirror in my satchel," said Simeon after a moment. "I'll fetch it."

He climbed out of the pool, a great quantity of water draining from him, and padded across to his gear. Opening his satchel he laid it out on the bench and took out a small oval mirror that was mounted on the end of a short metal rod, used for looking down throats.

"What are you going to do with that, Doctor?" called out one of the Musketeers, whose attention had been drawn to this sudden movement of wet mammoth. She was almost as tall as Simeon, and corded with muscle, though nowhere near as bulky.

No one was, save Sesturo.

"Are you volunteering to find out?" asked Simeon.

"No, no!" laughed the Musketeer. She had smiling eyes and was very attractive.

Simeon picked up a pair of tweezers as well.

"I have to investigate a splinter of stone, probably from a courtyard flagstone thrown up by a badly misaimed musket ball," he said with mock seriousness. "Were you one of those firing down from the counting house?"

"No, not I," replied the Musketeer again. She smiled at Simeon again. "I missed that fight; I have merely had the honor of a long slog through a sewer, with a minor tussle with some toshers along the way. But if I feel faint, Doctor, will you come and feel my . . . forehead?"

The other Musketeers and Simeon's friends laughed. He smiled himself and shrugged as if to say perhaps he might, and quickly moved back to the pool, trying not to think about the naked body of the Musketeer. It was odd, he thought to himself again, that he felt no physical feelings for Agnez or Dorotea, though both in their different ways were just as attractive as that Musketeer. Or Henri, for that matter, who was a handsome man. Though Simeon usually preferred female partners, he had experimented with chapters four to six of Janossa's *Ways of Love*.

He got back in the water and moved close to Dorotea, his bulk shielding her from the other occupied pools.

"Here," he said, handing over the small mirror. "Have a look while I pretend to extract a splinter from your ear. Best to give them a reason."

"They're not watching anymore," said Agnez. "You've made a conquest there, Simeon. I heard Demesnil likes her lovers to overtop her, and there's few who—"

"Yes, well, I have . . . we have . . . other more important matters," said Simeon hurriedly.

"Yes," said Henri. "Like not being executed for . . . for whatever . . . I mean if Dorotea can see this 'shadow' in . . . in us . . . what if other people can? What if the Cardinal can? Or Rochefort?"

"I've never heard of anyone else being able to see like this," said Dorotea quietly. "It's like feeling the presence of an icon. I've never known or even read about anyone else being able to do that either."

"What?" asked Simeon, Henri, and Agnez together.

Simeon continued, "But you told us, when we found the Refuser . . . the Worm . . . you said it was normal for scholars like you to sense the presence of powerful icons!"

"Well, I thought it might be," said Dorotea. "Except, on consideration, it isn't. Though I suspect there is someone who probably can see like I can."

"Who?" asked Agnez.

"Milady."

"I really don't understand," said Agnez. "Is she some sort of Alban spy? A specially talented mage? She's not an *assassin*, is she?"

"No, no, surely not," soothed Henri, as Agnez appeared to be about to levitate out of the bath, grab sword and boots and charge toward the Queen's Palace, semi-naked through sleet or hail or freezing winds or whatever was now happening outside. "The Cardinal and Dartagnan and everyone must have investigated her, and she's had plenty of chances already, and hasn't done anything."

"Besides," added Simeon, "why would she be? The Queen and the Atheling might have their disputes, and there was that business with Deluynes's letters, but they are cousins after all, and we haven't been at war with Alba since . . . what . . . fifty years ago?"

"Forty-six," said Agnez. "The Cod's-Head War."

"I don't even know that—"

"It lasted only a week, and one battle, an inconclusive one at that. It started when one of our fishing boats was captured by an Alban brigantine—"

"I thought a brigantine was an armored coat—"

"That's a brigandine," said Agnez scornfully. "Anyway, they had a full hold of cod and—"

"Let's hear about that later," said Henri diplomatically. "I think we can discount milady being an Alban assassin. Though she might well be a spy. But why can Dorotea see the same shadow as she sees in the four of us? And what is it? I don't like—"

"It's not the same," interrupted Dorotea. "It's . . . sort of fainter in us. It's hard to explain."

"Try."

Dorotea pursed her lips, thinking.

"Well . . . ," she said tentatively. "You know the sensations most people have when they summon angels, or are near an angelic summoning? The harp sound, the clash of wings, thunderclaps? Warmth sometimes, or cold?"

"Yes," confirmed the others.

"I see things as well," said Dorotea. "I always have. When an angel is present, from summoning to release or banishment. Which for most angels is only seconds, perhaps minutes, with a few exceptions, what they call the prophylactic angels, the defenders and so on. Like your Requaniel, Henri."

"Do they actually look like their icons?" asked Simeon curiously.

"No," replied Dorotea. "It's . . . it's more formless, shapes that change and flicker. Though there is nearly always a kind of visual hint of wings and haloes. I can see how the earliest icon-makers tried to show what they saw and it ended up as haloes and wings. Then over time . . . certain illustrations were most successful at capturing the . . . the essence of the angel . . . and so they got used over and over again."

"So you think seeing angels is how icon-making got started in the first place?" asked Simeon. "But now most icon-makers don't actually see the angels? They just illustrate what people have done before?"

"Yes," said Dorotea. She frowned. "Though now I think about it, I never talked about seeing angels because no one else did, and I never read about it either. But that doesn't mean other people can't see them too. They're probably just keeping quiet like me."

"I learned the basics of icon-making," said Simeon. "And

I summon lesser angels frequently in my work. I hear and feel them, I have never seen anything."

"I never have either," said Henri. "And my father summons Huaravael once a week. No one in my family has ever mentioned seeing the angel. Just hearing the weird crippled bird sound she makes with her wings."

"Crippled bird sound?"

"Kind of fluttering around in a circle," said Henri. "She's not much of an angel. . . ."

"We need to keep quiet about this," said Simeon firmly.

"But it's important," protested Dorotea. "We all have the presence of some angel within us, that's our connection! And then these Diamond Icons show up in front of us, and it turns out they belonged to Lady Dehiems, and she has an angel . . . angels . . . within her too. It must mean something!"

"I don't feel like I've got an angel in me," said Agnez doubtfully. "If I did, surely there would be more signs? Not just you squinting not quite at me and seeing things?"

"What do you think the Cardinal would do if she thought we had angels inside us?" asked Henri.

Everyone looked at him. After a moment, Simeon drew a finger across his own throat.

"That's what I reckon," said Henri. He looked at Dorotea. "So you can't tell anyone about what you think you see."

"We need to know," said Dorotea. "Who is this angel within us?"

"Do we?" asked Agnez. "Like I said, even if it's there, which

I'm not sure about at all, what does it matter? Provided no one knows, that is."

"I reckon Lady Dehiems knows," said Dorotea, staring out of the pool. Her eyes suddenly narrowed, and she raised her hand to her mouth in shock. "Oh, heavens!"

"What?"

A Refuser was pouring water on the hot stones in a bronze barrel nearby. Dorotea was staring not quite at him, her eyes scrunched to the barest slits.

"The Refuser . . . there's the same faint shadow of an angel in *her* . . ."

No one said anything for what felt like several minutes but was actually only several seconds, before Henri finally whispered, "We are doomed."

"No we're not!" said Agnez automatically.

"No . . ." said Simeon. "Are you absolutely sure you're really seeing angels, Dorotea?"

"Echoes and fragments," said Dorotea absently, still squinting, this time at another Refuser. "The Refusers . . . it is very faint, like flickering light and shadow in the distance. With us, it is stronger, the light more pure, but still . . . distant. And Lady Dehiems has many layers of light and shade that throng thickly . . ."

"But what can we have to do with Refusers?" asked Agnez, bewildered. "We aren't Refusers! We all use angelic magic, we've all had it used upon us. We'd be dead from the Ash Blood, or have become beastlings."

"No, we cannot be Refusers," said Dorotea. "I do not understand this. Nor this vision I have now. I need to talk to Lady Dehiems—"

"No!" exclaimed Simeon, Henri, and a moment later, Agnez.

"But—"

"No, no," said Simeon. "We don't know if she's an Alban spy, we don't know what she wants. She already has the ear of the Queen. What if she tells the Queen, who tells the Cardinal? Don't you understand, Dorotea? All of this makes it seem more and more like you really are Liliath reborn."

"You aren't, are you?" added Agnez. "I mean, *we* wouldn't mind, but—"

"I'm not Liliath! I just would like to understand! This is what I do, what I'm supposed to do, I'm a scholar of the Belhalle!"

"You'll be a dead scholar," said Henri.

"And we'll be dead too," added Simeon.

"So we do nothing?" asked Dorotea.

"We probably should flee," said Henri gloomily. "To the Eighty-Six Kingdoms, or even Alba—"

"We can't flee," interrupted Agnez. "I'm a Queen's Muske-teer. We don't flee. It would be abandoning my duty. And why should we? If we keep it quiet that Dorotea can see angels in people, and Milady—"

"Dorotea is being questioned by the Cardinal tomorrow," said Simeon heavily. "No. Today. In about ten hours."

"Then we're done for," said Henri.

"Not necessarily," said Dorotea.

"What do you mean?" asked Henri. "I told you, when she

questioned me, she had an angel look inside my head!"

"But only a Cherubim, or at worst a Throne," said Dorotea. "She's old. She won't risk summoning a more powerful angel."

"What does it matter?" asked Simeon. He was watching Dorotea closely, and she wasn't meeting his eyes.

"Well, I can . . . I can probably misdirect or fuddle a lesser angel's interrogations," said Dorotea. "Angelic magic is all about the expression and focus of will— What?"

"You can sketch icons, sense powerful icons, and see angels," said Simeon. "Now we hear you can *resist* angelic magic."

"You *are* Liliath reborn, aren't you?" said Agnez.

"No, I'm not!" shrieked Dorotea, very loudly. Every Musketeer in the huge room looked over at the four friends, many rising up out of their pools and beginning to reach for weapons.

"Laugh," whispered Henri urgently. "Everyone laugh!"

He started laughing, rocking his head back. Simeon joined in, then Agnez. Finally Dorotea chuckled a bit. The Musketeers around them laughed too, as if they'd all shared the same joke, and settled back down with splashes into their own conversations.

"We know you're not Liliath reborn," said Henri. "At least, I believe you when you say you're not. And if you're sure you can misdirect the Cardinal's questioning, then perhaps we aren't doomed after all."

Dorotea looked at Agnez and Simeon, very fiercely for her.

"I believe you're not Liliath reborn," said Simeon quickly.

"I never really thought you were," said Agnez untruthfully.

"Then stop asking me if I am," said Dorotea. "And I will do

my best not to reveal anything to the Cardinal, or talk to Lady Dehiems, or do anything else that will cause problems."

"Good," said Simeon. "Because I think lying as low as possible is the best thing we can all do. Just do our work. Stay out of sight. Make no trouble."

"I wish we could leave the city for a while," said Henri. "You know the old saying 'What you don't see doesn't exist'?"

"No," said the others.

"That doesn't even make sense," said Agnez. "There are plenty of things I don't see I know exist. We can hear the rain on the roof but not see it, right now."

"Look, it just means . . . I just think if we were not here, the Cardinal and everyone would forget about us—"

"I don't want to be forgotten," protested Agnez. "How can I ever be Captain-General of the Queen's Musketeers if I'm forgotten? That wouldn't do at all."

"Never mind," replied Henri faintly. "We'll just have to lie low in general. Like Simeon says, simply do our work. Speaking of which, I'd better get back to the New Palace."

"What?" asked Agnez. "You've forgotten! The Captain asked the Queen for you to be accommodated here."

"Ah," said Henri. "I had forgotten. With everything that's happened tonight . . ."

"You sleep here in the barracks from now on," said Agnez. "All four of us, in my chamber. Derangue, Delamapan, and Desouscarn will be furious about having to move. But it's Dartagnan's order, for your safety from toshers and the like."

She slapped Henri hard on his bare back, making him squeak, and added, "You're halfway to being a Musketeer! Probably as close as you'll ever get, but still!"

In Demaselle House, Liliath was in the royal bed watching Bisc pace in front of the fire, which was heaped high against the cold, the flickering red and orange flames casting interesting shadows on the wall and across the half-closed drapes of the four-poster.

"We've warned as many as we could, but at least fifty of my best people have already been arrested!"

"Don't be concerned, my Bisc!" said Liliath, idly patting the bed next to her, letting the covers slide down from her shoulder, to show she was naked beneath them. It was a mark of how upset Biscaray was that he kept pacing, only stopping when Liliath continued. "I have a plan to bring them out of the Cardinal's clutches. Most of them."

"You do?"

Liliath nodded, and crooked her finger. Bisc hesitated, then slowly approached the bed.

"Of course I do," said Liliath. She reached out and drew Bisc in, slim fingers unlacing his breeches as he lay down next to her.

"You *have* killed that man who told the toshers Lady Dehiems and your Serpent were one and the same?" asked Liliath, idly running one finger down Biscaray's cheek and across his mouth, while she did interesting things to him with her other hand. "If they know the deeper secret still, that the Serpent is Dehiems is Liliath, then all may be lost."

"He didn't know more," gasped Bisc. "It was only . . . cir-
cumstance he saw you as both Dehiems and the Serpent. . . .
They killed him. . . . We have the body. . . ."

"I was greatly displeased," said Liliath. "My four were there, the
four I need. One of them could have been killed or badly hurt."

"I heard . . . I heard there was a beastling—"

"Yes, there was," said Liliath, her eyes fierce with anger, though
her body was calm, intent. "I called on Sarpentiel, unobtrusively,
and I directed the course of the Ash Blood. There should have
been no beastling at all, but . . . but I could not fully exert my
will, not there, not with so many mages so close. Fortunately, I
was able to inform Descaray of the creature's weakness, without
her knowing who it was. But I should not have been in that
position!"

"No . . . no, that's . . . that's my fault!" gulped Bisc.

Liliath shifted onto him, her eyes half closing, though the
glitter of anger remained. Bisc moaned and tried to bend himself
upward, but Liliath pressed a finger on his forehead.

"Stay still, my Biscaray," she said, though she moved herself,
very slowly. "I told you I am displeased. Fortunately, it seems
the toshers themselves will be dealt with anyway, by the servants
of the lovely Queen."

"She . . . she . . . liked . . . She wants you . . ."

"Yes," purred Liliath. "She does. And that is the second thing
I have put in her mind."

"What's . . . the . . . oh . . . the other?"

"You know," whispered Liliath, bending close, her lips

brushing his ear, her impossibly strong hands holding his down on the bed. "Treasure in Ystara. A great treasure, close to the border, very close . . . very close . . ."

"Yes!"

"She wants it, and she shall have it," whispered Liliath. "Or so she thinks. But all she will be doing is helping me. . . ."

Just as Bisc was at that moment.

TWENTY-FIVE

ROCHEFORT CAME AS PROMISED TO ESCORT DOROTEA TO the Cardinal at eleven the next morning. She did not deign to enter the Musketeers' Barracks, merely waiting outside the gate while Dorotea was called. The scholar was ready, and walked out, doffing her cap as Rochefort came near.

"No coach?" asked Dorotea. "Do we go by the river?"

"The Cardinal is visiting the Tower," said Rochefort. She looked tired and cross and was still wearing the same coat as she had been the night before, and there were bloodstains, somewhat wiped, on her sleeves. "Her Eminence awaits you there."

"The Tower," sighed Dorotea. "So I am to go back after all."

"Momentarily," replied Rochefort. "Where are your three constant companions?"

"My fellow Bascons?" asked Dorotea. "Agnez . . . that is Descaray . . . has gone hunting toshers with her troop, Doctor MacNeel to heal the sick in the Infirmary, and Dupallidin to run about at the whim of the Queen's Architect. I am the only one who is not able to pursue their work."

"You serve Her Eminence, and thus the Queen and Sarance,"

said Rochefort, offering her arm. After a moment's hesitation, Dorotea tucked her hand into the crook of the taller woman's elbow, and they walked away together. Dorotea glanced back and saw the commiserating looks from the Musketeer guards on the gate. They'd heard she was going to the Tower, to see the Cardinal. They probably didn't expect to see her again.

Rochefort surprised Dorotea by talking only of unimportant things as they walked. The day was unseasonably cold but clear, and she spoke of the weather, the unusually early hailstorm of the night before, without mentioning the battle in the palace courtyard. She asked about the food in the Musketeers' Barracks, long rumored to be better than the Pursuivants', and inquired if Dorotea had experienced the famous bathhouse.

"Are you trying to put me at my ease?" asked Dorotea, as they rounded the corner of the Pursuivants' Barracks and the entrance to the Tower became visible ahead. A line of chained toshers, the sewer stink strong, were being led inside, under the close attention of a dozen Pursuivants. One wielded a whip, lashing the back of the last Refuser who was slow to climb the steps. The lashing did not make the woman move faster. Instead she fell, slipping down several steps. Even fifty paces away, Dorotea heard the angry shout of the Pursuivant, who lashed her again without effect, before stepping up herself to lift the tosher and hurry her along.

"Because your Pursuivants are having the opposite effect," she added.

"They are only Refusers," said Rochefort, with a shrug.

"Toshers of the Night Crew, thieves, and worse. You have never been treated so. And will not be."

"I am no different to that Refuser who fell," said Dorotea quietly. "We are the same."

"What are you talking about?" asked Rochefort. "You are . . . are like a bright star above, and that Refuser a muddy reflection in a dirty pond. They were forsaken by their Archangel; they should have died in Ystara like the others."

"Or be turned into beastlings?" asked Dorotea sadly, looking up at Rochefort.

"The beastling transformation is a punishment from the other Archangels," said Rochefort, with great certainty. "The Refusers brought it on themselves."

Dorotea did not reply, biting back her disagreement. She had heard this explanation before, usually as part of an argument that Refusers deserved what came to them, particularly if it was mistreatment or not being paid for their work, or something similar.

They walked on in silence, Dorotea silent and glum, Rochefort's face set like stone, her facial scar paler than ever. On the first step, the Pursuivant-Captain spoke again, leaning close, her voice low.

"Her Eminence is not in good sorts this morning," she said. "Please do not fret her."

"Why?"

"Why? Because I do not wish harm to come to you because you make Her Eminence angry!"

"No," said Dorotea. "Why is she in a bad mood?"

Rochefort didn't answer for a few steps. Then she sighed and said, "The Alban. Lady Dehiems. The Queen is already infatuated with her. She sent everyone else out of her levee. Including Her Eminence. This has never happened before."

"She *is* very beautiful," said Dorotea. She was watching Rochefort so carefully her foot slid on a step, and she had to grip the Pursuivant's muscular arm more forcefully. "Did you not think so?"

"She is," agreed Rochefort. "In her way."

She mumbled something after that, which Dorotea didn't catch. There were a lot more Pursuivants on guard ahead than when she had been there before. They were drawing themselves up to full attention, one pushing open the smaller portal within the great iron-studded door.

"What did you say?"

"Not as beautiful as you," said Rochefort, gently drawing her arm away from Dorotea so she could return the salute of the Pursuivants, and then ushering her ahead, into the gloom of the Tower.

"Don't," whispered Dorotea. "You're taking me to a prison, to be questioned. I can't forget that, and you shouldn't."

For the first time since Dorotea had met her, she saw Rochefort suddenly wrong-footed, unsure of herself.

"I . . . I am sorry . . . I had schooled myself to say nothing. I do want you to know I will do my best to keep you from harm—"

Why just me? thought Dorotea. *What about the Refusers? What about everyone else?*

But she did not say it. Rochefort was still talking.

"But . . . there is little I can do, if the Cardinal wills it otherwise."

"Have you slept since yesterday?"

"No . . . no, there has not been time. It is of no matter. Come, we must not keep Her Eminence waiting. As I said, she is already distempered."

After the guard room, they did not climb the stairs as Dorotea expected, but rather a Pursuivant led Rochefort and Dorotea down the steps, with another Pursuivant falling in behind. The scholar could not help but take a little dry swallow as she started down. She had not been afraid when she first came to the Tower, but that had been ignorance as much as anything. Dorotea knew more now, and had greater reason to be afraid.

They were well beneath the rock, below the Tower, when the Pursuivant ahead stopped at a half-lit landing and knocked on the door there. Though the steps continued down, it looked like a very long way. After a moment, another Pursuivant opened the door. She nodded to Rochefort.

"This is Scholar Imsel?"

Rochefort inclined her head and gestured for Dorotea to step forward. She did so, while trying to slow her breathing, to stay calm.

"I must search you, ser," said the Pursuivant, and she quickly passed her hands over Dorotea's head, running her fingers through her hair and then over her body, feeling for any weapon. Rochefort turned away and looked at the wall.

"You have no icons?"

"None," answered Dorotea. Her voice sounded a little scratchy, but it was stronger than she'd thought it might be.

An elegant man, in a very rich version of the Cardinal's livery, with a gold chain on his tunic, came out behind the Pursuivant who had just finished searching Dorotea.

"Captain Rochefort, Her Eminence wishes you to examine the Night Crew Refusers who have just been brought in," said the man. "It is suspected one is the Night King."

Dorotea looked at Rochefort, but the latter did not meet the scholar's gaze.

"I doubt it, Robard," said Rochefort wearily. "We have had nine or ten people claim they can point to the Night King, in the hope of leniency for themselves. None of their descriptions matched, and I doubt we have managed to arrest anyone in the upper ranks at all. But I will go, as ordered."

She clattered away down the stairs.

"What's bitten her?" muttered the Pursuivant to Robard. Dorotea was not meant to have heard, but she did.

Robard ignored the question. He bowed slightly to Dorotea.

"Please follow me, Scholar Imsel," he said.

Dorotea followed the Cardinal's Chief Secretary into the room. It was a surprisingly large chamber, though badly lit by two apparently randomly placed standing candelabras, each holding a dozen candles in wrought-iron claws. Hewn from the stone, the chamber was made more habitable by the addition of a number of thick carpets, laid crosswise and overlapping each other, and there were tapestries hung along the walls. Old tapestries, most in shadow, but the ones Dorotea could see depicted scenes from Sarancian history. The one nearest the door portrayed a stylized overview of the Great Flood of 1309, with Cardinal Saint Erharn shown turning back a curling wave. Or rather standing in front of it while above her in the air Ashalael pursed her lips and puffed her cheeks and blew the water back. It caught Dorotea's attention for a moment, because it was not the usual rendition of Ashalael. The Archangel was usually shown as male with red skin, but in this one she had a bosom wreathed in cloud, her face was quite feminine, and her skin was silver. Yet the seven-pinioned wings behind made it clear who she was meant to be.

"Come."

The command was preemptory, the voice forbidding. Dorotea looked back from the tapestry, toward the end of the room. It was well beyond the farthest candelabra, but she saw a hooded lantern on a long desk, and standing by it the tall figure of the Cardinal. She was wearing a heavy furred robe, all black, so she was hard to see in the semidarkness, save for her crimson face.

Dorotea walked toward her. Robard stayed near the door, but there were two Pursuivants in the corners of the room, behind the Cardinal, who stepped forward a few paces as if the visitor might be dangerous, their hands on sword hilts.

When she was a few paces away, Dorotea stopped and bowed low, almost as low as she had bowed to the Queen.

"Eminence," she said. "I am Scholar Dorotea Imsel, come as you commanded."

The Cardinal reached out and unhooded the lantern. She wore gloves as well as the heavy fur robe, and a close woolen cap instead of miter or ducal cap. It seemed she felt the cold, though this chamber was quite warm, or so it seemed to Dorotea, though she could not see any fireplace or stove.

The unfettered light fell across the desk. Not the famed ivory desk in the Cardinal's palace, this was of old, heavy wood, one corner notched with ax or sword cuts. There were six icons placed on the edge of the desk facing Dorotea, all in a row. Most were painted and gilded, gesso on wood or ivory, but there were two of engraved metal, and the sixth of enameled glass. She knew without looking that none were particularly powerful.

"Tell me which angels these icons summon, Scholar Imsel, and their scope," said the Cardinal. She stepped back out of the light herself, and her hand moved. Dorotea knew it was to touch an icon, for she felt the looming presence of an angel, and a moment later heard the harp strings and the clash of wings. She kept her eyes down, looking straight at the desk, though even then she caught the flash of the strange shapes of light she saw when angels were present.

"May I look closer, Eminence?" asked Dorotea, her throat dry. She could feel the angel prying at her mind. It was Pereastor. She knew him, and blanked her thoughts, focusing entirely on the icons ahead of her.

"Orgentiel," she said. "Seraphim. Whose scope is malleability of metals, excluding gold and silver."

The Cardinal nodded, only her face and eyes visible in the

gloom. She was watching Dorotea intently, head cocked slightly to one side, no doubt listening to Pereastor's report.

"Beherael. Seraphim. Closing and shutting."

She paused at the third icon. It was a painting of three interlocked wheels, each with spokes that extended beyond the rim, and a gilded halo above. It was reminiscent of several that she knew, but she did not know it.

"A Throne," said Dorotea. "One I do not know."

Pereastor tested the truth of that in her mind, and the Cardinal nodded again.

"It is of the Ystaran host," she said. "Xaniatiel, whose scope is hooved beasts."

"The fourth is of my own making," said Dorotea steadily. "Horcinael, whose scope is to make liquid solid or solid liquid. The fifth is Gloranael, whose scope is . . . uncertain, but she is employed to arrest decay, in both the animate and inanimate. Some say her scope is therefore time, but I do not agree."

"And the sixth?"

Dorotea bent to look more closely at the icon of enameled glass. It was extremely fine work, and though she had done little work with glass or enamels of any kind, she knew it was both extraordinary and unusual. It took her a few seconds more to realize that it also seemed familiar, not because of the angel—a fairly typical aged woman's face, with golden eyes and mouth, brown skin, and a halo of sky blue—but because of the style of the illustration, even in glass.

"I do not know the angel," she said. "But I would say this is by Chalconte. I did not know he ever worked in glass, or with enamels."

"Where have you seen Chalconte's work?"

"In the Belhalle," said Dorotea, and once again she felt Pereastor testing the truth of that, and the cold spike of the angel's power inside her head, seeking more, knowing there was more to find. "And my friend Doctor MacNeel has a family heirloom, an icon of Requaniel, rumored to be by Chalconte. I examined it and in my opinion that is true. Also, I looked closely at the Diamond Icons when we first found them."

"You have never seen others?"

"No, Eminence," answered Dorotea, wincing as Pereastor made sure this was true.

"Have you ever seen an icon made by Liliath, the so-called Maid of Ellanda?"

"No," said Dorotea truthfully. "Not as far as I know."

"You are not Liliath reborn?"

"No," said Dorotea, forcing back the anger that arose at once again being asked this ridiculous question.

"What does the expression 'killer mage' mean to you?"

"Nothing, I mean nothing in particular," answered Dorotea, puzzled by this question.

She felt the presence of Pereastor retreat from her mind and heard the faint, receding harp strings of his departure. The Cardinal swayed in place and reached out her hand, the closer Pursuivant swiftly coming forward to support her.

"So you are come honestly to this icon-making talent of

yours," said the Cardinal slowly, her voice weary. "Though it still might lead you to heresy, like Chalconte."

Dorotea didn't say anything. She kept her head bowed, and slowed her breath, hoping also to slow her racing heart. She felt the Cardinal's presence like a sharp blade, stopped in the moment before striking her head off, or being pulled back to rest.

"Captain Rochefort has spoken for you," said the Cardinal. "She wishes you to join my Pursuivants."

"What?" burst out of Dorotea's mouth.

"You are a very powerful and skilled mage," said the Cardinal. "Entirely suited to my service. And that of Ashalael."

"I . . . I am a scholar . . . ," said Dorotea. Thoughts were racing through her mind. Was this a choice between serving the Cardinal or execution? Or imprisonment?

"Come, take my hand," said the Cardinal. She slipped off her right glove. "I hold it out to you, and should you take it, all suspicion of heresy is removed. You may make icons as you will, in my service."

Dorotea gulped back hasty words, frantically trying to think how she could refuse. Be a Pursuivant? Carry out the Cardinal's every whim, even when that meant bringing people to the Tower to be interrogated, perhaps tortured, even executed?

"I thank Your Eminence," she said. "This is a great honor . . . but one I cannot accept . . ."

"Cannot?" snapped the Cardinal, withdrawing her hand. "Or will not? We fight an unceasing struggle against the enemies of Ashalael and Sarance, one that requires the services of the most skilled mages, as you are. You shirk your duty."

"I truly am only a scholar, Your Eminence," said Dorotea. "I can best serve the Queen and the kingdom in the Belhalle."

She risked lifting her eyes a little, expecting the Cardinal to be glaring back. But the older woman was shaking her head, and looked more frustrated than angry—and very, very tired. She was still held under her left elbow by the Pursuivant.

"Truly, it would be so much easier if you were Liliath reborn," grumbled the Cardinal. "The block is very close here, and I have yet to meet a mage who could summon angels after meeting the executioner's ax. But you are not Liliath, as I suppose I knew all along. After all, how could she come again? She is long dead. And the Queen has seen you, thinks well of you . . . she is too kindhearted . . . if I could remove all Refusers from the kingdom, cast them into the sea perhaps . . . and now this temptation of treasure, the Diamond Icons . . . "

Dorotea stayed as still as she could, a new fear rising. The Cardinal was mumbling to herself, her words becoming incoherent, as if she had forgotten Dorotea was even there.

"Ystara is infested with beastlings, the cost of an expedition, the risk of failure . . . yet the treasury would benefit . . . the King such a drain on the exchequer, and he can always play upon her guilt . . . even that small amount of gold would have proven useful . . . then there is the Alban woman, the Atheling's agent no doubt . . ."

The Cardinal's muttering became a gasping moan. The second Pursuivant rushed forward to hold the aged priest under her right elbow, as her legs sagged and her head lolled forward . . .

Dorotea jumped as someone else touched her shoulder. She jinked her neck looking too fast behind her, but it was only Robard, the secretary, who didn't speak but made a gesture for her to stand up. He immediately grabbed her arm and hustled her from the room.

"Say nothing of this!" he hissed urgently as they hit the landing, the guard Pursuivant slamming the door behind them. "Her Eminence has overtaxed herself, she will recover soon. But you must not speak a word, or I will see you go to the block myself!"

"I understand," replied Dorotea, considerably shaken. "May I . . . may I return to the Belhalle?"

"No!" spat Robard. "You must stay within the Star Fortress until Her Eminence orders otherwise. Nothing changes until she orders it."

"Then I go back to the Musketeers' Barracks?"

Robard hesitated, and looked at the closed door.

"I suppose so," he said grudgingly. He gestured to a Pursuivant. "Escort Scholar Imsel from the Tower."

"Yes, ser."

"Remember," said Robard. "Say nothing of this to anyone!"

"I wondered why Magister Hazurain was needed in the Tower so hurriedly," said Simeon quietly. He and Dorotea were in a corner of the physic garden at the Infirmary, and she had just told him what had happened. "I suppose it makes us safer. For a while."

"Will she recover?" asked Dorotea.

"I don't know," answered Simeon. "It might simply be the exertion of summoning, on top of general weariness, in which case she will. But it could be apoplectic bleeding in the brain. If the latter, it depends on how swiftly Magister Hazurain can investigate and act. And whether she considers it worthwhile summoning the angels required, because there would be considerable cost."

"It's the Cardinal!" said Dorotea. "Surely, she would do whatever is needed."

"Months or more, taken from Hazurain's own life," mused Simeon. "It would depend on the chance of success. We start with lesser angels to gauge what might be done, before calling on the great. If there is little chance of success, Hazurain won't intervene. Even for the Cardinal."

"Anyway, I have kept my head attached to my neck," said Dorotea. "And yours, I suppose."

"Thank you," said Simeon gravely. "Henri will be relieved. I think he was the most fretful. Agnez seemed to think nothing could possibly happen to her, being a Musketeer and all."

They both laughed at that.

"Do you still see the angel in me?" asked Simeon, very quietly.

Dorotea squinted and looked off to one side.

"Yes."

"Can you tell which angel it is?"

"No," said Dorotea. "There isn't enough . . . shape, I suppose. And it's not part of an angel I've ever seen before, either as an icon or manifested. Though if I could get to the Belhalle and look through Marcew and Depremival and perhaps Alarazon . . ."

"It's best left a mystery," warned Simeon.

"I'm not going to do anything," protested Dorotea. "I promised."

"Curiosity killed the lion keeper," said Simeon. "I must get back to my patients. Lots of Musketeers and Pursuivants in today, with minor wounds. Mostly from falling over in the sewers, not from fighting toshers."

"I saw some being taken into the Tower," said Dorotea. "Refusers, that is. Has anyone found out why those toshers attacked us in the palace?"

Simeon was silent for a moment. He looked across at the walls of the garden, and then up at the blue sky above.

"I don't think they were attacking us," he said. "I think they were attacking Lady Dehiems. They waited until she was close."

"But why . . . ?"

Simeon held up one large hand.

"As we said before, best we lie low. Do our work. Leave the mysteries to those who can afford the consequences of discovering what they mean."

"I am not allowed back to the Belhalle," said Dorotea. "So what do I do?"

"Finish painting the sign at the tavern?" suggested Simeon. "See if there's any other similar work around? I have to go. I'll see you at the barracks this evening."

PART V

The Expedition to Ystara

TWENTY-SIX

DOROTEA HAD JUST STEPPED DOWN FROM HER LADDER and was staring up at the finished tavern sign with a critical eye when her friends arrived, rather cautiously in the case of Henri and Simeon, as it was Thursday and once again the King's Guards were in possession of the tavern. But there were none of the green-clad soldiery outside, only half a dozen inside, and they did not pay any attention to the new arrivals.

"I thought there were meant to be six golden cups," said Henri. "I mean, there were six splodges before."

"Seven balances better within the space," said Dorotea.

"But the place is *called* the Six Cups—" said Henri.

"Six or seven on the sign, all I care is that I get an actual cup in my hand!" exclaimed Agnez, sitting down on a rough-hewn stool by one of the large barrels. She looked over to a Refuser server and waved her hand. "Wine!"

The girl nodded and rushed inside. But before she could emerge again with the wine Agnez greatly desired to wash the foul taste of trooping through sewers all day out of her mouth, a familiar booming voice made her jump up, and all the others start.

"Drinking out of turn, Descaray! Today the tavern is not for Musketeers!"

Sesturo stood in the road, laughing.

"You are summoned, all of you," he continued.

"Summoned? By whom?" asked Dorotea.

"The Queen," said Sesturo. "Haven't you heard? You're joining the Expedition!"

The four friends spoke as one, with the same question.

"What expedition?"

Sesturo sighed.

"What is it with the young folk of today? Never paying attention, going off to taverns in defiance of regulations—"

"What expedition?"

"The Expedition to Ystara. All your fault, of course. You find three of the Diamond Icons and everyone gets excited. Now you have to go off and get the rest. It'll be easy, or so I'm told, a mere jaunt into the mountains on the border with Ystara, fight a few beastlings—a few dozen beastlings perhaps—gather up the treasures, and come home. Come on, we have to go and muster up everyone else."

"Everyone else?" asked Agnez.

"Well, it isn't just the four of you going," said Sesturo. "Some of our fellow Musketeers will be along to make sure you don't get lost. And an assorted lot of those other fellows we trip over about the place from time to time. Like those drunken fellows inside."

"I take it you mean the King's Guards, the Cardinal's Pursuivants, and the Watch?" asked Simeon, with a faint smile.

"So that's who they are," replied Sesturo dubiously. "I have wondered. Oh, and some cannons and suchlike from our friends the Loyal Royal artillerists. Some think that such things might be necessary for dealing with beastlings."

"There's really going to be an expedition to Ystara?" asked Agnez, her eyes sparkling. "And we are to go?"

"You are to go," said Sesturo, scowling. "While better folk must stay behind."

"You mean . . ."

"The Queen stays in Lutace, I must stay with Her Majesty," said Sesturo. "But you are particularly required to go expeditioning, it seems."

"No time for a single glass of wine?" sighed Agnez.

Sesturo smiled and marched away, whistling. The four friends looked at each other and followed, running to catch up. Sesturo's paces were long.

"You're not really summoned by the Queen," said the huge Musketeer, as they left the tavern behind. "I only said that to impress the guards inside."

"What?" asked Agnez. "You mean the whole Expedition thing is—"

"No, that's true enough, you'll have your adventure," said Sesturo. "But it's the Captain who wants to talk to you about it. At our barracks here, not over at the Queen's Palace."

"The Captain?" asked Agnez. She straightened her back and took an apprehensive breath. "Dartagnan?"

"None other," said Sesturo blandly. "She won't eat you alive.

Probably cook you a bit first."

"This expedition, I guess it is going to the place specified in the directions from the letter we found, and that sketched map from Lady Dehiems's second chest?" asked Simeon.

"Not my affair," replied Sesturo. "Ask the Captain."

"Why are *we* included in this expedition?" asked Dorotea.

"Because we found the Diamond Icons, right?" suggested Agnez.

Sesturo shrugged, refused to answer any more questions, and marched on. With the day almost done, there were many people about, leaving their work. Most were skilled workers, masons, and carpenters and the like, but there were several gangs of Refuser laborers as well, now escorted by the Watch, whereas previously they had moved about on their own—though many Refuser children still ran around unsupervised, presumably carrying out the minor tasks, message taking, and deliveries that secured them a precarious living.

Dartagnan was waiting for the four friends in her study on the third floor of the barracks. Sesturo expertly led them up the central staircase past Musketeers waiting for orders, Musketeers waiting to report, Musketeers loitering for no reason at all, Musketeers practicing holding a stair against multiple attackers below them, Musketeers betting on the progress of a child's spinning top across a landing; and all the usual hustle and bustle that was typical of the place.

Dartagnan's study was an oasis of calm by comparison with the rest of the barracks. A long, broad room with tall windows that faced the New Palace construction site, it was spare in its furnishings, having only a twelve-foot-long table, a stand for several swords, and a half-dozen chairs, which were mostly pushed up against the wall. The table was currently strewn with maps, papers, and ledgers. Two clerks, both older Musketeers who these days labored more with pen than sword, were at work on one end, while Dartagnan stood in the middle, surveying the maps. She turned as Sesturo entered, swift and straight-backed, her silver hair glinting in the light from several oil lamps suspended from the ceiling on short bronze chains.

"Ah, Sesturo. You have brought them. Please, sers, come to the table, gather around; yes, there, opposite me. No, no, don't bother to salute, I know who you all are; you know who I am. There are important matters to discuss and time is of the essence."

Hats that had been in the process of being doffed were restored and everyone gathered close, facing Dartagnan across the table. She hardly waited for them to get in place before continuing.

"Her Majesty has decided upon an expedition to Ystara to recover the remaining nine Diamond Icons and whatever other treasures may be in the Temple to Palleniel Exalted founded by Liliath, the so-called Maid of Ellanda. Though this temple is only some seven leagues from our border, Ystara is infested with beastlings, and it is unknown how many there are, or indeed, their peculiarities, strengths, and weaknesses. Consequently, this will be a military expedition, commanded jointly by myself and Captain Rochefort of the Cardinal's Pursuivants, composed of two troops of Musketeers, two of Pursuivants, two companies of the Watch, and two companies of the King's Guard, plus an attachment of light artillery from the Loyal Royal Artillery Company. In addition to this, Her Majesty has also ordered that the Refusers, suspected to be members of the Night Crew, arrested in the past day and night, be sent not to the galleys, but to serve in the Expedition as porters, laborers, and so forth, and if they so wish, and it proves possible, to then stay in Ystara, their ancestral home."

Dartagnan paused, allowing her listeners to take stock of what she had just imparted. Varying degrees of shock, confusion, and concern could be seen on everyone's faces.

"As I said, this is to be a military expedition. We will call for volunteers from the regiments, and make our selection. But Her Majesty has decided the four of you are to be given the opportunity to also go on the Expedition, as a reward for finding the three Diamond Icons in the first place. I should say that apart from the recovery of the heirlooms of Her Majesty's house, a proportion of any other treasure found will be distributed among members of the Expedition."

"Given the opportunity, Captain?" asked Simeon cautiously. "We don't *have* to go?"

"It is an opportunity," said Dartagnan. "Which cuts both ways. I suspect Her Majesty would be most displeased to have this generous offer refused."

Simeon nodded. It was as he thought. They had been drawn into the affairs of the great and could not easily escape.

"I take it you will all be joining the Expedition?"

The four nodded. Henri enthusiastically, his mind already full of great mounds of Ystaran double dolphins and piles of gems. Dorotea slowly and thoughtfully, for she was curious about Ystara, and beastlings, and Palleniel, for reasons that had much to do with what she saw in the Refusers and in herself and her friends. Simeon reluctantly, because it would take him from the Infirmary, where he was learning a great deal, and he was afraid of beastlings, and he feared the worst. Agnez with simple acceptance, because Musketeers were going to battle and she was a Musketeer.

"Very well. Another question arises. As I said, this is a military expedition. I will not permit those not under orders to be part of this campaign. Descaray, of course, is already a Musketeer. But for the duration Sers Dupallidin, Imsel, and MacNeel must also become soldiers of one of the regiments concerned. I have spoken to Franzonne and Sesturo and they tell me that my Musketeers would not be averse to allowing you a special, temporary status among them. But if for some strange reason you wish to march and possibly die among the Pursuivants or those others, I believe that could be arranged."

Agnez started to say something, most likely in outrage that anyone could be allowed to even temporarily join the Musketeers without going through the trials she had endured, but Sesturo trod on her foot, stifling whatever she was about to utter as she instead had to restrain a gasp of pain.

The others stared blankly at Dartagnan for several seconds, before Simeon was the first to answer this proposal.

"Captain, I am aware of . . . of the high honor . . . " he began hesitantly, "the high honor you would do us. But I am a doctor and magister, not a soldier, not a swordsman . . ."

"You would be our doctor," said Dartagnan. "I should have said, while you *temporarily* wear the tabard of a Musketeer, I shall employ you where you will be most useful. Each regiment will have its own doctor; you would be ours. Similarly, Dupallidin, I believe you are extremely adept with numbers, money, and ledgers, and so no doubt would be useful to my clerks and quartermaster. And Scholar Imsel, I would ask you to study, to discover as much as you can about this hidden Temple of Palleniel Exalted, to ferret out whatever the Royal Archives or the Belhalle libraries may hold about it, and any writings on the nature of the beastlings we will face. This latter, perhaps most of all, given we know so little about the beastlings of Ystara, as opposed to those created here by misuse of magic upon Refusers."

"We know they can be killed," said Agnez boldly.

"Ah, the rashness of youth!" exclaimed Dartagnan, though she did not seem displeased. "Indeed, you slew one. But I daresay you don't know that every beastling is different? No two beastlings have the same weaknesses, the same vulnerabilities. You were fortunate to shoot the one at the palace in a barren patch without armor, but the next beastling might have a throat that is proof against a pistol ball."

"Oh . . . I . . . I didn't know," said Agnez. "But it wasn't just luck. Someone told me to shoot there."

"Someone told you?" asked Dartagnan quickly. "Who?"

"I don't know," replied Agnez. "I thought it was Dorotea, but she said not. One of the courtiers, I suppose."

"A pity," said Dartagnan. "Perhaps they only guessed. But it would be of considerable assistance to us if we could call upon anyone with greater knowledge of beastlings."

"Magister Delazan, who was killed at the hospital . . . he had quite a collection of books about beastlings," said Simeon. "Dissections and so forth. I had not considered that their differences would make them difficult to fight. Though the books he had were only about the beastlings made by angelic magic here, not the original transformees of Ystara. Or their descendants, I suppose."

"If they have descendants," said Dartagnan. "The folk on the border, who see beastlings from time to time, claim there are no young, the beastlings do not breed, nor do they age. It is true some seem to be the same individuals, unchanging over time. I am a Bascon too, as perhaps you know, from Acques, right on the border. I have seen beastlings on the mountain path above my village. One we called the Yellow Head, for its plume of feathers or something akin to feathers. I saw it as a child, and I have seen it in more recent years. It looked the same, unchanged."

"Is the Lady Dehiems to come on the Expedition?" asked Dorotea.

"No," said Dartagnan.

"I wondered. She seemed to be suggesting exactly such a thing last night. . . ."

"And did so again today," said Dartagnan. She paused for a moment and then continued. "Lady Dehiems has been with the Queen since the morning levee. In fact, she suggested the Refusers be used as laborers for the Expedition, rather than sent to the galleys. But she did not at any point suggest she be a part of the Expedition herself, and in fact, said she could not be, as her health is poor and severely affected by travel."

Dartagnan added, without emotion or inflection, "Besides, though she is new to the court, clearly Her Majesty already holds Lady Dehiems in very high esteem and affection, and would not wish her absence from Her Majesty's side, particularly to go on a mission fraught with danger, as this undoubtedly will be."

"Where are we going, exactly?" asked Henri. "Where is Baranais?"

Dartagnan looked at him sharply.

"So you did decipher the letter. I wondered."

Henri gulped and flushed at the same time, and then squeaked as Simeon trod on his foot.

"Ah yes, yes we did, ser," he said. "But we thought it best not to . . . not to bring attention . . ."

"I understand," said Dartagnan. "Is there anything else you chose not to mention? Any of you?"

There was a general shuffling, and an exchange of downcast glances.

"Very well."

Dartagnan leaned over the map, and put her finger down.

"Baranais is here, to the south of Monthallard. It is one of the lesser passes through the mountains. The 'twin peaks' referred to are probably the greater and lesser peaks of Mount Cabiromera, with the temple in the saddle between. It is unclear whether there is a path or road from the pass, or beyond it. All this will have to be carefully scouted, no doubt in the face of beastlings. We will proceed cautiously, preparing a fortified camp each night once we cross the border. The Refuser laborers will be useful for that. It will make for slow progress, but better to be sure than dead."

"How long will it all take?" asked Simeon.

"Ten days to prepare here, perhaps longer," said Dartagnan. "If it were just we Musketeers, half that time. But it is not, and I know the Watch, for one, do not have enough horses or mules or carts. They will have to be procured, as will numerous other supplies. Once we get under way, even in our lands it will be slow. Twenty days to the border, if the weather grows no worse. Then a day or perhaps longer to climb to the top of the pass, after that, perhaps another day to locate and get to the temple . . . if there is a great treasure, a day or two to load again and a similar time to return. All depending on the weather, on the exact nature of the ground, on the beastlings.

"And, of course, on ourselves. I shall count you as Musketeers, and expect far more of you than of any others. The Pursuivants are not mean fighters, but they rely overmuch on their icons, on angels and magic. The King's Guard are, at best, individually brave. The Watch . . . well, as their name suggests they will be useful to watch the Refusers and little else. The artillerists are reliable, and know their business. But even their light sakers and falconets may prove too difficult to get through the pass. When it comes to fighting the beastlings, it is Musketeers who must carry the day. Remember that."

No one said anything. They were all thinking of the beastling in the palace courtyard. What would it be like to face more than one such creature?

"Descaray, you may see them fitted out. You can discover your duties tomorrow, sers. You know what I want of you, look into how it may be done."

"I may go to the Belhalle?" asked Dorotea. "Leave the Star Fortress? Only, I was forbidden by the Cardinal . . ."

"I believe Her Eminence is not well and not to be disturbed by such small matters," said Dartagnan. "But for surety, Captain Rochefort will be informed you have leave to pass the gate. I do not believe there is any more danger from the toshers—if there was any to you four in the first place. However, have someone accompany you whenever you go out of the fortress. And all of you, wear your swords!"

This last instruction was clearly a dismissal, emphasized by Sesturo stretching one great arm toward the door. The four friends filed out, into the hubbub, their place inside immediately taken by Lieutenant Decastries, who raised an eyebrow as he passed them.

"So it seems we have three more Musketeers!" exclaimed Sesturo, rubbing his hands together. "After a fashion!"

"The fish has bitten the hook all the way down into its greedy stomach," said Liliath with satisfaction to Biscaray. They were standing on the small platform between the peaks of two roofs of Demaselle House, so that Liliath could examine the heavens. As always, she scanned the part of the night sky that related to the Ystaran angels, noting with satisfaction there were no changes that would give away the movements on the earth that were destined to restore Palleniel, and most particularly the Archangel's star had not suddenly reappeared. She did not expect to see anything, but it was like a nigglesome tooth. She did not want to see changes, but could not resist looking, just in case.

"You were all day with the Queen," said Bisc. "In her bed-chamber too, or so I hear."

"What, are you jealous, my Bisc?" asked Liliath, running her finger down his cheek.

"I know I have no right," said Bisc. "But yes . . . I am jealous."

"Do not be," said Liliath. "You will come with me to Ystara, you will be with me—and she will not. And in time, Sarance will be nothing, there will be no queen. A governor perhaps. Maybe you would like that? To rule where once you were reviled?"

"I want to be wherever you are," said Bisc, drawing her close. They kissed, and Liliath slid her hands under Biscaray's coat and shirt.

"Your hands are always warm," murmured Bisc. "Your skin has heat . . . no matter how cold the air . . ."

"I am not as other mortals," whispered Liliath.

A knock at the door to the attic, which led to their small walkway, made them move apart. Liliath's warm hand went to her sleeve, where she still wore the bracelet with three icons.

"Yes," called out Biscaray. His hand was on the hilt of the dagger at his belt. He had given orders they were not to be disturbed.

"It's Sevrin," said the doorwarden, opening the door a crack. "News, Bisc."

"What news?"

"The jailer we bought at Riversedge, he says the prisoners . . . our people . . . are not being sent to the galleys at Mallassa. They're to go to Ystara! There's going to be an expedition!"

"I know," said Bisc. He looked over at Liliath. She nodded. "We will be going too."

"We will?" asked Sevrin, poking her head around the door, her eyes wide in amazement. "You too, milady?"

"Well, the often sickly *milady* will stay here," said Liliath, smiling. "Sadly, she will be too ill to see the Queen, and too ill to receive visitors. But *I* will become a Refuser, most scarred or afflicted in some way, and yes . . . together we will return to Ystara. We will restore Palleniel. And all will be made whole!"

"We should have told Dartagnan," said Agnez to Dorotea. They were in their shared chamber at the barracks, preparing for bed, at least notionally. Dorotea was drawing something very small on a torn scrap of paper, Simeon was making notes from Deraoul's *Abstract on the Establishment of a Battle Hospital and the Provision of Medicines, Icons, and Sundries*, and Henri was leaning on the door to make sure no one else came in. "About what you see in milady, and the Refusers."

"And in us?" asked Simeon. "No, we should not!"

"Surely it doesn't matter," said Henri hopefully. "I mean, Dehiems isn't going on the Expedition. Perhaps by the time we get back, with the treasure, things will have changed. Maybe whatever Dorotea sees will be gone by then."

"I am concerned for the Queen's safety," said Agnez. "If milady is not what she seems . . ."

"The Cardinal will be here, and Franzonne and Sesturo," said Henri.

"Let us concentrate on what we know lies ahead," said Simeon, tilting his book so it was better illuminated by the hanging lamp. "This expedition. I think it good we will be out of the city, and out of the sight of Cardinal and Queen."

"If we aren't killed by beastlings," said Henri.

"Apart from that," conceded Simeon.

"Rochefort is in joint command," pointed out Agnez. "She won't forget us. She was already suspicious, even when we didn't know ourselves there was anything to be suspicious about."

"There may not be anything!" protested Henri. "All we know is Dorotea can see something! Maybe . . . maybe that's all there is to it. A hallucination!"

Dorotea looked up from her drawing, which was an abstract of thick, swift strokes that didn't seem much by themselves but when taken together and looked at aslant, suggested very much the towering wings of an angel.

"The Refusers definitely have the same . . . residue or taint . . . that we do," she said baldly. "From the same singular angel. But Dehiems is different. It seems to me hers comes from *many* angels."

"We are not Refusers!" exclaimed Henri. "Again: all of us have summoned angels. All of us have had angelic magic practiced upon us! Yet we live and are not beastlings!"

"I know," sighed Dorotea. She squinted and looked not quite at Henri. "I am sure it is the same angel, but the . . . the quality of the residue is different. In us, it is bright flame, in them a clouded slurry, but moving like fire . . . oh! I can't properly describe it. I know I can't ask Dehiems about it, but the Rector at the Belhalle perhaps—"

"No!"

Dorotea looked around at the others, who had all expressed themselves at once.

"I didn't say I was going to," she said, putting her scrap of paper and charcoal stick aside with a sigh. "Just that I would like to!"

"We should sleep," said Agnez. "Tomorrow will be busy. Very busy."

She stood up and lifted the glass of the lantern, pursing her lips to blow it out.

"I am still reading," said Simeon, not looking up.

"Yes, who put you in charge?" asked Henri. He was tired but did not want to admit it.

"I am the *real* Musketeer here," said Agnez, surprised to be questioned. "Of course I'm in charge."

With that, she extinguished the lantern, to a small chorus of complaints, and the sounds of Simeon's book being angrily snapped shut and Henri tripping over a sword scabbard on the way to his own bed.

TWENTY-SEVEN

DESPITE DONNING THE HATS AND TABARDS OF MUSKETEERS, and forced into the habit of wearing their swords, Simeon, Henri, and Dorotea were not transformed into soldiers and were not sent on the continuing patrols against the toshers in the city's subterranean layers, nor to practice their swordplay as Agnez was, with Franzonne and Gruppe, the latter being expert in brawling and unconventional techniques. As Dartagnan had said, the "temporary Musketeers" were put to work where their particular skills and experience would be most useful for the Expedition.

Simeon found himself back at the Infirmary, though he now spent little time with patients or assisting Magister Hazurain. He was mostly in the back rooms of the hospital, with dispensers and bandage makers and clerks, working out exactly which medicines, instruments, consumables, and other items could be packed into the two horse-drawn wagons or onto the six mules the regimental medical teams would share.

On the fourth day after the announcement of the Expedition, when the initial excitement had given way to some extent to dull routine, a rumor sent Simeon from the apothecary's store, where he had been overseeing the packing of bottles of calamine lotion in straw-filled boxes, to search out Magister Hazurain, who he found examining a King's Guard who had been badly injured by discharging a musket with a barrel blocked with earth, the result of carelessly using it as a crutch while inebriated.

"We shall have to take off that hand," said Hazurain conversationally to Simeon. She had already employed Sarpentiel to put the Guard into a very deep sleep.

"Would not Gwethiniel . . ."

"Perhaps," said Hazurain. "But I have called upon her once this month, and that is my limit. You know my methodology, Simeon. I must calculate the cost to my own life span, not expend it willy-nilly. She will survive the amputation, I judge. Never employ an angel unless it is necessary, and you will live to not regret it."

Simeon nodded. Gwethiniel, who could make flesh and bone whole again, was a Virtue and according to the calculations of Handuran, to summon her would cost two months of a mage's life.

"I will use the number two and three saws and my Turingen knives," said Hazurain to one of the attendants. "Have Detheren prepare them. Tell her I wish her to use my icon of Charysylth for the cleansing. Now, what can I do for you, Simeon? I take it you wish to borrow more of my essential equipment for your expedition?"

"No, Magister," said Simeon. "Well, perhaps I may, later. But I heard something and I wanted to ask you about it."

"Ask," said Hazurain. She sat on the end of the wounded Guard's bed and rubbed her eyes. "Ah, I am weary. I don't suppose you would take off this fellow's hand for me, would you?"

"If you'd like me to, Magister!" replied Simeon, delighted to be given such a responsibility. He forgot his question for a few minutes as they both examined the terribly crushed hand and discussed the technicalities of the amputation, which of the Seraphim and Cherubim to summon for their assistance and so forth. Only when the attendant returned with a box of bone saws and Simeon's fellow student Detheren did he remember what he wanted to ask, just as Hazurain was about to bow out and leave him to the operation.

"Oh, ser! What I wanted to ask . . . I heard you were called in to see Lady Dehiems, the Alban?"

Hazurain wiped her forehead.

"Oh, yes," she said vaguely. "Her Majesty was concerned, Lady Dehiems not being able to attend her at the palace. But it is only a case of some river fever, an Alban strain Lady Dehiems is prone to. Not serious, but it sits in the lungs. Rest and quiet is the most appropriate remedy, except in extreme cases or where the patient simply must be moved, and then angelic intervention is warranted. Dehiems was adamant she would soon recover, and I judge that is true, though perhaps not as swiftly as she hopes. A few weeks, rather than days."

"What were Dehiems's symptoms, Magister?" asked Simeon. He wanted to ask about the strange internal fires Dorotea could see but dared not. Presumably Hazurain couldn't see them any more than Simeon could himself, but there might be other signs of oddness.

"Oh, just the fever, she was very warm to touch, and extreme lassitude," yawned Hazurain. "It was all absolutely typical of the illness. I must retire, Simeon."

"Thank you, Magister," said Simeon, walking a little way out of the chamber with the older doctor. He lowered his voice and leaned close to say, "And Her Eminence, the Cardinal? She recovers well?"

Hazurain glanced at Simeon in puzzlement.

"You are very interested in the high and mighty," she said. "The new Queen's favorite, oh I know who Dehiems is, even if word has not spread more widely, and then the Cardinal herself as well. Why do you ask?"

"Uh, curiosity," stammered Simeon. "And . . . er . . . to be honest, self-interest. This whole expedition, it was set in train while the Cardinal was unwell, and absent from the Queen's side, and I thought perhaps when she is recovered, she might decide it isn't a good idea after all . . ."

"I see," said Hazurain. She hesitated, then spoke very softly, "Her Eminence is considerably older in body than her years, because she has used herself unmercifully to serve Sarance, summoning angels. She does recover, but it will be slow. Very much slower than Lady Dehiems, who has youth on her side, and is not a mage. I expect the Alban favorite to be at the Queen's side far sooner than the Cardinal will be. Does that answer your question?"

"Yes, it does," answered Simeon. "The Expedition will go ahead."

"I wish you good luck," said Hazurain, and left.

Simeon knew she wasn't talking about the amputation.

Dorotea, allowed to return to the Belhalle, threw herself into the required researches with great gusto. Accompanied by a silent, reserved Musketeer called simply Huro, whose company she valued because he hardly seemed to be there, she went back and forth to the Belhalle by boat.

Her initial searches, concentrating on finding maps of the border area with Ystara, went reasonably well, though many appeared at first glance to contradict each other on the placement of geographic features, and none were of the extraordinarily valuable type made by flying angels in conjunction with expert cartographers, but those were rare for any part of the world.

After a few days, when she moved from maps to looking for useful references on beastlings, Liliath, Palleniel, and the Doom of Ystara, Dorotea could not find most of the volumes she needed, even though they were listed in the great bibliographies chained to the desks of the Upper Reading Room in Belhalle's chief library (known colloquially as "Petal," for the flower motif repeated everywhere throughout its oak wainscoting).

There were many titles like *Flight from Ystara and the Fall of*

Palleniel by Villeska or *An Examination of Five Beastlings Fished from the River Agros,* or *Letters of a Bascon Marcher to Her Ystaran Counterpart, in the Time of the Ash Blood Plague* listed in the bibliographies but not present on the shelves. Initially Dorotea had presumed this was just the usual problem of books not being put back where they were supposed to go. But after consulting with junior librarians, a great shaking of heads, and the movement of many stacks of books that had been awaiting sorting or cataloging for decades at the least, it became clear the books, journals, and papers were no longer in the Belhalle libraries at all.

It was one of the most senior librarians who explained what had happened.

"Confiscated by Cardinal Dumauron," she said, looking over the bibliographic entry Dorotea showed her. "You see this sign, here?"

Dorotea leaned close. The bibliographies were written by many different hands, over centuries, and there were many blotches, crossings-out, and other marks that might or might not be entirely accidental. There was a blot above the third letter of the title, which could be construed as deliberate.

"Green ink," said the librarian.

Dorotea peered still closer. The Reading Room, like the Rotunda, had angel-clarified glass panels in its roof, but the day was not bright.

"I suppose it is," she agreed. Very dark green, hardly different from the purple-black oak gall ink most used in these volumes.

"Green dot," said the librarian with a sniff. "Removed by

order of Cardinal Dumauron. Which was, let me think, about eighty years ago."

"Removed where?" asked Dorotea.

The librarian shrugged.

"Ask the Pursuivants. Though as you're a Musketeer, I suppose you won't want to do that."

"I'm not really a Musketeer," protested Dorotea, looking down at her tabard somewhat distastefully. She had left her sword with Huro by the front door. "It's temporary, for the Expedition. I'm a scholar here."

"Oh, you're going on the Expedition!" exclaimed the librarian. "You will look for books, won't you? The Ystaran King was supposed to have a copy of Mallegre's *Mystery Plays*, the last one extant. If you could find that!"

"I will certainly look," promised Dorotea. She brightened at the thought of long-lost books that might still exist in Liliath's secret temple. "I hadn't thought there might be books! Everyone has been so excited about the Diamond Icons and gold and so on."

"Pah! Trumpery stuff, compared to *knowledge*. Please, please do make sure anything of interest is brought back."

"I'll do my best," said Dorotea. "And I will see if I can find out where the books taken from here have got to as well. I'll ask Rochefort; she'll know."

"Captain Rochefort?" muttered the librarian. She coughed and moved away slightly. "Yes, well, good luck. And please don't mention my name."

"I don't know your—"

But the librarian had disappeared, back between the shelves.

Henri was enjoying himself far more as a kind of Musketeer clerk than he ever had as one of the Architect's assistants. Instead of scurrying all over and under the Star Fortress trying to get recalcitrants to do what they were supposed to do, he was working with practical records and meaningful numbers, and he was appreciated for his talent and hard work.

He had already discovered a cunning scheme where the Musketeer's brewer was selling one barrel in ten on the side to the Angel's Tower in the city, an inn much frequented by Musketeers, perhaps for the surprising familiarity of its ale. Henri had wondered about that, and his calculations showed the amount of production did not meet the amount of consumption in the barracks; it was then relatively easy to enlist the support of Decastries to have barrels secretly marked. A day later, the whole scheme was uncovered.

Decastries also asked Henri to consult with Lieutenant Deramillies of the Artillery on the quantities of powder, shot, and prefilled cartridges the Musketeers would require for the Expedition, the safe transport of such, and the arrangements for distribution while on campaign.

Henri had a long-standing interest in artillery and blowing things up. Now that he wore the uniform of a Musketeer and was on Expedition business Deramillies and her fellow artillerists happily involved Henri in their practices, and adopted him almost as one of their own.

He was particularly interested in the six falconets that were to be taken on the Expedition. Light cannon, they were slim bronze tubes about as long as he was tall, as round as his arm, and fired what was effectively a double-sized musket ball twice as far as any musket could shoot. Mounted on wheeled carriages, they were drawn by a team of two horses and could be easily loaded and fired by a gunner and one or two mates.

Modern artillery, Henri declaimed to his friends, was the answer to any threat posed by the beastlings. Even their armored or rugged hides could not turn a ball from a falconet. The artillerists were also making grenadoes, like the one Franzonne had carried at the palace, cast-iron balls packed with black powder, and a slow match for a wick. Every Musketeer was to carry two or three of them, and the early practice—again outside Lutace on the martial field—had indicated they would be effective, though dangerous to friend as well as foe.

There was a slight resentment among some of the Musketeers that three places in the Expedition that perhaps might have been their own had gone to Simeon, Henri, and Dorotea. But even the grumblers, when pressed, had to admit that they had earned the privilege, first by finding the Worm's chest and then by their victory over the beastling in the palace courtyard. And as they proved useful, in their own ways, the resentment waned, or at least was not shared in public.

Henri was returning from one of his outings with the artillerists when he saw Musketeers on a side street he was passing, escorting a line of newly captured toshers, their hands tied behind them and their ankles hobbled with rawhide cords. Agnez was one of the escorts bringing up the rear, a sorry sight, for she was covered from her boots to her waist in what he hoped was merely mud.

Slipping off the horse he rode, Henri bade farewell to the artillerists and moved quickly through the passing crowd, who, noting his hat and tabard, gave him as wide a berth as they were giving the other Musketeers and their Refuser prisoners. The city as a whole was still on edge, there had been riots both for and against the Refusers, and everyone was being cautious of soldiers.

"Ho, Agnez!" called out Henri as he got close.

Agnez turned, her hand on her sword hilt. "From the smell of burnt powder, you've been shirking your work and off firing cannons."

"I don't want to say what *you* smell like," said Henri companionably, wrinkling his nose as they resumed following the prisoners and he fell into step with Agnez. "Besides, I needed to see if we use the same powder in our muskets as is used in the falconets."

"Is it?"

"No, but it could and should be," said Henri. "The artillerists agree; I just have to convince the Captain. Where did you capture this lot?"

"Under the Garden of Ashalael," said Agnez. "There are natural caverns in the rock. This lot were hiding out in one of them. It was half-flooded from the river; I suppose that was why no one looked before. But one of the priests saw them slinking in and out at night."

"Was there a battle?"

Agnez shook her head.

"Take a look at them! I'm not sure they're even real toshers, or part of the Night Crew. They're certainly not fighters like the ones we took on earlier. Some of them are little more than children, half are crippled in some way. Two of them are blind! They didn't have any weapons anyway."

They walked on in silence for a while. Henri could tell Agnez was dispirited by her current task, basically acting as nothing more than a common jailer, overawing the despondent and pathetic-looking Refusers, who trudged on with their heads down, occasionally stumbling from their hobbles.

"They're branding them at Riversedge," said Agnez after a while. "An 'R' on the back of the left hand. So they're marked for the Expedition and won't ever be able to come back to the city."

"They might be able to start a new life in Ystara," suggested Henri.

Agnez looked at him scornfully.

"The place is overrun with beastlings! Everyone who could flee when it all started did so, or they died. No one has ventured back since, or at least come out alive to talk about it. How do you think this lot would go fighting against something like that beastling I shot?"

"I don't suppose we'll just leave them there," said Henri weakly.

"That is exactly what is planned," answered Agnez shortly. "We use them as laborers on the way, and I suppose on the way out, and then turn them back into Ystara at the border to whatever fate awaits."

"It might be our fate too," said Henri thoughtfully.

"Not ours," said Agnez with much greater certainty than Henri felt. "We can fight!"

"I can't believe Captain Dartagnan would just abandon them, if the beastlings are pressing us."

"It won't just be the Captain's decision, remember? Rochefort is in joint command. And remember what Dorotea told us the Cardinal said? Her Eminence would like to put *all* Refusers into the sea, not just the Night Crew and the toshers, and Rochefort is the Cardinal's right hand."

"The Cardinal wasn't herself though," said Henri. "I mean, Dorotea said she was mumbling and practically falling over . . ."

"Plenty of people think the same," said Agnez. She looked ahead at the trudging prisoners. "I'll allow I'd not considered the matter, until I had to start collecting them."

"Well, they brought it on themselves," said Henri. "Or their ancestors did."

"Did they?" asked Agnez. "Dorotea doesn't think so. And remember what the Queen said about not being responsible for crazy ancestors?"

"Well, I don't know," said Henri uncomfortably. "I mean, it's just the way it is. There's nothing we can do about it. Besides . . ."

He looked around and leaned in close.

"Besides, we don't want to get involved with Refusers. You know, just in case whatever Dorotea sees in them does have something to do with us. Simeon has it right. Lie low, do our jobs."

Agnez grunted, but it wasn't really in agreement. She quickened her pace, moving up closer to the last Refuser in the line, and Henri had to skip to keep up. They didn't talk the rest of the way to Riversedge, following the Refusers and the other Musketeers through its thrown-open outer gates and into the shadow of the long tunnel that led inside.

TWENTY-EIGHT

ROCHEFORT WAS NOT PRESENT AT THE CARDINAL'S PALACE, or at least the gate guards would not tell an apparent Musketeer that she was within. Dorotea had a similarly uninformative reception at the Pursuivants' Barracks in the Star Fortress, despite the oft-repeated orders from on high that all regimental enmities be set aside for the Expedition.

That left the Tower, Dorotea thought. Huro wanted to accompany her there, but she asked him not to, and since his orders were only to stay with her outside the Star Fortress, he reluctantly accepted her sword and returned to the Musketeers' Barracks while Dorotea meandered on to the Tower, pausing every now and then to look at things that caught her interest, either as potential subjects to sketch or for reasons she didn't know herself. Things just interested her, or they didn't, be they people, animals, insects, objects, landscapes. . . .

Eventually, shortly before sunset, she arrived at the Tower and climbed the steps. The main gate was shut, so she knocked on the smaller portal set within and looked at some interesting lichen on the capstone while she waited. Eventually, the sally port opened and Mother looked out. She seemed surprised to see Dorotea, for her eyebrows rose up into her hair and she leaned back and then forward again as if buffeted by a strong wind.

"You!" she said. "Where's your arresting guards? And why are you wearing a Musketeer's tabard?"

"Well, to answer your second question first, I am a Musketeer now, after a fashion," replied Dorotea. "And for the first, I'm not under arrest, I'm not coming back to my cell. I want to see Captain Rochefort, if she's here."

"The Captain's here," said Mother dubiously. "Did she send for you?"

"No," said Dorotea.

A Pursuivant looked out over Mother's shoulder. He wasn't one Dorotea had met before, a sullen-looking fellow, straw-haired and ruddy.

"If you've got a message for the Captain, hand it over, Musketeer," he sneered. "And then be off. The Tower's no place for the likes of you."

"That's what I thought when I was staying here," agreed Dorotea. "Even if Mother said it was one of the best cells. I haven't got a message for Captain Rochefort. I have a question. Could you please let her know Dorotea Imsel is here?"

"You? Asking Rochefort questions? I don't think so," said the Pursuivant, pushing past Mother, who began to raise a hand to stop him and then let it fall. He was heavier and taller than Dorotea, and clearly bad-tempered. He clapped a hand to his sword hilt and was just beginning to draw it when he noticed

Dorotea wasn't wearing one.

"Where's your sword?"

"I sent it back with Huro," said Dorotea. "Really, I do think Rochefort would be perfectly happy to talk to me, she always has—"

Her last word didn't come out because she had to dodge a blow from the Pursuivant's meaty fist, aimed straight at her face. He hadn't expected her to move so fast, so he overbalanced. Dorotea helped him along with a kick to his backside, sending him to the rail of the landing. He collided with that hard, swore and spun back just in time for Dorotea to get a firm grip on his nose. Her fingers, strengthened by years of carving woodblocks, engraving copper, and other surprisingly arduous artistic tasks, twisted one way and then the other, the Pursuivant shifting his head to try to ease the pressure.

"Ow! Ow! Ow!"

Dorotea let go at the moment she had the Pursuivant's nose fully twisted to the right. As he was throwing himself into moving with it, he flew through the air and collided with the other section of railing. Slumping to the ground, his scabbard tangled between his legs, he cursed again, and touched an icon on his tunic.

"You'll pay!" he shouted, though his nose was so traumatized it came out more as "Wool bay!"

Dorotea heard the sound of rushing wings, and the chime of bells, and she saw the angel begin to manifest above the Pursuivant's head. She knew it immediately. Mazrathiel, whose scope was movement, and she saw the Pursuivant's plan. Mazrathiel would not intentionally harm her, but would push Dorotea off the platform if the Pursuivant was forceful enough to make the angel obey, and the fall to the ditch below would do the rest.

The Pursuivant was muttering his commands. Dorotea moved close and pushed her hand into where she saw the shape of fire and light, and spoke to Mazrathiel too, but only in her mind. She bent the full strength of her will upon the angel and issued an overriding instruction.

Begone, Mazrathiel! Return to the heavens, and answer no more to the icon that brought you here. Begone!

The icon under the Pursuivant's finger crumbled into dust. There was a clap of thunder, a flash of light, and Mazrathiel was gone almost before he had manifested.

Dorotea drew her knife, the one she used to cut the nibs of her quills, and bent down to the Pursuivant. He was staring at his stained fingers and the remnants of the icon: tiny fragments of wood, gesso, and gilding that had collected like crumbs on his jerkin.

"What! What are you . . . ?"

Dorotea slipped the point of her knife into his left nostril and said, "Don't move. I don't want to cut your nose off your face, but I will if necessary. I simply want to have a word with Captain Rochefort. Your attack was entirely unnecessary, and impolite."

"Not to mention incompetent," said a cold voice from the doorway.

Dorotea removed her knife and stood upright, inclining her head.

Rochefort nodded back, and looked down at the Pursuivant.

"You are a disgrace to Her Eminence's coat," said Rochefort. "Get out of my sight."

The Pursuivant gulped and bent his head. He got to his hands and knees and then rose slowly half upright, to grovel past Rochefort and go inside. Rochefort looked at Mother and said, "Shut the door."

This left the two women alone on the landing.

"The angel," said Rochefort. "You resisted its power."

Dorotea nodded slowly, thinking she had really done it this time. Not just swift icon-making, but something potentially even worse and bound to be extremely heretical in Rochefort's eyes.

"It is a rare gift," said Rochefort. "I have done it. I know of two others who can do likewise. They are all Pursuivants, as you should be. I . . . it is an affront to see you in that Musketeer's tabard. You should be with *me*."

"It is not heretical?" asked Dorotea. "To banish an angel summoned by another?"

"Not for a Pursuivant," replied Rochefort. "Otherwise? I do not think Her Eminence would smile upon a Musketeer displaying such power. And she might reconsider her recent conviction that you are not, in fact, Liliath reborn."

"That Pursuivant will speak of it," said Dorotea. "I shouldn't have done it, but I was afraid, and angry, and I—"

"He will not speak of it," said Rochefort, with grim certainty.

"Oh, no, don't kill him! Not for that!"

Rochefort raised her right eyebrow.

"Kill him? I don't kill my own Pursuivants! He will be sent to one of our outlying chapters tonight, with no hope of return unless he keeps quiet! Furthermore he has lost his place on the Expedition, which will doubtless hurt him all the more. But he was a fool, and deserves the fate he has earned himself."

Rochefort frowned, and then added quietly, "But what this says of how you see me . . . am I just a bloodstained murderer to you, Dorotea?"

"You can be . . . very cruel," said Dorotea.

"In the service of Her Eminence," protested Rochefort. "I do what must be done for the safety of the state, and nothing more."

"I think it is perhaps too easy to say something is for the safety of the state," said Dorotea. "This collection of Refusers, for example, and their expulsion to Ystara. Most of them aren't toshers, they aren't part of the Night Crew, they're just poor and afflicted and they wouldn't or couldn't attack anyone even if their lives depended on it!"

"Their inclusion on the Expedition and 'resettlement' in Ystara is neither the Cardinal's notion nor my own," said Rochefort, nettled.

"Whose, then?" asked Dorotea. "You wanted to arrest them!"

"I want to find out what is behind the toshers attacking other Refusers!" exclaimed Rochefort. "I want to find out why those three Diamond Icons have surfaced now! I want to know why I see this light inside you—"

Rochefort stopped herself midword, and looked around

quickly, making sure there was no one in earshot, then pulled Dorotea close.

"You know?" whispered Dorotea.

"Since I saw Lady Dehiems," answered Rochefort, very quietly. "Something was quickened in my sight. I saw her, and you, and your Bascon friends . . . and then the strange shadow or reflection within the Refusers, all the Refusers . . . but I do not know what it means."

"Have you told the Cardinal?"

"No," answered Rochefort heavily. "She is very weak . . . and I feared for y— I feared what she would do, in her weakness and terror. I must know more before I can act."

"My friends don't want to do anything," said Dorotea. "They hope it will just go away. That we can go on the Expedition, and come back, rich and free of . . . whatever this is."

"The Expedition is pure folly," said Rochefort bitterly. "We will be fortunate if we do return. But there is some wisdom in watching and waiting."

"What of Lady Dehiems? What is she?"

"I know not," said Rochefort. "I have made inquiries, my agents in Alba confirm her husband's death, her passage here, her wealth. If only I could arrest her, put her to the question . . . but of course, that is impossible. Imagine the Queen . . . and in any case, it may be she has no knowledge of what shines inside her, just as you do not know . . . or do you?"

Dorotea shook her head.

"No. As I said, my friends . . . I agreed we should lie low, do nothing to investigate or bring attention to ourselves."

"It is probably fortunate the Alban has fallen ill," replied Rochefort. "Confined to her bed. A river fever, according to Hazurain. Debilitating, but not serious. The Queen is afire with concern and . . . and unrequited longing. I hope she may die . . . Dehiems of course . . . she was too swift to turn Her Majesty's head, and to plant the idea of the Expedition. Though that may also have come from the King. But it was definitely the Alban's idea to send the arrested Refusers to Ystara."

"Why?"

"She said to save them from the galleys, which was what the Cardinal preferred," said Rochefort. "That may be true. Or it may be some deep and terrible plot. But I cannot see what Dehiems has to gain from either the Expedition or expulsion of Refusers. Nor why she is not pursuing her interests with the Queen now, in the first flush of infatuation. Dehiems could send messages, love letters, requests, or demands. Her Majesty would give her almost anything she wants now. But milady doesn't ask for anything!"

"I feel . . . more than think . . . that somehow the answer to these mysteries lies in Ystara, and in the Fall of Palleniel," said Dorotea, very carefully. She held Rochefort's arms, the tension in the Pursuivant's muscles obvious. "Which is why I came to you. I need to look at books about these things, books removed from the Belhalle under the orders of Cardinal Dumauron. Where would they be?"

"Gone," said Rochefort bleakly. "Like beastling blood, turned to ashes. Dumauron burned many books and papers, not just to do with Ystara and the Fall of Palleniel, and not only from the Belhalle. She was afraid of knowledge. She died from a heart attack the first time she summoned Ashalael, you know. Some said it was a miracle, the Archangel saving us from our own Cardinal. A different time . . ."

"Perhaps not so different. I am afraid our present Cardinal might want to destroy anything she does not understand," whispered Dorotea, leaning still closer to Rochefort. Her nose was almost nestled in the hollow of Rochefort's neck, her lips not quite touching the skin where the Pursuivant's shirt lay open just above her breastbone.

"I will not let you be hurt, Dorotea," whispered Rochefort.

"I know you will *try*, Camille," sighed Dorotea. She stepped back out of their near embrace and smiled. "Thank you for telling me about Dumauron and the books. I had best get back to the barracks. My friends will be concerned for me."

Rochefort nodded slowly, her eyes sad.

"Watch and wait," she said. "If you learn anything, can tell me anything . . ."

"I will," said Dorotea. "I will."

The door behind Rochefort opened, and another Pursuivant looked through. She held a sheaf of papers in her hands and looked harassed.

"Captain! You said you would be but a moment, and we have so much to do!"

"The Expedition waits for neither Pursuivant nor Musketeer," said Rochefort. She bowed to Dorotea, and doffed her hat, much to the watching Pursuivant's surprise.

Dorotea bowed back, turned away and ran down the steps, her mind already racing ahead as to what she could tell the others, and what she should not.

In the event, it was simpler for Dorotea not to mention meeting Rochefort at all, or so she told herself. The hustle and bustle of the barracks, always great, had increased to a fever pitch with the preparations for the Expedition. By the time she'd got through the throng of Musketeers, Refuser servants, horses, mules, wagons, barrels, chests, boxes, bags, and sacks in the courtyard, the others were already halfway through their supper in the refectory: white bean soup, accompanied by a test of the hard "campaign" bread that would go on the expedition, more biscuit than bread washed down with the rough but robust and travel-resistant red wine of Berass. Her friends already crowded at one of the long tables with many other Musketeers, there was no chance for private conversation.

After supper, Henri was called away to examine a suspect bill from one of the farriers shoeing Musketeer horses; Agnez was inveigled into a game of dice; and Simeon was summoned to negotiate with the doctors of the other regiments in the unending struggle for space on their shared wagons. Dorotea retired alone to their chamber and swiftly went to sleep.

Nor was there time in the morning, the demands of the expedition calling everyone immediately to their tasks, breakfast snatched along the way. On reflection, Dorotea had decided it would only alarm the others to know Rochefort could see the angelic taint that linked the four of them to the Alban noblewoman . . . and to the Refusers. They did not want Dorotea to stir up trouble. Henri had already criticized her for her newly developed habit of squinting indirectly at people, to see if she could spot any more people who had a similar internal light.

Dorotea put it out of her mind, something she was always well able to do, and in company with the silent Huro, returned to the Belhalle in search of anything useful about Ystara, Palleniel, or beastlings that might have escaped the attentions of Cardinal Dumauron.

In Demaselle House, Liliath listened to the reports of Biscaray and Sevrin, on the progress of her preparations for the Expedition, which were as varied and complex as the more legitimate ones taking place in the Star Fortress.

"There were three of the Worm's lieutenants among those held at Riversedge," said Biscaray. "They have been dealt with. Two others are in the Tower. They know my name, this mask, and at least two of our houses, which are, of course, now abandoned. There has been no indication any of them know any more of you than what they saw of 'Biscaray's Serpent' at the Pit."

"You are confident of this?" asked Liliath.

"I am sure there are no toshers alive who can connect Lady Dehiems and the Serpent."

"Good," said Liliath. "What else at Riversedge?"

"Most of them will be useless," said Bisc. "There are currently one thousand eight hundred and sixty-two Refusers held there, who will be sent with the Expedition. Of that number, only two hundred and eleven are Night Crew, and a hundred of them useful if it comes to fighting."

"It will come to fighting," said Liliath. "One way or another."

"When do we join them?" asked Sevrin.

"It depends on how well the jailers keep *their* count," said Liliath.

"Not well," answered Bisc. "It's been left to the Watch . . . ."

Sevrin and Bisc chuckled; Liliath allowed herself a faint smile.

"So it will be simple enough to add ourselves at Riversedge," continued Bisc. "However, with Dartagnan and Rochefort in command, there will doubtless be another, more careful count when everyone is mustered to leave."

"Which is now in three days?"

"The latest word is four," said Bisc. "The Watch, naturally, could not be ready in time."

"We must be in Riversedge the night before," said Liliath. "Best not any sooner, to limit the chance of discovery there. You have worked out how to fake the branding, Sevrin?"

"A tarry paint, with a bit of scuffing and rasping to bring up the blood around, it looks just as the real ones do," said Sevrin.

"What about Lady Dehiems?" asked Bisc. "Rochefort has spies watching this house, and almost every delivery to the kitchen is by her agents. The Queen's people too are ever curious. That present yesterday . . . those two 'servants' who carried the vase in, they were Musketeers."

"I have been showing myself at my bedroom window from time to time," said Liliath, smiling. "Looking suitably weak. That will continue."

"How?" asked Bisc.

"A simulacrum in my clothes, animated by Horvaniel, whose scope is mimicry of life," replied Liliath. "Why do you think I've been carving and whittling these past few days?"

Neither Bisc nor Sevrin replied, but from their faces it was obvious they thought Liliath had been preparing something far more frightening and horrible than a wooden model of herself.

"It will need those clothes changed each day, as if it were I. On command it will rise and walk before the windows, wearily rest its head in its hands as it gazes out and so forth. But it will not bear close examination. Someone must remain behind to secure the house and deter visitors. That will be you, Sevrin."

"Oh no, milady!" protested Sevrin. "But you said—"

"It is decided," said Liliath firmly. "But fear not, Sevrin. Once Palleniel is restored, I will call all Refusers back to Ystara. You will be healed."

She said this with total conviction, though it was a barefaced lie.

Bisc glanced at Sevrin, a look of slight puzzlement on his face. Sevrin was one of the few Refusers who showed no sign of affliction or past ailments. Nor had she ever spoken of any physical problem. But his thoughts were swift, and it took only a moment for him to reach the correct conclusion, common to many Refuser women, due to childhood ailments or the lover's pox. Sevrin was unable to bear children and wished for a baby of her own.

"I understand," muttered Sevrin, bowing her head.

"You were not concerned your summoning of Horvaniel would attract unwanted attention?" asked Bisc.

Liliath laughed.

"No," she said. "It is great good fortune that the Cardinal has overreached herself and lies on her sickbed. Ashalael may gripe in the heavens, but none here will know. I had considered calling upon Darestriel too, for my disguise, but that would not last into Ystara. So we will both need some more mundane rearrangement of our features, my Bisc."

Bisc waved a hand airily, dismissing this as of little difficulty.

"The beggars are great artists in these matters," he said. "I am to have a ridge of painted clay glued across my cheek, my teeth blackened, my hair razored off in strips and the remnants dyed, and my hand bound with two fingers back, holding a day-old piece of calf's liver. I am sure they can do something similar for you, milady."

Liliath wrinkled her nose.

"Without the rotting meat, I fancy. You have studied the map I drew for you?"

"I have," said Bisc. "But what exactly do you plan?"

"My plans depend on several circumstances," said Liliath. She thought for a moment. "For now, I think you and the twelve best fighters must stay close to me. Of the rest, divide them into teams of four. Assign four teams to watch Descaray, Imsel, MacNeel, and Dupallidin. To protect them, if necessary, but also later to secure them. The other teams will target the Watch who guard them. When it is time to strike, they are to wreak havoc, while heading for the mustering place. I expect this will need to happen at the top of the pass, where the secret temple path rises."

"When do we tell them who you are?" asked Bisc. "It will make a difference. They will fight so much harder than they would even for the promise of treasure."

"Yes," replied Liliath thoughtfully. "But if it should be known to others, all would be lost."

"On the day?" asked Bisc.

Liliath hesitated. But she knew Bisc was right, and she would need his Night Crew to fight with conviction.

"Only to the fighters," she confirmed. "On the day, when they will be told the mustering place as well. And they must *not* speak of who I am, even among themselves. All they have to do is stay together, keep quiet, and act when they see the sign."

"And the sign? What will that be?"

"It will be a great pillar of fire," replied Liliath and she smiled her cold smile, which never reached her beautiful brown eyes.

TWENTY-NINE

AT LAST THE DAY CAME, NOT FOUR BUT SIX DAYS AFTER Bisc's report to Liliath. With the Watch finally as ready as they would ever get, the Expedition departed Lutace.

The four friends rode in the vanguard, on fine horses thanks to Henri's work with the quartermasters, sumpters, and horse copers. They each also had two remounts farther back in the long, long line that already stretched two leagues along the road from the south gate of the city.

At the very front came the vanguard composed of one troop from each of the regiments save the Watch, all mounted; then half the Refusers, not so much marching as ambling in roughly organized clumps with thin columns of the Watch guarding them on either side; then came the forty-four commissary wagons, slow bumbling vehicles, each with four or five guards from the regiments they would later feed or supply riding alongside; after them came a herd of cattle, food on the hoof, with their drovers; then the six falconets, with the artillerists riding the left-hand horses of the teams that drew the gun carriages, and behind them six very well-spaced wagons loaded with powder and shot, guarded by the artillerists' own well-disciplined train guards; after them came a small contingent of not terribly useful priests from the Temple of Ashalael, ceremonial mages for the most part and none of them a match for the least mage among the Pursuivants ahead; then the four medical wagons, also guarded by the soldiers that hoped not to need the services or supplies within; then more Refusers, loosely watched and guarded by the remaining troops of the Watch; then the remounts, lines of horses mostly led by the trusted Refuser servants from the Star Fortress barracks, who would not go on into Ystara; then the last official component of the Expedition, the rear guard, composed of more Musketeers, Pursuivants, and Royal Guards, again on horseback, though they could do no more than walk, with frequent halts, given the congestion ahead.

But behind the rear guard there was a greater crowd strung out a further league or more, without order or shape. Camp followers of all kinds, from genuine spouses, companions, and children to male and female whores wanting to stay with their best customers; peddlers, shysters, and thieves; among all these categories many Refusers who hadn't been arrested or branded but who were leaving Lutace anyway, in the hope of somehow finding their fortune in the wake of the Expedition.

Among the general riffraff there were also merchants with their own guarded carts and laden donkeys, acting on the strong likelihood that the supplies in the Expedition's own wagons would run out and the towns and villages along the route would not be able to supply their wants.

Finally, straggling along behind everyone else were children old enough to seek adventure or unwanted enough to strike out on their own, or some combination of both.

"Well, we're finally on the way," said Agnez cheerfully. "And not eating dust. Aren't you glad you're not with your fellow doctors all the way back, Simeon?"

"I am not sure whether the dust might not be preferable to this horse," answered Simeon, who hadn't ridden for quite some time and was already anticipating badly chafed inner thighs. "At least I could ride on a wagon with the others."

"And to think of the trouble I had to get horses that were up to your weight," protested Henri. "You'd be riding a yellow cart horse if it wasn't for me."

"I'd be asleep in the back of a wagon," said Simeon.

"No you wouldn't," said Agnez. "Remember you're a Musketeer now, at least in part. The Captain would never allow the *Musketeer* doctor to sleep in the back of a wagon."

"Hmmph," grunted Simeon. He shrugged his shoulders, making his massive black and silver tabard flap.

"What are you reading, Dorotea?" asked Henri. Dorotea had a small, leather-bound book in her hands, and was studying it intently, her reins carelessly draped over the pommel of her saddle, clearly trusting that her friends who rode on either side would come to her aid if her horse took it in mind to bolt or misbehave.

"What?"

"What are you reading?"

"A journal," answered Dorotea. "Supposedly of an Alban hunter and mountaineer with the unlikely name of . . . Cecily Jenkins . . . who some hundred years ago traveled in Ystara for several weeks, and survived."

"Supposedly?" asked Simeon.

"I am not sure it is authentic," replied Dorotea. "While I can read Alban moderately well, there are nuances that either lend it credibility or deny it altogether. I am not sure whether she is inventing or being amusing. Or just Alban. She keeps mentioning the importance of clean undergarments and bemoans her inability to buy salt beef rather than pork in Troumiere before she crossed the border."

"Sounds like an Alban," said Agnez.

"So you found something in the Belhalle after all?" asked Henri.

"No . . ." replied Dorotea, tucking the small volume into the useful pocket inside her tabard, where most Musketeers kept small daggers, lockpicks, and the like. "Rochefort sent it to me. She found it in the Cardinal's personal library. It is almost the only useful reference to survive the burnings of Dumauron."

No one said anything to this, and Dorotea did not notice the exchange of raised eyebrows between Henri and Agnez.

"If it is a true account, it might be useful," continued Dorotea. "For one thing, she says the beastlings generally shun the higher elevations, for they fear proximity to the heavens. That is how she escaped them, several times, by climbing peaks."

"Easier to kill 'em," grunted Agnez. She gestured back along the road. "An army like this can't climb any peaks. The pass will be hard enough. We'll probably have to leave the horses behind in any case."

"What else does she write?" asked Simeon.

"She says the beastlings are mostly solitary," said Dorotea. "There were occasions when she was able to escape only because she was pursued by a single creature, or at most two, and if there had been more she would have been taken and eaten."

"I wonder what they do eat?" mused Simeon. "Alban diarists would be sparse, and few people must ever come into their territory."

"Jenkins wrote about that too," said Dorotea. "In her time, at least, there were plenty of goats, sheep, and cattle around, presumably descended from the herds of the time before the Doom. The beastlings stalk and eat them. And once she watched from on high as a beastling and a wolf pack fought."

"With what result?" asked Agnez.

"The beastling killed three of the wolves and the rest fled," said Dorotea thoughtfully. "The beastling then ate the dead wolves. All of which seems credible . . . I will note the salient points from this book for the Captain."

"Which one?" teased Agnez. "Dartagnan or your *friend* Rochefort?"

"Dartagnan of course," replied Dorotea, calmly ignoring the jibe. "But I daresay Rochefort will read it as well."

"Where do we stop tonight, Henri?" asked Simeon.

Henri had spent a great deal of time with the officers organizing the route of the Expedition and had taken particular care to assist and ingratiate himself with those in charge of the billeting and camping arrangements, and the placement of advanced stores of food, wine, and other comforts.

"The plan was to reach Charolle," he said, looking back along the column, the far reaches of it obscured by dust. "But we left late, and at this speed . . . I suspect we shall sleep on some meadow tonight, and gnaw at whatever rations are in our saddlebags. I *had* arranged for us to be accommodated at the second-best inn in Charolle, the Silver Sheaf. The best being reserved for the senior officers."

"Perhaps we might find a farmhouse we can inhabit . . ." began Simeon, who did not relish the prospect of sleeping under stars or canvas, though he knew it would come to this sooner or later.

"Captain Dartagnan has forbidden us to commandeer private lodgings," said Agnez.

"Only inns, livery stables, ale houses, victualing houses, and the houses of sellers of wine may be requisitioned, and must be duly paid for," recited Henri. "Though I daresay those concerned would prefer coin to the scrip our quartermasters will be handing over. A promise to pay when the Expedition returns . . . I would not like to be paid that way."

"Better than not paying at all and taking over wherever we want. My mother told me that is the surest way to set everyone's hands against us," said Agnez. "Better to lie under the stars alive than be stabbed in your sleep in some stolen bed."

"I wonder if I can sleep in my hospital wagon," said Simeon.

"Surely, the Captain wouldn't be against that?"

"We do have a tent for those nights no suitable town or village is along the way to provide lodgings," said Henri. "And plenty of Refusers to put it up and take it down. But there won't be time tonight. It's for later, for shorter days, when we leave early enough, and arrive before dusk. Today will be long."

"Very long, I think. If it stays fine, and the night is not too dark, I think the Captain . . . the captains . . . will decide to press on," said Agnez. "Dartagnan was talking about the importance of a good start on the first day. And they might release the vanguard to go on ahead, in which case, we at least would be there by nightfall."

"Ashalael, save us from rear-guard duty," said Henri. "Wherever *we* stop, they will be three or four hours behind."

"Heavens forfend," muttered Simeon. "Would this Silver Sheaf of yours have a bath, Henri?"

"Baths, good wine, excellent food," replied Henri. He looked back along the lengthy column, the far end of it now totally obscured in dust, and then forward—only fifty or sixty paces ahead—to where the two captains led the vanguard, trailed by lesser officers and with mounted messengers constantly leaving them or catching up, riding to and fro on the sides of the road. "Though we will have to be sure to be among the first arrivals. No matter the advance arrangements, there are bound to be Pursuivants or more likely King's Guards who will try bribery to get our chamber, and eat our choice viands. Which reminds me, how much money has everyone got?"

"I haven't spent any of the Queen's gift," replied Simeon, reaching under his tabard and feeling around various objects before drawing out the small leather purse, leaning well over in his saddle with a disturbing creak of leather girth straps to hand it to Henri. "Here, you have it. I have a little more of my own money, in addition."

"I lost all my money at dice," said Agnez. "But we shall soon enough fill up our purses again with Ystaran gold!"

"Which is not terribly helpful right now," complained Henri. "I'm glad I at least spent my money for all our benefit."

"I have the purse still," said Dorotea. She tapped her left saddlebag. "But I spent its contents on paper, charcoal, paints, and gold leaf. I had thought we would not need any money, now we are Musketeers upon campaign? Surely, that is what you have been so busy about, Henri, with the Captain's clerks, and that one-eyed quartermaster? Organizing food and accommodations and so forth?"

"Up to a point," said Henri. "The . . . ah . . . foundational level of that supply is a blanket on a muddy field, wine watered nine parts out of ten, and that tooth-breaking campaign bread to eat. Well, I suppose I shall do my best with Simeon's purse. But we have twenty days or more upon the road . . ."

"Give it to me," suggested Agnez. "I have had my bad luck at dice. It's bound to change if I try Triple. I will win us enough to buy all these luxuries it seems you think we'll need along the road."

Henri shook his head, burying Simeon's purse deeper under tabard, jerkin, and shirt.

"You betray a complete ignorance of the mathematics of chance, Agnez," he said. "Not to mention the skills of too many of our fellow Musketeers, to say nothing of the Pursuivants or Guards. Spent wisely, I think Simeon's purse will suffice. Though once again I regret those Ystaran double dolphins . . ."

"They were never ours," said Agnez.

"They could have been," answered Henri.

Bickering, they rode on.

Almost an entire league behind the four Musketeers, a young Refuser man, sadly disfigured by a lumpy, raised scar upon his face partly hidden by a kerchief, strode beside a much older woman, who though she had a long staff to assist her, did not rely on it overmuch. Or in fact, only did so when reminded by the scarred man in a soft voice, that while she looked the part of a middle-aged, beaten-down Refuser, Liliath wasn't always acting that way.

"Pah! No one is paying the slightest attention," said Liliath. She was cross because her coarse gray shift was itchy and ugly; angry at the various slights she had suffered from the Watch since being introduced into the prison population the day before; bored with walking; and disgusted with the gruel and thin ale, which was all they had been given to break their fast that morning.

"A disguise must be maintained all the time," soothed Bisc. "If it is to work."

"I know, I know," muttered Liliath. She bent her back and leaned on her staff, which was in fact a repository for more than a dozen carefully selected icons, cunningly hidden inside. "It is necessary. It is my own plan. But I wish I had thought of some more comfortable way to accompany the Expedition without arousing suspicion."

"It will not be for long," said Bisc. There was the light of the true believer in his eyes as he continued. "What is twenty days of discomfort, when at the end we shall see Ystara restored and Palleniel come to heal all our broken people?"

"Yes," said Liliath. She smiled, a smile Bisc had not seen before, one almost of rapture. "Yes. *Palleniel.*"

The Expedition did reach Charolle that first night, though as Henri predicted, the rear guard did not arrive until just before midnight, marching under the moon. Also as he predicted, there was some minor brangling with some King's Guards outside the Silver Sheaf, but the four friends were victorious and secured both room and board.

This good fortune seemed to be a harbinger for the rest of the journey. An early start was achieved the next day, and the next, and the distance from Lutace steadily increased as Monthallard grew closer. The autumn rains, expected at any moment, did not arrive in full force, confining themselves to evening showers and the occasional downpour just before dawn. The weather was so good, in fact, that it was generally considered the Cardinal must have called upon Ashalael himself to help the Expedition on its way.

But the Captains, and some chosen few like the four friends, knew otherwise from the dispatch riders who were in constant motion between Lutace and wherever the Expedition found itself. The Cardinal was still recovering, as was Lady Dehiems.

There was another factor at work in the speed of the Expedition's progress, besides the good weather and the belief that they were aided by the Archangel. Every day took them closer to the fabled treasure, and speculation rose everywhere about just how much there was to find, and how much would be distributed among the ordinary soldiery.

Strangely, the Refusers, too, seemed to grow more cheerful and less despondent as the distance to Ystara decreased, even though there was no prospect of them sharing in the treasure. Yet when Rochefort had several of the most cheerful taken for questioning about their changed attitude, none could say why they lifted their heads more, or laughed a little when they never laughed before. And shortly after those questioned were returned, so did the usual somber mood of the Refusers, as if they had collectively felt a momentary happiness, now gone. The Watch officers responsible for guarding them put it down to the autumnal sunshine, unblocked by hovel walls or the ceilings of sewers. Whatever Rochefort thought, she did not share it with anyone.

Two weeks out of Lutace, Dorotea realized the strange illuminations she could see within her companions were becoming more definite, and easier for her to see, as were those in the Refusers. But her friends did not want to know and refused to discuss the matter when she brought it up, leaving her with only one person she could talk about it with.

At the end of the day's journeying, as yet another temporary camp was set up (without the palisades and entrenchment that would later feature when they reached Ystara), Dorotea sought out Rochefort for a quiet word, both things more difficult in execution than she had hoped.

The encampment, as it had been every night, was really a conglomeration of many smaller camps, overlapping each other and rarely in the same pattern or relation, despite constant attempts to impose order. Particularly good fields would be claimed by Musketeers, Pursuivants, or King's Guards regardless of the plan; kitchens would spring up next to them, those of the better regiments always having to turn away "guests" seeking superior provender; somewhat less appealing fields would become an artillery or wagon park, or utilized for the field hospital or stores; and the Refusers would get whatever was left, always the least salubrious area on offer, and perforce the Watch who kept guard on them also suffered from being last and least.

Consequently, finding anyone in particular was a different and difficult task each day, though at least the Captains' tents were larger and more obvious than any others. Dorotea left the Musketeers' higher meadow, descending to the low stone wall that separated it from the next, much muddier field down slope, where the hospital wagons were circled. She waved to Simeon, whose Musketeer's tabard was being held by an attendant while he shrugged on his doctor's coat in preparation for an operation outside in the last of the afternoon light.

Passing the hospital field, she joined a stream of people treading a path into a morass along the line of a hedge, until they reached a gap, currently being widened by Refusers with axes, doubtless to some farmer's annoyance. Though they would not dare protest while the Expedition was in residence.

Through the gap, the ground rose again, and Dorotea saw another pleasant meadow, with orderly rows of dun-colored Pursuivants' tents, each with a scarlet flag, and right in the middle of them, the larger, more imposing and entirely scarlet tent of Rochefort, guarded by Pursuivants at each corner.

Remembering her reception at the Tower, Dorotea hesitated before continuing on through the hedge. The Pursuivants on guard watched her approach but did not reach for swords, pistols, or icons, and in fact when she drew near, one of them came to meet her, doffing his hat. Dorotea recognized him as Dubois, one of the Pursuivants who had been with Rochefort when Dorotea was taken from the Belhalle.

"Scholar Imsel," greeted the Pursuivant. "Or should I now say Musketeer Imsel?"

"Something of both, I think," replied Dorotea. "I would like a word with Captain Rochefort, if I may."

"Indeed, she has left instruction that you are always to be admitted," replied Dubois. "But may I ask you to wait a few minutes? The Captain is hearing a report. Would you like a cup of wine?"

"I would," replied Dorotea, suddenly finding herself thirsty. She had not paused to drink or eat before looking for Rochefort, and after a long day's ride she was, as always, both parched and hungry.

Dubois gestured, and a Pursuivant wandered off, returning shortly thereafter with a cup of very good wine, better than anything Dorotea had drunk on the journey so far, despite Henri's best efforts. She sipped it, wondering exactly what she would say to Rochefort, and what she wouldn't say, and found herself uncharacteristically nervous. She wasn't afraid of Rochefort, as such, but she was afraid of something to do with Rochefort. Or herself. It was confusing.

"Perhaps I will come back," she said, draining her cup. "Tomorrow, or—"

"No, no, the Captain will want to speak with you," said Dubois. "Listen, the scouts are coming out now."

Dorotea heard the jingling of spurs, and voices raised in farewell. The tent flap was lifted and two nondescript people who looked like hunters in their dirty, bloodstained buckskins limped out. Only the scarlet scarves wrapped around their arms proclaimed they were, in fact, Cardinal's Pursuivants.

Rochefort was behind them, towering above the woman and man, as she towered over almost everyone except Simeon and Sesturo, though both of the latter were also considerably broader. She saw Dorotea and her eyes lightened.

"Dubois," said Rochefort. "Vautier and Dufresne are to have a skin each of the good wine, and find them a comfortable tent. If that is possible."

"As you command," said Dubois. He indicated Dorotea and said, "Musketeer-Scholar Imsel is here to see you, Captain."

"Come in," said Rochefort. "You are, as always, most welcome. I had hoped you might visit me before now."

"I . . . I wanted to ask you about something we discussed before, at the Tower," said Dorotea cautiously, following Rochefort back into the tent. Though it was sparsely furnished, it was still far more luxurious than the tent she shared with her friends. It had a folding table, a carpet laid down over the clover, three open-backed chairs, and a camp bed.

"I see," replied Rochefort. She turned to the Pursuivant who stood by as an interior guard. "Derambouillet, you may join the others outside."

Derambouillet inclined her head, and slid outside. A moment later, she tugged the cords that closed the tent flap tight, giving Rochefort and Dorotea greater privacy.

Rochefort gestured to a chair and sat herself. Dorotea did likewise, and for several seconds they just looked at each other, over the table.

"What I saw . . . in my friends . . . it seems to be stronger, more definite," said Dorotea. "The same with whatever is in the Refusers."

Rochefort's eyes narrowed, and she looked a little to the left of Dorotea.

"Yes," she said. "I had not noticed . . . with so much to oversee . . . do you have an explanation for this?"

"No," said Dorotea. "Because I don't know what I was seeing in the first place! Is it an actual angel or angels lurking in our flesh? The residue of an angel?"

"I don't know," said Rochefort. "But if it has grown stronger as we draw nearer to Ystara, the answer may well lie there."

"I hope so," said Dorotea. "I don't like not knowing, not being able to understand! And my . . . my friends do not wish to speak of it, or discuss what these strange . . . shadows . . . might be."

Rochefort nodded and pressed her long fingers against her temples.

"So you came to me. But I fear I, too, can spare no thought for anything other than the Expedition."

"I know," said Dorotea. "I just wanted you to be aware . . ."

"Yes," said Rochefort. She smiled at Dorotea, the first time the younger woman had ever seen her full smile. Or perhaps anyone had seen such a smile on Rochefort's face. "Thank you for thinking of me. I thank you too for your close reading of that Alban adventurer's journal. I had hoped it would be useful. I did not have time to read it myself."

"You consider it authentic?"

"I do," said Rochefort. Still looking at Dorotea, she reached for the cup of wine near her hand and almost knocked it over before her fingers snatched it midfall and set it upright again, without a drop spilled. "Those two Pursuivants you saw just now, they are my best scouts. I sent them ahead a week ago, to cross the border and go up the pass, to the highest point before it drops down again. They say the land is much as described in that journal. They saw a few beastlings, far apart, several wild goats . . . and little else. The road through the pass has degraded of course, but it was originally built in Imperial times, and so has lasted better than more recent works. Unless it snows—which is extremely unlikely at this time of year—we should make good time, and I am greatly relieved by the scarcity of beastlings."

"I hope it stays that way," said Dorotea fervently. She shifted in her chair, nervously, and then added, "I wondered if I might also have permission to . . . to talk to some Refusers. Because it seems to me some of *them* might be able to see—"

"Refusers can have no intercourse whatsoever with angels," replied Rochefort dismissively. "The merest touch of angelic magic, and they die from the Ash Blood, or are made beastlings."

"Yes, but perhaps they may know more about why this is so," urged Dorotea. "Maybe they have stories about seeing angels in people, Ystaran fables, I don't know . . . some faint knowledge, disguised as stories for children, you know the sort of—"

"This was all gone into when they first fled Ystara, and so many came to Sarance!" interrupted Rochefort. "None knew where the Ash Blood came from, or why some died and some were transformed. The only thing that was clear is it had to be Palleniel's doing, and this was confirmed by the ban placed upon the country by the Archangels."

"The ban?" asked Dorotea.

Rochefort sipped her wine, and frowned.

"It is something of a secret of the temple," she said. "Suppressed knowledge, as with the books Dumauron burned. The Archangels of the states bordering Ystara—Ashalael for Sarance, and Turikishan of Menorco—laid down a ban that pens the beastlings in. That is why they did not spread from Ystara."

She took another, deeper draft of wine, emptying her cup. Immediately refilling it from the bottle, she continued.

"Unfortunately for us, there is a corollary to the ban on the beastlings. It has long been known that no angel can cross the bounds and enter Ystara. Otherwise I could have sent Reahabiel to spy out the temple and Quarandael to retrieve any treasure. What has also been suspected, but hitherto not proven, is that no angels may be *summoned* there either. At least no angels not of the Ystaran host."

Dorotea digested this news.

"Unproven until now," said Rochefort bitterly, drinking again. "It has just been confirmed by my scouts. The icons they carried there were just pictures, dull and lifeless."

"So that's what Dartagnan hinted at . . . ," said Dorotea.

"What?"

"Oh, just . . . um . . . she thinks you Pursuivants rely too much on icons and angels," said Dorotea with a blush. "But I think she suspected our icons might not answer in Ystara."

"Dartagnan has always been very clever," muttered Rochefort, taking a deep swallow from her cup, which left a red stain around her lips.

"But what does it mean?" asked Dorotea. "That Ashalael allows none of his angels to enter Ystara, and none may be summoned there?"

"It doesn't matter what it means! We should leave the cursed country alone," replied Rochefort, drinking again. "But we are ordered otherwise, without possibility of it being countermanded. Her Eminence chose a bad time to overexert herself, as I warned her! She should never have questioned you herself."

"Do you mean you would have questioned me?" asked Dorotea. "*You* wanted to put me to the question? To have Pereastor grope inside my mind for *you*?"

"No!" protested Rochefort, slamming down her cup, red wine exploding and the table's legs collapsing. "No! I did not want to, I would not have . . . save for a direct order from Her Eminence. But she was already exhausted. She should have let someone else . . ."

"I will leave you now, I think," said Dorotea, her chin up. She pushed her chair back. Rochefort leaped up too, and for a brief, terrible moment, Dorotea thought the Pursuivant would try to restrain her. But she did not. She stood there, swaying, her arms hanging loose by her sides.

"I said I will do you no harm," muttered Rochefort. "I hold to that."

"You also said you hoped I would never fear you," said Dorotea. "Yet I was afraid then, for a moment."

"I do not want to be what I have . . ." Rochefort began, but she stopped and said no more as Dorotea looked at her, waiting.

"Yes?" asked Dorotea.

Rochefort shook her head very slowly, as it was made of stone, too heavy to easily move. She gestured hopelessly at the tent opening. Dorotea went to it, unlaced the cord and strode out into the dusk, uppermost in her mind the fact that Rochefort had not actually refused her permission to question Refusers. . . .

THIRTY

"ONE OF THE FOUR HAS BEEN ASKING OUR PEOPLE QUES-
tions," said Biscaray quietly to Liliath, as they laid their rough
blankets on the ground in the lee of a large boulder. They were
close to Monthallard now; they would reach it the next day. The
road had been climbing slowly but steadily for the past week as
they neared the mountains that marked the border with Ystara,
and it was considerably colder, particularly in the wind. The
Refusers had taken to sleeping packed close together on the
ground, which now was more often bare earth or rock, and not
muddy fields. "The scholar, Dorotea Imsel."

"What is she asking?" asked Liliath. She kept her voice low,
despite the fact they were surrounded by Bisc's fighters on all sides.

"She wants to hear stories, the things we tell our children,
or were told as children," said Bisc. "About the Doom of Ystara,
about Palleniel."

"What has she been told?"

"The usual two tales, the ones she must already know,
nothing else. That we sinned beyond redemption, and Palleniel

cursed all Ystarans, and we carry that curse forever. Or the other one, the one the Sarancians don't like, that it was a war in the heavens and enemy angels cursed us, with Palleniel unable to save us. Either way, according to the stories, we're forever doomed. I must admit I am curious to know the truth of the matter . . ."

"I have told you before, Palleniel did not curse anyone. His enemies caused the Ash Blood plague and the beastlings," said Liliath angrily, twisting to remove a thorn or burr from her side. "The other Archangels, directed by their cardinals and high priests, they attacked Palleniel. He has been banished . . . but we will bring him back. All will be restored, Bisc."

"But will not the enemy Archangels strike again?"

"Palleniel was taken by surprise," said Liliath. She had told this lie before, long ago, and it came easily to her tongue. "His icon was held by a weak old woman, Cardinal Alsysheron. When Palleniel returns, it will be because *I* will summon him, and *I* will direct him against our foes. It will be different. All will be healed, the beastlings gone, Ystara restored to greatness."

Bisc nodded, his face barely visible in the falling darkness and the shadow of the stone. Even Liliath could not make out his expression.

"But why do you need those four?" he asked. "Descaray. MacNeel. Dupallidin. Imsel. They are not of Ystara—"

"Enough of these questions," said Liliath testily. "For now understand I need them alive and unharmed, in the temple."

"But—"

"I have spoken," said Liliath, through her teeth. "See my orders are obeyed."

"As always," replied Bisc. "Your will shall be done."

"I have seen higher passes," said Agnez, with a sniff.

"It looks cold," said Henri, who had been wearing his heavy cloak for the past three days. It was the black wool with silver fox fur trim worn by all the Musketeers, and he wrapped it close. The sun had only just risen, and though the sky was clear and the day begun, there was no warmth in the air. "That is to say it looks even colder up there."

"Be thankful for your cloak," remarked Dorotea. "The Refusers have nothing so warm."

"And be thankful for the weather," added Simeon. "It could easily be much colder than this. And wetter. We have been fortunate, so far."

They stood together on the crest of a low ridge that paralleled a narrow, nameless stream that marked the border between Sarance and Ystara. There was a broad, pebble-bottomed ford below, marked in part by the stumps of several ruined piers, all that remained of the old Imperial bridge. The road, or rather the remnants of the ancient road, rose from the ford in a straight line toward a gap in the mountains to the southwest, two-thirds as high as the peaks on either side, great spikes of gray stone, only their heights topped with ice and snow.

The four were afoot, their horses corralled along with the Expedition's other mounts a short distance away at what would be the final encampment in Sarance, around the village of Monthallard. Another, much larger though temporary village had grown up around this no longer at all bucolic settlement, as the camp followers who would not be allowed to proceed onward into Ystara settled down to await the return (or not) of their loved ones, customers, and marks.

The old road up through the pass was too broken and difficult in several places to allow the use of horses, so Dartagnan and Rochefort had decided the Expedition would henceforth march. The six falconets and a great quantity of powder and shot would be taken up in pieces by mules, along with other stores. The Refusers were also to serve in a similar fashion to the mules, and had been loaded up with tents, sharpened stakes to make a palisade, food, water, powder, shot, bundles of firewood, and much else.

Agnez, remembering her mother's stories of campaigning, had prevailed upon her three friends to carry a great deal more than they would otherwise have done, and each of them was now heavily laden with several days' food, a waterskin, a change of clothes, and two thick blankets in addition to their swords, muskets, and cartridge belts.

Nevertheless, they counted themselves lucky not to have halberds rather than muskets, as was the case for half of the Musketeers, Pursuivants, and King's Guards. Though these soldiers all trained with halberds for largely ceremonial use in the Queen's and Cardinal's Palaces and the King's House, their main purpose this time was to provide a heavy melee weapon against armored beastlings.

Certain individuals were also issued grenadoes, but only to those soldiers considered to have both a calm nature and an excellent throwing arm. Henri had been disappointed not to be accounted among this number, though it was only because he was not known to have these qualities as opposed to being known to definitely lack them.

Simeon had refused a musket, given he was also carrying his surgical kit and sundry medical supplies upon his large person. It did give rise to a taunt from a Royal Guard about a musketless Musketeer being a kind of eunuch, but this was only said once and not continued by anyone else, and the Guard concerned was expected to recover from the concussion.

Henri shivered as he saw the Musketeer and Pursuivant scouts, the first to cross, wade into the stream, their boots tied around their necks, the long-barreled, rifled fowling pieces they favored held over their heads. The water wasn't deep anywhere, and only came up to the scouts' knees at the ford, but he knew it would be freezing. And he knew he would be crossing it within the next half hour, since they were once again assigned to the vanguard.

"Strange to think that is Ystara over there," said Dorotea, gesturing toward the mountains, with their sparse coverage of birch and rowan below the bare rock. "It looks no different from any other mountains. Yet our angels will not come to us there, and long ago, the Archangel of this place destroyed his people."

"Did you think there would be some physical sign of the Doom?" asked Simeon.

"No," said Dorotea, with a sigh. "It's just interesting. Scope and borders, they're deeply intertwined. I am sure *both* are mortal inventions. I think perhaps we press a scope upon an angel, rather than discover it—"

"Ssshhh!" exclaimed Simeon. He looked around quickly, but no one seemed to have heard Dorotea, or taken note of what she said.

"What?" asked Dorotea. "I was only thinking aloud."

"Well don't," said Henri. "It sounded heretical."

"It's not heretical," protested Dorotea too loudly, gaining her another round of shushing.

"Well, it sounded like it might be," said Simeon. "We decided it was best to keep out of all that sort of thing, remember?"

"Yes, yes," agreed Dorotea, with a long sigh. "But I wish I was back in the Belhalle, where people can talk sensibly!"

"I would not object even to my stall in the New Palace stables," said Henri.

"Or I, the Infirmary," said Simeon.

"What is wrong with you all?" asked Agnez. "You have become Musketeers! We are on a campaign! Great wealth and fame await us."

"I hope so," said Henri, brightening a little. The chest of double dolphin coins rose up in his mind again, his memory of the weight of the gold in his palm so strong he could almost feel it. . . .

"I suppose there might be *real* treasure," acknowledged Dorotea. "As a librarian suggested to me. Long-lost books and papers . . ."

"Well, we shall see soon enough, one way or another," said

Simeon pragmatically. He pointed to where Dartagnan's trumpeter was readying his instrument, about to blow the call for the vanguard to assemble, doubtless soon after that to also sound the triple peal that meant "Onward, March!"

Three hours later, it was Liliath's turn to cross, amid the throng of heavily laden Refusers. She had felt the border long before she reached the ridge and could look across, above the dust of all those who had gone ahead. Though it was not so much the proximity of Ystara that caused her skin to tingle and her heart to beat more rapidly. It was Palleniel, who, though broken and dispersed, was more present in the land ahead than he was anywhere else, and would be even more so once this throng of Refusers drew closer to the temple.

Soon, she would speak with him again, for the first time since she had awoken in the tomb of Saint Marguerite. And soon after that, they would be together. She smiled, a smile suddenly cut off—

"Come on! Pick up your feet!" called out one of the more foul-tempered members of the Watch, a suspicious-eyed woman who the others called Reinette, though the Refusers had to call her simply "ser" and keep their heads down while they were doing it.

Reinette was not carrying one of the huge wicker baskets that were now on the backs of nearly all the Refusers nearby. Packed with lead shot and cartridge papers for muskets, they were even heavier than the sharpened stakes the group ahead were lumbered with, though possibly lighter than the water carriers behind. Liliath, who had been excused a basket by reason of her apparent advanced age and infirmity, still had to carry a bag of musket wads slung over one shoulder.

"Hurry it up, hurry it up!" shouted Reinette again, casually buffeting the nearest Refuser across the back of her legs with the haft of her halberd, a blow designed to goad and hurt without inflicting serious injury. "Got a long way to go today, all the way up to the top of the pass! You'll like it there, very refreshing I'm told! Pick it up!"

"She'll be the first to die," muttered Bisc, pausing momentarily to rebalance his load and retie his ragged gray smock at the front. "Maybe I'll take her cloak and stake her out in the snow, let her die slow. You did say there would be snow?"

"Oh yes," replied Liliath, smiling. Happiness was bubbling up inside her, as with every step she grew closer to the lingering presence of Palleniel, and the prospect of completing her life's goal. "There will be snow, when it is needed."

Something of her mood was transmitted to the Refusers around her, and they walked faster, with more of a spring to their step. This in turn spread to the Refusers farther ahead and behind, so that the whole great mass of gray-clad carriers moved more swiftly. Those guarding them had to walk faster too, and some grew angry at this, and struck out even more with fists, boots, and halberd shafts. But they could not shout "slow down" without attracting the unwanted attention of their officers, or worse still, from the soldiers of the other regiments.

As the lead Refusers neared the ford, a susurration of whispers began. Not in rebellion, for they kept marching forward and made no movement to attack their guards or do anything other than they were told. There was just one word, repeated over and over, soft as breath, hardly audible by itself, until magnified by its repetition in fifteen hundred mouths.

"Ystara. Ystara. Ystara."

Liliath heard it and smiled again as she neared the river. She could feel all the tiny motes of Palleniel in the Refusers around her, and in the beastlings on the mountain slopes beyond, though the latter were as yet few and far between. The creatures would come, drawn to her, as she knew to her cost. She had fled down from the pass ahead one hundred thirty-seven years ago, along this road, across this ford, with her guards fighting a valiant and losing rear guard action against these same beastlings who had begun to gather.

They would sense her presence as soon as she stepped into Ystara. Liliath was a living beacon to the beastlings, a beacon that would grow brighter and brighter as she worked her magic. A fire to summon them from every corner of Ystara. They would come to slay the one who had made them what they were. They had little intelligence, but their instincts were strong. They knew she had something to do with the torment of their long, unnatural lives, and if they could somehow kill her, this would end.

Liliath chuckled to herself at this false hope of the fallen creatures, and began to wade across the stream. She ignored the chill of the icy water, the cries of shock from the Refusers around her and the shouts of the Watch. Halfway across the stream, a sudden warmth filled Liliath from toe to head, and she heard the chime of silver bells, just for her, above the sounds of the rushing water.

I am here, said Palleniel, in her mind. His voice was very faint, but it was there. *I await you.*

Liliath shut her eyes, for a fleeting moment, and hugged herself, reveling in the contact.

The Maid of Ellanda had returned to Ystara, and soon all would be well.

For Liliath, at least.

Far off in Lutace, Cardinal Duplessis heard the terrible chatter and rustle of the icon of Ashalael again, and the deep, warning jangle of a discordant harp. She struggled from her sickbed, blinking as she staggered into the fall of sunlight from the window. She tried to call out, but could not make her tongue move, and her throat was dry.

She crawled to the bureau and tried to pull herself up it. Not only was the icon of Ashalael vibrating and humming, it was emitting a harsh, white light, brighter even than the sunshine, something the Cardinal had never seen before.

"Ashalael."

She managed a croaking whisper but could not rise up high enough to touch the icon. Nevertheless, she felt the presence of the Archangel gathering, manifesting in the room. There was a tremendous thunderclap of his enormous wings, like a cannon blast, rattling the window frames and shattering glass, and then the peal of a thousand trumpets, drowning the shouts and cries of alarm outside her door.

The Killer Mage! The Killer Mage! screamed Ashalael inside the Cardinal's mind, every word like the thrust of a slender knife piercing her brain.

"I don't understand," whispered Duplessis.

She kills angels! *Stop her! Stop her! Stop her!*

The Cardinal did not answer, could not answer. Her fingers slipped off the edge of the bureau. Muscle and sinew slackened, no longer able to hold her up. She fell sideways to the floor with an anticlimactic thump, soft after the clamor of the Archangel. Bright red blood gushed from her eyes, ears, nose, and mouth, the visible sign that her already weakened mind had been utterly destroyed by the force of the Archangel's shout.

Ashalael, denied his summoner, retreated to the heavens, even as the door to the Cardinal's chamber flew open. Anton, Robard, and three sword-wielding Pursuivants rushed in, only to halt as if they'd run into a wall, such was the impact of seeing the mistress of all their fates, the woman who had ruled angels and mortals alike for decades, dead upon the carpet.

THIRTY-ONE

PROGRESS UP THE PASS WAS A STOP-START AFFAIR, WITH numerous skirmishes between the vanguard and single beast-lings. Though formidable enemies in melee, the beastlings were easily spotted at a distance in the rocky, bare ground of the pass. The soldiers would stop at first sight, form lines and fire several volleys. On the rare occasion when the beastling wasn't killed by massed musket fire, it was still wounded badly enough to be easily dispatched by half a dozen halberdiers.

Four or five of these successful encounters cheered everyone, except perhaps Dartagnan and Rochefort and some other vet-erans, who mistrusted the accepted wisdom they would only be fighting a single beastling or at worst, a couple, at a time. Cer-tainly, a hundred Musketeers could finish a single beastling if it was spotted three hundred paces away. But what would happen if there were a hundred beastlings? Or a thousand?

Dorotea, like everyone else following behind the fighting vanguard, paused to look over the fallen beastlings. It was an excuse to take a moment's rest from the hard slog up the pass, and she was fascinated by how different they all were. Some had walked upright on two legs, some down on four, one had many legs, and though Dorotea hadn't seen it in motion, it must have scuttled like an insect. Some were armored with scales in many different hues, some had knobbly hide of gray or dark purple, others had matted fur in white and brown and russet. All seeming to be equally good at turning bullets or steel. Most of their wounds were shallow. It was simply the quantity of shots, or halberd strokes, which had finished them off, or had struck a weak point and dealt greater damage.

Farther back down the pass from Dorotea, Simeon was looking at the wounds on a beastling too, using probe, ruler, and tongs, and occasionally a knife to open the wound up, though this took all his strength and he wished he had the larger of the four saws that were currently on the back of a mule farther up with the hospital supplies.

He very much wanted to conduct a full dissection, but there was no time. His limited examination confirmed what Dartagnan had told them: every beastling was different, and none shared the same weak points. They had different kinds of hide or bony armor or insect-like chitin. It was thicker in different places, the skeletal structure beneath was not the same in any two beastlings, and they even had entirely different arrangements of internal organs. Though they all had something approximating a heart, these differed too in how they pumped or forced the gray dust that was their blood through their bodies.

"Come on, Simeon," said Henri. "You'll probably get more to cut up later."

"I just need a few more minutes," replied Simeon. He was examining the beastling's left eye, which had a tough, transparent lid he was able to move backward and forward with the point of his knife.

Henri shook his head.

"Everyone's gone past but the rear guard. You want to stay here on your own?"

"What?"

Simeon looked around, wincing as the echoes of another musket volley came down from higher up the pass, reverberating between the cliffs of the mountains to either side. Apart from Henri, no one was close. A group of the Watch were shepherding a gaggle of Refusers farther up, and there were perhaps fifty or sixty Musketeers and Pursuivants farther down the slope, quite spread out. The rear guard.

"No, I don't want to stay here!" he said, quickly gathering his instruments and packing them back in their case.

"Didn't think so," said Henri. Pulling his cloak tight around himself again, he started plodding up the slope, with Simeon close behind.

Despite a dozen skirmishes, the Expedition reached the top of the pass earlier than expected, in the early afternoon. Immediately everyone set about establishing the camp and the defenses, while a dozen scouts continued on, looking for side paths or other clues that would point to where Liliath's Temple of Palleniel Exalted was located, and how to get there. None had been found during the ascent.

There was a surprisingly flat area at the top, before the pass began to descend again, probably smoothed long ago by the old Imperial builders. It was also much narrower than it was lower down on either side, with the high cliffs of the mountain peaks pressing close. Even better, there were the remnants of old walls about a hundred fifty paces down from the top of the pass, on both sides, so the palisade makers needed only to fill in the gaps and build up the remnant walls with found stone. A ditch was attempted, but abandoned, as there was only a foot or two of topsoil and rubble above solid rock. Sufficient to plant stakes for the palisade, but not to dig deeper.

Between these western and eastern lines of defense, the Expedition settled itself, and for the first time the plan of encampment was rigorously enforced.

Dartagnan and Rochefort had their tents set up right in the middle of the flat, next to each other, with some selected soldiers of their regiments camped nearby as body guards, but the majority of the Musketeer and Pursuivant tents were raised in a line set back some fifty paces from the western defenses. This was the dangerous side, facing whatever might come up from the interior of Ystara. Four of the six falconets were emplaced here, but higher up toward the flat, and raised farther on mounds of rammed earth and stone, revetted with leftover stakes not needed for the palisades.

The tents of the King's Guard were placed on the opposite side, back toward Sarance, in a line that ran along the eastern wall and palisade, with the remaining two falconets emplaced to cover the approach deemed less likely to be attacked.

The Watch were not positioned to garrison the defenses. Their tents were pitched closer to the Captains in the center of the flat, surrounding a large space where the Refusers would gather to sleep. If they could sleep, lacking tents or any other cover, though they had now each been given *two* of the rough blankets.

The hospital and store tents were erected on the flat on the northern side of the camp, right up against the almost-vertical mountainside, while the gunpowder store was established on the southern side, under a rocky overhang. Artillerist sentries marked out a line fifty paces away, which no one might cross with lit match, pipe, dragging spurs, or other source of fire or spark.

As the last sections of the two palisades were raised, tied together and bedded down, the firewood was distributed, and campfires began to snap and crackle throughout most of the camp. Generally good-natured arguments arose about who was going to cook what, attempts to procure rations were made, and sentry lists arranged, rearranged, and received with enormously varying degrees of happiness.

Yet despite the swift construction of the defenses and the orderly establishment of the camp, there was a general air of uneasiness about the place. The Pursuivants, in particular, were unhappy they could not start their fires with the assistance of Ximithael, or have Horcinael dry the wet blisters on their feet, or do any of the things they had long been used to call upon angels to carry out.

Everyone had been told their angels would not answer before crossing the stream that marked the border. But somehow the sharp truth Rochefort and Dartagnan spoke had become diluted in the passing into mere possibility, or a chance, and none of the Sarancians were happy to discover they were definitely beyond the reach of their angels.

Dorotea, of course, found it very interesting. While Simeon directed the establishment of his part of the field hospital; Agnez stood guard with her troop over palisade-building Refusers and watched for beastlings; and Henri moonlighted with the crew of a falconet when he was supposed to be checking the allocation of firewood, Dorotea retreated to their shared tent in the Musketeer lines, and experimented with her icons, which Rochefort had returned to her along with the Cecily Jenkins book.

Neither Dramhiel or Horcinael would answer at all, try as she might to summon them, regardless of the techniques she employed. They were just painted rectangles. Dorotea put them away and spent quite some time trying to think of a Ystaran angel, mentally working through a catalog of celestial beings. But she could not remember ever seeing the name of a Ystaran angel, apart from Palleniel himself. That, in turn, made her wonder how the first mages had summoned angels at all. They hadn't known any to summon, they didn't know their shape or feel to make icons . . . so how had that worked?

She was pondering this, and may have in fact dozed off, when a trumpet suddenly sounded nearby, and there was a sudden scurrying and shouting outside, followed by the boom of the nearest falconet, a concentrated flurry of musket fire and then the rapid cadence of drums, calling everyone to stand to arms.

Dorotea stuck her head out the tent and saw the artillerists of the closest falconet, unsurprisingly assisted by Henri, frantically swabbing out their smoking cannon, preparing to reload. The Musketeer sentries who'd just fired, including Agnez, were reloading, ramrods flying up and down, while scores more Musketeers were rushing to the palisade. Refusers were running back the other way, and there was a great deal of smoke and noise and confusion in the air.

Dorotea ran to the falconet platform and clambered up, being careful to keep out of the way. A gunner's mate jumped down past her as she did so, and sprinted for the gunpowder store shouting something. Henri didn't even glance over at Dorotea. He was looking down the pass to the west, shielding his eyes against the red glare of the setting sun.

The dozen scouts who had gone out so confidently several hours before were running up the slope, racing flat out, scrambling over boulders and broken ground as if their lives depended on speed and speed alone. None still carried muskets or other weapons, and as Dorotea counted them, she saw there were eight, not twelve.

The reason for the haste, and for the missing four scouts, came a scant hundred paces behind them.

A tide of beastlings.

Scores of beastlings swarming up the slope. Some upright on two legs, some down on four, one with many legs, scuttling.

Many were bigger than Simeon, a third again as tall or long, but most were roughly the size of normal humans, with a few smaller and more sinuous. All had oversized jaws and many sharp teeth, and claws or talons, most also had spurs or jagged extrusions of bone along their limbs as well.

They howled and shrieked and hissed as they ran forward, noises neither animal nor human, more like the sound of hot metal quenched in water, or teeth grinding on bone, magnified a thousand times and made more horrible.

Three of the scouts at the rear were not fast enough, several beastlings grabbing and rending them, tearing them apart and then fighting each other over the pieces. More and more beastlings joined in the feast, a huge squalling, writhing mass of monsters, making a perfect target for every musket and the four falconets. There was a ripple of gunshots, several bigger booms and a great drift of white smoke billowed overhead.

But all it seemed to do was annoy the beastlings. Not one fell, though all were bleeding gray ash from multiple wounds. The leading ones swallowed down chunks of human flesh, watching each other and the soldiers ahead. Yellow and orange and black and green eyes, some round, some almost rectangular, some oval, all hostile and strange.

At least it was a pause, even if it was going to be brief.

"Musketeers, hold your fire! Reload and wait for volley orders! Halberdiers, take your positions! Falconets, fire as you will!"

That was Dartagnan, leaping down the slope to stand on the platform near the middle falconet. Her voice was loud and steady, already calming every soldier in earshot, her commands being picked up and repeated by lieutenants and sergeants along the line.

Rochefort was doing the same thing on the right for the Pursuivants. Dorotea could see her and could almost catch her words, likely to be very similar to Dartagnan's.

Five of the scouts made it to the palisade, ran along it for a short distance to one of the lengths of old wall, were helped up and over it. Three fell down at once to lie prostrate, one knelt and vomited, but the fifth ran to Dartagnan to report.

A movement among the beastlings caught the corner of Dorotea's eye. She turned to look and realized it was not movement. It was that strange vision she had. She'd got the angle just right by accident, and had been squinting from the lowering sun. She moved her head and squeezed her eyes almost shut, looking slightly off to one side. She could see it clearly now. The beastlings had the same shapes within them as the Refusers, the roiling darkness, the patches of light and shadow . . . denser in different parts of the beastlings' bodies, with wisps moving between. . . .

"Oh!" exclaimed Dorotea. "I can see their weak points!"

"What?" asked Henri, who had stepped back to stand next to her, having just pricked the charge through the touchhole of the falconet with the quill in his hand. "You can?"

"Or their strong spots," said Dorotea. "I'm not sure, light or shadow. Look, that one with the yellow scales and the ridge of spines, shoot it near its tail, where the legs join."

Henri looked at the gunner, who shook her head. She was looking down the barrel and held a burning slow match in a linstock well out to one side.

"If it sat still we might hit such a target," she said quickly, shouldering the slim bronze barrel to move it an inch or two. "Have to aim for the mass of them with this. A rifled fowling piece, that's what's wanted. Stand clear!"

She moved aside, glanced around to make sure everyone else was clear, and applied the slow match. There was a fizz, a plume of smoke, a sharp crack, and the cannon recoiled several feet on its high-spoked wheels, bumping up against the ledge of rocks placed to stop it hurtling backward off the platform.

"Sponge out!" shouted the gunner.

"Go, go, tell Dartagnan what to shoot at!" shouted Henri. He picked up the long sponge and dipped it in the water tub, before swiftly ramming it down the falconet's barrel and giving it a few turns to extinguish any errant sparks or burning scraps from the paper that had wrapped the charge.

Dorotea jumped down behind the emplacement and raced toward Dartagnan. The Captain bellowed something and there was an organized crash of musket fire, very different from the scattered shots of before, and the horrible screeching from the beastlings grew even louder and more fever-pitched.

The monsters dropped what they were eating, and charged, and there were more and more beastlings coming up behind.

"Steady!" roared Dartagnan. "Steady! Wait for my order!"

"They all live," reported Bisc.

Liliath sighed with relief, for this was her greatest fear. In the end she might only need one, but better to have all four . . .

"The Musketeer was struck down but only bruised. Are . . . are more beastlings coming?"

"Yes," answered Liliath. "But not soon, and the snow will slow them coming up the pass. It will not matter to us, not then."

"There is no sign of snow," said Bisc, looking up at the night sky. It was clear, and cold, and many stars glittered in the narrow band between the dark bulk of the mountains that enclosed the pass.

"There will be snow," said Liliath. "Do you doubt me, Bisc?"

"No, no," muttered Biscaray. He was a city dweller, and out of his depth in this chilly wilderness, with the freezing wind blowing up the pass, and the beastlings only just defeated. They had kept attacking and attacking and in the end almost all the soldiers from the eastern side had to join those on the west. No beastling had ever turned away, or retreated. They just kept charging and charging until they were dead.

"Who is at the gate?"

"I left Karabin and Alizon T there; they're working as hospital porters," said Bisc. "But there's so many wounded now, they're laid out right up to the cliff, and there are some lying right in front of the gate. How does it open, anyway? I could just see it, when you showed me, but there's no catch or handle or keyhole. . . ."

"It will open, when I need it to," said Liliath. "Where are the four now?"

"MacNeel is in the hospital, cutting off limbs and the like," said Bisc. "Wishing his icons worked, as the wounded scream for their angels. . . ."

"Did you enjoy that, Bisc?" asked Liliath. "The wounded calling for the help of angels they cannot have? They are all no better than Refusers now."

"I had thought I would," said Bisc slowly. "But I did not."

Liliath looked at him sharply, but he did not say anything else. He just stood there, his head bowed as always, in deference and respect.

"And the others?"

"Dupallidin and Imsel are in their tent. Exhausted, asleep. Dupallidin fought with a cannon crew all evening. Imsel . . . she could see the weaknesses in the beastlings. She pointed them out to Dartagnan to give firing orders. Later, someone gave her a fowling piece; she shot well with that. Without her, I am not sure they would have held. . . ."

"So she has that sight," mused Liliath. "It is rare, but not unexpected, particularly in her. She has the swift icon-making too. Perhaps she will be the one . . . so like me . . ."

"The one?"

"It is not your concern," said Liliath. "Send out word, everyone is to prepare and on the—"

"Hey, you two! Come out of there!"

Liliath and Bisc were standing between the rows of tents belonging to the Watch. Clad in gray, shadowed by a tent from the moon and starlight, they were well out of sight. But some slight movement had caught the eye of a Watchwoman passing along the lines. She was stepping over guy ropes and coming toward them, everything in the way she moved suggesting belligerence, her halberd at the ready.

It was Reinette, the obnoxious, who Bisc had wanted to stake out in the snow.

"There's work to be done! Palisade's got to be fixed! No shirking, curse you malingering graybacks!"

A slim knife appeared in Bisc's hand. Liliath smiled. Reinette faltered and opened her mouth to shout for assistance, just as Bisc threw his blade. It flew straight and true, striking the Watchwoman in the throat. She dropped her halberd and got her hands to the weapon, choking and coughing blood. Another knife appeared in Bisc's hand, but he didn't throw it. The woman's eyes rolled up and she fell against the side of the closer tent, sliding down it in a welter of blood, leaving a long stain, black in the moonlight.

"Well done, my Bisc," said Liliath approvingly. She kissed him lightly on the temple, under the scrap of cloth he'd wound around his head in a vain attempt to keep his ears warm. "As I was saying, tell everyone to be ready. Watch for the sign."

"You shouldn't stay here," warned Bisc, going over to retrieve his knife. He had to work it backward and forward to get it out of the woman's throat. She was still not quite dead, and he danced a little, to keep from being splashed with blood.

"I'll be near the gate, in the hospital place," said Liliath. She unscrewed her staff, separating the two halves, upending each to catch a cascade of icon rings and brooches, which she put in a pouch under her ragged smock. Like all the other Refusers she also wore one of the blankets she'd been given wrapped around her as a coat, though she didn't need it for warmth. "Watch for the sign."

She went out past one tent, and Bisc out by another. Just two of the many Refusers who were working everywhere now, or skulking, or had even fled back down the pass toward Sarance. The Watch were only making half-hearted attempts to organize them. Too many of them were dead, or wounded, or shivering on the western palisade, hoping no more beastlings would come.

Liliath picked up an abandoned basket just beyond the tents. Bending low, she carried it toward the northern side of the flat, where the field hospital was set up. It was easy to see, a bright part of the dark camp, as many oil lanterns had been strung up, where the doctors were hard at work doing what they could without the help of angels.

Closer, Liliath had to step around the dead who were laid out farthest from the light, until they could be buried, or more likely have a cairn raised over them in the morning. The ground was too hard to dig graves, and there was already a shortage of firewood. Liliath smiled again, thinking how she could help with Irraminiel, the Ystaran angel whose scope was fire, oft used for cremation. But she had other plans for Irraminiel.

Closer to the lights and the doctors, the wounded were laid in rows, awaiting attention or already treated. Many lay still, close to death, but many more writhed and coughed and cried and clutched at anyone passing by, begging them to help.

Many called on angels, particularly Ashalael, forgetting where they were.

Liliath skirted the central area where the doctors worked at their trestle tables, sodden with blood, and continued on past more dead and wounded people toward the cliff face.

This seemed to be a solid slab of grayish stone, jutting up hundreds of feet until it joined another set farther back, one of many such slabs balanced against each other, right up to the very peak so high above.

Liliath sat down with her back against the rock, the basket at her side, and began to put on her icon rings and fasten brooches to her smock. A wounded Pursuivant lying near her watched, his eyes reflecting the starlight, the rest of him just a dark silhouette on the ground. He tried to call out, to shout an alarm, but only a sad rattle came from his throat.

Liliath ignored him. She touched the icon of the first angel she needed, a Power called Hayrael, whose scope was the interaction of air and water, and her geographical limitation the northeastern marches of Ystara.

Hayrael answered, very reluctantly, for she knew who summoned her. But as always, Liliath prevailed. The angel tried to sound trumpets of alarm, to alert anyone near, but that was quashed. She flexed her wings, or the metaphysical equivalent humans understood as wings, and that too was prevented by Liliath's adamant will.

All Hayrael could do was obey, to marshal wind and moisture, flitting here and there about the sky.

Soon, there would be snow.

THIRTY-TWO

TOWARD MIDNIGHT, DARTAGNAN AND ROCHEFORT MET in the middle of the western palisade, near the destroyed number three falconet, its bronze muzzle just visible under the body of the huge beastling who had briefly seized it and swung the barrel as a club. Its blubbery, wart-covered hide was dappled with holes from musket balls and crosshatched in deep cuts and slashes from swords and halberds, most still dribbling slow streams of ash.

"I have been half a mile down the pass, into Ystara," said Rochefort. "No beastlings, nor any movement under the moon, as far as I could see with eye or glass. Even as swiftly as they move, I doubt there will be another attack before the dawn. If then."

"Any attack like the last would finish us," said Dartagnan quietly. She had a bandage around her upper left arm, the stain of red human blood on it seeming all the brighter in comparison with the beastling's pools of ash. "We should retreat back across the border, as soon as the troops have had a few hours' rest."

Rochefort, who was unhurt, nodded wearily. "Dufresne . . . one of my scouts . . . I've just heard . . . she says they saw the Temple."

"What!"

"A few minutes before they encountered the beastlings. She looked back toward the camp and saw a coppered spire high in the mountain. It's up there, almost directly above us."

Rochefort pointed to the northern mountainside.

"Dufresne didn't see any way to get to it," she continued. "It seems likely the path or road begins on the other side of the pass."

"Rochefort, there is no chance we could push through," said Dartagnan. "Retreat is the only—"

"I don't disagree," said Rochefort mildly. "I just thought you should know. To be honest, I am somewhat surprised the Watch hasn't all run already. Or the King's Guard."

"Some of the Refusers have run," said Dartagnan. She sighed. "I cannot bring myself to blame them."

Rochefort didn't answer. She sniffed the air and watched the fog of her breath roll out as she exhaled. She took off one glove and held out her hand, turning her palm up and down.

"There is a change in the air, yet it grows no colder. . . ."

She looked up at the sky, Dartagnan following suit. The night had been clear, the stars and the moon bright. But now there was a dark front slicing across, moving swiftly. A great mass of cloud, blotting out the light. Even in the few seconds they watched, it rolled overhead, and the world grew much darker, the only light the flickering orange glow of the nearby watch fires.

"We should go *now*," said Dartagnan suddenly, still looking up. "Before it snows—"

A snowflake fell in her mouth, and then another hit her eye. She blinked, and in the next instant the whole sky was full of snow, snow falling thick and fast.

"The snow will slow any beastlings coming up the western side," Rochefort pointed out.

"It will slow us, too, but at least we will be descending," said Dartagnan. "Are you agreeable to we Musketeers playing rear guard, Rochefort? There may already be beastlings between us and home, so I would prefer to have your Pursuivants lead the way back, rather than the Watch. The Refusers can carry the wounded. We should abandon the guns, and all stores. We can always eat the horses, if we get to Monthallard."

"Agreed," said Rochefort. "Provided it is not my horse we eat."

She touched her hat in salute and stalked away, already calling out orders to the Pursuivants who accompanied her. But she stopped midword and midstep, only a short distance away, listening.

Far off and muted, yet she knew instinctively also very close, she heard the sound of harp strings, the rush of wings, the roar of a brazen trumpet, almost as if in warning . . . and the sensation of impending heat, like the doors of a forge thrown open . . .

"Dartagnan! Run!" screamed Rochefort. "Dive!"

The Musketeer Captain obeyed instantly, diving for the ground, snow flurrying around her cloak. In the space where she'd been—where they had both stood a few moments before—there was an enormously bright, boiling column of fire, so hot Rochefort flinched and shielded her face, though she was a good twelve feet away. The fire rose up and up, snow swirling wildly and melting all around it, and then it winked out as if it had never been, not even leaving any smoke.

As this blinding column of fire died, the Night Crew struck.

Simeon was seized from behind by two of the porters who had worked tirelessly with him all night, bringing the wounded up from the palisade. Taken totally by surprise, exhausted from performing hours and hours of the most horrendous and basic surgery without angelic assistance, he didn't even realize what was happening until they had his arms back and tied with a bandage, and even as he struggled against them a sack was pulled over his head and he felt a blade prick him just under his ribs.

"Do as you're told and you'll live, Doctor," said a harsh, unfamiliar voice. "Walk, and don't be foolish."

"My patients—" Simeon began to say, but he could already hear screaming and shouting, gunshots and the clash of steel. The sound of battle again, but a different battle than before, because there were no beastling shrieks.

"Walk!" commanded the voice again, and someone pushed him in the back.

Simeon walked.

Henri and Dorotea weren't taken so much by surprise as by sheer exhaustion. Both were asleep in their tent, wrapped in cloaks and blankets, including those belonging to Agnez and Simeon.

The roar of the fiery column and the sudden clamor woke them, but they were still muzzily trying to free themselves of their many-times-wrapped blankets when the four Night Crew fighters slid into the tent and simply wrapped the blankets tighter, secured them with cord, and then the two largest and strongest ruffians slung the blanket-wrapped, struggling captives over their shoulders and ran for the meeting place.

Those who sought to capture Agnez did not fare so well. She sat on a rock among a circle of walking wounded, gathered around a campfire near the hospital. They were waiting for a Refuser to finish heating a pot of wine, wine of uncertain vintage since it had been gathered from the dregs of everyone's personal bottles or wineskins, flavored with the addition of a handful of cinnamon sticks from a King's Guard who lay against the rock Agnez sat on. The Guard's broken, splinted leg was thrust out with her foot toward the fire, and her big toe had broken out of the woolen stocking. Agnez herself was tightly bandaged around the waist, Simeon having assured himself she had been only bruised when overborne by a beastling, perhaps with some ribs cracked, but nothing more.

When the column of fire roared up, Agnez was on her feet in an instant, sword in hand. The four Night Crew nearby who were assigned to collect her were slower, and by the time they had dropped the litter with the dead Pursuivant they'd been taking to and fro for the last half hour, Agnez saw them drawing weapons.

The closest barely had his club out from under his blanket coat when he went down with a sword thrust to the chest. The second jumped back to avoid a similar fate, fell over the broken-legged King's Guard and tried to crawl away, only to be gripped and stabbed in the neck by that same Guard, who could not get up but could fight perfectly well from the ground.

The third bully, used to back-alley brawls and unsuspected assassinations, was not prepared to face a furious swordswoman. She backed up as quickly as she could, parrying one thrust with her dagger, before risking a complete turn so she could sprint away. But she had fatally underestimated Agnez's reach and fell with Agnez's sword impaling her chest, the point sticking out just below her breastbone.

But this overpowered thrust, in turn, proved to be an error on Agnez's part. As she put a boot on her enemy to pull her sword free, the last of the four Night Crew rushed forward and struck her hard on the back of the head with one of the sharpened stakes that had never made it to the palisade.

Agnez crumpled. She tried to rise again, to renew her grip on her sword, but another Night Crew quartet had rushed over. They held off the wounded soldiers who tried to interfere. Agnez's hands were swiftly bound and she was lifted up and dragged toward the mountainside at a frantic pace.

She feigned unconsciousness as she was taken away, a subterfuge severely tested as they passed through the prone ranks of wounded toward the mountainside and through lidded eyes she saw *Lady Dehiems*, clad in Refuser rags, standing by a gaping hole in the cliff, with many rough-cut steps beyond leading up into darkness.

Or not exactly Lady Dehiems, for this young woman's eyes blazed with a commanding intelligence, she spoke entirely without an Alban burr, and she had an icon ring on every finger and more icons pinned upon her smock.

"Hurry! You're the last!"

Agnez felt herself lifted up and her bearers moved forward fast. She caught their fear of this woman, their instant obedience, and then they were lifting her so her feet didn't drag on the steps, and she realized they were carrying her up a stairway in the mountainside!

Behind her, she caught the chime of bells, and three perfect harp notes, followed by a faint rumble, as if the earth was shifting deep below. The steps shivered beneath her bearers' feet, and they slowed, lowering her down for a few moments, but then the rumble and vibration stopped and they picked her up again.

"She's awake," said the woman who was not Dehiems. "Make her walk."

The Night Crew lowered Agnez, but she tried to carry through her deception, slumping on the step.

"Such mummery," said the woman. "If you want to be unconscious and carried like a sack of meal, I will have my people oblige. Better if you walk."

Agnez thought about that for a moment, then slowly got to her feet, which was difficult with her hands bound behind her back.

"Who are you?" croaked Agnez. She must have bitten her tongue when she was hit from behind, because her mouth was caked with dry blood.

"Liliath, the Maid of Ellanda."

Agnez coughed and choked out a single word.

"What?"

Liliath did not answer her.

"Move aside," she instructed the two ruffians. "I am going ahead. Watch her carefully, she may be the most dangerous of the four."

The passageway was narrow, so the Refusers had to turn sideways, with Agnez held tightly between them, to allow Liliath to pass. Agnez looked at her carefully, noting the nimbus of light around her, centered on one of her icon brooches. She was using an angel to provide illumination, and she had certainly called upon a much more potent one to open and close the way below. Yet she did not look in the least bit tired. Or aged in any way, not even so much as by a line on her face, or a single white hair.

Beyond her, the steps continued up and up in a very straight line, at an unvarying angle of about thirty degrees, indicating this tunnel was itself the work of angels. There were many other Refusers climbing ahead of them, some holding lanterns, and Agnez's jaw clenched as she recognized the bulk of Simeon, looming above his captors. Something familiar about the two blanket-wrapped prisoners ahead of him suggested they were Dorotea and Henri.

"Why have you captured us?" she asked her two Night Crew captors. "Where are you taking us?"

"Shut up and walk!"

Agnez was lifted onto the next step, and put her feet down. She felt her ribs ache with the movement and knew that she would soon be very stiff. Not that this would stop her fighting, when the chance arrived.

Perhaps there would be such a chance at their destination, she thought, for the "where are you taking us" *had* been an unnecessary question. Given that the woman was indeed Liliath, still somehow alive or reborn after all these years, and that the tunnel clearly rose high into the mountain above, Agnez thought she knew their destination.

The Temple of Palleniel Exalted.

It was all done so swiftly, in the dark, that it took some time for everyone to realize it was not another beastling attack: it was the Night Crew. But most of the soldiers did not and could not know they were under attack by only a small element of the Refusers, or that the attacks were only to confuse and delay while the main object was undertaken, the capture and removal of the four friends.

It was the Watch who started the slaughter first. Always most fearful of what might happen if the Refusers turned against them, they waded in with halberds and swords. Musketeers, Pursuivants, and Royal Guard returned fire against Night Crew sniping at them, and then more generally began to shoot any Refusers who moved.

"Kill the graybacks!"

"It's the Refusers!"

"Kill them!"

"Kill! Refusers! Kill them!"

The shouts were angry and fearful, and came from all quarters, almost drowning out the drums calling the soldiers to take their posts on the palisades and the commands of Dartagnan and Rochefort and lesser officers, as they tried to restore order.

It was almost an hour, and many more deaths, before discipline was reestablished, and the surviving Refusers herded to their sleeping field. There they were surrounded by the Watch, who were themselves intermingled with the most trustworthy Musketeers and Pursuivants and King's Guards, to make sure they did not go wild again, while almost every other able-bodied soldier stood ready on the palisades.

By this time, Dartagnan and Rochefort were at the hospital field, both kneeling by the side of a dying Pursuivant, who lay close to the sheer mountainside. They had been led there by consistent stories that had to be true. The Refusers who had suddenly turned on the Watch and seized their weapons, and then rampaged through the camp, had all come here. They had not fled to the east or west; they were not anywhere else within the camp.

And they had kidnapped four people. Many people had seen Agnez's fight and capture; two other doctors had seen Simeon removed; a great many soldiers had noted the Refusers carrying away two bundles of squirming blankets.

The Pursuivant on the floor had seen where they all went. But she could barely speak, her voice so soft Rochefort actually lay flat next to her and bent an ear as close as possible, while Dartagnan spat "Be silent!" to everyone else and gestured with her hand.

It grew very quiet, but still only Rochefort could hear. She listened for thirty seconds . . . forty-five . . . a minute, then slowly slid away and pulled herself up, glancing across at the sheer stone of the mountainside, then back down to the Pursuivant who would never speak again.

"She summoned an angel, who rolled away a great stone," said Rochefort. She bent close to the cliff, gesturing for one of the doctors who held a lamp to bring it close. "There was a tunnel beyond, slanting upward. They all went through it, the mage last of all, commanding the angel to close the way again."

"She? The mage who called down the fire?"

"Lady Dehiems, in aspect," said Rochefort. "Or so Dangenne said."

"Dehiems! The Alban? But she's back in Lutace!"

"We have been gulled," said Rochefort, her eyebrows gathered in the fiercest scowl, her scar white as the snow falling beyond their shelter. She bowed her chin almost to her sternum, took a deep breath, and lifted her head again with visible effort.

"I must presume Liliath *has* returned. It was as the Cardinal feared. I cannot believe . . . yet it must be so . . . Dehiems is Liliath; Liliath is Dehiems. And we have helped her."

Dartagnan didn't answer. She went close to the rock, feeling it with her fingers, tracing the very faint outline that in fact might mark the presence of a hidden door.

"What is the use of marking it out? Dangenne said a *great* stone! We have no angels to move anything so large," said Rochefort. She slapped the wall with her hand. "Ah, I have been slow, and stupid!"

"Fetch Deramillies," Dartagnan snapped out to the closest Musketeer, who turned and ran.

"Why would we need Deramillies?" snarled Rochefort. "We must find another way up—"

"Deramillies is a siege expert, a master with powder, and many of her gunners were miners," said Dartagnan. "I can feel the faint line of a doorway. We'll chisel it out, blow the stone away."

"And pursue?" asked Rochefort.

"Naturally," said Dartagnan. "The Musketeers will pursue. The Watch, the King's Guard, and your Pursuivants will escort the Refusers and retreat down the pass."

"No! Allow me to command the pursuit!" said Rochefort. "You command the retreat!"

"The four they took are Musketeers," said Dartagnan. "We will go after them. *You* will command the retreat."

"No!" exclaimed Rochefort. "It is temple business! If it is indeed Liliath . . . I do not know what she intends, but it cannot be anything but disastrous for all. And Dorotea . . . that is, Scholar Imsel . . . she was my charge, my prisoner, I mean she was my guest. I said I would never see her harmed . . . and that . . . and that . . . it is certain both Cardinal and Queen would insist it is I and my Pursuivants who deal with Liliath. We are best suited!"

Dartagnan tilted her head wonderingly to one side and looked closely at Rochefort.

"I do not believe I have ever heard you make such an inarticulate speech, Rochefort," she said. "Though your points are salient . . . in any case, the matter is moot. Deramillies may not be able to open the way, or might bring the whole mountain down. Knowing we are to leave the powder anyway, she is bound to overuse it."

"Please, Dartagnan," implored Rochefort. "You ready the retreat. Take everyone but my Pursuivants. Leave us to the pursuit, just as our name suggests."

"The beastlings *will* take the pass," said Dartagnan. "You will not be able to come back this way."

"That is of no matter to me," said Rochefort coldly, her face once more devoid of emotion.

Dartagnan started to say something, stopped, frowned, and then snapped out four words.

"The pursuit is yours."

THIRTY-THREE

THE NIGHT CREW LEFT THE TUNNEL SOME FORTY MINUTES later, emerging in a flurry of snow and wind on a road that wound up from somewhere much deeper in Ystara and continued into the heights. Liliath clapped her hands and cried out in triumph. They were so close now, they would reach the Temple of Palleniel Exalted by sunup.

"We have to rest, milady, and treat our wounded," said Bisc, running to catch up with her, as she started to stride up the road. Whichever angel she had summoned for light still wrapped her in a pearly aura, so much brighter than the flickering lanterns carried by some of the Refusers.

"We have to rest!" repeated Bisc, as Liliath showed no sign of stopping to listen to him.

The climb had come at the end of a long and taxing day, and many of the Night Crew were practically sleepwalking already. Several had fallen down the steps, from fatigue or weakness. Many were suffering from minor wounds they'd received either in the battle with the beastlings or the running fight to escape the camp. The more badly wounded had been left behind.

"But we are so close!" cried Liliath. She clenched her fists, trying to hold in the excitement she felt, the rage that anyone might delay her now! All the years of planning, the first failure, the long sleep . . . all of it leading up to a moment that would come so soon, they *had* to get to the temple. . . .

"We *must* have some rest," repeated Bisc. He brushed snow from his face and added, "And shelter. Is there any on this road? Before the temple?"

"It is the pilgrims' road," said Liliath sulkily. "There are . . . there were caravansaries along the way . . . there is one a little higher up, I do not recall how far. Or what state it will be in now. If we press on, we could reach the temple by dawn."

Bisc shook his head.

"Not with this snow. Not now. We must rest."

Liliath's mouth flattened into a grim line. Bisc saw it and added, "The four prisoners need rest more than anyone."

Liliath relaxed a trifle, her hands unclenched.

"Very well," she said reluctantly. "We will rest at the caravansary. But no more than two hours, Bisc. We must go on!"

"Thank you, milady!" said Bisc.

He turned back to the gaggle of Night Crew, dim figures in the snowy night, many quite invisible outside the flickering pools of lantern light. The last Refusers were just leaving the tunnel. It was not blocked by a boulder at this end, just a cunningly concealed trapdoor, which they were lowering back in place.

"There's a shelter, a place to rest not far ahead!" he bellowed, the snow eating up his words. "Help each other! It's not far! Ystara!"

A weak chorus of "Ystara!" answered him. The Refusers picked up their feet and shouldered those who needed it, and set out along the road, with Liliath pacing out in front, burning with impatience. Bisc ran again to catch up with her.

"Not so fast, milady," he panted. "What if there are beastlings?"

Liliath paused for a moment, shutting her eyes. She felt snow falling on her face, light touches of cold that melted immediately on her ever-warm skin, leaving traces of moisture that reminded her of long ago, when she could still shed tears. Long, long ago, when as a child she had first been called the Maid of Ellanda, miraculously gifted summoner of angels. Some had even called her the *Angel Mage*, but the priests had put a stop to that. While they still held any sway over what she did.

"Beastlings . . ." murmured Liliath. She stood on the spot and slowly turned about in a circle, opening her mind to the world about her. She could sense all the tiny fragments of Palleniel strewn everywhere, though they were different in their nature. The Refusers about her, the four prisoners, the beastlings . . . her lip curled as she identified bands of the creatures coming up the pass, and on the mountainside, and there were indeed some on the old pilgrims' road, but much lower down . . . she hated the beastlings so much, the evidence of her failure . . .

"There are none close," she said. "They are drawn to me, but even more so to where I have summoned angels. There will be a horde at the top of the pass below, by early morning. They will finish off the Expedition."

"But what—"

"They will all soon be gone," said Liliath, waving her hand as if to brush away some annoying insects, snowflakes leaving wet trails across her hand. "Soon."

She started off again, still too fast. Bisc ran after her and clutched at her elbow, and she turned like a beastling herself, one hand ready to claw, but at the last second she smoothed her fingers out and merely patted Bisc on the side of his head.

"I am impatient, I know," she said. She looked back and saw the Night Crew were straggling, the dull glow of lanterns faint in the snowy night, illuminating dark, trudging shapes disappearing into darkness. Most important to her, the four prisoners were almost out of sight in the swirling snow.

As she looked, the ground shuddered beneath her feet, and there was the muffled sound of some distant explosion. She looked at Bisc.

"Blowing up their powder dump," said Bisc. "They must be retreating back down the pass. Or it could be an accident."

Liliath nodded slowly and lifted her hand, examining the icon rings on her fingers. She thought of dispatching Esperaviel to see what had happened, but dismissed the thought. A summoning here would lure more beastlings to the high road, and though she doubted any could arrive in time, it would be best not to risk it. . . .

"Time," she said aloud. "We must hurry."

"Yes, milady," said Bisc worriedly. Liliath appeared to be so fixated on reaching the temple she had forgotten their discussion about the need for rest. "The caravansary?"

"Yes . . . yes," replied Liliath. She shook her head, wiped snow from her face, looked through the white gloom. "I remember . . . there is one, not far . . . around the bend ahead."

Bisc nodded. He could not see a bend in the road ahead. It was too dark and the snow was falling too thick and fast. But as always, he believed his mistress. Stamping his feet in an attempt to warm them, he followed her up the road, and the Night Crew and their prisoners followed him.

Well back from Liliath, Henri slipped and fell heavily into the snow. The Refusers had stripped him of his many blankets and tied his hands at the bottom of the stairs, and though they had left him his cloak, it was spotted with tiny burn holes from sparks, and the fur trim had been singed off. He lay in the snow groaning for a moment, too tired to even try to get up, and wondered whether he would ever be warm again. Though staying alive might be an even greater issue than being warm. . . .

Refusers lifted him up, not gently, and pushed him next to Dorotea, who was moving with the dumb regularity of an underpowered waterwheel, fed only by a trickle from the millstream. Barely lifting her feet above the snow, she didn't leave footprints so much as dragged lines that looked like a sled trail.

As Henri's shoulder bumped hers, Dorotea looked across blearily, and smiled.

"Treasure," she croaked. "And hardly any beastlings."

Henri couldn't quite manage a smile. He looked around. The Refuser who had pushed him had paused a half-dozen paces behind now, and was trying to coax her lantern to shed more light. The next closest was half a dozen paces ahead.

"Do you know what's going on?" he whispered. It was hard to talk; his throat was so parched. He stuck his tongue out to catch some snowflakes as he waited for Dorotea to gather the strength to answer.

"No," said Dorotea quietly. "But they've got Simeon and Agnez too. They're behind us."

Henri turned to look but could see only the Refuser with the lamp, and some dim shapes beyond her, obscured by snow. He tried to twist around more for a better look, slipped, and fell over again, this time into Dorotea, sending them both sprawling into the snow.

But again, they were picked up, pushed in the back, and made to trudge on.

Agnez saw them fall, recognizing them by shape and movement, for they were not much more than silhouettes. She had managed to catch up to Simeon, who now walked stolidly at her side. A Refuser with a lantern had been close behind them, but could not keep up the pace, and they were now in almost total darkness. Henri and Dorotea, lit by a lantern bearer near them, were forty or fifty paces ahead.

"I am fairly sure I can break my bonds," whispered Simeon. "They only used a bandage. There's no one that close behind us, not close enough to see."

"Best to wait," cautioned Agnez. "There's too many of them.

Besides, she commands many angels, and there is nowhere to go."

"She?"

"You didn't see her?" asked Agnez.

"No."

"Lady Dehiems. Or as she told me, Liliath, the Maid of Ellanda."

"Ah," said Simeon, possibly the most understated response Agnez had ever heard to a revelation of such importance. "Henri will be surprised. He still thought it might be Dorotea. . . ."

Agnez almost laughed, and would have if her ribs hadn't hurt, her hands weren't tied so tightly, and the snow hadn't got down the neck of her cloak.

"Can you think why they've taken the four of us?" asked Agnez, a dozen steps later. "And no one else?"

Simeon did not answer for some time. But after several dozen more steps, he did.

"I fear it has something to do with what Dorotea can see in us. We are somehow connected to the Refusers. To Ystara. And thus to Liliath."

"I will kill her," said Agnez, with great decision.

"You know, despite your lack of any weapon, and with your hands bound behind your back, I almost believe you," said Simeon.

"Speaking of bonds," said Agnez. "I changed my mind. We should take advantage of this darkness. If you can break your bonds, then do so."

Simeon grunted. Agnez couldn't see what he was doing. She could barely work out where his face was, it was so dark, the snow falling so thickly. But she heard him grunt again, and then there was a soft snapping sound.

"Undo me," she said. "But wrap the bonds around again, and I'll do yours, as if we're still tied up."

Walking close, and fumbling somewhat in the darkness, Simeon did so. Agnez returned the favor, loosely retying his hands, both of them slipping and stumbling, so much so the lantern bearer who'd fallen behind closed the gap. As her light fell upon them, they turned shoulder to shoulder to march forward again, heads bowed low.

The roof of the caravansary had fallen in, but the walls were mostly intact, providing some shelter from snow and wind. Refusers quickly went to work assembling fires from the fallen timbers of the roof, assisted by lamp oil, and soon had four huge blazes going in each corner of the large courtyard. Food was shared out, and water, though many Refusers simply went to sleep as close to the fires as they could get.

Agnez and Simeon made for Henri and Dorotea, and their immediate guardians were either too tired to stop them, or figured it didn't matter. The four friends exchanged tired looks of welcome and settled down together to bask in the warmth of the northeastern fire.

They had only sat for a few moments when the young Night Crew leader approached them. They'd heard the Refusers use his name, or names, sometimes Bisc and sometimes King. He was quite handsome, had a definite air of command, and unusually for a Refuser, no visible signs of past disease or current infirmity.

"Do you know why she wants you?" he asked, looking down at them, his back to the fire.

There was no question who "she" was, even without him glancing over to the fallen archway where the gate of the caravansary had been. Liliath stood there, enveloped in bright, angelic light, staring up the road, oblivious to the heat, food, and water being shared within.

"No," answered Dorotea, after a few moments when it was clear no one else was going to reply. "You don't either?"

Bisc didn't respond. He just kept looking at them.

"Is she really Liliath?" asked Agnez.

"What!" exclaimed Henri, jerking upright. But Dorotea was silently nodding, as if what she had just heard made perfect sense.

"She is the Maid of Ellanda," confirmed Bisc.

"And who are you?" asked Henri.

"I am the Night King of Lutace," replied Bisc, with a faint smile. "A little out of my kingdom, I admit. I suggest you try to sleep now, we will be moving on quite soon."

"To the Temple of Palleniel Exalted?" asked Dorotea. "What is she going to do there?"

Bisc shrugged and turned away, with a curt aside to the Night Crew nearby.

"Take turns to stay awake. I want them watched."

The four friends watched him go toward Liliath, who still stood staring up the road.

"I suppose we had best rest," said Agnez. She glanced over at the nearest Refusers, none of whom appeared to have paid any attention to Bisc's order, perhaps as he hadn't actually addressed it to anyone in particular. They were already settling back down to sleep. "If we go back to back, we can lean on each other."

They wriggled around on their bottoms and leaned back to back. A few moments later, Agnez was quietly struggling with Dorotea's bonds, and Simeon had already undone Henri's.

"Don't move," whispered Agnez. "We'll retie them loosely, so it looks like you're still fastened up. Don't forget and wave your arms around or anything. Then we'll just have to wait for the right opportunity to escape."

"I wouldn't forget!" protested Dorotea.

"Do you know why Liliath wants us, Dorotea?" asked Henri anxiously. "I mean, why us?"

"I think it has to do with what I can see," whispered Dorotea. Simeon nodded in agreement.

"In us and the Refusers," continued Dorotea. She paused as the wind shifted, and the smoke from the fire billowed round, briefly blowing over them, stinging their eyes and making them choke down coughs before it went round again.

"It's in the beastlings, too."

"Really? The same?" whispered Simeon.

"Variations on a theme."

"And Liliath?"

"No. She is different," said Dorotea. "Entirely different. She has entire angels within her. Many angels."

"So what's in us? And the Refusers and the beastlings and

whoever? Other angels?"

Dorotea took a breath.

"No. I think they are all the same angel, or rather pieces of one. Shards of a broken angel . . . spread across us all . . . or rather, shards of a broken *Archangel*."

There was an awful silence. Everyone was thinking it, but no one would say it, until Simeon whispered the word but with an inflection that made it into a question as if he still couldn't believe this could be true.

"Palleniel?"

THIRTY-FOUR

"THERE ARE EMBERS AND COALS; THEY LEFT NO MORE than a quarter of an hour ago," said Vautier. The scout kicked the log she had partially pulled out of the fire back in, and fresh flames licked up around the wood.

Rochefort nodded. She looked around, noting that the four big fires were already being coaxed into new life, her Pursuivants hoping to take advantage of the warmth and shelter. They were exhausted; there was no point in charging on, much as she wished to do so.

"We will rest here one hour," she announced. "Derambouillet, have food prepared and wine heated for everyone. Vautier, see to sentries, up and down the road. In threes, to be changed every twenty minutes. I want *us* to do the surprising, not the reverse."

Rochefort took out her pocket watch, opened it, and held it toward the light of the fire so she could read the twin dials, one above the other, the top one indicating hours, the lower minutes. Five and twenty, which meant the dawn was perhaps two hours away, though this might be notional, if the cloud stayed so thick.

Perhaps it wouldn't, she thought. The snow was easing. In fact, as they neared this ruin she had thought she'd felt an opposing, warmer breeze contesting the one that had brought the snow. She looked up and confirmed this. There was a faint patch of clear sky, with several twinkling stars, and it was growing noticeably bigger as she watched.

That was good, Rochefort thought, tapping the butt of her pistol. Without angels of their own, they would need the advantage of their powder weapons. Her Pursuivants were all expert shots. Which in turn reminded her that they should take the time to unload, draw powder and shot and reload, for everyone's weapons were sodden with melted snow.

"You should rest too, Captain," said Derambouillet. "Come, by the fire here . . . I will bring you wine as soon as it's warmed."

"You are right," said Rochefort. She sat down by the fire, and took her hat off to shake away the collected snow.

But she did not rest. Instead, she stared at the flames, and over and over again heard her own voice say, "I will not let you be hurt."

The road wound around the mountainside one final time and turned straight as an arrow to the north as it reached the saddle between two peaks. It was already growing lighter, with the first rosy hint of the sun in the west, and it had stopped snowing some time since, with the sky clearing. What cloud there was lay beneath them, for they had climbed high.

Liliath stared at the Temple of Palleniel Exalted. *Her* temple, her home for a half-dozen years. She had come to it as a child, under the sway of others, and had made them her slaves. The temple was the site of her greatest works of angelic mastery, and also of her greatest failure. One she was soon to make good.

The temple was still a mile away, across a frozen lake that drained over the western edge in a jagged waterfall of ice. Nestled into the side of the opposing mountain, it was a modern-looking L-shaped house five floors high, built of a cream-colored stone, now somewhat darkened, with large shuttered windows, the shutters a faded red that was almost pink. There was a considerably higher tower at one end, also square, topped with the classic temple spire of beaten copper shingles, bright under the sun.

It would be a pretty house, somewhere else, with gardens about it. Here, it just looked incongruous, perched on bare rock and ice. The spire was the only indication it was a temple.

In the early light, the four friends saw they all looked terrible. Simeon was still in his doctor's coat, which was deeply stained with blood, though he also had a blanket over his shoulders as a kind of makeshift cape. Agnez was bruised down the side of her face, her cloak had been ripped right up one side, and she looked strange with an empty scabbard at her side, and no pistols or daggers in her belt. Henri resembled a runaway smith's apprentice or the survivor of a powder mill explosion. He had powder stains all over his face, hands, and tabard, and the fur trim of his cloak was singed to rag ends. Only Dorotea looked relatively neat, though like them all, her face was drawn with weariness.

They dared not speak to each other, for Bisc and Liliath stood close by. Everyone watched Liliath, as she stared and stared. Finally, she turned her head away from the Temple, but still no one spoke.

"We go across the lake," she said. "It is frozen in the middle, all year round. There is no danger."

"What do you intend with us?" asked Dorotea, daring a question.

"You will see," said Liliath. She looked back at the temple again. "Soon. Oh, soon . . ."

She started off without another word. Bisc looked after her, then gestured to the Refusers to move.

"Alizon T, you and yours stay with the prisoners," he said. "Watch them. Remember the orders."

"Aye, King," said Alizon, a tall, nervy woman with only one arm. Her left was a stump above the elbow, with a sock tied over it poking out of her blanket wrappings. But she had a long knife thrust through her belt, close to her right hand, and the scars on her face suggested she had survived many fights in her thirty or so years. She was one of the older Refusers. They did not live long in general, and the Night Crew's lives were shorter than most.

"On you go, then," said Alizon to the four friends. She drew her knife, and her three cohorts stood closer. They all had long knives, and two had pistols. "Don't give me any cause to bleed you. Orders are you're not to be hurt. Unless necessary, that is."

"We will give you no difficulty," Agnez assured her coldly. She looked at her friends.

"Shall we go?" she said, and then mouthed the word "slowly," turning her head so Alizon and the others would not see.

They started walking, close together, with Alizon and her

trio behind, but not too close behind. Most of the Refusers were ahead with Liliath, keen to keep up with her, as if her presence offered safety from beastlings, but there were still plenty behind. Too many to risk trying to escape. There was nowhere to run to, or to stage a last-ditch defense. Just snow and ice and stone, and ahead, the frozen lake and the jagged waterfall.

They reached the shores of the lake half an hour later. The wind had died down, and the sky was now entirely clear, a beautiful blue, with the sun sitting in it warm and golden. A little of its warmth reached them, sufficient to cause Refusers to take off excess blankets and roll them to carry, rather than wearing them as coats. The warmth also seemed to ease the mood, which had been of desperation and exhaustion and constant fear.

The prisoners, who had dragged their feet as much as they could without being too blatant, found themselves closer and closer to the rear of the whole drawn-out column. It was even easier to go slow on the ice, and within a few paces, Dorotea's feet slid in different directions and she slowly went down, rolling across Henri's legs so he fell over too, and Simeon promptly sat down as well, almost cracking the ice. Agnez laughed, drawing Alizon's attention as the other three Night Crew went to lift up the fallen prisoners.

Liliath had reached the other side of the lake, almost skating her way across, her feet so light upon the ice. The Refusers spread out behind her were generally not so graceful, and their progress was marked by a lot of slipping, sliding, falling, and cursing.

Just before the lakeshore, Liliath stopped. She had been like a hound returning to her kennel and dinner, her head up, sniffing the wind, eyes on the temple. Now she stood still, and then turned in a full circle, her eyes shut. Several seconds later, those fierce eyes snapped open and she stared to the west, where the lake drained in high summer.

"Beastlings!" spat Liliath. She raised her arms in fury. "Beastlings!"

"Where?" asked Bisc, looking anxiously in all directions.

"Climbing the waterfall!" said Liliath. "I had not thought they could . . ."

She stared back across the ice, taking in the long line of Refusers, saw the prisoners fallen on the far side of the lake.

Liliath's mouth moved into a snarl.

"Hurry! Bring the four! Hurry!"

Bisc shouted, his voice carrying across the ice.

"Move! Get 'em up! Make 'em run!"

Then he saw something else and his jaw dropped. He turned to Liliath to tell her, but she had seen them too.

Agnez glanced over her shoulder, to see how many Refusers were still close. This was a chance to escape, no matter how small. There was only Alizon and her three, and some real stragglers even farther behind . . . Agnez's eyes narrowed. They weren't stragglers, and they weren't beastlings. There was a large number of soldiers in scarlet cloaks trimmed with red fox fur, and some ways out front four buckskin-clad scouts, who were kneeling, leveling long-barreled, rifled fowling pieces—

"Stay down!" shouted Agnez, pulling her hands free of her

bonds to fling herself onto the ice. The others, about to be helped up, threw themselves flat.

The sharp crack of fowling pieces was followed by the thud of bullets striking home and the cries of the struck. The Refuser closest to Agnez fell, clutching at his stomach. She raced on all fours to him and took his knife and pistol, immediately cocking it and turning it on Alizon T, who was gaping at the Pursuivants charging down the road. Agnez pulled the trigger but there was only a click and a soggy, spluttering whoosh as it misfired. Alizon whirled, drawing her own knife, and came at Agnez, only to be tripped by Simeon, who snaked out one huge foot.

Agnez stabbed Alizon, left the blade in and snatched the Refuser's own knife out of her slowly opening hand. Standing up, she half slid, half ran across the ice to where Henri was grappling with a Refuser, holding his wrist with both hands as the man tried to plunge a dagger in his chest. Agnez stabbed him through the ribs and pushed him off, as Simeon picked up the remaining Refuser, who was trying to open the pan of his pistol, and hurled him across the ice.

"All down?" gasped Agnez, looking around. The closest Refusers were a good thirty or forty paces across the ice.

"Dead, or unconscious," confirmed Simeon. He took off his hat and waved it over his head at the Pursuivants. There was little chance of him being confused for someone else.

The scouts did not fire again, but nor were they rushing forward. For some reason, the Pursuivants were spreading out along the road and halting. Their muskets were going up, but *not* pointing toward the bulk of the Refuser force near the lake, who were well out of range anyway.

"What are they . . . ?" Dorotea started to say, but she had looked where the muskets pointed, and saw for herself.

Beastlings were appearing over the lip of the frozen waterfall. Scores of them. Again, they were of many different shapes and sizes, but all had claws or spurs or talons that made it easier for them both to climb the frozen waterfall, and to move over the ice. They spread out in a long line and moved forward, very swiftly.

"Curse it!" spat Agnez. She looked at the beastlings, at the Pursuivants, at Liliath and the Night Crew on the other shore of the lake, and instantly worked out the tactical situation. The only chance of evading the beastlings meant running toward their enemies on the other side of the lake, and the potential shelter of the temple beyond, if it could be barricaded or held.

Running back to captivity.

"Run!"

Liliath made a noise Bisc had never heard from her before, a kind of gasping cry, as if she had been stabbed or badly hurt.

"Go to the temple," she said to Bisc. "Prepare to defend the lower levels. I do not know what state it will be in."

"I'm not leaving you," said Bisc.

"I will bring the four," said Liliath.

"But . . . they . . . the beastlings will have them," said Bisc. Their former prisoners were running across the ice as fast as they could, but the beastlings were gaining on them. A few of the monsters toward the rear had fallen from the Pursuivants' musket fire, and Rochefort's force was advancing by leapfrogging ranks, the front rank firing and then reloading as the rank behind ran forward to fire from the advanced position, the whole action continually repeated. But it made for slow going, and they would never catch the foremost beastlings, nor be able to shoot enough of them to make a difference.

"Go," repeated Liliath. "I will summon an angel."

Bisc went, calling to his Night Crew. They needed little urging, with the beastlings so many and so swift, but everyone looked back at Liliath on the ice. Bisc was reassured as he saw her lift her hand and place a finger on one of her icon rings, though he had no idea what she planned to do. Angelic magic could not be used on beastlings, or at least no one else had ever been able to force an angel to act against them . . .

The icon Liliath chose was of a Virtue whose scope was the movement of air. The plaque depicted a gold-eyed woman with wildly puffed-out cheeks, lips pursed and blowing.

"Mairaraille, Mairaraille, come to me," whispered Liliath, the name repeated in her mind, reinforced and concentrated. She had not wanted to use magic here, for it would lure still more beastlings, but it was too late for that.

The angel heard at once but tried to twist away, to recede farther into the heavens. Liliath grimaced and ground her teeth, before speaking louder and focusing her mind on her quarry, the world around her forgotten.

Still the angel fought. Liliath felt lines crinkle around her eyes and smooth again with the effort of summoning. An incandescent rage built up inside her, a desire not just to summon the angel but destroy her. Mairaraille felt that anger and grew frightened, suddenly giving in to manifest with a jangle of discordant bells and misblown trumpets, the winds she wielded whipping around Liliath without daring to touch her.

"Go to the four who run upon the ice," instructed Liliath steelily. "Wrap them gently and lift them aloft, ensuring they are not hurt in any way, and fly with them here. Then you will lift me up also, as gently and with equal care, and take us all to the front of the temple I point out now. You will set us down again gently and do us no harm."

I cannot lift so many, protested the angel.

"You must!" commanded Liliath.

It is too difficult, the air is too cold, too thin—

"Go or I will end you!" screamed Liliath. "Go!"

There was a clap of thunderous wings and a blast of trumpets. Ice chips flew in tight circles, drawn up into a whirlwind that howled across the frozen lake, toward the four Musketeers.

Dorotea sensed Mairaraille before she saw the angel, out of the corner of her eye. A whirling column of light and shadow, seconds later visible with her ordinary sight as well, as the angel gathered still more ice and shredded it into smaller fragments and water vapor, to form a towering column of white. She did not know which angel it was, but she knew its kind, and guessed it had to be sent for them, since there was no point attacking the Pursuivants when the beastlings were closer, and no angel would act against the beastlings of Ystara.

"Close up!" she shouted, clutching at Simeon's shoulder. "Close up!"

Simeon saw the widening gyre of white rushing down upon them. He reached over and pulled Henri close and Agnez too saw what was coming and slid over to get an arm over Henri's shoulder, and they all skidded to a stop and almost fell into a heap.

"Shut your eyes!" screamed Dorotea.

The whirlwind hit a second later and they were blown violently backward—but not down onto the ice. Mairaraille lofted them up and up, and they lost their hold on each other and were violently tumbled about, but the angel kept them separate, so their weapons and everything in pouches and pockets fell without causing harm, and Mairaraille did her best not to entirely tear their cloaks from their shoulders, and she only took one of Agnez's boots and all of their hats.

The angel carried them back across the lake in just a few seconds, and blew low, the icy whirlwind bowing down to pick up Liliath, who curled herself in a ball and clenched her fists against her stomach and thus kept nearly all her icons, save two, pinned to her robe, which flew off when her smock was shredded into tatters.

A few screaming, frozen moments later they were all dumped in a deep bank of snow near the front gate of the temple. Mairaraille fled before Liliath could dismiss the angel, taking advantage of her fingers slipping from the icon as she fell. Angrily Liliath climbed out of the deep imprint her body had made, meeting Bisc who was pushing through the snow to help her. The Refusers had reached the temple only as the angel spun past overhead.

"Secure the prisoners!" snapped Liliath, and Refusers obeyed instantly, to drag the blinking, dizzied Musketeers from the snow. Like Liliath, they all had dozens of tiny stinging cuts from flying chips of ice on their hands and faces, but were otherwise unharmed.

But in Liliath's case, those tiny cuts were already healing, and the noticeably silver tinge of her blood was fading as her skin returned to its customary, unblemished and beautiful brown smoothness.

The temple loomed above. There were no windows in the ground-floor walls of thick stone, and the windows on the floors above were all tightly shuttered. When a Refuser tried the huge central door of solid, iron-bound oak, it did not budge. There was a keyhole the size of a child's fist on the right-hand side, but no key. It was firmly locked.

A frisson of panic ran through many of the Refusers as the door resisted the impact of several larger Refusers kicking at it, and there were many glances downhill.

The beastlings were almost across the lake, only five or six minutes behind. They weren't even shrieking, but silent, which was almost worse. The only sound was the rolling boom of the Pursuivants' musket volleys, coming steadily, two or three a minute. But Rochefort's troops hadn't quite reached the side of the lake. They were still slowly advancing by fire and movement, and though their massed fire was taking its toll on the rear ranks of the beastlings, there were still at least a hundred of the monsters who would stay out of range and reach the temple.

None had turned to attack the Pursuivants. All the beastlings' attention was fixed on Liliath. Or as the Refusers saw it, on them.

"There is a door in the base of the tower," snapped Liliath. "It is . . . or was, unlocked. Follow me and bring the prisoners. I need them alive! Take no chances."

She ran along the front wall, toward the tower. Refusers grabbed Agnez, Simeon, Henri, and Dorotea, interpreting Liliath's command to pile on. Each of the Musketeers had a Refuser on each side, holding their arms, and one behind ready with the pommel of a dagger or pistol butt.

The door in the tower was made of iron, rusted and flaking. Liliath turned the ring that would raise the bar inside. It came away in her hand, but she gripped the bolt itself with her impossibly strong fingers and turned it, the bar inside groaning as she forced it up. The door stuck too, but she pushed and it could not withstand her, sliding back with the shriek of iron on stone.

Liliath did not pause, but ran inside.

"Bring the prisoners!" she shouted. "Bar and prop the door!"

THIRTY-FIVE

THE INTERIOR OF THE SQUARE TOWER WAS LARGER THAN it looked from a distance, the entry chamber easily fifty feet on each side. It was hard to see in the fall of light from the door, but it was some sort of guardroom, with simple wooden chairs and a table, a sword rack and some barrels. Everything was falling apart and covered in a greenish mold. Liliath was already running up the stone steps on the left side, toward a heavy wooden door, which opened easily.

Agnez kicked off her remaining boot as they crossed the threshold, earning a tap from a pistol butt. Like the others, she was hustled up the stairs after Liliath, Refusers crowding ahead and behind. The air of barely restrained panic was still strong.

"Last one in drops the bar!" Bisc shouted. "Grandin, Ratter, you take charge here. Break that table, prop the door. You have to hold it. We must give Liliath time to summon Palleniel and then he will destroy the beastlings! All will be well! Ystara!"

The Refusers answered with a weak chorus of "Ystara!" and sent clouds of mold flying as they started in to dismember the table, wrenching planks from it ready to set at an angle against the door when everyone was inside. Bisc watched them for a moment, then followed the rush upstairs.

The room on the next floor was a kind of antechamber, adjoining the house proper, the tower chamber opening out to join a great hall, which had shuttered windows, a long table and well-padded chairs, in much better condition than the furniture in the tower guardroom. There were dusty, discolored paintings on the walls, which all seemed to be of Liliath or were scenes of angelic powers in use.

"Everyone who's got a pistol or musket, get to those windows!" ordered Bisc. "Open them up and start shooting! Everyone else, go and load and watch with sword or knife! Remember those beastlings can climb! You go too, Kreel and Basco, Jevens."

Most of the remaining Night Crew poured from the tower into the hall, fifty or sixty of them, leaving only two people on each of the Musketeers. There was no shouting "Ystara" now, no joking or chatter. Just grim women and men hoping to stay alive. The shutters did not open easily, and some fell off when pulled, and no one wasted time trying to open the windows, simply smashing the glass.

The prisoners and their reduced escort, with Bisc, continued on in the wake of Liliath.

The next room up was a library, and Dorotea almost had her right arm dislocated as she was hauled back when she instinctively turned toward the closest shelf to inspect its contents. The shelves, of a dark wood with long glass doors of angelic make, ran from floor to ceiling, on three of the four walls, the fourth taken up by the stairs, but there were shelves there too, necessarily foreshortened at the start, running under the steps.

The massed shriek of many beastlings, the crack of pistols and muskets, and the gong-like boom of something striking the iron door below all sounded at the same time as they reached the next room. This had been a bedroom, the remains of a feather mattress eaten away by rodents and insects strewn around much of the room, the bed it came from a tarnished relic of bronze and timber in the corner. Two chests of drawers stood next to it, so covered in dust it was impossible to tell what timber they were made from. A tall looking glass across from them was in a similar state. A copper bathtub in one corner was green and horrid, and there were piles of what were probably once clothes rotting away near it.

They continued up the stairs, emerging into brightness. This room had floor-to-ceiling windows of pure, angel-clarified glass, which never needed cleaning, and it was warm, the sunshine pouring in. There were perspective glasses on tripods on each side, and low lounges, somewhat the worse for the wear, where those not using the telescopes could wait their turn to look out over lake, waterfall, and mountains, and into the lowlands of Ystara beyond, or to the east, Sarance.

But everyone looked to the waterfall now. The jagged spikes of frozen water were hardly white at all, there were so many beastlings swarming up this broad ladder for their invasion. Thousands and thousands of beastlings.

"Palleniel preserve us," whispered Bisc, all his attention on the terrible sight below. The other Refusers were just as distracted, gaping at the vast horde of beastlings.

Simeon was the first to act. He pulled his arms free of the men who held him, grabbed their heads and threw them against the window. Being angel glass, it cracked but did not break. They bounced from it and fell sprawling on the floor. Simeon turned and ripped the nearest telescope from its tripod, brandishing it as a club.

Agnez arched back and sideways, head-butting her left-hand captor, while she kicked the woman on the right, placing her heel deep in her stomach. Both went down, and she snatched a dagger to engage Henri's right-hand guard, who let go to draw her own dagger, while Henri wrestled with his left-hand Refuser, both of them trying to throw each other.

Dorotea, who was closest to the steps that continued upward, got a leg around one of her guards, but could not bring her down and was carried to the floor. Her other captor, seeing her secure, drew her sword and ran to attack Simeon.

Agnez saw her, and turned about, parrying the first attack, running her dagger up the sword blade as the Refuser tried to disengage, closing so fast she was able to punch her in the nose, and take her sword, smacking her with the pommel to send her down.

Bisc started back down the stairs, drawing his own sword. Liliath was already halfway through the door above, but she whirled around.

Even as she did so, the glass cracked by Simeon's two Refusers shattered, and a beastling sprang into the room. Taller than Simeon, but thin as a sapling, it was entirely covered in black, iridescent scales, and it stood on four spiked legs and had two forelegs with long, crablike claws. Its head was still grotesquely, impossibly humanlike, save for the mouth, which was a gaping, round hole of tiny teeth, rather than a horizontal slit.

It shrieked and grabbed a Refuser in its claws, mouth descending on his shoulder to chew.

"They're climbing the walls! They're climbing—"

The shout came from somewhere below. Refusers and Musketeers turned as one on the beastling. Simeon hammered it with the telescope, breaking the bronze tube, the lenses flying free. Agnez stabbed at its eyes with her sword, and Henri took the pistol he was wordlessly offered by his opponent of moments ago and fired with her, both of them ducking in to aim at its lower joints, so they wouldn't hit anyone else.

"Bring her!" screamed Liliath, pointing to Dorotea. "Bring her!"

The Refuser who held Dorotea had let her go to fumble with his pistol. Dorotea was just about to steal a dagger from his belt when Bisc grabbed her by the arm and bent it back behind her, hustling her up the stairs, almost carrying her as she tried to struggle free.

Liliath slammed the door behind them, and dropped the bar.

This room was also full of light and warmth, but it had no windows. At least, not in the walls. Dorotea looked up and saw that what had seemed a copper roof from outside was something else, something of angelic make beyond her knowledge, a variation of the angel-clarified glass used in the Rotunda of the Belhalle. Light streamed through as if there was nothing there. She could see the frame that supported the roof, nothing in between the beams.

The room was an iconer's workroom, an ideal studio. There were four workbenches, and many cupboards for paint and paper and gold leaf; wooden and ivory and metal plaques; for brushes and tools and stirring rods and knives and burins, all the paraphernalia of the craft.

In the very middle of the room, there was an easel, with an icon sitting on it. A large icon, as big as Dorotea's hand. She felt its presence faintly, and was surprised it did not emanate the overwhelming sensation of power she expected.

It was clearly Palleniel. There were the seven-pinioned, enormous wings, surrounding a figure that was featureless, all burnished, shining gold, so bright it was hard to look at. But the halo above his head was gray, not gold, something Dorotea had never seen in an icon before.

It was the same gray as beastling blood.

She was so intent on the icon it took a second for Dorotea to notice there was a body on the floor by the easel. A desiccated corpse, laid out on a pallet. He or she had been a priest of some kind, for the remnants of a habit lay around the yellowed skin and protruding bone, and there was a hood folded back behind the head, which was not quite yet a skull.

"Bring her close," instructed Liliath, who had run to the easel.

She was in a fever of anticipation and anxiety, her hands shaking, her eyes bright. "Sit her here. Keep her still."

She pointed by the corpse, close to the easel. Bisc thrust Dorotea down heavily, but his face was a mixture of puzzlement and trepidation.

"What . . . ?" he started to say, but thought better of it, as Liliath laid one hand on Dorotea's head and placed the other on the icon, and laughed, a laugh of relief and joy, so strange in counterpoint to the muffled screams, shrieks, shouts, gunshots, and general noise of battle that emanated from below.

"What are you doing?" asked Dorotea. She tried to sound calm, though her heart was hammering under her ribs. "That icon . . . it isn't finished . . . or something."

"It is finished," said Liliath. She glanced down at Dorotea. "You know much, but then so little."

A resounding bang on the door made Bisc flinch and then press down harder on Dorotea's shoulders, before he realized it was an errant gunshot and not a beastling trying to knock it down. But that relief was short-lived, as a shadow fell on them from above. Looking up, they saw a beastling clambering across the roof. A sinuous, multijointed beastling with elongated, almost human hands, but with only four fingers, ending in hooks.

"It will not get in that way," said Liliath. She laughed again. "They are too late. So close, but too late."

"Summon Palleniel," urged Bisc. "Set all to rights!"

"Not with that icon," said Dorotea.

"Really?" asked Liliath. "You haven't seen to the heart of

the matter, Dorotea? I am told you have seen what lies within Refuser and beastling, in your friends and—"

"Summon Palleniel!" interjected Bisc. "Don't waste—"

"Quiet!" ordered Liliath. "I was going to say, and in *me*."

"You have angels within," said Dorotea slowly. "Angels entire. Whereas we others have . . . broken motes. I presume of Palleniel . . ."

"So you do see," said Liliath. "Perhaps all along you were fated to be the one. You must be the one. You must be."

"Liliath . . . ," begged Bisc. The sounds of fighting were growing louder, and someone was screaming at the top of their lungs just outside the door, screaming in pain. The beastling above was scratching at the glass or whatever it was, with those horrible hooked fingers.

"I am not going to summon Palleniel from the *heavens*," said Liliath. "That is why you feel a wrongness in the icon. There is hardly anything of Palleniel there. He is in this mortal world. Spread thin, in the Refusers and beastlings. And a little, a very little, but the most powerful and true fragments of all, in you— and in your friends."

"So you will bring him back together," said Dorotea. "But you broke Palleniel apart, in the first place, didn't you, one hundred and thirty-seven years ago?"

"Yes," agreed Liliath, a fleeting expression of pain crossing her face. "I made a terrible error, a mistake, now to be corrected."

"I don't understand," whispered Bisc. He let go of Dorotea, and stood upright, facing Liliath. "*You* broke Palleniel apart, Liliath?"

"Yes," said Liliath. "I didn't *mean* it to happen, it wasn't supposed to—"

"But then . . . the Ash Blood plague . . . the beastlings . . . you—"

"Yes! I told you! But now I will . . . I will make everything right."

Liliath raised a hand to touch Bisc's face, stroking his cheek to remind him of what she had done for him, to soothe him. "I am sorry, my dear Bisc. I am going to put everything to rights. You will be with me, Biscaray, dear Biscaray, we will be together always—"

There was no sincerity in her words. She hardly looked at him, her eyes upon the icon on the easel.

Bisc's face twisted in sorrow and anger combined. His fingers flexed, to drop the dagger from his sleeve into his hand, but Liliath was far faster, lowering her hand, her steely fingers gripping his throat. Bisc choked and gasped as she lifted him clear from the floor and then flung him away, off to one side.

A servant used, discarded, and immediately forgotten.

"What were you trying to do?" asked Dorotea, swallowing her fear. "Back then, I mean?"

She tried not to look at Bisc's dagger. The weapon lay four or five feet away, well out of immediate reach.

"We are destined to be together," said Liliath, once more placing one hand back on the icon, the other on Dorotea's head. The scholar felt the weight of Liliath's fingers, far heavier than they should be.

"You and Bisc?"

"Palleniel," snapped Liliath, and the icon flashed beneath her hand, and Dorotea heard the Archangel answer too, far away and yet close.

Inside her head.

I begin.

Dorotea leaped for the dagger. Or at least, that's what her mind told her body to do. But she didn't move. She was transfixed, pinned down by the power that flowed from Palleniel to icon to Liliath to Dorotea's head.

"My true love always," whispered Liliath. "I wanted to bring him down from the heavens, clothe him in mortal flesh . . . feel his kisses, his love . . ."

Dorotea could not move, but she still breathed, and her eyes had some volition. She peered sideways at the body on the pallet.

"You tried to put Palleniel *in* someone!"

"The best of my human lovers," said Liliath. "I strengthened him. Fed him small angels, as much as he could hold. But it was not enough. I did not know then it could never be enough, that was not the way. And I summoned Palleniel—"

Yes.

"And he came, but as a vessel too small will overflow, that body could not contain him. My love sought other bodies, flowing into one, then another, and another, and another, across all Ystara. But none could hold *Palleniel* and he was spread too thin and I couldn't, I couldn't bring him back, and my love was split asunder, broken into thousands and thousands of pieces, mere mortal pieces, who could not contain even the least of him, and so the Ash Blood ran, the beastling transformations began . . . and everything was *spoiled*."

She looked down at Dorotea, tears welling from her lovely eyes, the first tears in a hundred forty years to splash down her face.

"But there was hope," she said, and then sharply, in answer to some refraction on the part of the Archangel that Dorotea could not sense, "Palleniel!"

I gather myself. I obey.

"There was hope," repeated Liliath. "Some few mortals were almost strong enough to hold my dear love, to give him flesh. But they needed to be changed, to be made stronger still, strengthened with each generation. Their grandchildren, I thought, would be numerous, strong, I could choose any one of them to host my lover. I went to my sleep, knowing I would wake when this work was—"

She paused, spat out a word.

"Palleniel!"

I obey. I obey!

"When this work was done," said Liliath. She cocked an ear, listening, and Dorotea realized the sounds of battle were fading. The screaming outside the door had stopped. The musket fire diminished. There was no shrieking from the beastlings. She could not look up, but it seemed to her the one above had also gone, or was no longer moving.

"The closest beastlings will be gathered first," said Liliath, with a faint smile. "And Refusers too."

"What . . . what will happen to them?" whispered Dorotea. She could move her tongue, but only just. She tried biting the tip, to see if the pain would help free her, but she could not close her mouth.

"It matters not. I suppose the beastlings will die; they have been so much transformed, kept alive so long by my love's power," said Liliath. "The Refusers . . . the residue is small. They may survive—

"Palleniel!"

Soon. Soon.

"And me?" whispered Dorotea, though she already knew.

"It was not the grandchildren but the seventh generation who finally became what was needed," said Liliath. "And so few . . . I had not considered the Ystarans who escaped would fear to breed—

"Palleniel!"

Upon the brink.

"I never knew," said Dorotea. But her mind was not on her words. She was steeling herself for the struggle to come, drawing breath not to speak but to fortify her will. "An ancestor from Ystara, and not a Refuser. My mother will be shocked."

"She will never know," spat Liliath. "Oh, my love, my love, it has been so long, but we will be together! Palleniel!"

I am here.

Palleniel manifested in the chamber with a crash of wings so loud Dorotea was deafened, her teeth rattled, her hair blown back. But she was prepared, neither stunned nor put off guard.

She felt the heat of his presence, the light, so much brighter than the sun, so bright she saw it through her shut eyes, every blood vessel in her lids in stark relief.

Angelic power pressed against her skin, entered her blood. Dimly, she was aware of Liliath's will urging the Archangel on, directing Palleniel to move inside her, to inhabit her body, to purge her mind and make everything his own.

No, said Dorotea quietly, a tiny voice in the deep center of herself, somehow clear amid the raging torrents of power.

No. I do not surrender.

Take her! Take her! Take her! urged Liliath. *We must be together. We must!*

Palleniel gripped Dorotea even more tightly, pushing her deeper and deeper into herself. She lost all feeling in her arms and legs and then her sight and hearing vanished, leaving only one tiny voice, that deep center, in a void of disconnected darkness. There was only this small remnant of herself, and the Archangel, and Liliath.

No, declared Dorotea. *No.*

Take her! screamed Liliath, inside Dorotea's head. *We must be together! You don't understand!*

Dorotea laughed, even as Palleniel began to press against the last redoubt of her mind.

Why do you resist? You must, you must surrender!

You've got it all wrong, you silly girl.

What?

You've got it back to front.

No, you try to trick me, but it is too late, we must be together—

You can be together. Like I said, you had it reversed.

I . . . I . . . we must—

Palleniel must return to the heavens. And you should go with him, Liliath.

Dorotea felt a sudden cessation of the pressure from Palleniel, the dawning doubt in Liliath. The scholar's sight came back, darkness ebbing away at the edges of her vision.

"Be together," said Dorotea, aloud. Her mouth felt numb and strange, but it worked again. She had pins and needles in her legs and arms, she could move them again as the Archangel retreated from her body, no longer forced on by Liliath to do something he . . . or rather it, in Dorotea's opinion . . . didn't want to do.

"Be together *in the heavens.*"

Dorotea infused her words with a total sense of rightness. Earth and heavens had been knocked awry by Liliath, and now they had to be brought into balance. Dorotea made herself believe there could be no other course. She could afford no sense of doubt, offer nothing that Liliath might latch on to that would make her change her mind.

Liliath slowly lifted her hand from Dorotea's head. Instantly, the last of the broken remnants of Palleniel left the little scholar's mind and body. But the Archangel's physical manifestation remained within the room, an overpowering, shifting shadow play of brilliant light and deepest darkness, moving and whirling, suggesting great sweeping wings, blinding halo, a fiery sword . . .

"Yes," said Liliath, very slowly. "Yes. We will be together. In the *heavens*."

The tip of one of the Archangel's great wings swirled around Liliath. Her skin took on his brilliance, and the shapes of light and darkness Dorotea had seen within Liliath, the remnant powers of the angels she had slain, began to stream from her eyes and mouth, joining and blending into the even brighter and darker swathes of Palleniel.

Dorotea staggered over to the closest workbench. She reached blindly for a stick of charcoal, one hand pressed against her eyes, peering through her fingers, shielding herself against the terrible angelic light. With the stick in hand, she went back to the easel, her head bowed. Every step was a struggle, as if she moved against a tide.

Liliath was just an outline now, a vague human shape within the swirling currents of Palleniel. But her hand, a strange extrusion from the bright nebula of light and darkness that was the Archangel, still touched the icon, though palm and fingers had grown translucent, not showing bones and blood beneath, but streaks of sunshine and starry night.

"Be together!" said Dorotea, once again.

Liliath's hand fell from the icon and she was pulled into the incandescent heart of Palleniel, with a great cry, part peal of trumpets, part human sigh of ecstasy.

Dorotea flicked the existing, priceless icon of Palleniel off the easel, and sketched quickly with her charcoal stick on the bare board behind, doing the swiftest and purest work she had ever done.

Blood was easy. She drew the stick savagely across the back of her hand, reopening all the tiny cuts from the flying ice, and drew again, with bloodied charcoal. The Archangel who loomed behind her grew still, light and shadows slowing, as it saw its essence—its new essence—captured so simply, and yet so well.

Dorotea touched the icon and spoke with infinite decision.

"Begone, *Palleniath*."

EPILOGUE

THERE WAS A HAMMERING ABOVE. DOROTEA LOOKED UP, and saw the beastling that moments before had been trying to force its way in was still alive. But the hooked fingers were shrinking, gray ash falling from . . . from human fingers . . . gray ash boiling away in a cloud, to be instantly swept up and away by the wind. An entirely human woman remained, naked on the transparent roof. A young, brown-skinned woman with lively green eyes, staring in shock . . .

Bisc was alive too, and unscathed. He stared up at the woman on the roof, tears streaming down his cheeks.

"She turned back," he cried. "A beastling turned back! Liliath was wrong! So my people . . . my people too . . ."

"Yes," said Dorotea.

"I didn't know what she wanted to do to you," said Bisc. "She healed me. I believed her; I believed what she told me about the Doom, about how she would restore Ystara. She said we would all be healed, we could come home. We would no longer be denied angelic magic . . ."

He bit back a sob and wiped his eyes.

Dorotea looked at him from the corner of her eye and squinted.

"That part will be true," she said. "For those of your people who need it. There is no taint in you now, nothing to stop angelic healing."

"Liliath was so beautiful . . ."

"She was so *young*," said Dorotea, shaking her head. "She had such power, from childhood on, it was too easy for everyone to forget she was only nineteen. I don't count being asleep for a hundred something years. And obsessed beyond the point of madness . . . well, she is with her lover now."

She went to the door and unbarred it, adding with a frown, "Not that I am sure she still exists as an actual person. If she does, it will be an experience for her to have to do someone else's bidding. You know, now that I think of it, I wonder if she is the first mortal to become an angel . . . how do angels begin . . ."

"I don't know," said Bisc uncomfortably. He looked up at the woman above and waved. She hesitantly lifted her hand and waved back. He pointed to the top of the wall below her, where the very faint outline of some sort of hatch in the strange, transparent material could be seen. She nodded and began to crawl toward it.

Dorotea stepped away from the door as Agnez, Henri, and Simeon burst in, their various weapons ready. Agnez, of course, had managed to get a sword; Henri had an empty pistol reversed as a club, and Simeon a very bent telescope. They saw Bisc staring up, Dorotea looking pleased with herself by the door, and no one else.

No Liliath.

"The beastlings are becoming human again!" exclaimed Agnez. She surveyed the room for enemies, carefully also looking up. "Ah, here too, I see. They all seem rather stunned, like fish cast upon a shore. The Refusers, too."

"It is your doing, I take it?" asked Simeon, looking down benevolently from his great height at Dorotea. He was absently pressing a finger against a deep cut under his eye, to stop the bleeding.

"Look at her," said Henri, in mock indignation. "Of course it's her doing. Thank the heavens."

His gaze swept across the benches and at the cupboards, the board sketched with charcoal and daubed blood on the easel, and the complete absence of small bronze chests. Or very large chests, for that matter.

"I don't suppose there's any treasure here, is there?"

"There is a great treasure below," said Dorotea.

Henri's smile grew eager, which turned into a groan as she continued.

"In the library. I believe I even saw a copy of Mallegre's *Mystery Plays*."

"But where is Liliath?" asked Agnez, as ever intent on the immediate matter at hand. She stood ready to engage, or more hopefully, lunge at any enemy who might suddenly appear. "What has happened?"

"I . . . *assisted* . . . Liliath to become an angel," replied Dorotea, gesturing to the icon upon the easel. She paused to allow the others to take this in. "Part of one, anyway. Together we restored the Archangel of Ystara, from all the broken pieces of him that were in the beastlings and Refusers and . . . in us . . ."

"So you were right about that," said Simeon.

"Up to a point," replied Dorotea. "I didn't know we were meant to be vessels for Liliath to make herself an earthly paramour from her angelic lover—"

"What!"

Dorotea explained, pausing frequently for cries of horror and amazement. But as she talked, she kept half an eye on the window, watching the Pursuivants approaching over the ice, the foremost of them a tall, dark woman, racing ahead as if she could not bear any delay.

"I should go and tell Rochefort," she said finally. "To make sure there is no fighting with the Refusers. That is to say, the Ystarans."

"Ystarans?" asked Bisc. Though not stunned, as the former beastlings appeared to be, he spoke slowly and it seemed with great effort. "You mean you're not going to . . . to take us back, execute us as criminals for what we've done?"

"Why do you look at me?" asked Dorotea. "It's not my decision."

"You do hold the icon of the Archangel of Ystara," said Agnez. "Even if you've left it on that easel for now."

"I'm not staying," said Dorotea quickly. "I'm going back to the Belhalle. Some Ystaran will learn to summon Palleniath, I'm sure. Or will make another icon."

She paused, then added kindly to Bisc, "But I will talk to Rochefort about letting you Refusers stay and, well, become Ystarans in truth, like the former beastlings. You will need to look after them. I think Rochefort will listen to me."

"I'm sure she will," said Henri drily, as the others nodded. Dorotea blushed.

"Thank you," said Bisc. He gave a slight, embarrassed bow. Then he looked up and shouted, "I'm getting a ladder!"

"Good idea," said Henri.

Bisc started for the door, talking as much to himself as the others. "Um, I'll . . . I'll get a ladder . . . We'll have to gather the beast— I mean our people who used to be beastlings, get them clothes first, they'll be frozen, food . . ."

He paused in the doorway, then spoke to Henri in particular, "You mentioned treasure . . . the other nine Diamond Icons . . . they're still in Lutace. *She* left them in Demaselle House. There are great riches there, in the strong room."

"While I'm glad to know the whereabouts of the Diamond Icons after all this," declared Henri. "I'm going to look for other treasure *here*. There must be some in this temple, somewhere!"

"I need to find some boots," remarked Agnez. "And my own sword. I suppose it's out on the ice. . . ."

"And I must find someone competent to sew up this cut," said Simeon. "Or a mirror, so I can do it myself. Not that one downstairs, before anyone mentions it. I doubt it would show a reflection at all."

But despite these statements of intent, none of the four friends moved. They stood in a circle, facing each other, the doctor, the scholar, the one-time clerk turned artillerist, and the real Musketeer.

"I feel no different, even without the angel you say we shared among us, Dorotea, which drew us together," said Agnez. "You are my sister, my brothers. And always Musketeers, whether you will or not."

"I too have not changed, no matter the angelic amputation within," rumbled Simeon. "You are my strange siblings, who I never thought to have, and value most highly. Though I take the Musketeer part under advice, Agnez, for I fully intend to return to the Infirmary and learn from Magister Hazurain. But I suppose I will never have any shortage of patients from the regiment."

"If the Musketeers should purchase cannons, I will happily continue to wear this tabard," said Henri. "But I think I see a future I never thought to have. In the Star Fortress of all places, with culverin and saker, and of course, the falconets. As for the rest, take it from someone who has plenty of sisters and brothers by blood. You are better friends and closer to me than they have ever been or ever will be."

"Love is strange," mused Dorotea. "I love the Belhalle, making icons in the Rotunda, under that golden light. But people use the word for so many different things. Liliath's love was in fact obsession, the cause of so many deaths and so much misery. Then there is the love based on simple physical attraction, the desires of the flesh, which may or may not be part of some greater love, such as we four share . . . though how it has survived the removal of its catalyst, the motes of Palleniel within . . . there is much to think on, to examine, the whole nature of angels and icons. I think Rochefort would like to pursue this also, in the Belhalle. She has served the Cardinal too long, at too great a cost—"

Agnez nudged her, and pointed out the window.

"Speaking of Rochefort, she's almost at the tower. And she's picked up my sword. I wonder if a duel would be . . ."

"No," said Dorotea and Simeon and Henri, all together. For a moment it seemed Agnez would take offense, but then she began to laugh.

Laughing, the four went to the door, and started down the stairs, their past adventures done, their new ones just begun.

ACKNOWLEDGMENTS

An author's work when writing is a solitary affair for the most part, but what is eventually produced is a manuscript, not a finished book. I have been very fortunate to team up with very clever, thoughtful, and experienced publishing professionals who have worked with me to take my bundles of straw and spin them into gold.

My agents are always there, in the very beginning and throughout the process: Jill Grinberg and her team at Jill Grinberg Literary Management in New York; Fiona Inglis and the gang at Curtis Brown Australia; and Matthew Snyder looking after film/TV at CAA in Los Angeles.

My publishers make beautiful books, and I am honored to be on their lists: Katherine Tegen and the HarperCollins crew; Eva Mills and everyone at Allen & Unwin; and Gillian Redfearn and the team at Gollancz.

Many booksellers have been absolutely essential in helping my books reach readers. I am grateful to all booksellers, not just for supporting my own books but for everything you do to connect people and reading.

Thanks are also very much due to my wife, Anna, who as a publisher has to deal with enough authors at work but gets me at home as well, and despite this is endlessly supportive; and to my sons, Thomas and Edward, who cut me a lot of slack when I am deep in a book.

Lastly, I would like to thank and remember our family dog, Sam, who recently passed away. Sam and I went for many late-night walks together during the course of writing this book, when I was in trouble with the story and needed to think things through.

Read on for a sneak peek at

THE LEFT-HANDED BOOKSELLERS
OF LONDON!

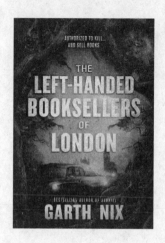

CHAPTER ONE

> ⊱ ⊰ ⊱ ⊙ ⊰ ⊱ ⊰

A clerk there was, sinister gloved
Dexter scorning, his sword well-loved
Wielded mirror-wise, most adept
Bookes and slaughter, in both well kept

> ⊱ ⊰ ⊱ ⊙ ⊰ ⊱ ⊰

A SLIGHT YOUNG MAN WITH LONG FAIR HAIR, WEARING A PRE-OWNED mustard-colored three-piece suit with widely flared trousers and faux alligator-hide boots with two-inch Cuban heels, stood over the much older man on the leather couch. The latter was wearing nothing but a monogrammed silk dressing gown, which had fallen open to reveal an expanse of belly very reminiscent of a puffer fish. His fleshy face was red with anger, jowls still quivering with the shock of being stuck square on his roseate nose with a silver hatpin.

"You'll pay for this, you little f—" the older man swore, swiping with the cut-throat razor that he'd just pulled out from under one of the embroidered cushions on the couch.

But even as he moved his face lost rigidity, flesh collapsing like a plastic bag brushed against a candle flame. The young man—or perhaps it was a young woman who was dressed like a man—stepped back and watched as the tide of change continued, the flesh within the pale blue robe falling into a fine dust that ebbed away to reveal strangely yellowed bones poking from sleeves and collar, bone in its turn crumbling into something akin to the finest sand, ground small over millennia by the mighty ocean.

Though in this case, it had not taken an ocean, nor millennia. Merely the prick of a pin, and a few seconds. Admittedly a very special pin, though it looked like any other pin made for Georgian-era ladies. This one, however, was silver-washed steel, with Solomon's great spell of unmaking inscribed on it in letters too small for the unaided eye to see, invisible between the hallmarks that declared it to have been made in Birmingham in 1797 by Harshton and Hoole. Very obscure silversmiths, and not ones whose work was commonly sought after, then or now. They mostly made hatpins, after all, and oddly sharp paper knives.

The young man—for he was a young man, or was tending towards being one—held the silver hatpin in his left hand, which was encased in a pale tan glove of very fine and supple cabretta leather, whereas the elegant fingers of his right hand were free of any such covering. He wore a ring on the index finger of his right hand, a thin gold band etched with some inscription that would need close examination to read.

His gloved left hand was perfectly steady as he slid the pin back into its special pocket in the right sleeve of his suit, its head snug against the half sovereign cuff links (1897, Queen Victoria;

the jubilee year, not any old half sovereign) of his Turnbull & Asser shirt. His *right* hand shook a little as he did so, though not enough to make the hatpin snag a thread.

The slight shake wasn't because he'd disincorporated crime boss Frank Thringley. It was because he wasn't supposed to be there at all and he was wondering how he was going to explain—

"Put . . . put your hands up!"

He also wasn't supposed to be able to be surprised by someone like the young woman who had burst into the room, an X-Acto craft knife in her trembling hands. She was neither tall nor short, and moved with a muscular grace that suggested she might be a martial artist or a dancer, though her Clash T-shirt under dark blue overalls, oxblood Doc Martens, and her buzzed-short dyed blonde hair suggested more of a punk musician or the like.

The man raised his hands up level with his head. The knife-wielder was:

1. Young, perhaps his own age, which was nineteen;
2. Almost certainly not a Sipper like Frank Thringley; and
3. Not the sort of young woman crime bosses usually kept around the house.

"What . . . what did you do to Uncle Frank?"

"He's not your uncle."

He slid one foot forwards but stopped as the young woman gestured with the knife.

"Well, no, but . . . stay there! Don't move! I'm going to call the police."

"The police? Don't you mean Charlie Norton or Ben Bent-Nose

or one of Frank's other charming associates?"

"I mean the police," said the young woman determinedly. She edged across to the telephone on the dresser. It was a curious phone for Frank Thringley, Merlin thought. Antique, art deco from the 1930s. Little white ivory thing with gold inlay and a straight cord.

"Who are you? I mean, sure, go ahead and call the police. But we've probably only got about five minutes before . . . or less, actually—"

He stopped talking and, using his gloved left hand, suddenly drew a very large revolver from the tie-dyed woven yak-hair shoulder bag he wore on his right side. At the same time the woman heard something *behind* her, something coming up the stairs, something that did not sound like normal footsteps, and she turned as a *bug* the size of a small horse burst into the room and the young man stepped past her and fired three times *boom! boom! boom!* into the creature's thorax, sending spurts of black blood and fragments of chitin across the white Aubusson carpet and still it kept coming, its multi-segmented back legs scrabbling and its hooked forelimbs snapping, almost reaching the man's legs until he fired again, three more shots, and the huge, ugly bug flipped over onto its back and spun about in frenzied death throes.

As the deafening echoes of the gunshots faded, the woman realized she was screaming, and stopped, since it wasn't helping.

"What . . . was that?"

"*Pediculus humanus capitis.* A louse," replied the young man, who was reloading his revolver, hitching up his waistcoat to take rounds from a canvas bullet belt. "Made bigger, obviously. We really have to go. Name's Merlin, by the bye."

"Like Merlin the magician?"

"Like Merlin the *wizard*. And you are?"

"Susan," said Susan automatically. She stared at the still-twitching giant louse on the carpet, then at the pile of reddish dust on the lounge, contained by the pale blue robe. The monogram "FT" was uppermost, as if pointing out who the dust used to be.

"What the hell is going on?"

"Can't explain here," said Merlin, who had gone to the window and was lifting the sash.

"Why not?" asked Susan.

"Because we'll both be dead if we stay. Come on."

He went out through the window.

Susan looked at the phone, and thought about calling the police. But after a single second more of careful but lightning-fast thought, she followed him.

CHAPTER TWO

A left-handed bookseller I did spy
In a wood one darkling day
I durst not ask their business, why
Best not to know, I do say

THE WINDOW OPENED ABOVE THE ROOF OF THE CONSERVATORY, which ran from the back of the house to the fence. Beyond that lay the dark mass of Highgate Wood. Merlin was walking out along the steel ridgeline of the conservatory, Cuban-heeled boots notwithstanding. The flat ridge was no wider than his hand, with long sloping panes of glass on either side. But he acted as if they were of no account, though if he fell he'd smash through them and be cut to pieces.

Susan hesitated and looked back. The monstrous bug was still writhing, but there was something else happening now. A dark fog was flowing up the stairs. It looked like thick black smoke, but it moved very slowly and she couldn't smell burning. Whatever it was, she instinctively knew it was wrong, something inimical. She shivered suddenly, bent down, and crawled out onto the ridge of the conservatory, moving swiftly on hands and knees.

"There's a weird black fog coming up the stairs," she panted as she reached the end. Merlin was standing in front of her, but as she spoke he jumped, clear across to a branch from an ancient oak that overhung the garden fence.

"How can you do that in those heels?" gasped Susan.

"Practice," said Merlin. He held on to a higher branch with his right hand and extended his left. "Jump."

Susan looked behind her. The extraordinarily dense, dark fog was already coiling out the window. It didn't move like normal fog at all; in fact, one broad tendril was coiling out towards her specifically. Reaching for her. . . .

She jumped. Merlin leaned out to her but Susan didn't need help, landing close to the trunk and immediately steadying herself by wrapping her arms around it.

"Down," said Merlin, climbing quickly. "Fast!"

Susan followed him, jumping the last five feet, her Docs splattering hard into the leaf mulch and mud. It had been raining most of the day, though it had eased off at nightfall. Now, past midnight, it was simply clammy.

The wood was very dark. All the light was behind them, spilling out of the houses and streetlights onto Lanchester Road.

The black fog was streaming over the conservatory, flowing down the panes on either side of the ridge. Spreading and extending, blending into the night once it moved outside the fall of light from the houses and street.

"What *is* that?"

"More to explain later," said Merlin. "Follow me. We have to get to the old straight track."

He led off, almost jogging, zigzagging between trees. Susan followed, hands up to ward off snapping-back branches and saplings. She couldn't see anything clearly. Merlin was a dark shape ahead; she had to trust he could see where he was going and try to stay right behind.

A few minutes later she almost ran into Merlin's back as he came out onto a path. He hesitated for a moment, looking left and right and then up at the cloudy sky, and the very few visible stars.

"This way! Come on!"

Meet the magical fighting booksellers who police the mythical Old World of England.

An entertaining new fantasy from the masterful GARTH NIX!

From bestselling author Garth Nix comes the story of an ageless young woman with terrifying angelic powers, bent on reuniting with her lover—no matter the cost to anyone else.

An epic feminist fantasy set in a dazzling new world

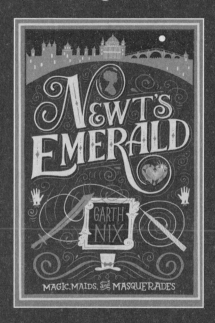

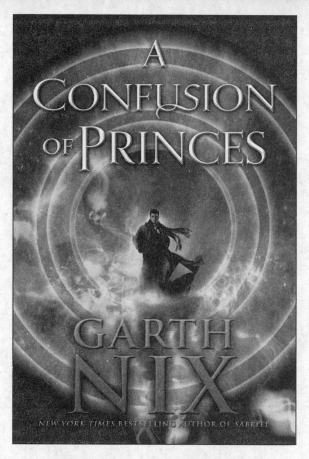

JOIN THE

Epic Reads
COMMUNITY

THE ULTIMATE YA DESTINATION

◀ **DISCOVER** ▶
your next favorite read

◀ **MEET** ▶
new authors to love

◀ **WIN** ▶
free books

◀ **SHARE** ▶
infographics, playlists, quizzes, and more

◀ **WATCH** ▶
the latest videos

www.epicreads.com